D1929758

Back to
WANDO
PASSO

ALSO BY DAVID PAYNE

Confessions of a Taoist on Wall Street
Early from the Dance
Ruin Creek
Gravesend Light

ONTARIO CITY LIBRARY

JUN   2007

ONTARIO, CA 91764

Back to

WANDO

PASSO

DAVID PAYNE

WILLIAM MORROW

An Imprint of HarperCollins*Publishers*

Grateful acknowledgment is made to reprint excerpts from *Memories, Dreams, Reflections* by Carl Jung. Reprinted by permission of Random House. Copyright 1961, 1962, 1963.

This book is a work of fiction. The characters, incidents, and dialogue are drawn from the author's imagination and are not to be construed as real. Any resemblance to actual events or persons, living or dead, is entirely coincidental.

BACK TO WANDO PASSO. Copyright © 2006 by David Payne. All rights reserved. Printed in the United States of America. No part of this book may be used or reproduced in any manner whatsoever without written permission except in the case of brief quotations embodied in critical articles and reviews. For information address HarperCollins Publishers, 10 East 53rd Street, New York, NY 10022.

HarperCollins books may be purchased for educational, business, or sales promotional use. For information please write: Special Markets Department, HarperCollins Publishers, 10 East 53rd Street, New York, NY 10022.

FIRST EDITION

Designed by Sarah Maya Gubkin

Printed on acid-free paper

Library of Congress Cataloging-in-Publication Data

Payne, David (William David)
    Back to Wando Passo : a novel / David Payne.—1st ed.
      p. cm.
    ISBN-13: 978-0-06-085189-7
    ISBN-10: 0-06-085189-9
    1. Rock musicians—Fiction.   2. Separated people—Fiction.   3. Myrtle Beach Region (S.C.)—Fiction.   4. Triangles (Interpersonal relations)—Fiction.
5. Plantation life—Fiction.   I. Title.

PS3566.A9366W36   2006
813'.54—dc22

                                 2005044907

06 07 08 09 10 WBC/RRD 10 9 8 7 6 5 4 3 2 1

For Will Payne, superhero
sans portfolio and itinerant energy beam . . .

From the old yellow cat who keeps coming back

Early this mornin', you knocked upon my do'
Early this mornin', you knocked upon my do'
I said, "Hello, Satan, I b'lieve it's time to go."
                                          —Robert Johnson, "Me and the Devil Blues"

If I die, I will forgive you.
If I recover, we will see.
                        —Spanish proverb

CONTENTS

Part 1

TALKING IN MY SLEEP

ONE

*R*ansom Hill had fallen hopelessly in love with his own wife. If there was any doubt of it—there wasn't, but had there been—it ended in Myrtle Beach, as he deplaned and found her waiting with the children at the gate. Tall and thinner than he'd been since high school, Ran had on his good black coat, which still stank of cigarettes, though he'd given them up in anticipation of this trip, the first of many sacrifices he was prepared to make. His slouching jeans were held up by a concho belt in which he'd lately had to punch three extra holes, and his Tony Lamas clapped along with a delaminated sole. His Stetson, though—the new three-hundred-dollar white one he'd seen and really felt he owed himself—was as crisp, serene, and towering as a late-summer cumulus. In its shadow, under memorable blue eyes, two dark crescents stood out against his inveterate New York City pallor, smudged as though by Christmas coal, the lumps that Santa Claus reserves especially for fallen rock stars and other habitual offenders. Ran, as always, was carrying two guitars, the ones Claire called "the Gibson girls" and, again, "the mistress and the wife." His road-worn but still handsome face seemed clarified by recent suffering for which he had nobody but himself and maybe God to blame. As he came up the ramp, a bit short-winded, with that slapping sole, he looked like someone who had served a stretch in purgatory, and now, there, in paradisal light at

the end of the square tunnel, was Claire. And paradise turned out to be
South Carolina. Who could have guessed?

Amid the tourists headed for the links and Grand Strand beaches, the
rushing bankers on their cells, his wife and children looked like a subversive
little carnival unto themselves. Hope, his four-year-old, had on a pink
dress-up with blue and silver sequins and boa trim. In dandelion-white hair
tinged with the faintest faint blond rinse, her plastic tiara featured sapphires
one shade bluer but only half as incandescent as her eyes. Over the summer,
her legs had sectioned out like telescopes and suddenly acquired a shape like
Claire's. At their distal ends, her nails were painted chipped hot pink. So,
too, Ran saw—with an alarm he rapidly suppressed—were his son's.
Wrapped around his mother's waist, Charlie, not quite two, had on a Cody
Chestnut T-shirt with a grape juice stain and a hard-shell plastic fire hat:
FDNY. As he shyly grinned with two new serrated teeth, Ran saw with a
pang, for the first time, who his son was going to be, which had carved it-
self from formless babyhood while Daddy was away.

"Dute! Bi'truck!" he said, and banged his plastic lid.

"Fire truck, dude." Putting down his cases, Ran took a knee, removed
his hat, and raked his fingers through his sandy hair. With a hint of the grin
that once upon a time had opened many doors (quite a few of which he
would have been wiser to eschew), he held out his arms, not quite in time
to catch the kids as they smashed into him like rocket-propelled grenades.

"Dad! Da-*dee*!" Hope squealed.

"Hey, Sweet Pete!" He keeled over, laughing, on his seat.

"Daddy, how come you're so skinny?"

"I'm not skinny, am I?"

"Yes, you are. How come?"

"Bi'truck! Bi'truck!" Charlie said, lacking skills, but concerned to have
his contribution recognized.

"Man, I really like that hat," said Ran. "I don't suppose . . ."

He commenced a swap, but it was ill-advised. "Mine!" said Charlie,
clamping down with two big little hands.

Hope tugged his sleeve. "How come?"

"Well, Pete . . ."

He lost her on the hesitation.

"Look what I have on!"

"Umm-hmm. Très chic," he said.

"You bought it for my birthday." Her tone flirted with severity, as though she suspected he'd forgotten.

"I remember," Ransom said, and now he did. "It fit you like a sack."

In New York, cruising the garment district one day in his cab, he'd seen the item on a rolling rack disappearing up a ramp and haggled out the passenger-side window with a nervous Puerto Rican kid in a black do-rag. This was after the label dropped him; after his well-meaning friends rallied round and got him a stint producing a band from the U of Alabama called Broken Teeth ("the next Hootie," they were touted as). After five days at the Magic Shop in SoHo, he was ready to kill them all or commit suicide, preferably both. In lieu of either, he showed up at home that night behind the wheel of a lurching, shot-shocked cab, making good a long-term threat. Five songs into an album he was hell-bent on self-producing and distributing, he bought studio time by running up huge debts on MasterCard (at one point, he had six he had to rotate every time the promo rate expired). One morning he came back from the garage after a shift and found the closets empty. He sat for a long time at the kitchen table, with Claire's bran muffin and her coffee—sweet and extra light—in a bag, before he read the note. It was on her good stationery, heavy linen stock with the address blind embossed on the verso of the envelope. Even nineteen years in a rock band couldn't burn some good habits from the heart of a Charleston girl who'd grown up south of Broad. They left in April, and Ran hit bottom, or what looked like bottom then. By that September morning in the airport, he'd discovered that, beneath the basement, the house we know as life has several unsuspected floors; and, below those, several more.

"We missed you, Daddy," Hope said.

"I missed you, too," he would have liked to say, but Ransom, briefly, didn't trust his voice. Sitting on the floor as the traffic veered like a stream around a rock, Ransom squeezed his children hard and smelled them like a stricken animal recovering the scent of its lost cubs, and then he opened his red eyes and looked at Claire.

Standing barefoot on the Astroturf, in defiance, probably, of several laws, she had on a pair of faded, cutoff OshKosh overalls he recognized far better than Hope's dress and from much further back, the sort that date from those brief years when you're as close to physical perfection as you're ever going to get and later put away in the unlikely hope that you'll fit into them again. They not only fit her, they were loose, and her tan was almost shocking—a fearless and unapologetic mahogany the likes of which no one who listened to *All Things Considered* and read the *New York Times* had dared in recent times, as though in coming here she'd thrown away whole levels of caution and regressed to a wild, natural state. After years of threats and promises, she'd finally cut her hair, the long bolt of heavy chestnut silk she'd both prized and half resented, having had to tend it dutifully like an aging parent or the grave of a lover who'd died young. It barely brushed her shoulders now, the ends chopped in different lengths that looked gamine and unconsidered in a way nobody had to tell him cost a lot of dough. The gray threads he'd begun to notice in New York had been replaced by red-gold highlights, and all this somehow contributed to, but did not explain, the peculiar, throbbing vividness she had, which Ransom wanted to attribute to her coming home, to starting a new job and being mistress of her own demesne again, any cause, any possibility but one: that his absence had been good for her, had allowed certain parts of her long eclipsed by certain parts of him to reemerge and shine.

"That's some hat, Sheriff," she said as the kids hauled him to his feet.

Ran held the crown and stared inside. "It's white."

"Duly noted." She smiled at him from eyes that were the color of the glaze on good crème caramel, with that same burned, limpid sweetness. "You are skinny, bud."

"The Tragedy Diet," he said, making light. "Do I look bad?"

"Fuck you, Hill," she whispered as she tiptoed up. "You look twenty-five."

"Twenty-five?" His tone mingled incredulity and pleasure. Thinking "cheek," Ran was happily surprised when Claire gave him her lips.

"Well, thirty-five." Her eyes had now turned sly. "Forty, tops."

"Hey, I'll take forty," said Ransom, who was forty-five. Never shy of taking chances, he glanced his fingers through her hair. "It's great."

"Thanks," she said, and her expression sobered—not rejectingly, but taking his touch the way you might a friend who says *We need to talk,* when the matter is a serious one on which you know the two of you may not agree.

Her kisses were allowable, then; reciprocal privileges, if any, had yet to be determined.

Pondering the state of play, Ran let his hand drop to her shoulder, wanderingly. On one side of the flap, a replacement button had been sewn. Thumbing the suspender, he drew his hand away. "I remember these."

Claire looked down, then up again. "You do? From where?" Her face was innocent and clueless.

Ransom pressed his lips and shook his head.

In the baggage area, he chatted with the kids and held their hands, trying not to look at her too much. His lovesickness for his wife of nineteen years was like a tumor in his chest, one he didn't know if he could live with, but had proved beyond all shadow of a doubt he couldn't live without.

And the carousel went round and round and spit out his black bag, and away they went, back to Wando Passo.

T W O

*Y*ou wait here."

With an ambiguous smile, Claire put on her Wayfarers and her Yankees cap and disappeared with the kids into the dark maw of the parking deck, leaving Ransom at the curb.

The heat was something. He took off his coat. Ransom had forgotten heat like this. Even in the second week of September, it hit you like a comforter hauled prematurely from the dryer, scalding and wringing wet.

Before long, they hove to around the curve. Amid the late-model Tauruses and minivans, they looked more carnival-like than ever in a torch red Thunderbird convertible, the old country-club-style '56 with the Continental spare that had once belonged to Ransom's dad, who had sewed seams on the line at the Dixie Bagging mill in Killdeer, North Carolina, Ran's hometown. Mel had bought the car the one and only way a seamer could afford: from the salvage yard, with the shotgun side stove in and suspicious stains on the white Dial-A-Matic seats. Since his death, it had been parked beneath a tarp in Wando Passo's crumbling stable. Claire wanted to trade it for something more kid-friendly and familial, but for Ran, the Bird represented something he could neither put his finger on nor quite let go.

As they drew abreast, loud music thumped the air like a damp rug, and the kids were syncing out a little Motor City dance routine:

We said, "It's so tru-oo-ue,"
We said, "It's so deep,"
But all it ever was, baby,
Was talking in our sleep, that's all,
Just talking in my sleep. . . .

Their little faces screwed up in impassioned winces, they whined the
lyrics like world-weary, hardened rockers who'd sweated blood for every
word, and it was sweet and funny and, for Ran, like having someone open
his belly with a knife and extract his small intestines link by smoking link.
"Talking in My Sleep," you see, was the biggest hit the Ransom Hill Band
ever had, but the version booming off the box in the front seat was RAM's,
and the singer wasn't Ransom, it was Mitchell Pike.

"Do you like it, Daddy?" Hope asked.

"Where'd you learn those moves?" he said, struggling to keep glumness
from his tone.

"Mommy teached us them."

"Taught them to us," Claire corrected.

"Taught them to us."

"Yea, Mommy! Yea, Doddy! Yea, me!" Unshy of self-advancement,
Charlie hitched his wagon to the chorus as it circled back.

"Talky nana seep, bay-bay, talky nana seep, aw-haw . . ."

"They've been practicing all week." Over her rims, Claire shot him a
look of friendly mischief and jangled the keys like forbidden fruit.

Ignoring them, Ran slipped into the shotgun seat and punched Eject.

"Don't tell me. You don't like what Mitchell did." Her dark eyes
looked preemptively fatigued.

His blue ones flashed. "You're kidding, right?"

"Come on, Ran, it's sweet."

"Sweet?"

She stood her ground. "Yes, I think they found a sweetness in it we
didn't see. Why not just give it to them? Did Mitch ever call?"

"No, Mitch never did."

"How about the check?" Her smirk invited him to schuss past hurt feelings and let other people's money wax the runners on his sled, but Ransom felt resistance, and though this might have been predicted, his forecasts had unilaterally called for clear blue skies. In New York last night packing up to come, as he moved about the apartment on West Jane, he returned over and over to the kitchen table and over and over slid the royalty check out of the music publisher's envelope. $17,631.27. No fortune, true, but it had been quite some time since Ran had seen a check that large, quite some time since he'd seen any checks at all. Defying doctor's orders, he uncorked a celebratory red from better times and poured a glass and put on *Tosca,* music Claire had turned him on to all those years ago, when he was on the cusp of stardom, yet still, at heart, the same hick kid who'd grown up in a company row house in the shadow of the great twin stacks of Dixie Bag with Mel, a fearful, angry drunk whose happiest hour came after the whistle blew on Friday afternoons. Returning from the package store, Mel ritually climbed behind the wheel and punched the buttons on the Town and Country radio of this car, which sat for years on blocks in the backyard awaiting restoration, as the rain and snow and dust and autumn leaves fell into it. At eleven, with money saved from scrubbing down the urinals at Dixie Bag, Ransom bought his first Chet Atkins self-instruction course and taught himself to Travis-pick, pledging himself to rock like a Famine Irish orphan to the church. When he arrived in New York on a Greyhound six years later, he could lay down, note for note, every lick Keith Richards played on *Let It Bleed,* yet he lived there for eight years and never set foot in the Met. And it wasn't that he feared the music—actually, he was curious. What Ransom feared was the moment at the ticket window, when some poised, well-turned-out girl with her hair up and a string of pearls would ask him what he wanted, and he wouldn't know the proper protocol for ordering, and he'd go hot and red like a specimen pinned beneath her clement 10x gaze. Claire—who'd had every chance, every reason, to be that girl, and wasn't—had changed all that.

And as Maria Callas sang "Vissi d'arte," vibrating that silver treble E string in the spine that Ran, in his own way, still reached for every time he picked up his Les Paul, he got a little drunk. More relaxed and closer to himself than he'd felt in months, he turned the check facedown and wrote, "pay to the order of Claire DeLay," and signed his name. All the way to South Carolina on the plane, he felt it in his wallet, radiating subtle heat, goodness, and he imagined the conversation he and Claire would have, her relief that things, which hadn't been okay in quite a while, could begin, from here, to be okay again. And now she asked him, "How about the check?" and the old resistance cropped up and surprised him, though it really shouldn't have. Somehow, in all his fantasy preenactments of this reunion, the one thing Ran had never counted on was the future being like the past.

"Can we talk about it later?"

"Suit yourself." Claire answered his evasion with no light in her face and put the key in the ignition.

He touched her arm. "Let's just wait till we get home, okay?"

Her expression came back a little ways in his direction, as far as "mature and fair." But it had started warm and lost some ground.

"Maybe I will drive. . . ."

She reached for the chrome handle, but Ransom gripped her waist and slid beneath her, switching seats the way they used to do. As they passed, he felt the difference in her body, slighter but more dense, the bone and sinew closer to the surface, smelled her plain good soap, the perfume at the pulse-point under her left ear and, below that, an emergent hint of her BO, like turned black earth. Briefly, in his lap, there was something radiant and almost hot, and some of it was her, some him, and which was which and what was what was past parsing out. But though there wasn't any stiffness in Claire's body, there also wasn't any give.

Rebuffed, he pulled them out into the hot wind and took 17 south. As they crossed the double bridges over the Waccamaw and the Black, Ran saw the voluminous billow hovering over Georgetown like a benignant mushroom cloud. It always looked so white and clean emerging from the smokestacks, as if the south side of town concealed a cloud manufactory. Then you caught the sulfur smell of a paper plant.

Ran dropped off his prescription at the CVS, and when he returned, Claire and the children—who'd picked up T-bones and instant mac and cheese next door—were working out to Marvin Gaye. When Ran heard Charlie belting out the Hooked on Phonics version of "Sexual Healing," he laughed aloud.

"In fifteen years, they'll be telling this one on the couch for sure," he said, slipping behind the wheel.

"You don't end up on the couch for that." Claire nodded to the rearview, and, together, as they hadn't been in quite a while, they contemplated their offspring cutting loose. Ran picked up the jewel case.

"So, Marvin G . . . I guess you've been warming up for my arrival."

"I've been warming up," Claire said. "But who says for you?" She poked her tongue into her cheek, and her eyes flashed, toying with him now.

Ran's gaze narrowed a degree. "What's this new je ne sais quoi, DeLay? You seem different."

She flushed at the acknowledgment and looked away. "Not different so much as . . ."

"As?"

"Getting back to who I used to be."

"Hey, seems to me, I remember her." He smiled and put the key in the ignition. "That chick."

Claire's gaze, limpid now and bright, rested on his; then she reached out and straightened his collar, allowed her knuckles to graze his cheek. Something in Ransom soared, and, turning off the highway, he joined them on the chorus.

> . . . *when I get that feeling*
> *I want sexual healing—sexual healing*

The words flowed back into the slipstream, and for twenty minutes, as they shot through the blue Carolina afternoon, happiness was with them, like a fifth, completing presence in the car, a familiar stranger Ran had lately doubted he would ever see again.

They took 701 twelve miles inland toward Planterville, a tunnel, ribbon-straight and flat, through walls of pine and cypress forest, broken occasionally by marsh and estuary, gold-and-silver-spangled black this time of day.

It was coming on to dusk by the time he turned into the allée of ancient water oaks. Three-quarters of a mile long, there were over a hundred trees on either side, like deposed gods from some old pantheon, brooding wrongs the wider world had moved on from.

A cool exhalation from the river, not quite mist, further softened the soft light as the car moved up the potholed, sandy drive under heavy branches draped with Spanish moss where cicadas whirred. The whole scene possessed a riverine lushness composed of countless shades of green, and at the end of the tunnel of great trees, the house sat like a sepia-toned visitation from an old daguerreotype set down in the middle of a modern color photograph.

Wando Passo was none of the things Ransom had expected on his first visit, when Clive DeLay—Claire's vindictive, jolly, aquiline-nosed uncle— was still alive. "The true old Carolina style," Clive jeeringly explained— after ascertaining, in a quarter of a minute, everything he cared to know about Claire's rock star husband—"wasn't Tara, wasn't Greek Revival, wasn't elegant and white. What it was was *this*." And his eyes—his bright, narrow, happy, entitled, avian old eyes—seemed to Ran to gloat: "And it belonged to *us*, not you, you ill-bred North Carolina cracker." Clive was in the backyard now, taking his dirt nap beneath the cypress tree by the black pond with all the other dead DeLays, but Ran still sometimes felt he was here on sufferance, at the master's—now the mistress's—whim.

Under a tin hipped roof with six crumbling chimneys sticking out, what Wando Passo really was was a giant unpainted saltbox, a saltbox of seven thousand square feet and fifteen rooms. Massive and faintly carious, with the occasional window missing where symmetry demanded it, others where no Crayola-toting five-year-old with an ounce of self-respect would have placed them, the house was like a great ambition marred by insufficient planning and excess afterthought. At ground level, a wide porch elled around two sides under a shed roof. Its exposed rafters were supported not by columns, but by simple posts whose sole detail was a chamfered edge, irregularly cut with foot-adzes by the old slave carpenters who hewed them out of native cypress logs hauled up by mule team from the swamp.

Inside, though, despite a half century's neglect, the house revealed its charms. The foyer cut up through two stories. Hung on fifty pounds of sterling links, the massive crystal chandelier was framed by a horseshoe staircase. Along its two curved walls, the paneling was faux-painted to resemble verde marble, and stepped above the rails were portraits of Claire's ancestors, old planters of rice and, before that, of indigo, in crimson British uniforms, powdered wigs, silk hose, with silver buckles on their shoes.

A spacious center hall with three large rooms on either side led to the kitchen. Claire took the kids out back as Ran unwrapped the steaks in one of the deep bays of the old rust-spotted enamel sink that dated—like the pearl-tone Formica and the Frigidaire, with its heavy nickel latch and hinges and the top compartment made to hold a block of ice—from Clive's renovation in the thirties. Overhead, the dusty chandelier harked back to a still more distant era, when the room had been a parlor and the kitchen house had been somewhere out there in the yard where Ransom headed now.

On his way, he left the check at Claire's place on the table, smoothing it over the rough old heart pine planks.

"Look at this a minute, Ran, would you?" Claire said as he poured charcoal in the grill.

Brushing his hands, he joined her where she stood, arms akimbo, frowning at a boil of rot that had erupted in a foundation timber on the river side. Ran squatted on his hams and palpated a discolored patch of paint. The wood around the sore was punky and unsolid. When he poked, his index finger sank fist-knuckle deep.

He looked up, wiping mildewed wood pulp on his pants.

"Not good," she surmised.

He shook his head. "You've got a rotten sill."

"Just tell me how much it's going to cost."

"If it's gone, a fair amount," he said, standing up again. "They'll have to jack this bad boy up and—"

Hearing him begin to wax enthusiastic, she held a hand up like a cop. "Stop. Don't tell me. I don't want to know."

"The core may still be solid, though," he repented. "I'll check it when there's better light."

"Well, unless the house is going to fall down on our heads," she said, starting off, "it's going to have to wait until I start my job."

"Maybe not . . ."

She turned.

"I left something for you inside on the table."

Her stare interrogated him, but Ransom, under pressure, didn't break. "I guess I'll see about that grill."

In the first *whoosh* of exploding fire as Ransom tossed the match, he saw an ant, a large black one, crawling across a pale expanse of trodden clay. Dancing from the Weber's cauldron, the tall blue flames revealed another, and another, a whole line marching across the lawn, flanked by their distorted, much larger shadows. Following them in the direction of the graveyard, Ransom, halfway there, came to a patch of old-growth periwinkle, where the tiny regiment vanished into cover. With the insole of his boot, he brushed the greenery aside. The earth within had been milled into friable red grains, the telltale sign. Trying to ascertain the colony's extent, he waded deeper. The ground turned spongy underfoot. Feeling his way gingerly, his boot struck something solid, upright, like a stob. Squatting on his hams, Ran swept aside the leaves and looked. Protruding from the ground was what appeared at first to be a nub of upthrust tree root, possibly a surveyor's pin. In the failing light, it was impossible to make it out. Touching it, he felt a shock. "Shit! The damn thing's hot!" he said, reverting to old habits from the cab.

As he rubbed his hand and looked, Ran noticed smoke rising from the ground around him, a thin, subtle cloud, drifting over the periwinkle in the direction of the river. Suddenly, a boat horn blew.

"What the hell . . ." Startled, he fell over on his seat.

At that moment, he heard the fluttering of wings and looked up to see a flock of birds passing up where afternoon preserved a late, last note of blue. Wheeling in dark formation, they threw their shadow earthward as they went, creating the illusion. Trying to make out what they were, Ran watched them drift eastward in a twittering green cloud. Shelving his eyes, he stared toward the river, waiting for the boat to come around the bend. A beat passed. Then another. Ransom, as he waited, could feel his heartbeat pounding out a heavy klaxon in his chest.

THREE

*I*n the Nina's bows, Addie, with the breeze of the boat's headway blowing her loose hair, watches six black oarsmen in a lighter off the starboard side put their backs into the strokes, redoubling their efforts as the little steamer overtakes them.

"Look, Aunt Blanche, they're racing us—isn't it lovely!" She points with the hand that holds her book—a new edition of Byron, in red morocco, picked up at Russell's for the trip. In the excitement, she has yet to cut the pages. . . .

Last evening, as they crossed the bar at Charleston, the Niagara fired across the bow, and all night long, as the crew tumbled casks and bales into the sea, the big Federal frigate gave chase—so close at times, Addie could hear the creaking of the warship's masts. Today, just at dawn, the Nina slipped, safe, into Winyah Bay.

Addie barely closed her eyes, and her first encounter with the Pee Dee has ravished her so wholly that her beloved Byron has received short shrift.

"Oh, and listen . . . Listen, Aunt Blanche." Now she holds a finger up.

Above the engine and the rush of wind, the song drifts up:

In case I never see you anymo'
I hope to meet on Canaan's happy sho'. . . .

Addie's eyes, which are blue and mobile, showing every change of mood or thought, film with happiness as she looks at her aunt, who stands holding down her bonnet, under stress from the dazzle of sunlight on black water, from the fresh, raw wind.

"Yes, dear, but sparks . . . The smoke is blowing toward us." Blanche eyes the imported silk of Addie's dress regretfully. From Mrs. Cummings's shop on Meeting Street, the centerpiece of the trousseau, it is pale blue to match her niece's eyes, with darker horizontal stripes to bring them out, a style called bayadere, all the rage this winter past, the gayest social season anybody can remember, with a Secession ball or supper every week, a Secession something somewhere every night. "And your hair, Addie . . . Please come in before we have to hire a team of mules and drag a hay rake through your hair."

"Do I look a fright?" she asks, laughing as she touches it. "I'm sure I must. But, oh, Aunt Blanche, I feel happy. Have you ever seen such a sky? If you struck it with a mallet, it looks as though it just might ring. And, look, the birds!" she cries now, pointing, as a sudden flock swoops down. "They're racing, too! What are they? Are they the ones that Nellie makes?"

"No, dear, those are bobolinks," Blanche answers. "These are green. I don't know what they are."

"Maybe it's an omen!"

"A good one, let us pray."

"I'm sure it is," says the new bride. "Seeing this, I feel it will all come right. It must. It simply shall, Aunt Blanche."

"I hope so, dear," says Blanche, with notably less enthusiasm than her niece. "Though I can't speak from personal experience, Addie, I've seen many marriages that start in passion come to bad results, while those built on prudence and good sense endure and thrive. Though Harlan isn't whom I would have chosen for you once upon a time, you and he are well matched in several ways."

"You're right, Aunt Blanche, we are. And I thank you for all you've done. You've been both mother and father to me."

"Dear girl."

As the women press each other's hands, Addie looks at Blanche's face, at what is circumscribed and fearful there, put out by last night's events and the disruption of routine this trip upriver represents—at what is afraid, essentially, of life—and it strikes her how narrowly she has escaped this fate. And that she has escaped it is due, in no small part, to Blanche herself.

Both the birds and the oarsmen have disappeared now, and Addie's face, in contemplation, as she stares after them into the wake, takes on a melancholy cast.

When she first came out in society, she was courted by Paul Hayne, a poet who has now achieved a minor fame, yet when he proposed, she turned him down. And *why? Because when Addie searched her heart at seventeen, she couldn't say she loved Paul in the way Evangeline loved Gabriel Lajeunesse in Longfellow's poem, which she first read at Mme. Togno's school, in the dear old double house on Tradd Street two doors east of Meeting, where Addie walked each morning from her aunt's. She felt certain then that such love—love like Evangeline's, that would be proof against the power of distance, time, and even Death—would come to her; it seemed impossible that it should not. And as Addie waited for her Gabriel—like Sleeping Beauty for the prince—one season became two; two turned, suddenly, to ten, and she had passed, without perceiving any inward change, from debutante to the succeeding stage in the female life cycle that in Charleston is euphemized as "chaperone." Instead of dancing at cotillions, to her bemusement and surprise, it became expected that Miss Huger would take the piano bench and play for the enjoyment of the younger crowd, who suddenly threw themselves into the round dances, the mazurka and the waltz that in her day were just the other side of proper, practiced only in the fastest set.*

And there came a point—where was it?—when Addie learned to smile at the girl she'd been, who had believed that love like Evangeline's exists outside the imaginations of poets and the pages of their books. She swallowed down her disappointment and reconciled herself to the fact that she would never marry, that she would have her morning walks in White Point Garden and spend her afternoons with books and visits to the sick, and take the family pew at St. Michael's every Sunday and fold her spotted hands and listen, nodding, to the sermon and die an old maid like her aunt and be buried in the churchyard there, with Great Michael, the deep bell in the carillon, to mourn for her and count the hours into years. There were worse fates, after all. Far worse. And then, just when this future seemed assured, when Addie had accepted it, one night Harlan DeLay, who was rich but from a family that was not quite proper—not proper by a stretch— came to supper. He made her a compliment about her gown and laughed at a remark she made. Their eyes met over it, and something passed. Even now, Addie cannot say what. But she does not deceive herself that it was love, not even the sort she felt for Paul. Yet she liked Harlan's jollity and size. In his slightly hazy ginger eyes there was a spark of play, something eager, childlike, reckless, that sought confirmation of its effect in her and did not appear to entertain the possibility of disappointment. And, too, there was the sympathy of one motherless child for another. She quickly saw the effects the lack of female governance had had in him, the way he laughed too loudly and sought to draw too much attention to himself, but these were things she felt that she could help to temper and correct. He seemed to want correction in that way, and even said so.

And so she took the gloves and sugarplums he sent her during Race Week in the mad runup to Sumter and felt eighteen again. But what moved Addie more than these was a simple gift of flowers. In a time when Charleston's gallants relied upon the florists, who made up trite bouquets of pinks and bud roses wired stiffly to a stick, with geranium leaves and silver paper frills beneath, Harlan had the wit to pick a quart of white musk roses from Wando Passo's hothouse. The morning after the Jockey Club Ball—where, in the carriage riding home, she first allowed a kiss—he sent them to her in a little wicker creel. Somehow those flowers, hinting at a sensitivity, an original turn of mind she hadn't clearly seen before, set Addie irreversibly upon her course.

And so, when Harlan asked her for her hand, she said yes, and did so gratefully despite the tales she'd heard about his father. Percival DeLay's alliance with Paloma—the Cuban Negress he brought back from Matanzas years ago—is infamous throughout the Lowcountry. (Some say he won her in a game of cards!) Paloma's children serve in privileged roles on the estate. Due to these peculiarities, no few wedding invitations were declined, a slight that not even the Huger name could prevent. Harlan tried to speak to her about the situation once, but he grew flustered, and Addie, having accepted him already, felt that it would be indelicate to press. "When I'm master, things will be different," is all he really said. "I mean Wando Passo to be a proper home for us and for our children, Addie, the way it never was for me. With you as mistress, it can be a great house again."

Actually, in the moment, he seemed rather fine, and his dream was one that she could share. The truth is, when he asked her, Addie fairly leapt. And it was not for land or money or any of the things that social Charleston understands and cares about. Part of it was the chance for children and a family, things Addie longed for as a child, growing up a ward in her aunt's house. The deeper reason, though, the one that only comes to Addie now, as she first looks at, then looks away from, Blanche, is this: she married him because she felt or feared that Harlan's offer would be the last she would receive, her final chance to join the dancers in the dance.

And now, still holding Blanche's hand, Addie turns and smiles, though her eyes do not participate. For a moment, they take on the oddly mesmerized and mesmerizing quality they've had since she was four months old, as she lay nursing with her dah on the sun-drenched beach at Pawleys, when her young parents walked, hand in hand, into a sparkling, calm sea, and did not come back.

"Look, Addie!" Blanche points.

And suddenly here they are. As the Nina rounds the final bend, the captain blows the horn and Addie catches her first glimpse of Wando Passo, her new home. There is the park; there, the six great chimneys rising up above the canopies of the old trees; there, on the rolling greensward that slopes down to the river, a crowd of *well-dressed people mills beneath a tent with colored ribbons flying at the poles. Now, thinks Addie . . . Not tomorrow, not next week, next year, but today, this hour, my true life starts. . . .*

And there, surrounded by his friends, stands Harlan on the dock. It's the first time she's seen him since the wedding, the first time she's seen him in his handsome, worrisome gray uniform. There, to his left, is Tom Wagner, his commanding officer at Fort Moultrie. (Just three days, she thinks, three days before he must report.) Both Harlan's face and Tom's—all the faces in the crowd, in fact—are turned expectantly one way, as if waiting, yet, oddly, not for her. Odder still, Harlan holds a gun.

FOUR

*E*yes still shaded with a hand, Ransom gazed southward toward the river bend, waiting for a boat that never came. He could still make out the birds, though, away there in the distance. Like spindrift from a breaking wave, they hung a moment, a curtain of bright green high in the air, and then they veered and Ransom lost them, too. Through some trick of light, or of perspective, they vanished as though never there.

"*Daddy!*"

Coming to as from a fugue, he found Hope glaring from the edge of the periwinkle.

"What?" he said.

"What are you looking at? I called you *three times!*"

"Did you see those birds?"

"What birds?"

"You . . ." He took a sounding from her face and stopped.

"Mommy said the coals are ready. Everybody's hungry."

Some doubt of him had been instilled, he recognized. "All right, then, come on," he said, deciding it was going to be his project now to banish it. "I'm deputizing you as my assistant."

"What's 'deputizing'?"

He smiled and put his hand on her small shoulder. "It means you're going to help me cook."

They were really there, though, weren't they? As he walked toward the fire with Hope, Ran posed the question to himself, or, rather, a little voice asked him, the familiar one that, in the morning, when you hesitate between the blue shirt and the red, reminds you, *Red is better with your coloring.* This conversation, for the most part, in most of us, goes on subliminally, yet for Ransom, in the months since Claire had left, when he had no one else to help him choose his clothes, this voice had broken through; he had befriended it, or it, him, and he sometimes answered it aloud. This didn't seem too worrisome—the voice, after all, was his—yet in the cab and elsewhere, it had occasioned looks, so Ransom, heading south to rehabilitate his life, had decided to forgo further conversations in this line.

"Absolutely," he muttered now, forgetting that resolve.

"What, Daddy?"

"Nothing, Pete."

She watched, frowning, as he forked the first steak on the grill. "Is that zebra?"

Ransom laughed. "Zebra? What, does your old man look like a poacher, a horseflesh-eating kind of guy? Nope, Pete, plain old beef."

With her hands clasped behind her like an Oxford don, scratching one big toe with the painted toenail of the next, Hope contemplated the meat with the oddly mesmerized and mesmerizing stare she'd had since infancy. "Scar eats beef."

"Who's Scar?" he asked as he seared one side and flipped.

"He's the bad brother in *The Lion King.*" Brushing dirt smudges from her knees, Claire emerged from the garden with Charlie and a shirtfront full of Silver Queen and baby mesclun leaves.

"He isn't bad," Hope said. "Scar's my daddy."

Surprise made Ransom's laugh a little sharp. "So who does that make me?"

"Silly, Scar's my *real* daddy. Let's play the Scar game!"

Claire's look said, *Don't pursue,* but Hope dropped to her knees and reached her fingers up to him, curled like claws. *"Help me, brother, please!"* she said, and her eyes glowed like two small illuminated swimming pools at night.

"No, ma'am." Claire hauled Hope to her feet. "I need you inside to help me shuck this corn."

"Mommy, *please!*"

"Madam, in the house. Right now. March."

"*Mo*-om!"

"Move it!"

What's this? Ran's look said to Claire, and hers answered, *Later.*

In the square of mottled, antique yellow light, he watched them stripping tassels and green shuck into the sink, the same home movie he'd screened every night in New York all these months when he turned out the lights. Twice, Claire passed the table without looking, but the third time she glanced at the check, as though to reassure herself that it was really there. She glanced toward the window, seeking him outside in the darkness. Ransom, though—outside in the darkness, looking back—could tell by the vagueness in her face that Claire couldn't see him through her own reflection in the glass.

"I think I may have diagnosed your problem," he told her, slightly later, as he poured the wine.

"Do tell."

"Carpenter ants."

Claire glanced up, surprised. "You're kidding."

"There's a mongo nest out there in the periwinkle patch."

"Carpenter ants . . . They're not that bad, though, right?"

Ransom shrugged. "Not as bad as termites. From what I understand, they only bore in wood that's wet. That sill felt pretty damp to me."

"So where's the water coming from?"

"That would be the question."

Claire considered. "That side of the house is always muddy when it rains."

"Maybe it's runoff from the roof. I'll see what I can see tomorrow. By the way," he said as he sat down, "there isn't power to the cabin, is there?"

"No, why?"

"When I was feeling around out there, I got a shock. I wondered if there could be a buried line."

Claire shook her head. "I don't think so. The house line comes in on the other side, from that pole in the allée. It must be five hundred yards from there."

Ran considered. "Maybe I just scared myself."

"Look at me."

Feeling this parental tête-à-tête had gone on long enough, Charlie put his bowl of macaroni on his head.

"Nice chapeau," said Ransom, feeling some paternal comment was required.

Encouraged, Charlie strafed the china in the corner cupboard, twelves of this and that, an hour's cleanup for a second and a half. Another volley hit the chandelier and plopped back down like muddy rain. With a big, pleased, slightly nervous grin, he looked around, assessing impact. Knowing better than to laugh, Hope polled Mom and Dad with a jewelly gaze that said, *Bring on the dancing bears!*

"So, Monster Man, that all you got?" said Ran.

They howled like happy hell on that, like happy hell broke loose. Charlie took his bowl and tossed that, too.

Claire's chair skidded with the sound of a bad traffic accident. "Okay, buster! That's it for you! Upstairs in the bath!"

"I've got him." Swigging Pinot Noir and taking one quick bite of steak, Ran tossed the squealing miscreant across his shoulder like a twenty-five-pound sack of Idahos and headed up the servant stairs.

As the tub filled, Ran undressed his son and, with a finger-sized black comb, raked melted cheese and white sauce from his hair. Charlie took advantage of a lull and bolted down the hall. From twenty feet away, he looked back with that gleeful, defiant, anxious grin that seemed to say, *You can't catch me (but please try).*

"You'd better get your little ass right back here, Hoss," said Ransom, with an ominously Mel-like note, as the fun wore thin.

Charlie, in response, raised his arms, cocked one knee like an impertinent dauphin, and burst into a stomping, penis-flapping version of the Highland fling, cantering down the hall in one direction and then, widdershins, back again. From the landing, Claire looked at Ran, and Ran looked back. Astounded and indignant, they both blinked and burst out laughing the way they hadn't laughed that day and probably that year.

In the rocker, though, the little animal stilled, and as Ran read, he could see the pink curve of tongue working the plastic nipple from beneath the way no adult remembers how. With his buttery pomade, he looked choirboy trig and innocent, and under the smell of residual cheddar, under the watermelon of his no-tears shampoo, there was something that reminded Ransom of the smell of jute that, along with sweat and gasoline, was always in his father's clothes and which, in spite of everything, he'd loved.

When Ran finally put him in the crib, Charlie said, "Stay, Doddy, stay," so plaintively that Ran turned off the light and sat back down.

"Doddy?"

"What, buddy?"

"Doddy?"

"I'm right here, sweet boy."

"Doddy?"

"Close your eyes now."

"Shadlow, Doddy . . ."

"It's just the bedpost."

"Doddy?"

"Shh."

"Doddy?"

"Charlie, damn it, go to sleep!"

Forty minutes later, he made good his escape.

Claire was in the bathroom, washing up.

"Jesus."

She mugged in the mirror, knowing all about it.

"How do you deal with two?"

She shrugged. "One minute it's five o'clock, the next I know it's nine and they're both in their own beds in their own rooms and neither one is dead, and how they got there—poof!—before I'm five steps down the hall, it flies out of my head."

"How is it I don't remember any of this?"

"Post-traumatic stress, babe."

She'd hung her coveralls on the door and had on just her sleeveless linen blouse and underpants—new ones, Ransom noticed, hot pink briefs the color of her nails, with darker fuchsia trim. "Nice undies."

With a droll look, she put a cotton ball on a bottle of green witch hazel and shook like Lady Luck about to roll the dice. The room filled with sweet astringency.

"You excited about teaching?"

"More nervous." She began to swab her face. "A lot of this stuff I haven't thought about since Juilliard. I mean, four-part tonal writing? I barely—and I mean *barely*—remember what it is."

"They're lucky to have you, Claire," he said. "You've got ten times more real-world experience than anybody in that dump. To say nothing of talent."

She glanced at him uncertainly. "Yeah, well, thanks, I guess. Harlow's not a dump, though, Ran. It's really not."

There was just one way the conversation could go now.

"So, how's Cell Phone?" Ran's attempt to make this sound offhand came off like skywriting four-story capitals in multicolored smoke.

Claire's reflection frowned at him, and then her face. "For starters, no one calls him Cell Phone anymore."

"I guess it's not in keeping with his newfound dignity as dean." Ran's single bite of steak—or something—threatened to repeat.

She turned. "It's been seventeen years, Ran. . . ."

"Eighteen," he corrected. "Not that anybody's counting."

"Eighteen years," she said, building up a head of steam. "After Marcel left . . ."

"Marcel?"

"After he left RHB, he toured with Olatunji. He was the principal percussionist with the fucking Boston Philharmonic. His dignity isn't 'newfound,' and it doesn't stand or fall by you."

"You remember, though, don't you?" Ransom said. "That first one he got at Crazy Eddie's back when even the roadies had no idea what a mobile was? I think it was some sort of prototype. It weighed about six pounds and came with its own vinyl tote . . . more like a holster for a ray gun?" He laughed with happy malice. "The only place he could make calls was from the observation deck of the Empire State on a clear day when the wind was blowing from the south-southeast?" Doubled over now, hands on knees, Ransom gasped and tears streamed down his cheeks.

Claire slapped the countertop and stamped her bare brown foot. "Ransom! Look at me!"

Looking at the quiver in her pretty thigh instead, he swallowed hard and straightened up. A look of less-than-convincing penance filmed his eyes.

"Marcel Jones is my oldest friend. I've known him almost thirty years. For eighteen of them, I didn't call him because of you and your various wounds and sensitivities, but when I was desperate and about to sell this place to pay the taxes, I picked up the phone and asked him for this job. I didn't even know what a fucking CV was, Ran, and he hired me, no questions asked, and I love him for it, I'm grateful to him, and I need this thing to work for Hope and Charlie, I need it for myself, and I'm not going to have you fuck it up over old bullshit and hurt feelings."

"That's fairly clear," he said. "Anything else?"

"Actually, yes. There's a cocktail party at the college tomorrow afternoon, and if you really mean it when you say you want to be supportive, I'd like your skinny ass in situ. Correction, excuse me: I'd like it very much if you would come. In my dream, you will arrive in your white hat; you will walk across the floor; you will look him in the eye; you'll say 'Marcel'—not 'Cell,' not 'Cell Phone'—'Marcel, it's good to see you'; you will shake his hand; there will be peace in the valley. Do you read me, Ransom? Sir?"

"If Cell Phone wants peace, why can't he come see me?"

Her frown turned terminal. "You don't read me. Ransom, I'm not asking this for Marcel, I'm asking this for me."

He let a beat elapse. "I guess this is what they call a Mexican standoff."

"I guess it is."

"That's a hard one, Claire. You know it is."

"Suck it up," she said.

"Can I sleep on it at least?"

"Please do. And sweet dreams to both of you." She turned away, dismissing him, but Ransom didn't go.

"So what is this Scar business, anyway?"

She doused another cotton ball. "It's 101, Ran. He scares her. If she makes him her father and pretends he's good, then he won't hurt her, see?"

"So it's about me. . . ."

Claire laughed a short, bitter laugh. "Why not? Isn't everything?"

Ran held up his hands, surrendering, and turned around.

"I'm sorry," she called after him. "Ran?"

He turned.

"That was a cheap shot."

"Okay."

"And thank you for the check. It'll help with that repair."

"It should do more than that."

"Great," she said. "Because I still owe seven thousand in back taxes, and this year's are coming due."

"There'll be more."

Her face turned sober and attentive.

"Want to know how much?"

"You know I do. Don't make me jump through hoops."

"Come on, guess," he said in a tone of sportive wheedling.

"Fifty?"

He pressed his lips and shook his head.

"More?"

He pointed toward the roof.

"A hundred?"

He shook his head again, trying not to smile.

"Oh, shit, Ran, just tell me, would you! What?" Her excitement had an edge of childlike terror.

He shot her a V.

"Two?" she said. "Two hundred?"

He let the grin come now, and Claire's eyes filmed. She leaned back against the counter, staring blankly into the white void of the clawfoot tub, and then she covered her face and her shoulders shook.

Ransom hadn't seen this coming and took it like a hard punch to the gut. He put his arms around her. "It's been a bad patch, Claire."

She looked up with streaming eyes. "It has for you, too, Ran. I know it has, and I'm sorry."

"It wasn't your fault. You did what you had to."

The happy news led them down the alley, around the corner to revisit the dark place they'd escaped. For years they'd lived like gypsies and never cared for money—or thought they hadn't, when there was enough—and then they'd found out what it was to be without it and have children. They'd found that what they took to be their basic and inalienable rights— to have a decent place to stay, to feed and clothe themselves, to take care of their children—weren't rights at all, were nowhere guaranteed. The moment the spigot of their cash flow had shut down, the moment Ran had ceased to be able to meet his obligations, their inclusion in the human family, in fellowship of people of goodwill, had become tenuous in the extreme, and they had looked as near as their own families—Claire's, that is—and far through the wide world and failed to find a single other person who would go to bat for them or stand up for Hope and Charlie's right to eat and breathe and occupy a space on earth and serve out their allotted term of years. Ran had understood this growing up with Mel, who would have let him starve and advanced starvation as a character-building exercise before he would have forked out for an unearned Happy Meal; Claire had learned the news for the first time. The experience had been stinging and transformative for both.

"Listen, Claire, you don't have to do this Harlow thing."

She sniffed and gathered. "No, it's done, Ran. They're counting on me. I promised, and I want to."

"That's okay, too."

"I'm glad you think so."

He drew the inference, and her look, more sad than confrontational, confirmed the inference he drew. There had been a fundamental shift, and in the resounding childless stillness of the house, they contemplated each other, uncertain what came next.

"You know," she said, "despite your God-given talent for driving me insane, I've missed you. I've missed you every day."

"I've missed you, too," Ran said, "but more at night."

She smiled at this, her lips did, but her eyes were grave. "You know what my therapist said when I told her you were coming?"

"Unless it's complimentary, I encourage you to keep it confidential."

"She looked at me and said, 'Do you know what the definition of insanity is, Claire? Repeating the same action and expecting a different outcome.'"

"Hey, therapists don't know everything," he said. "Doesn't the exception sometimes prove the rule?"

"Let's just try not to blow it."

Ransom shook his head, and his eyes shone.

"Because I don't know how many more tries I have left in me, Ran. I truly don't."

"I've changed, Claire," he said, and he was earnest now. "I know it's up to me to prove, but this time apart, however hard, has made me have a come-to-Jesus with myself. We aren't going to blow it. I'm not. Okay?" When she didn't answer, he repeated it. *"Okay?"*

"Okay. You must be tired." She laid her hand along his cheek. "Aren't you?"

"Not particularly."

"I'm wiped. Let's go to bed."

To his credit, Ransom didn't pump his fist or click his heels or sprint.

Uncharacteristically shy with him, Claire switched off the light and turned her back as she undressed, a moving cameo against the starfield in the window frame. She lay down and Ransom brushed away her hair. Claire's face was grave but open. Feeling a permission he formerly took for granted, a confidence he formerly assumed, he slipped his hand between the mattress and her breast. The nightgown she was wearing, soft and sheer as tissue with repeated washing, revealed the changes time and motherhood had wrought. Her breasts, once just enough to fill a dessert compote, were enlarged and lax. Their indolence aroused him. As he cupped and lifted, Ransom saw the telltale softening in Claire's face and shoulders. Rising on an elbow, he leaned in and kissed her. She kissed back. The negotiation, at first, was as punctilious as that between two Confucian bureaucrats, and then he felt her tongue and they tumbled down a staircase into some loud, sweaty honky-tonk, and the tastes they took became like stinging hits of raw grain alcohol.

"Ran."

"What?"

"We need to be real about this."

"About what?" He drew up to look at her. "Real about what?"

"The money."

He groaned and rolled heavily onto his back. "Can't we have fantasy hour first?"

"I'm serious, asshole. I need to understand this. I need to be clear on what we're doing here."

"We're trying to have sex—I am, at any rate."

"You can't just endorse the checks to me," she said. "What are you supposed to live on? You need to keep some for yourself."

Ransom sighed. "All I want is enough to cut the album."

She took a beat before she asked, "How much will that take?"

He took a beat before he answered. "Seventy-five? Worst case, a hundred."

In the silence, Ran could all but hear the clacking abacus.

Claire rose on an elbow. "So, we pay, what, forty percent in taxes? That leaves one twenty; you spend a hundred on the album; there's twenty left, and you just gave me seventeen. What about the rent on Jane Street? What about groceries, bills, insurance? I mean, how does it work?"

"We just have to make it to the album, Claire. Even if it only sells as much as last time, we'll clear fifty. That's respectable for a year's work. We can live on that down here."

"Whoa," she said. "Hold on, bud. We've never discussed you living here. That's further ahead than I can think right now. And you've already been working on this album for a year, haven't you? You've got, what, four songs?"

"Five," he said, feeling everything begin to slip away. "I had a setback, Claire. Be fair."

"I'm trying to be, Ran, but the truth is, there are always setbacks in your writing. You need six more songs, and if it takes another year, that fifty's down to twenty-five, and that's not enough to live on, here or any-where. So tell me how it is that I don't have to work."

Ran, however, had never thought it out in such detail. "Jesus Christ," he said. "I just told you we have two hundred thousand dollars coming in, and you act like I whacked you with a bat."

"What I heard you say," she countered, as hot as he was, "is that we have a hundred and twenty after taxes, of which you've earmarked a hundred for yourself. Does it work? If it doesn't work, it doesn't work."

"Well, it certainly fucking won't if we don't believe in each other. It won't if you don't believe in me. Do you?"

She didn't answer.

Ransom's feet hit the cold floor. "What do you want me to do, Claire, quit? I've been playing rock and roll for thirty years. For twenty, it took damn good care of you. What else am I supposed to do?"

"I never asked you to quit, Ransom. Never. As long as you have the stomach for it, I think you should keep on, but let's face it, the fact that Mitchell Pike covered 'Talking in My Sleep' was basically a fluke, a onetime deal. The kids and I have needs, and we can't count on you hitting the lot-tery every year or two to provide for them. And I really don't need you breezing in like Mr. Bigshot and telling me I don't need to work, because I do, I just fucking do. And, speaking of which, I have to be up at the crack of dawn, so if you don't mind, I'm going to try to get some sleep."

She turned away, and Ransom started out, then turned back at the door.

"Tell me something, Claire, okay? Why am I here? I'm suddenly having trouble understanding why you wanted me to come."

Claire sat up. "You asked to come, Ran—remember? Not once. A hundred times. Ninety-nine of them, I turned you down."

"And you said yes the hundredth because . . . ?"

"Because you're Hope and Charlie's father, and they need you. Because I keep thinking, if only we can turn the corner, maybe we can spare them the unhappiness our parents did to us. I'd do almost anything to spare them, Ransom. And, along with Hope and Charlie, I'd also like to spare you and myself. I said yes because we've loved each other since we were children. Because I'm your family and you're mine, and because I couldn't stand to leave you moping around the city in that cab the way you were. No matter what my shrink or anybody says, I won't stand by and watch you sick and suffering, and whatever happens between us, I never will. Do you understand that? Why are *you* here, Ran?"

Ransom should have had the answers ready. Moping around the city in that cab, and all those nights alone on Jane Street, when he closed his eyes and screened the tape, he'd had ample time to work them out. What he'd imagined, though, were tender declarations delivered in a moment of passion and shared sympathy, not being put on the spot like this and answering in self-defense. Yet Ran was forty-five and knew he ought to make those tender declarations anyway, knew full well the better man he'd always hoped to be—despite Mel Hill and Clive DeLay and many more—would say them anyway, despite the circumstances. But the real man Ransom was was too hurt and frightened by that "whatever happens between us," and he said, "You know, Claire, I'm really not that sure."

"Yeah, okay, great, whatever."

And at that moment, as she rolled away toward the window, as Ransom hit the trail into the hall, something white flashed along the wall in front of him, moving toward the stairs. For an instant, only one, he felt a sense of free fall. Then the explanation came—*headlights*—and he reached out and grabbed it like a branch and stopped himself. That was all it was—someone passing on the road outside. He started to relax, and then there was a crash downstairs.

Claire sat up. "What was that?"

"Stay here."

Blindly patting down the library wall, he stumbled over something on the threshold. The first switch clicked without result, the second brought on the brass portrait lamps. By that light, Ran found himself straddling an antique double-barreled shotgun lying in a scattered pile of books. Bemused, he studied it, and then a trail of plaster dust led him to a hook above the door and the small hole where the second hook had been. He knelt.

"What are you doing with that?"

Claire stood in the doorway, her hand over her breastbone. The barrel, as it leaned against his knee, pointed straight at her.

"It fell."

Claire frowned, as though inclined to doubt his explanation. The tension, for that moment, was like a spell.

Then he nodded to the place the gun had hung, and she stepped in and looked. "Oh," she said. "Oh, right, the Purdey."

"The what?"

"It's an English bird gun, Ran. It was made for one of the DeLays. Have you got this?"

He nodded. "I've got it. Get some sleep."

After she left, he stacked the fallen books and laid the shotgun carefully beside them on the antique partners desk. "I doubt the damn thing even works," he muttered to the empty room. A twenty-five-pound bag of 08 shot presently contradicted this assertion, as he opened the side drawer. A UPS box with several other items—a tin of FFG black powder, five hundred packs of overshot and overpowder wads, percussion caps, a brass ramrod still in shrink-wrap—was addressed to Clive DeLay from Dixie Guns in Tennessee. There, too, quarter-folded on slightly yellowed paper, was a diagram entitled "The Proper Sequence for Loading a Muzzle-Loading Shotgun."

An indefinable misgiving stole over Ran as he examined this. A lover not a fighter, he shut the drawer, poured a drink, and sat down on the scuffed green leather sofa. There were five thousand volumes in this room, Clive had told him once. Looking at the shelves, it was easy to believe. Ran preferred to close his eyes. Sipping Clive's old single-barrel Kentucky whiskey, he settled back, and his exhaustion overcame him. Within a second and a half, he was back at CBGB, 1982. . . . Someone led him to her table between sets. (This is where the tape began.) Amidst the Capuchins in downtown black, Claire wore a pastel linen summer dress with her heavy hair pulled forward over one bare shoulder. A critic of no less chops than

Lester Bangs at *Creem* had just called *Talking in My Sleep* "the debut of the year," but Claire, a pianist at Juilliard, did not read *Creem*. "Hello, Mr. Hill," she said in a voice that conjured fountains plashing in the courtyards of gated Charleston homes, and cream-cheese-and-olive finger sandwiches on crustless triangles of white bread. "Hello, Mr. Hill"—at CBGB, on the Bowery, amidst the Capuchins, at two A.M. And then regarding him, the young rock wunderkind, with a deflationary but warmhearted irony, she pursed her lips around the straw in her Coke and Maker's Mark and took a sip. That was it for Ran.

Within a month, she'd moved into his apartment overlooking Tompkins Square Park. They were so wild for each other then that sometimes he looked up and found her watching and groaned, "Oh, Jesus, not again." Her eyes would widen with malevolence and she'd punch him—playfully, then hard. "Quit, DeLay." Under pressure, he regressed to the idiom of Bagtown.

"Quit, DeLay?" she mocked. *"Quit?"*

And he remembered those OshKosh overalls, how the button—the original they never found—made a tinny ping on the wood floor as he ripped the strap. Claire reached out and slapped him hard across the mouth, and they ended wedged against the armoire with Ransom's white-knuckled hand atop the bathroom door, straining into her as Claire fought back, exhorting, "Come on, come *on*," desperate to shed some skin and merciless on both of them till they broke free.

With a soft groan, Ran, working himself between three fingers and a thumb, came now, alone on the sofa, as he had then, when they fell down, drenched, together, on the bed. As they lay there, "Talking in My Sleep"— not Mitch Pike's version, but the true, original, and only: his—had drifted up from a boom box or a car passing on Avenue B, and it seemed to them that this was the beginning of an arc that could only rise. The certainty of it was tinged with a ferocious joy, like found religion. And she left school and played keyboards in RHB. She gave up her dream for his, or not gave up so much as found her dream, not quite so confident and fully fledged, sucked into the undertow of his. And Ransom came up to the brink of stardom and somehow failed to make the final push. They learned, in the hard school everyone attends, that there is no entitlement to glory. Maybe in the next life, but not here. And in the twinkling of an eye, nineteen years had passed and they'd had Hope and Charlie, and poorer with the rich, and sickness with the health, and worse together with the better, and Ran, at forty-five, still loved her with the heartsick love he'd felt at twenty-six and didn't know if Claire loved him, or ever would again.

He didn't even realize he'd drifted off till he started awake and found it all repeating, found Claire in the door again, her hand over her breastbone as before. Only it wasn't Claire, and it wasn't the doorway. It took Ran a moment to reorient. He was staring at the opposite wall, where a painting hung. Blue-eyed and fair, the subject bore little resemblance to Claire. With her unruly mass of thick blond hair, full of waves as stiff as beaten egg whites, she looked more like Botticelli's Venus, not the youthful goddess, but the model reencountered in a farmhouse or a tavern somewhere, twenty years beyond the seashell and the bubbling foam, lost in middle life. It was her hand, that specific gesture solely, that connected them across the generations, something in the camber of her wrist as she queried a mother-of-pearl button on another era's dress. Ran briefly lost himself in the alkyd gleam of her fine eye, and then, for the second time, the blast of a boat horn startled him. Now, though, in the great, watery black windows, it appeared, its deck hung with lights like strings of incandescent pearls. Ran heard disembodied laughter carried over water and watched it pass like something from a dream.

When it was gone, he noticed something protruding from the gilt-edged pages of a book—a cobweb or perhaps a catkin. He picked it up and saw it was a feather, almost transparent where it had been exposed to light and air. When he opened to the place it marked, however, the part protected by the book was still bright green.

FIVE

*H*arlan, now, has seen the boat. He smiles at her, puts a finger to his lips, and, with that finger, points across the water to the rice dike on the opposite shore. Through an open trunk gate, water from the hidden field behind the high clay wall pours back into the river on the falling tide. Above the Nina's engine, Addie can't make out the splash, but then, far louder than the engine, comes another sound, an eerie ululation, like crickets or cicadas, yet made by human tongues. "E-e-e-e-e-e-e-e-e." It is like women keening in grief or warning, and as they cry, they accompany themselves with pots and sticks, and Addie hears the tink and thunk of wood on tin and bone on bone.

And then a new sound drowns out all the rest. From behind the dikes, as from a hidden amphitheater, something like a cloud of smoke arises, green smoke shot through with flashing trails of red and yellow fire, and the smoke is birds, and the new sound, the overwhelming sound, is the chittering they make. Her hand goes to the button on her breast, and she can feel her heartbeat, quickened, under it. The cloud rises higher. There are thousands, perhaps hundreds of thousands, of birds—so many and so loud she doesn't hear when Harlan fires the gun. She sees the muzzle-flash, though—once, and then again. The shot moves through the flock like a hand through smoke, and six or seven birds from low to high drop down. The cloud breaks in two, then heals and drifts across the river toward the house. Addie shades her eyes *and something stings her face. Pellets of spent shot ping the metal rail and pelt the deck like fine black hail. One hot iron bead has landed on her sleeve!*

"Goodness! Goodness mercy!" Blanche begins to swat at it.

Too late, though. It melts the watered silk like butter and leaves a tiny black-rimmed, smoking hole.

Addie takes a step and has to brace herself against the cabin wall. The captain cuts the engine now, and in a strange, ringing silence, the Nina *glides toward dock through water studded with dead birds, like strange bromeliads, feathered, warm and apple-green, bobbing in the patch of dazzle, where the sun casts demilunes in the dark river.*

"Welcome to Wando Passo!" Harlan hails her, smiling as he waits. His gun—the new percussion fowler that Percival DeLay had built on Oxford Street in London as a wedding gift (with a certifying letter from James Purdey himself)—rests across his forearm. Two wisps of matched blue smoke rise from the barrels of Damascus steel. The air is heavy with black powder and cigar smoke, and Addie hears his friends laughing in the soft, coarse way men take when blood sport has been successfully concluded.

The crew have secured the lines and gangway now, and as Addie starts down, at a signal from the groom, the revelers link arms and start to sing, drunkenly, but with their hearts, "She Walks in Beauty Like the Night," the very song Addie sang her guests the first night Harlan came to supper at her aunt's. How many times has she told him of her love for Byron, whom Addie holds in esteem above even Longfellow. And that Harlan should remember, that she should be holding in her hand the very book . . . (When she saw the youthful portrait on the frontispiece in Russell's, it brought back her days at Mme. Togno's; it was the dead poet's sensitive and melancholy face with which she frequently invested her own Gabriel, when Addie still allowed herself to imagine him, when she still believed that he would come. Some little voice she used to hear more often then spoke up, and Addie, just three days before her wedding, her last three as a maid, put her money down.)

Harlan's thoughtfulness is wonderful, too wonderful for words; at any other time, she would be moved, but in this moment—with the dead birds bobbing in the wash (and others she tries not to look at flopping softly on the lawn), with the men regarding her with their glazed, slightly drunken smiles—Addie is too unnerved. Some heaviness has stolen over the bride, creeping like a spell. A thought flies into her head like a sparrow through the open window of a house, upsetting everything: she barely knows Harlan—he, her—can it really be they stood before the altar at St. Michael's and vowed to God to love each other until parted by death? What if the wisdom of the girl of seventeen—who never doubted that Evangeline must wait for Gabriel no matter what, however long it takes, even if she dies before he comes—was

*truer than the wisdom of the bride of thirty-three that said get on with it and live?
The little voice she remembers, though not from where, clearly forms the words:* All
this is a lie that everyone believes but you. *For one moment, this thought seems
truer than the party, truer than the smiling guests, truer than the house with its six
chimneys, truer than the oaks and the magnolias in the park, truer than the world itself. But, no, this is only nerves. Of course it is! A brief stir; the bird has flown.*

*Has Harlan seen it streak through her blue eyes? God forbid! But, no, he's smil-
ing, welcoming her. They all are. All but one . . .*

*Standing at the corner of the dock—conferring with the captain about the
tierces of rough rice prepared for loading on the* Nina *now that her outgoing cargo
is ashore—he's already aware of her by the time her eyes find him. Tall and lean-
waisted, he wears a coat of fine black gabardine that is slightly worn, and this
slight wornness separates him from the other guests as effectively as his physical
distance from them on the dock. (Nor, on his lapel, does he sport the cockade of
blue ribbon worn by all the rest, with the gold palmetto, the lone star, and the coil-
ing snake.) What separates him still more is the extreme gravity in his agated,
dark hazel eyes that are like ocean water when it thins out in a rising wave and
the sun shines through it from behind. It is this gravity that draws the bride's attention like a compass needle to magnetic north, for though it cannot be, it is as if
this man (whom Addie feels she knows, or ought to know from somewhere), alone
among the revelers, has looked into her depths and seen the bird before it flew.
There is no judgment in his face, but no dissembling either. And it is only in the
second moment, as Addie tells herself this cannot be, that his expression must
mean something else, that she catches the resemblance—it is to the bridegroom. In
the third, she realizes who he is: this is the plantation steward, Jarry, Percival's
dark son, the brother whom the brother owns. Only in the fourth and final instant, before she looks away, does Addie note he's black. . . . A look sustained for
four long blinks—it is no more than that. Yet Addie will remember it for the rest
of her short life.*

*But, goodness, here is Harlan, beaming at her, even bigger than she recalls! A
strident flush has spread from his collar, lapped by a small pink fold of flesh, to his
hairline, which has receded to the crown of his large head. On his gleaming brow,
beads of perspiration have formed like seed pearls, and Harlan wipes them with his
handkerchief, which is heavy, gray with sweat. Handing his shotgun to an elderly re-
tainer, he takes a glass of champagne from the tray the old man holds, then sips and
offers it to her. Addie smiles, but, wait, there's something in it, several crimson berries
floating like suspended drops of blood. Now Harlan reaches in. A finger and a fleshy*

thumb, flushed the same pink as his cheeks, go down. Addie sees the black hair on his knuckle joint float out in the champagne and lie flat down again as he extracts . . .

"But, Harlan, what on earth?" she says. "Is it a pomegranate seed?"

"No, dear, a granadilla, a bit of passion fruit, all the way from Cuba, through the blockade, for you."

He holds it out, dripping on the grass. He cups his hand to catch the drops. For a moment, Addie doesn't understand. Now her face has turned as red as his. All around, the crowd nods its encouragement. And what else can she do but smile and eat?

The crowd applauds. Just that quickly, it is done.

Harlan takes her arm. As they start to cross the dock, the steward intercepts. "I'm sorry, but the captain says he cannot take our rice."

"He what?" *asks Harlan.*

"They were fired on running the blockade, and he's afraid the weight may compromise his headway. It may be possible to flat the tierces to the bridge at Mars Bluff and take them into Charleston via rail."

"See to it then." *Harlan starts to turn away.*

"There's something else. . . . We've lost the order."

"What order?"

"From the factor. The entire spring order was jettisoned into the sea last night. Cloth, tools, oil, salt, seed . . ."

"Damn it, man, I don't want a list. It's my wedding party. Don't bother me with this. Figure something out. Now is that all?"

Jarry frowns. "It's getting late. We should call the mincers back."

"I want them in the fields till all my friends have shot."

"They haven't eaten since this morning."

"Then measure them half a gill of rum when they come in and make it up to them."

"Only for the beaters?" *Jarry asks.* "I'm sure everyone in the quarters would gladly drink to the new mistress's health."

Harlan's face turns shrewd. "You see how they manipulate me?" *he says to Addie.* "All right then, damn it, Jarry, all. But I don't want them drunk. I want them in the fields tomorrow like any other day."

"I understand."

"You understand, what?"

Jarry doesn't answer.

"That's right. God forbid that you abase yourself to call me 'sir' or 'master,' which is what I am."

The steward's expression is neutral, his eyes direct, unflinching, like a pair of taps turned to their full flow. Meeting it, Harlan's narrow and their look of good cheer crisps like paper in a flame. They hate each other! *Addie thinks, and she's grateful when a bird, fallen in the grass nearby, gives a weak thrash and breaks the spell.*

"Oh, look," she says. "Poor thing. It's still alive."

Jarry picks it up.

It is some kind of parrot, bright green with a yellow head and a reddish-orange domino across the eyes. Its breast moves in rapid, frantic respiration and then stops. The eye grows fixed and clouds, and Addie becomes aware of Jarry's hand—large, long-fingered, and narrow, like a certain kind of trowel, the sort a gardener or arborist might use for some exacting work. Cupped the way it is, holding the dead bird, it strikes Addie as refined and gentle.

"How beautiful," she says.

"These? No, dear, they're vermin," Harlan contradicts her lightly. "But, come, you must greet our guests and have a glass of punch." Harlan takes her arm, but she holds briefly back.

"What is it?" She seeks Jarry's eyes now for the first time in the exchange, and he, for the first time, looks back, with that expression that is like a question that, once posed, you cannot rest until you have the answer to.

"A Carolina parakeet."

S I X

*R*eally? I had no idea there were parakeets in South Carolina."
Claire leaned toward the engraving for a better look. Featuring a little green and yellow bird posed in a cocklebur bush in six or seven dramatic, if implausible, positions, *Conuropsis carolinensis,* "The Carolina Paroquet," was part of a small exhibit of Audubons hung in the wood-paneled foyer of Harlow's dining hall, where she was killing time, waiting for the faculty breakfast to begin.

"Well, there aren't. Not anymore."

After her first glance, Claire had to struggle to avert her eyes from her interlocutor's amazing helmet of black hair. It was like a toupee so bad it could only be real, she decided. He might have been the George in a quartet of aging Beatles impersonators.

"They failed to endear themselves to the rice-planting interests," he continued, "and endeared themselves a little too well to makers of ladies' hats. The last one was taken in the wild in 1904, I believe it was. I'm Ben Jessup, by the way, college librarian."

"Claire DeLay."

"I know who you are." He smiled and shook the hand she offered. "We met in Umbria almost twenty years ago. My uncle was a judge at Casa Grande the year you competed."

"You're kidding. Who's your uncle?"

"Glenn Gould?"

"Glenn Gould was your uncle?" Her hand wandered to the O-ring on the breast of her suit, a peach-colored Vertigo she'd exhumed from dry cleaner's plastic in the closet, where it had hung for fifteen years. After considerable agony, she'd put it on, having nothing better, and the truth was, it still looked pretty smart and she looked good in it, even if the big chrome motorcycle-jacket-style zipper was a bit too 1989. "Glenn Gould was the reason I became a pianist in the first place," she said. "I grew up listening to the *Goldberg Variations*. I must have listened to that record a million times."

"A million—really?"

"No, you're right—*two* million is probably closer to it!"

Jessup laughed. "And do you prefer the '55 or '81?"

"Are you kidding—the '55! Glenn Gould was a god to me!"

"He liked your playing, too."

"He didn't! *He did not!* Did he?"

"Especially the slow movement. You did Brahms's second, if I recall."

"Not the third movement?" Claire said. "I was all over the map on the third movement!"

"Well, he was moved by it."

"Excuse me while I go outside and shoot myself!"

"Please don't!" Jessup said, still laughing. "Why would you? I thought you'd be pleased."

"I am! I am pleased!"

Still smiling, he narrowed his eyes, and how could Claire explain what it meant to her that Glenn Gould had listened to her play the andante of the second twenty years before in a competition she had lost and been moved by it? She couldn't, so instead, she resorted to the stratagem that twenty years of living with a strong, self-centered man had taught her to perfect. "So, tell me about you."

"I'm a librarian—I think I mentioned that." Ben made a funny little moue, and at this evidence of wit, Claire laughed, deciding she liked him. "I can claim credit for this exhibit, though." His nod returned her to the wall. "Next to *Conuropsis* is Say's least shrew, from the *Viviparous Quadrupeds*. Not one of Audubon's more attractive renderings, to be perfectly frank. All these prints came to us from the Harlow family, who also bequeathed us Samuel Hilliard's diary, which I expect you know. . . ." His eyebrows—which bore a familial resemblance to his hair—formed an interrogatory arch.

"I don't think I do," Claire said. "Should I?"

"It contains a reference to the disappearance at your house."

She blinked. "Disappearance? At my house? Wando Passo?"

"You don't know the story?"

"I don't believe I do."

"Good morning, Deanna," he said. "Join us. Claire, you know Deanna Holmes, don't you? Deanna, Claire DeLay."

"We've met," said the assistant dean, a woman in heavy-framed designer glasses, mahogany-toned lipstick, and basic black, like Ben.

"Deanna was on my interview committee," Claire said, beginning to doubt the wisdom of her suit, which seemed altogether too much like a drink with an umbrella in a cored-out pineapple on a black lacquer tray of dry martinis, up. "She had to tell me what a vita was. How embarrassing was that!"

"Yes," Deanna agreed, "but here you are. How does it feel?"

"To be honest, Deanna, I'm petrified."

"What on earth of?"

"Everything!" Claire said. "If you really want to know, I'm terrified Marcel hired me for purely nepotistic reasons—is that a word?"

"Are you related?"

"Practically. We're such old friends, you see, and I was desperate for work. But I'll tell you both, I made a promise to myself: if I'm not great, I'll quit. You won't have to fire me, I'll run not walk straight through that door!"

"We'll hold you to it!" said Deanna, with a bluff, collegial laugh.

"Please do!" Claire said, laughing back and putting this one in the column headed *Hate*.

"Claire lives out at Wando Passo Plantation, Deanna," Jessup intervened. "Her great-great-grandparents—no, make that great-great-great—disappeared from there at the end of the Civil War."

"You don't say," said Deanna. "Where did they go?"

"Don't look at me," said Claire. "I went to Wando Passo exactly once when I was small—for a picnic when I was twelve. No, thirteen. The year before I went away to boarding school. Since then, the two of you have probably spent more time in South Carolina than I have. Family history was never my long suit anyway."

Both women turned to Ben. "Well, as I was telling Claire, Deanna, what I know comes from Samuel Hilliard's diary. Hilliard was rector at the Episcopal church in Powatan during the war. Your great-great-great-grandparents were parishioners of his. The man—whose name escapes me at the moment—was a Confederate artillerist at Wagner."

"Wagner?"

"Battery Wagner. It was a sand fort on Morris Island that guarded the entrance to Charleston Harbor from the south. If you saw the movie *Glory,* you know the place. The Fifty-fourth Massachusetts made their famous charge there. The Federals sent their whole ironclad fleet down here and pounded it for months. Wagner was an awful place, from the descriptions. The men inside lived standing up, elbow to elbow, in a windowless room called a bombproof, the sick together with the healthy and the living with the dead. And this was Charleston, in the summer. Harlan DeLay—just when you stop thinking of it, right?—was killed when the battery was evacuated in '63. Hilliard went out to the plantation and performed the burial in absentia—or whatever the expression is.

"Then, two years later, in September 1865, one hot afternoon, who should stroll into downtown Powatan . . ."

"You're kidding," said Claire.

Ben nodded. "Harlan DeLay."

"Wait," said Deanna. "You said—"

"I know," he preempted her. "The casualty report turned out to be in error. DeLay had been captured and incarcerated at Fort Delaware, a Union prison in Delaware Bay. It took him five months after Appomattox to get home. Apparently, he walked. Several people—including Hilliard's wife—saw him on King Street that afternoon. They hailed him, but Harlan walked right past them like a ghost. He went into Pringle's Dry Goods Store, bought one item, a bag of birdshot, then set out for Wando Passo on foot. That was the last time anybody ever saw him. Or your great-great-great-grandmother either, Claire."

"Adelaide," she said.

"Is this beginning to ring a bell?"

"A small one. Her portrait's in the library. She had a child, I think."

"A little boy of three. He was orphaned when they disappeared."

"I do recall Clive and my aunt Tildy saying something about this."

"So that Sunday," Jessup continued, "right after Harlan reappeared,

Adelaide failed to show up at morning service. Hilliard rode out to pay a call and found the table set for dinner. Someone had made biscuits and fried chicken, but the food was scattered, and the house was full of flies. He looked for them, made inquiries, and finally paid a visit to the sheriff. A search was made—that was when they found the child. He turned up in the quarters, but his father and mother were never found. Foul play was suspected, but no proof came to light. No word was ever heard of them again. It was as if one September afternoon—right around this time of year, in fact—Harlan and Adelaide DeLay simply dropped off the face of the earth."

"That's quite a ways to fall. . . ."

Tucking a pair of jet-lensed granny shades into the pocket of his suit, Marcel Jones breezed into their midst, smelling of the outdoors and Grey Flannel aftershave. "Morning, all." Gazing down at them from canopy level—he was six foot six—Jones smiled a smile that was boyish, sweet, and ever so slightly sly with the innocent slyness of one who, from the confident redoubt of his good looks, can afford to be indifferent to appearances. "So, who was this who disappeared?"

"My great-great-grandparents."

Jessup frowned and held three fingers up.

"Great-great-*great*," Claire corrected. "From Wando Passo, just after the Civil War."

"The War of Northern Aggression, don't you mean?"

Claire smiled at this sly dig with lidded eyes.

"I don't think I've heard this story."

"You don't know them all," she said. "Apparently, neither do I. You've piqued my interest, though, Ben. I'm going to call my aunt Tildy when I get home. If anybody has the scoop, it's her." She looked back at Marcel. "Nice suit."

He looked down. "This?" A four-button one of English whipcord in a restful and arresting shade of isingreen, this was set off by a plain black T that gave the ensemble a thrown-together air that Claire, who knew him well, was having none of.

"'This?' What, little ol' me?" Taking her revenge belatedly, she laughed. "Why, I just reached into my closet with my eyes closed and the light off and pulled out the first thing that hit my hand. If it had been a Roman toga or a bearskin rug, I'd be wearing that." As she mocked, her finger came out of the O-ring, her shoulders dropped, something full of wicked, happy energy was set loose in her expression.

To the uninitiated, it might have appeared she disapproved of his clothes, but this was not the case. Her old friend's flair was just so un-Ran-like that it inclined Claire toward a giddy, comic mood. Jones was one of those large men who tower in any crowd, resembling visitors from some far country where people grow twenty-five percent larger than they do here. Against the backdrop of that physical imposingness, his taste in dress was unexpected and ran somehow counter to his personality as well, which was self-assured, soft-spoken, and reserved. Claire liked that reserve the way she liked her great-grandmother's heavy silver, but she also liked to rattle it. And she was well aware that Marcel, however he pretended otherwise, liked to have it rattled in just the way she'd made her specialty.

"Sorry, y'all," she told the company, regressing, for some reason, to a Southern accent. "Marcel and I have known each other since God was a boy in shorts; I'm like the maiden aunt and he's the five-year-old whose cheeks I sometimes have to pinch."

"You were in the Ransom Hill Band together, I believe," Deanna said, a trifle sternly.

"Oh, yes," said Claire, "I was part of Marcel's disreputable past. We knew each other way before that, though. We met when we were fourteen, in boarding school. I was at Northfield when Cell—excuse me, Marcel—was at Mt. Hermon. He had this terrible crush on my roommate, Shanté Mills."

"Not Shanté Mills, the mezzo," Jessup said.

"The same."

"*I* have a crush on her!"

"You and everybody else," Claire said, "including my husband, Ran-som. But that's another story. Do you see his earring?"

"I don't think we need the earring story, Claire," said the dean, who wore a small gold stud in his left ear.

"Should we take a vote?" Claire polled the group's expanding mem-bership, and everybody raised a black-sleeved arm, except Deanna Holmes.

"You probably know he's from Manhattan. His family has a manse on Morningside and a summer place in Vineyard Haven. They're fixtures at Abyssinian Baptist. Marcel was once the chapter president of a nifty little club called Jack and Jill. He came to Mt. Hermon from St. Bernard's, and his first year he went around in a blue blazer with a little crest on the pocket and these heavy oxblood shoes. Somewhere in England, little men with jeweler's lenses on their specs had a wooden last shaped to his foot, and when his mother, Miss Corinne, put in a call they took it off the shelf and whipped young Marcel out a brand-new pair. And he had these really awful glasses, too, like . . ." Claire glanced involuntarily toward Deanna Holmes, then caught herself and looked away. "These thick black things, and a fro like Sly Stone, circa 1969. It was generally lopsided from where he slept on it and had specks of towel lint and the occasional bird's nest. And he was in, like, Latin 6 or some ridiculous course they had to invent for him, and he carried around this special pair of drumsticks. What were they, Cell?"

"I don't remember."

"Uh-huh," she said. "And Linus doesn't remember his Binky. Come on, you know. . . . You know you know. Zildjian 5A's, right?"

"Zildjian didn't even make sticks then. They may have been Vic Firths."

"But he doesn't remember," she said. "And you know those shiny metal rails in the cafeteria? You'd be pushing your tray along, waiting for the lady in the paper hat to ladle gravy on your mashed, and suddenly, *rat-tatatta rattatatta*, 'Wipeout!' and that creepy little laugh? He had it down. The whole line, twenty, thirty people, would groan in unison, and pelt him with a hail of napkin balls. And, oh, yes, I should also mention that he was the worst basketball player on the team, possibly the worst in the whole history of the school, and, in short, he was just so hopelessly uncool that Shanté and I took pity and adopted him."

Claire knew she was getting on a tear with this, but something in Marcel just drew it out of her and always had. Though not Southern in the least, he was like Southern gentlemen she'd grown up with, and, most especially, like that Southern gentleman of Southern gentlemen, her father, Gardener DeLay, who, in the bloom of apparent health, was struck down by a massive heart attack when she was seventeen. Claire's mother had been the dominating figure in the household. Before her descent into Alzheimer's, Rose DeLay had been a noted Charleston personality, a tongue-in-cheek provocateuse who specialized in that peculiarly Southern, female form of humor, lobbing burnished epigrams of gay, off-color wit like Molotov cocktails at cotillions, garden parties, and assorted charity events. Rose sucked the oxygen from the drawing rooms where Claire grew up. After bringing down the house with her command performances, however, she frequently got vapors and retired to bed with a compress on her eyes. On these occasions, Gardener made Claire grilled-cheese sandwiches down-stairs, cutting off the crusts the way she liked. They dunked these in tomato soup, a trespass so egregious that Gardener put a finger to his lips and Claire crossed her heart, agreeing to conspire. Gardener and Rose . . . Their names so perfectly expressed their natures and their roles that the in-joke spread beyond the family and permeated the whole town. Claire blamed herself, but in her heart of hearts she always loved him more. In a crowd, Gardener did not require centrality the way her mother had. Rather, he conferred it. There was something in the quality of his attention that made you feel singled out and special, as though bathed in the gold light from a photographer's umbrella. Marcel's attention was like that, too. Even now, in this new crowd of virtual strangers not all disposed to be her friends, it brought Claire out. In their youth at boarding school, she'd taken this for granted, but now, since moving back to Wando Passo, she didn't anymore. Just lately, Claire thought about this subject quite a bit.

"Behind his back, we called him 'the mascot with the ascot,'" she went on. "Did you know that, Dr. Jones?"

The dean, however, was in distress and couldn't answer, choking on a hilarity he clearly wanted to suppress, and couldn't, and as he chuffed and panted and waved his hand in a negating motion—meaning, no, he did not remember, or simply that he wanted her to stop—his clear face beamed like a dry shell dipped in ocean water and restored to its essential gleam. He al-most seemed another person than the one who'd breezed so easily into their midst, and the same was true of Claire. Ransom and the children would hardly have recognized their wife and mother. Her old friend and schoolmate recognized her, though, and, more important, so did Claire. For the person she became with him—the way we all do, if we're lucky, with one other person one time in this life (and sometimes, if we're most un-lucky, twice)—was herself. Or was she simply channeling her mother's ghost? The question seemed important. Wanting to avoid it at all costs, Claire continued on her roll, diverting, together with the audience, herself.

"So one Saturday he comes over, and we had some hash and got him stoned and did a fashion intervention. When he realized what was up, he was, like, hey, this is me, take it or leave it, and we were like, Marcel, if you're ever planning—like *ever*, in your *life*—to have a date, much less to procreate and pass on your genetic package, the whole object you must strive for is *not* to be yourself, to try *very, very hard* to be someone else. So we made him lose the coat and glasses; Shanté cut his hair. The earring was the coup de grace. I don't remember who did the actual bloodletting. . . ."

"You did," said Jones, regaining self-control and affecting an ironic glumness with only moderate success.

"Did I? You may be right. I know we used the needle in the sewing kit, and I can also tell you that he screamed and fainted at the sight of his own blood."

"Now *that*"—Jones's baritone boomed out strongly on the word, and he was laughing—"*that* is a lie, and a damned lie!"

Claire's laughter ran a scale of glee. "Dead away. Right flat out on Shanté's bed, the only time he ever got there! And look at him now. . . . Look who the ugly duckling grew up to be. Not to give myself undue credit, but I have to say the earring was the start of the whole turnaround, the beginning of the change in fortune that led to the result you see."

"I'd like to point out for the record," he said, "A, this story is apocryphal. B, I don't recall smoking hash with you. . . ."

"He didn't inhale," she put in sotto voce, and the whole group cracked up, converted to her cause.

"C, they're ready for us in the dining room and I suggest we repair there at flank speed."

No one, however, made a move to go. The black-garbed members of the chorus looked at their new colleague and the dean as though not quite sure what they were witnessing. Whatever it was, though, they were hesitant to remove themselves from it, and Claire and Marcel in their peach and isingreen pastels—in what might otherwise have passed for an old RHB gig at the Mudd Club, circa 1983—resembled tropical birds, Carolina parakeets, let's say, who'd spelunked by accident into a cave of nesting academic bats. They were isolated from the others, enveloped in a field as charged and brilliant as their clothes.

"Dr. Jones?" A nervous waiter looked out from the inner door.

"People," he said forcibly, ushering them ahead. As Claire filed in, he caught her sleeve.

"Oh, God, Marcel! I'm sorry! What did I do?" She put her hand over her heart. "Do you have any nitro, because I think I'm going to have a heart attack! I can't believe I said all that! What came over me? It wasn't even like me."

"What do you mean?" he said. "It was exactly like you."

Claire blinked and mulled it, then said, "You're right, it was!" And they both laughed.

"So, tell me, how did last night go?"

On that, Claire's face went sober. "Oh, fuck, Cell . . . Fuck, fuck, fuck."

SEVEN

In the submarine of creation, Captain Nemo
Can be found kicking ass and taking names.
I ought to know 'cause he impressed me deeply
And I attended boot camp in his brains.

It never rains down here, there isn't any weather.
On maneuvers, blind fish osculate our masks.
I'd like to know their taxonomic listings,
But I fear Nemo would torpedo if I asked.

tretched across the partners desk, one hand in his tousled hair, the other twirling Clive's nib pen, Ran reread the lines by the light of the green-shaded lamp and laughed out loud. He had the spirit now, or the spirit now had him. Though a rent in the bedrock, there was magma boiling up from the deep world. He hadn't written anything so free in months. Could it be years?

He could see it all before him: the album title would be *Nemo's Submarine*, and "Nemo's Submarine" the title cut. The music—playing all around him, bouncing off the moldering walls of books as it came on to four a.m.—was the driving three-chord blare that Ran and his whole generation had gone to school to with the Clash and the Ramones. (And Joey, gone, and now Joe Strummer, too. Alone in New York City in his cab, Ran had taken their deaths hard, but he was past the fear of death tonight. More than that, Ran was in a place where he knew death did not exist.)

And the words kept tumbling:

> *It's not that he's a tyrant or a monster.*
> *In fact, he's like a father to us all.*
> *It's just that loneliness has made his heart ferocious. . . .*

"Mama?"

Upstairs, Charlie softly called and something in his father clenched. When Ran looked up, gray light surprised him at the window. Suddenly the clock read 6:15. "Go back to sleep, sweet boy," he whispered. Prayed. *Just another hour. Thirty minutes.*

"Maa-ma . . . *Maaa*-ma . . ." In a sweet, teasing singsong, Charlie, working off his own agenda, willed his mom to come.

> *It's just that loneliness has made his heart ferocious,*
> *And . . .*

Ran could see the next line, like a billfish on the gaffe beside the boat. He had to land it now or watch it slip away into the dark.

Upstairs, the bedsprings creaked; the soft pad of Claire's footsteps, tentative and groggy, gaining purpose as they gathered speed, moving down the hall . . .

> *And he . . . he's grown ~~hard deaf hard~~ deaf . . .*

"Mama? *Maa*-ma? *Mama!*"

"I'm coming!" Claire called. "Good grief, Charlie!"

Dopplering like the whistle of a train, the song gave Ran a final chance to board.

> *It's just that loneliness has made his heart ferocious,*
> *And he's grown deaf to any softer call.*

Frowning, he put down his pen. "I've got him, Claire," he called, and went to fetch his son.

———

It was quarter to eleven when he finally made it back from Powatan, after dropping off the kids at preschool. Centuries had passed, and Ransom was a different, humbler man.

Holding one somber child in either arm, he'd watched Claire drive off down the allée toward her first-day breakfast, and he'd smiled for the rearview mirror.

We gave three heavy-hearted cheers and plunged like fate into the lone Atlantic.

The lines from *Moby-Dick* played back, and Ransom, swallowing a Bluepoint of cold, briny fear, took Hope and Charlie in the house and scrambled eggs.

"Are eggs baby chickens?" Hope asked as she climbed into her blue and purple booster chair.

"Baby chickens come from eggs," he conceded, spooning some onto her plate.

"Do they die when we eat them?"

"Well, Hope," he said, searching for a valve for Charlie's sippy cup, "the baby chickens aren't alive yet, so I don't think you can really say they die."

"Do chickens mind when we eat them?"

"What? Charlie, come eat breakfast!"

"I coming, Doddy!" Carrying his little toy guitar—another street-find Ran had mailed down for the birthday he had missed—he skidded around the corner in his socks.

"Look at me! Look at me!" he said with his sweet serrated smile and such vulnerable, unvarnished need in hazel eyes, which were neither Ran's nor Claire's. Whose eyes were they? Holding the guitar left-handed, with the treble E string on top, he hit a jangling stadium chord. "Look, Doddy! Look at me!"

"I see you, bud." Fighting the impulse to turn the instrument around and tune it on the spot, Ran lifted him into his high chair. "Now eat your eggs, okay?"

"Do they, Daddy?"

"What?"

"Do the chickens *mind*?" Hope articulated very clearly, as though he were semicretinous.

"Well," he said, "when we eat a chicken, the chicken becomes part of us, okay? Part of something that can think and laugh and dream and do all sorts of things a chicken can't . . . So maybe the chicken *doesn't* mind. Maybe there's something in it for the chicken, too. Does that make sense?"

Hope listened soberly. "Uh-huh," she said, and pushed her plate away. "Let's play the Scar game, Daddy." Her eyes took on the wicked gleam.

He faced her, arms akimbo. "What exactly is the Scar game, Hope?"

"Look at me, Doddy!"

He raised a finger. "Just a minute, bud . . ."

"You be Scar, and I'm Mufasa climbing up the rock," she said. "I say, 'Help me, brother, please,' and you grab my paws and say, 'Long live the king!' and let me fall into the wildebeest stampede."

He frowned. "What happens then?"

"I get dead." Hope grinned.

"How about when you say, 'Help me, brother, please,' I lift you up onto the rock with me and everyone lives happily ever after?"

"No, Daddy!" She regarded him with shocked disapproval. "*No!* That isn't how you play. You have to let me fall."

"I'm sorry, Hope," he said, getting softly in her face. "I don't think I can play that game with you."

"Why not?"

"Because I'd rather fall into the wildebeest stampede myself than see you break the toenail on your little toe."

"I don't have toenails, I have claws," she said, and showed him. *"Rarrrrrr!"*

"Rarrr, yourself," he said, wondering how it was that Claire always seemed to know the proper move. And not just Claire. It was as if there were some universal primer course on parenting, and everyone had taken it but him. This was an old feeling, though. Catching it, he made a mental note to pick up the scrip he'd dropped off at the pharmacy last night.

"Doddy?" Charlie's voice was wilting plaintively.

"What, Charlie, *what*?" When Ransom turned, the smile came back.

"Eat my eggs."

"Yes, you did. Good job. Now, everybody, listen up! Attention! No more fooling, we have to get to school. Mama's counting on the team. Now where are everybody's shoes?"

Charlie shrugged with big, round eyes, and Hope said, *"Mama* knows."

They searched the house three times—all fifteen rooms—only to find them in the one place the Team Leader never thought to look: the closet.

"Do we have time to swing before we go?" Hope asked him on their way outside.

"What are we doing here, Hope?"

She frowned at his tone. "Going to school?"

"That's right. Going to school. Do I *look* like I have time to push you on the swing?"

"No, but Mommy does."

"Well, I'm not Mommy. *Obviously.*" He threw in this ad hominem aside against himself as he strapped them in their seats. At which point, the missing valve in Charlie's cup—the one that Ransom never got around to putting in—led to a drenching OJ spill; which led to an unbuckling; which led to an about-face to the house; a hosing in the tub; another Huggie; a new set of clothes.

Finally—to the tune of "Five Little Ducks"—they set out. They were down to four, when the opossum or raccoon—the remains had reached the state where it was hard to differentiate—disappeared under the hood. As the tires *tump-tumped,* Ran caught Hope's expression in the rearview. Her face had gone grave; her eyes had that scintillant and musing light. She seemed like a tiny mathematician working out a problem, and it struck her father that his little girl had found the deep equation that would occupy her life. She had the artist gene—Ran didn't know what else to call it, or if he would have wished her spared.

In a guilty need for reciprocity, he looked toward Charlie, and found his son's eyes waiting for him in the mirror.

"Hi, Doddy."

"Hi, buddy."

Ransom smiled, and Charlie's left eye blinked, then both, and then the left again. Ran had seen this last night, too, and maybe if he'd been here all these months, this tic would never have developed; Hope might have turned her powers to the bright side, say, Barbie dolls, some correct, updated version in Birkenstocks with a waist and a flat chest. Ransom couldn't blame himself, and yet he did. *I'm here now, Charlie,* his eyes said to Charlie's in the mirror. The affirmation sank without a trace.

After he'd parked and slung their bags across his shoulder; after he'd put Charlie's socks and shoes back on and tied them; after he'd crossed the parking lot with Charlie slipping from one arm while holding Hope's hand and reminding her to look both ways; after he'd surrendered them to their teachers and come back out with two dark moons of sweat in his armpits and a tremor in his picking hand; after having longed for them and missed them so, Ransom slipped into the driver's seat and breathed a sigh of profound and profoundly culpable relief. In the desperate hope that he might find a pack of two-year-old cigarettes from his last trip, he reached for the glove box, but no such luck.

> *Mother duck said quack, quack, quack,*
> *But only one little duck came back. . . .*

As he punched out the kiddy tape, the radio came on, and what else could it be?

> *We said, "It's so tru-oo-ue,"*
> *We said, "It's so deep" . . .*

Ransom laughed and reached reflexively to turn it off, the way he had a dozen times before, then didn't. Pulling into traffic, he gave up and listened, really listened, for the first time. Mitch Pike had taken the driving backbeat of the original, steeped in old-time Stax/Volt Afro-funk, and slowed it to a ballad tempo. It was this that had Ran contemplating suicide the first eleven times he tried to listen and could not. Now, though, as he crawled along the strip, he realized Claire was right, Pike had found a sweetness in the song. Not that sweetness had been missing in his version, but it was just one of many things he'd put into his recipe. Ran had written "Talking in My Sleep" about the devastating end of a great love—his for Shanté Mills. The grief and fury he'd put into it, the despair, the deep question he'd posed about relationships, his challenge to the gods—all gone. Mitch had simplified—that was his masterstroke. Ransom suddenly understood that this was why Pike's version had gone number 1, where RHB's topped out at number 23, and the ghost of his old agent, Ponzi Gruber, floated up, telling Ran, the way he had way back at the start of everything, *The cream always rises, Ransom. Always.* And Ran suddenly realized that RAM's version was a better song.

He'd reached the light now, and he turned. Out there on a two-lane between high walls of trees, it hit him with a clang of rare finality that the success he'd dreamed about and worked for was never going to come. Deep into the country now, it came home to Ransom that his work, the work into which he'd poured the best part of himself for thirty years, was going to disappear without a trace.

> *But all it ever was*
> *Was talking in our sleep, baby,*
> *Just talking in my sleep. . . .*

The tires went *tump-tump,* and Ran was home.

Only as he pulled into the spelled green of the allée did it occur to him he'd driven past the CVS without a thought of turning in. Ransom knew he really ought to turn around. After all, he wanted to be good . . . even if he'd slipped a tiny bit. He'd promised Claire. On the other hand, he was dog-tired and wanted to check his song on the off chance that it might prove him wrong.

Like Buridan's ass, suspended between a bale of righteousness and a bale of sloth, he hesitated, then chose sloth. He had to drive back for the cocktail party later anyway.

"Can't wait for that," he told himself aloud, as good intentions slipped a further notch. And maybe the old unimproved, unmedicated Ran wasn't too dangerous to unleash, for a few more hours, on the friendly world that had convinced him of his error.

Inside at the partners desk, he reread his song and laughed. Words that not five hours before had fallen with the heavy chink of gold doubloons now seemed like charred and pitted scoriae brought back by chimpanzee astronauts from the dark side of the moon. Apart from strangeness, they held no interest whatsoever, and even if they'd shimmered with immortal genius, Ran had no idea where he'd meant to go from here. The song, in short, was gone.

Rifling the drawer, he took out Clive's old box. "Hell, yeah," he told himself, "let's get happy and go shoot some freaking guns!"

Outside, he loaded both barrels per instruction, then fired the first, surprised when the recoil knocked him back two steps. The muzzle belched a thick black cloud of acrid smoke. Fanning his way through, he found the Costco can of black-eyed peas thirty yards from its original position, reduced to smoking shreds of unidentifiable shrapnel, not much larger than a pile of fingernails.

"Damn," he said, sobered. "This thing could saw a man in half, couldn't it?"

Woman, too.

"Woman, too," he said, agreeing with himself. Having satisfied the urge and even spooked himself a bit, he stared toward the back porch, noting how the yard sloped slightly downhill from the river toward the house. Kneeling like a golfer on the green, Ran assessed the lie.

"Two hundred years of runoff. Yep, that could do it."

Gassing his whacker in the old slave cabin Claire had turned into her gardening shed, he waded into the periwinkle, clearing the area where he thought the new swale should go. It would cost some bucks, but a few hours' dozer work could send the water toward the road. That solved, they could see about the ants.

As Ran revved the engine, the doubled hanks of nylon blurred into an orange-tinted cutting wheel. He kept a weather eye out for the stob as clump after leafy clump went down, hemorrhaging a green fragrance and filling his cuffs with vegetal dicings. Pretty soon, his sweat-drenched T was modeled to his back, suggesting uncooked chicken breast.

Pausing to catch his breath, he stared toward the graveyard, which was laid out beneath an enormous cypress tree, whose branches bristled against a threatening blue-purple sky. Beyond the river, threads of soundless lightning flashed in the direction of Columbia.

As Ransom waded in again, the stob found him, snagging the line so hard it almost wrenched the trimmer from his hand.

Kneeling, Ransom took a closer, daylight look, as the first raindrops fell like tarnished pennies, splatting overlapping circles in the hot red dust.

What he'd uncovered was actually a foot, an iron foot. Feline in appearance, a little larger than a thumb, it suggested some big jungle cat, a jaguar or a leopard. Its crudely fashioned pads still showed the blacksmith's hammer marks, and there were tiny claws that age or use had almost worn away. A rusty link of hand-forged chain protruded from the clay beside it.

"What the hell have you done now."

He reached toward it, then, thinking better, fetched a spade and gloves out of the shed. In short order, as the rain fell harder, two more feet emerged, then the domed bottom of an overturned black pot—one might have said a cauldron. Buried in the anthill upside down, it was wrapped with chain, a single length crimped back on itself in a continuous loop. When Ransom yanked, the links crumbled like cigarette ash, smearing his gloves with orange chalk. Reaching down, he heaved till, finally, with a sumping *whoomp*, it came.

Inside were many things—some identifiable, most not—suspended in a hardened composite of mud and clay. Like flotsam from an ancient shipwreck, bits and corners peeked out from the frozen waves of earth—a stone, a candle stub, a coin, a nail, a shell. There was a small glass vial half full of fluid. Ran lifted it and something clinked inside. He held it to the light but couldn't see through the blue glass.

Ran was hesitant to touch the pot with his bare hand, but his little voice said, *Oh, go on. . . . You just scared yourself last night. It can't do any harm.* And when he shucked his glove, he did feel something coming through the iron—not heat, but some subtler energy, difficult to name. It sent a tingle to his earlobes, another to his loins.

At that moment, a slanting sheet of sunlight broke out of the rain, setting the drops individually on fire like prisms on a chandelier. Ransom closed his eyes, and just like that, the song was back and had the heavy chink of gold doubloons again and all their deep-sea gleam.

> *When it began, nobody can remember.*
> *No doubt at the beginning: one fine day*
> *The surface world collapsed around his longing.*
> *The deep world yawned and took his life away. . . .*

Some Geiger counter was going off inside him, giving warning clicks, but Ransom found it hard to tear his hand away. Just before he forced himself, something glanced along his back, as though someone had passed a candle not quite close enough to burn. It was the pressure of a pair of watching eyes, and when Ransom turned around, he saw someone standing at an upstairs window of the house.

"Claire?" The word died on his lips, and even as he spoke, Ran knew that it was not his wife. All he could make out was a silhouette, but Ran was almost sure the figure was a man.

E I G H T

*M*adam, I insist! You must partake. This receipt is of a sacred provenance, brought down from Sinai with the tablets of the law. It's Colonel Lay's own punch."

"Colonel Lay?" says Addie as she takes the cup. Harlan, it would seem, owing to the late arrival of the Nina, is in a state of more advanced conviviality than she has seen him in before in Charleston. And she notes, too, that the crowd pressing in on them beneath the tent is mostly male and military—members of his regiment, the Twenty-first Artillery, some boys barely half his age, who seem to regard him as a roué uncle and are eager to be led astray. The women in attendance have withdrawn to the piazza, where they can be seen fanning themselves and watching the carousings from within the cinched circles of their bonnets, with narrowed eyes.

The event is teetering on a precipice, in danger of disintegrating, momently, into a whorehouse free-for-all, a fact underscored by the Purdey's unsettling, repeated roar from the landing below, and by the banquet table, which is wonderful, but like no Lowcountry banquet table seen before. Paloma and Clarisse, her daughter—who have yet to show themselves, though Addie looks continually, eager to ascertain what sort of creatures they may be—have thrown a wedding *al estilo cubano*. Instead of a roast beef or leg of lamb, the central offering is a pig—not a suckling, but a hundred-and-fifty-pounder—presented splayed out like a bearskin rug with head and trotters still attached, the latter decorated with pleated paper frills, like the perfumed cuffs of an Elizabethan dandy. The creature rests on a grassy bed, one might almost say a *field of cilantro, and smells quite pungently—yet appetizingly—of that herb, as well as of sour orange juice and garlic. In lieu of an apple, it has a mango in the cleft of its split chin, and is surrounded by piles of other tropic fruit—mameys, guanabanas, and papayas, some imported, others grown on the estate, transplanted here from Cuba long ago by Percival, who is—or was, before his health declined—an avid horticulturalist. Furthering the Cuban theme, a pair of girls in stiff new frocks wend through the crowd, dispensing curtseys together with refrescos—limonadas and panales—from a tray, as well as savory little pastries known as empanadas filled with crab or cheese and guava.*

But the greatest wonder is the cake, which represents a large imperial building in the colonial Spanish style. Constructed of fondant and royal icing, it features an arched arcade at street level that supports balconies above and fronts upon a boulevard. There are several small black carriages—the sort Habaneros call quitrines—with licorice wheels and horses and postilions—realistically contrived with field boots, quirts, and beaver top hats—of colored marzipan. Across the street is a park with gravel paths of nonpareils, grass of shredded, bright green coconut, and palms whose trunks are sticks of cinnamon.

"Colonel Lay of New Orleans, Addie," Harlan answers as he dips the sterling ladle. "He's the proprietor of the Santa Isabel, a hotel in Havana, the hotel in Havana, I should say. . . . His rum punch is famous. Besides himself, I am the only man in the Northern Hemisphere who knows the formula. And did he give it to me from the goodness of his heart?"

"Nooo!" say several of his youthful protégés, like good Episcopalians, anticipating the lay part of the responsive reading.

"He did not, madam," confirms the groom, their priest. "I won it from him at el monte, which is a blood sport as played by Colonel Lay. And I tell you truly, Addie, I do not exaggerate, that gentleman wept tears, large tears of blood, in fact, like Jesus Christ upon the cross, as he wrote down the ingredients and measures. I keep it with me always, here, next to my heart together with the gift you gave me." With two fingers and a thumb, Harlan actually parts his coat, but either this is in jest, or he's forgotten to wear the miniature she presented him, with her image—in tempera upon ivory—in one oval of the locket, closing face-to-face with his upon a fragile golden hinge. "But, come now, drink up! You must set an example for these effeminate, fainthearted children."

"It is . . . very strong," she says.

"Strong?"

"A bit like breathing fire."

"Yes, yes . . . Better . . ." He stirs the air beneath his chin, as though to summon lyricism.

"Rum-scented fire," she arrives at now, "with a mist of orange peel."

"Ha ha, boys, is she game?" he says. "I told you she was game. Those oranges are the little bitter ones that Father grows around the house. They make an excellent marmalade as well. But, look, you've had the last of it," he says, glancing in the bowl. "We must make another batch. Where's Clarisse? Well, damn her, never mind. Come, Addie, will you go with me to the storehouse? We'll fetch the rum ourselves." He leans close to whisper. "We'll steal a moment to ourselves." And, then, in his plangent public voice, offering an arm: "Come, shall we have a little tour about the grounds?

"Thank God!" He mops his brow as they stroll off. "I thought I'd never get you to myself." In the shade of the allée, he turns and takes her hands. "How are you, Addie?"

"I am well."

"And your trip? Were you terrified?"

"Exhilarated, rather, though I confess it without pride."

He smiles. "Then I am proud for you. And the party—are you pleased?"

She hesitates, but it is brief. "It's thoroughly original, my dear."

"Yes, original," he says, with a face as suddenly sour as his father's oranges. Reaching in his coat for a cigar, he bites off the end and spits. "I'm not sure our friends know what to make of it. They catch the reek of garlic and smile and wave away the tray. I should have known better than to entrust it to Clarisse. Damn it all, though, we had a terrible row here early in the week."

"You and she?"

"No, the whole damned lot of us," he says, puffing as he lights. "You saw how Jarry was with me?"

"Yes?" she answers, not quite sure.

He nods, waving out his match. "He and Paloma are still furious. Father hasn't spoken to me since or deigned to budge out of the house today. I thought Clarisse was angry, too, but then she came to me all smiles and said she wanted to bury the ax and throw this party. I said yes to keep the peace."

"But, Harlan, truly, though, it's quite remarkable. That cake!"

"Yes, the cake. Do you know what I asked her for? For Sumter. And this is what I get, the Plaza de Armas in Havana."

"So that is what it is."

He nods. "The building is Tacón's, the opera house."

"But it's lovely, Harlan. I've never seen the like."

"But, damn it all, I wanted Sumter. I wanted to remind you of that night."

"But I don't need to be reminded. I remember every detail perfectly."

He concedes a tentative smile. *"So you're happy?"*

"I am happy."

"You are fine?"

"I am."

"May I kiss you?"

She laughs. *"Certainly not! Not here, where everyone can see."*

"To the storehouse then!"

"But, wait," she says as they pass the kitchen house, a log-and-daub-walled building with smoke boiling from the two great fieldstone chimneys on the gable ends. Outdoors, under the attached shed roof, a line of women in headkerchiefs, arm-deep in suds, are creating an enormous clatter as they wash the plate and crystal in a six-foot wooden trough. *"Perhaps I should peek in and pay them my respects."*

"No, Addie," Harlan says. *"You'll meet them soon enough. I want to speak to you about this matter first. I meant to wait, but, damn it, it's plaguing me. We'll go to the storehouse. It's more private there."*

And now, with a slight heaviness upon their mood, they proceed south along the sandy road that parallels the river, past the gardener, Peter, who is placing woodpile manure on the black raspberry vines. The kitchen plot is enormous—eight hundred feet by eighty or eighty-five—and Peter's boy is dressing out the rows of strawberries. There are at least three varieties that Addie can see, including the tiny ones called *fragole Alpine*, which she tasted once in Italy with Blanche and has not had since. A short distance from the house, they enter a cluster of buildings that surrounds the great shake-sided rice barn like a village in New England might surround its church. The carpenter's and wheelwright's shops are here, and in the forge, the ringing of the hammer stops as they go by. The guests' phaetons and barouches are parked along the shoulder of the road beside the stable, where Harlan stops and points in through the door. *"Look, there, Addie, do you see the little yellow rig?"* Amid the farm wagons and family carriages, half obscured by hanging tack, is a child's cart. *"That was mine when I was small. I had a goat named Beelzebub, though we should have called him Satan, based upon his temperament. He pulled Jarry and me up and down this lane as fast as we could go, and more than once he threw us in the ditch. You see this?"* He bows his large bald head and shows her a white scar. *"I do."*

"I have Beelzebub to thank for that."

"There." Kissing the spot, she pulls back when a groom appears with both arms full of hay.

"Marse, mistis," he says, smiling shyly, tossing clumps before the tethered horses in the line.

"That, now, is a respectful greeting. Hello, James," he calls. *"Yes, we see you winking there."* His tone is friendly, bluff, but cool, yet when the hounds set up a cry and leap against the kennel fence, his face lights up.

"No, Sultan, I've not forgotten you." He takes a scrap out of his handkerchief and throws it to a large bloodhound, which turns viciously on the other dogs and takes his prize into the corner of the pen. *"That's right, boy, show them who is Lord God of the yard."* Harlan gives a lusty and approving laugh. *"But damn me, which one is the key?"* he says, examining the padlock on the storehouse door against his heavy ring.

"What a charming little house," says Addie, leaning over the fence of a white cottage with a begonia vine in bloom along the porch and flowers in the yard. *"But, Harlan, aren't these they?"* She cups and sniffs a fragrant, large white rose that's rioting along the palings.

"I'm sorry, dear?"

"The ones you sent that morning . . . after the Jockey Club Ball? I put them in my drawer with my . . . intimate things, and, ever since, every time I opened it, I thought of you."

"Oh, yes," he says, with a vague, false smile, *"yes, I do recall. They're banksias, I think."*

"These? Banksias?" she says. *"They're musk roses, Harlan. They aren't like banksias—not the least little bit!"*

"Well," he answers, caught, *"I was never good with common names. The Latin, though, I think, is* rosa muskaplentia.*"*

Addie laughs aloud. *"Harlan DeLay! You know I married you for them?"*

"I hope that was not the only reason."

"But it was!" she cries. *"The only one! Because you didn't send those silly flowers on a stick! Now we must call it off."*

"You are pleasant, madam." He is smiling, but his ginger eyes have narrowed a degree.

"Blame your Colonel Lay. His punch is quite insidious. It's gone straight to my head. Truly, though, who lives here? It must be a woman."

"No, it's Jarry's house. He and Father, though, are thick upon the floral theme." His expressive lips—which have always struck her as almost, but not quite, sybaritic—take a slightly sour twist as he says this.

"*I see the way of it. Your brother is your Cyrano.*"

The key now finds the lock, but when he looks back up, the smile is gone. "*He's not my brother, Addie. Never call him that. If a man said that to me . . .*"

"*My dear!*" *she says, her hand over her heart.* "*Forgive me, I only meant . . .*"

"*I know,*" *he says,* "*I know it was a jest. But I cannot smile at it, Addie—not at that. What I have to say concerns him, though.*"

Opening the great plank door, he extends his arm, and Addie precedes him into the redolent dusk.

NINE

hew! Fuck me!"
Climbing the stairs backward, Ransom power-
jerked the pot behind him, step by step.
"Damn, boy! You really need to get back to the gym!" Hands on knees,
he panted on the upstairs landing till his wind came back, and then he
dragged his heavy find into the bath. With a doleful harbor-buoy clang, the
pot landed in Claire's antique clawfoot tub, and Ran wheeled on the taps.

Setting the water to its loosening work, he gazed through the same
window where he'd seen the figure looking out. The ants . . . the gun . . .
the pot . . . now, the silhouette . . . Ransom had the sudden, fleeting sense
that he was being led. . . . But where? By whom? *Another clue,* some voice
whispered in his head. Was it the same that in the morning helps you
choose between the blue shirt and the red? How come, at times, that voice
seemed like *someone else?*

"Nah, you just imagined it, amigo," he reassured himself, smoothing his
hand over the swirls and eddies in the pane. The glare of sunlight on old
hand-blown glass . . . "That's all it was. . . . And while we're at it, let's stop
talking to ourselves, all right? You know, and I know, it's no big deal, but
certain other parties might not understand. So mum's the word, agreed?"
Ran zipped his lips and smiled, amused by his own wit. He knew, of course,
how this conversation would be viewed—hadn't he seen his passengers' ex-

pressions in the cab? But the truth was, he felt perfectly okay—Ran, in fact, felt better than okay: strangely *good*.

When he turned back to the tub, a drift of red earth had begun to bleed into the water, releasing a faint smell that seemed familiar somehow, though he couldn't quite say how. Ran felt suddenly hungry, though. Remembering his resolution to make nice, he turned the water off and headed downstairs to start dinner.

As fate would have it, there on the bottom shelf of the fridge a package of Perdue whole fryer parts sat waiting for him. The moment Ransom saw it, gleaming in Saran, he knew fried chicken was the very thing he had to have and set to work, assembling the sacerdotal implements like a priest for Mass. Into a brown paper bag, two heaped cups of flour—self-rising, naturally, with a double pinch of cayenne and black pepper. A deep-sided cast-iron skillet received a dollop of Crisco the size of a shrunken head. Firing the gas, he tossed in the secret ingredient, the quiddity and fundamental particle of proper soul-food cooking, a stick of butter, indispensable for proper blistering and flavor. And like our metaphoric priest, getting happy in the sacristy, indulging in a swig or two of the not-yet-consecrated wine, Ran decided that a glass of something was in order. And there, as if at his thought-command, was an open bottle on the countertop beside the Peugeot pepper grinder Claire had lifted from New York.

A terrible wine snob, Ran took a chance. "Damn!" he said approvingly. "*God* damn!" Lusty, spirited, full of youthful insubordination, fat as hell and wholly indiscreet—it had his name all over it! The label rang no bells, and when he saw the tag he blinked in disbelief—IGA: $1.99.

"Holy shit! Remind me to get some more of this," he said, forgetting his resolution. "Hell, let's buy a freaking case!"

And what *was* that smell? Now it had drifted down the stairs. As Ran inhaled, he suddenly flashed back to a hot September night in Killdeer almost thirty years before. . . . Seventeen, nursing a Colt 45, he was standing on the stoop of a small brick house, staring through the screen at a woman working in her kitchen.

It was Friday, payday at the mill, and behind him, Ran could hear Bagtown hopping with sounds of harsh and not-entirely-joyful revelry. Carrying his malt in a brown paper bag, he'd walked from seven blocks away, the corner of Bane and Depot, where he'd gathered with some friends beneath the light to listen to the new Stones album and to admire the Earl Scheib paint job on Tommy Hicks's candy-apple-red Trans Am.

At home, Mel would be breaking ground on his second bottle of Old Screwtop or Chateau Shotgun Shack—whatever Friday special Earl's happened to be running—getting worked into a lather over the editorial in the *Socialist Worker* and ready to lash out at Herbert Kincannon or the first convenient capitalist who came his way. Kincannon, however, hadn't run the mill for thirty years without the savvy to stay the hell away from Bagtown after dark, and Ran and many of his friends had also found it politic to steer clear of home on Friday nights till after ten.

The first place Ran found to go was that streetlight on the corner where his friends still were. The consensus of the crew was that *Exile on Main Street* was pretty good, but Tommy nailed it when he added, "But it ain't *Let It Bleed.*" They'd put the older album on the eight-track, and the music followed Ransom on his ten-minute stroll, floating, airborne, over an unmarked border that on the ground was as fraught as that dividing East and West Jerusalem.

Not in Bagtown anymore, Ran could still hear it playing on Delores Mills's stoop. Even distorted by distance, challenged by the notes of tree frogs and cicadas, by the rumble of cruising muscle cars and the clack of freights uncoupling in the yard, there was no mistaking what it was. The song was "Gimme Shelter," the first piece of music he ever knew, reliably, as great. On the hundredth listening as on the first, Ran marveled at Mary Clayton's Valkyrie-like harmonies and, still more, Keith Richards's mighty licks, which seemed to him, at seventeen, as fundamental, as always-so, as the opening motif of Beethoven's Fifth, a symphony first opened up to him by the woman frying chicken at the range in her nude hose, the old-fashioned kind with seams, whose flesh tone, Ransom noticed—as he sipped his beer, afraid to knock—was not the color of her flesh.

The organist and choir director at the New Jerusalem Church of God in Christ, Delores Mills had taught music at Killdeer High since integration. By the time they met, Ransom had been studying guitar for three years on his own. He bought his first electric at thirteen—a solid-body, sunburst Teisco single pickup, mail-ordered from Chicago for $49.99.

While other boys dreamed of touchdowns and winning buzzer shots, Ran tuned to open G and dreamed of playing Shea and Fillmore East, mounting the stage and letting them get a little nervous, letting them begin to sweat a bit—especially those girls in halter tops and braided hair bands, with the keys of their daddies' BMWs outlined in the pockets of their poured-on jeans. Then he would hit the riff, that one impossible riff that would be, to rock guitar, like Bannister's first sub-four-minute mile, like the triple lutz that Donald Jackson landed on the ice in '62. . . . Ran's inability to read music had begun to seem like a potential obstacle to this future by the afternoon he stopped by Mrs. Mills's office to see if she could help. Her suggestion: join the band.

"The band?" Ran looked over his shoulder, as though this might be addressed to some more credulous individual who'd stolen up behind him in the hall. "You're kidding, right?"

Delores Mills's expression made clear her lack of comic intent.

"Yeah, well, thanks a lot." Tossing his hair, Ran raked his fingers after it and started out. "See ya round."

"Mr. Hill . . ."

He turned back.

"Close the door."

Two weeks later, he was back. Forced to choose an instrument, he picked the most preposterous one he could think of in an effort to preserve his fifteen-year-old dignity and revolutionary credentials: the slide trombone. And he had to pay for his humiliation, too. When he asked Mel for a loan to buy his uniform and instrument, the old man laughed and gave him a playful smack up 'side the head. Mrs. Mills came to his assistance. So instead of wailing on his ax at Shea like Keith or Jimmy Page, Ran spent his Sunday nights at New Jerusalem, mopping up the banquet hall after a bunch of niggers for a nigger teacher at a nigger church. And that's exactly how he thought of it.

Musical notation, time signatures, scales, intervals, and forms—without regard for his political opinions or the color of his skin, Delores opened these and many other mysteries, and eventually cracked the outer shell of rock for him the way she cracked the egg she used to bind the flour to the meat. So when Ran heard "Love in Vain," he knew—unlike Tommy and the other redneck exegetes at Bane and Depot—that Robert Johnson wrote the song. He learned to recognize, beneath the flesh of rock 'n' roll, the older pattern of the twelve-bar blues, which are the bones. And when

Delores asked him to her house one Friday night for supper, Ransom—
nervous about his table manners and also half afraid of "nigger germs"—
went in order not to hurt his teacher's feelings and had the first and only
decent home-cooked meal he'd had in his short life. And this became a
standing invitation, and in addition to her other gifts, Delores taught him to
prepare the only genuinely accomplished meal he ever learned to make.

Once he learned the surprising news that black people were only superfi-
cially different from himself, Ran developed an unsurprising crush on her, and
Delores—who'd been married once and had a child, who was attractive, single, and not inexperienced with men—was perfectly aware of Ransom's feelings and used them shamelessly—but only for his benefit, encouraging his
passion and his focus on the work, always pushing him a little further than he
wished to go. She was the first person who made Ransom Hill believe that
there was something in him worth an effort on another human being's part.
And this, Ran knew, was the one difference between him and his friends at
Bane and Depot: he found a second, better place to go. And he still said "nigger" when he was with them. He still laughed and called the part of town Delores lived in Niggertown—even though her house was brick and better than
his own. But after Mrs. Mills, it never sat quite right, like some once-familiar
food his system had lost the ability to digest. And even if he said it, even if he
laughed, he knew Delores Mills had saved him. And so, when what he really
wanted was to mount the stage at Shea and hit that riff of riffs and make those
rich girls who had heaped such scorn on him grovel at his feet and beg for it,
Ran, instead, took his place in line and marched up and down the sodden football field in his cheap shoes and played the slide trombone for Mrs. Mills. And
he would have marched to hell for her and back by way of Selma, Alabama, if
only Delores hadn't had a daughter, if only her daughter hadn't been
Shanté. . . .

If only at the Christmas choral program in assembly—in the midst of
Handel and the standard fare, as Ransom, slouching somewhere in the
twenty-second row, feigned sleep—Shanté, home for break from prep
school, where early talent and her mother's doggedness had won her a full
ride, had not stepped forward from the chorus and begun to belt out "Jor-
dan, Roll" in a voice as rich and strong as Gladys Knight's, but with six or
seven colors Knight's did not possess. There was melting sexuality in it, and
sorrow, and, in its upper register, a joyful longing that threw itself toward
transcendence like a trapezist letting go the bar, careening through the spot

with arms outstretched, never doubting that an unseen hand would lift her where it was her destiny to go.

If only none of this had happened, Ransom, three years later, on that hot September night, would not have been standing on Delores's stoop with malt liquor on his breath, watching her fry chicken and afraid to knock. When he finally did, she glanced over her shoulder, wiped her hands, and came up to the screen and didn't open it.

"Something sure smells good," he said with a big grin full of desperate charm that would later open many doors. Not this door, though.

"I'm sorry, Ransom," Delores said, "I can't ask you in."

"Oh," he said. "Oh, okay, well." He was halfway down the steps before the impact hit him like a speeding car with a drunk driver at the wheel. He turned around and pressed his face against the screen. "Why not?" he asked in a soft, pleading voice. "Why not, Miz Mills?"

Delores looked him in the face, full in the face, for a long beat. In her expression, pity and sorrow had made peace with something else resigned and hard.

"Did I do something wrong?"

"No, Ran, you didn't."

"Then why can't I come in?"

Delores simply looked at him, and softly, slowly closed the inner door.

From the yard, he saw Shanté silhouetted in the dormer window. She put her hand against the glass. The train, by then, had left the station. In the distance, Mick was singing:

> . . . *it had two lights on behind*
> *Well, the blue light was my baby, and the red light was my mind*

Ransom turned away and threw his beer can at the streetlight. Punching someone's car, he stumbled up the street, cradling his bleeding hand, with two tickets in his pocket for the New York City bus he took alone. As he went, the smell of Delores's chicken followed him, which he never ate again.

Yet here it was today at Wando Passo, all around him now, the smell that wafted through the screen that night. And the curious thing was, Ran had not yet started cooking. Even before he floated the first breast, like a Viking longboat, out into the lake of oil to burn, the house was redolent with the smell of Delores Mills's chicken, released by water's softening action from the earth in a long-buried pot. And how this could be so, Ransom didn't know, any more than he could explain the nature of this wine.

The more he drank of it, the more magisterial it became, filling him with an exquisite sadness, like a long view from an eminence on a perfect autumn day, with a church bell ringing in the distance and a tang of frost. He'd never tasted anything quite like it, and this was saying something. For he'd had something to prove with wine, distancing himself from the threaded jelly jar that Mel was often clutching when Ran came home and found him passed out in the front seat of the Thunderbird, listening to the Town and Country playing softly off a charger from the house. None of the rare vintages that, in better times, had cost him many hundreds—and, on occasion, more than that—had ever affected Ran the way this one did, which hinted of imperishable truths in the very process of its vanishing.

And it was wholly vanished by the time he put the final piece of chicken on the plate and glanced up at the clock. "Holy shit! The kids! The party! Claire! Fuck me!"

And Ransom grabbed the keys and ran.

T E N

arlan catches Addie's wrist and wheels her to the store-house door as it snicks shut. Pressing close, he kisses hungrily—her mouth, her neck, her collarbone. Moving from below, his hand nudges her breast upward as he drops his face into her décolletage.

"Harlan! Harlan!" she whispers, in mingled scolding and entreaty.

"Is this unwelcome to you?" he asks with flaming cheeks and an expression that is suddenly indolent, almost dull.

"No! Of course not, no. I only meant . . ."

"I've waited so long, Addie. I've so looked forward to tonight."

"But, you must wait," she tells him, straightening herself. "You must wait till then."

"Must I? Tell me why I must. What if I cannot?"

She laughs, half complimented, half alarmed, and starts off down the aisle. "What a strange place," she says, wiping a spot of saliva off her breast as she gives her top a hoist. A few stray sunbeams work their way through cracks of daub and show dust motes rising from the earthen floor, where tubs of lard, rendered from the Christmas killing, have been sunk to cool. When Harlan lights the sperm-oil lamp, she makes out burlap sacks of coffee, row on row, and shelves of pickles and preserves; corned beef and pickled pork in tubs, hams and sides of bacon strung up from the rafters. There is flour by the barrel, soap and olive oil, candles, hogsheads of molasses, boxes of cigars and fancy sugar in the nine-pound loaves. And all across one side, the spirits, wine in racks, perhaps a thousand bottles, with a heavy representation of the vinos generosos—Jerez, Málaga, and Amontillado—the strong, heavy wines of southern Spain, which Harlan, like Percival before him, developed a taste for in his Cuban days. For the quarters, there are casks of the cheap Spanish red called vino Catalán and of the raw cane brandy Cubans call aguardiente.

"You see how much there is," he says. "It's absurd of him to plague me over one lost order. We'll be in Washington by summer anyway. This will more than see us through."

"It's like the granaries of Egypt," Addie says.

Harlan laughs. "Yes, and now you are the Pharaoh's wife. But come here in the light where I can look at you." He unrolls a bolt of flannel on the coffee sacks and pats, inviting her to sit. "I don't know what reception you're to have from Father and the others, Addie, so before I take you to them, I want you to know what has occurred.

"So, Thursday last," he says, removing the chimney of the lamp and relighting his cigar, "the day after my return from Charleston and the wedding, Father called us all together in the library—and by all, you understand, I mean myself, Paloma, Jarry, and Clarisse. With great solemnity and mystery, as though he were about to lead us in some arcane rite, he produced a key from around his neck, opened the drawer of the partners desk, and produced his final will and testament. Most people, Addie, have the decency to die before inflicting their intentions on their kin, but Father, knowing he was going to stir a fracas, could not deny himself the stimulation of observing it firsthand. So it was read. To be exact, Jarry read it to us. Father, you see, prefers Jarry's style of oratory to my own . . . or do I mean rhetoric? But, never mind, I'll spare you the catalog of petty insults I endure, which would no doubt bore you and keep us here into the middle of next week." Harlan smiles perfunctorily, as though he's tasted something spoiled.

Addie, who has never heard this tone from him before, folds her hands and, with some effort, manages to keep a neutral face. "I take it you were displeased by its provisions?"

"In a word, I was," he replies. "Though the document leaves the property to me—to us—as I expected, as it should, there were surprises. Paloma, for her years of . . . 'service,' shall we say, is to be freed. I didn't know of that, but, frankly, she's past her prime, and I'm content for her to live out her days in the pine barren cottage with Clarisse, if that is her desire. What came as a far greater shock," he says, puffing furiously, "what I can neither brook . . . nor tolerate . . . nor allow to stand . . . is Father's intention to free Jarry. Not to put too fine a point on it, this would be ruinous to us. It is, moreover, by current law, illegal in the state of South Carolina, and in every state of the Confederacy, to manumit a slave except by special action of the legislature. Father, of course, does not concede the authority of the

government in Montgomery. The law, you see, according to his settled view, is change-able according to his whim, whereas his word has a force equal to, if not somewhat in excess of, biblical decree."

"He gave it then?" she asks.

"Apparently, he did," says Harlan, pacing up and down with one arm squared behind his back. "They all knew of this, of course. It was only I—his legitimate son and heir—who was kept in the dark. Not until the day after our wedding, ten days to the day before my departure for Fort Moultrie, did Father see fit to enlighten me. His position—wholly preposterous—was that it had never occurred to him I might object."

"But you do?"

"Do I? Madam, believe you me, I do! I object most strenuously and told him so in no uncertain terms. If he persists in this folly, I mean to contest the will, and let them see how a South Carolina court views the rights of one spoiled, selfish nigger slave against those of a plantation owner and first lieutenant in the Twenty-first!"

"My dear!" she says. "What happened?"

"What happened? What happened?" Harlan fulminates. "Madam, had there been pistols in the room, I could not have confidently ruled out the possibility of bloodshed. They all took his side, of course—of course!"

"And Clarisse?" says Addie. "Is she to be freed as well?"

"Clarisse? Clarisse is free, Addie. Long since free. Have I not acquainted you with her situation?"

"I don't believe you have."

Harlan's features concentrate. He smokes and stares into the distance. "Clarisse is not my father's child," he says after a beat. "She is Wenceslao Villa-Urrutia's by Paloma."

Addie blinks. "Wenceslao . . ."

"Villa-Urrutia. You have no idea who he is. . . ."

She shakes her head. "I don't."

"Of course you don't. How could you. How to put this . . ." He begins to pace again. "Briefly, Addie, Father, in his youth, displayed a mechanical ingenuity—one would almost have to say a genius—that led him, after some professional misadventures, into relations with a man named Charles Derosne. Together, they developed what subsequently became known as the Derosne mill. Father was instrumental in the design of the vacuum pan. That's what first took him to Cuba, where he made his fortune. I feel certain I've mentioned this to you before."

"It has to do with sugar?"

"*Exactly. The mill produced a new and iridescent form of it, of a quality no one had dreamed possible before. It long ago transformed the refining process—in Cuba and elsewhere—but its early history was checkered. The machinery was complex, temperamental, and fabulously expensive. The prototype cost over sixty thousand dollars and was wholly unproved. In an effort to win acceptance, he and Charles traveled to Matanzas and personally installed the first one at La Mella, which was Wenceslao's hereditary estate.*"

"*Villa—*"

"*Villa-Urrutia. Yes, correct. Count Wenceslao Villa-Urrutia. Father served as chief machinist in La Mella's caldron and purga, the boiler house and refinery. That's where he met Paloma. She was a housemaid at the hacienda, Villa-Urrutia's mistress. Father was smitten and tried to buy her. Prime wenches went—in Cuba, in those days—for twenty onzas or a little more, around four hundred dollars. Father offered six, then eight, but the Conde, like many Cubans of his class, was an inveterate gambler and proposed a more sporting proposition. He offered to put Paloma against Father's stake in the mill. We're talking two and a half years of work.*"

"*He took the bet?*"

"*He took the bet.*"

"She must have been something," Addie says, with a slight smile.

"*She still is. Mucha mujer. Of course, she's old now, but you'll see. They made the wager in the purging house, over cigars, using the bocoyes of coarse sugar for a table. A single hand of faro, and Father won. When she came to him, Paloma was pregnant.*"

"With Jarry?"

Harlan wags a finger.

"Clarisse!" she says. "Clarisse?"

He smiles. "*Correct. She is Wenceslao's child. She was born in Cuba and raised in the Count's household, educated like his other daughters.*"

"And she came here?"

Harlan nods. "*When I went down for my apprenticeship, I brought her back to help her mother with the house. Villa-Urrutia, you see, left her little but her wardrobe and expensive tastes. It was essentially an act of charity, Addie, something Father undertook for Paloma's sake. Clarisse, you see, is not related to this family. She is Villa-Urrutia's upon Paloma.*"

"So you said."

"*Did I? Forgive me, I've lost my train of thought.*" He turns away from her and stares into the shadows, as though what he's misplaced might be lurking among the soft goods and comestibles in the dark, far corner of the room.

"You were telling me about your father's promise to Jarry."

"Yes, thank you. He did this for Paloma, Addie. From our vantage here in proper South Carolina, it may be hard for you to understand, but Father's racial views were formed when he was young."

"In Cuba . . ."

"In Cuba. Yes. Things are different there." Taking out his handkerchief, he dabs his brow and walks away from her. "The races mix more freely. One meets people of mixed blood in society all the time, even in the highest circles, and it is expected, Addie, it is socially de rigueur, for one to treat these people—for a young man, let us say, to treat these women, these well-connected mulatas—one calls them morenas there, 'brunettes'—as one would treat women of good family here. In effect, as I treat you."

"I see."

"And perhaps you can also see how easy it might be for a young man to fall under the spell of Spanish decadence and so forget himself. . . ."

"As your father did."

"As my father did." He stops and faces her. His expression turns forlorn. "I myself, in my time there . . . I was not perfect, Addie."

"I appreciate your forthrightness, Harlan," she replies, after a moment, when it appears an answer is required. "But if you think to shock me, you must take a different tack. I'm not a child."

He smiles. "You are good. The more I come to know you, the more convinced I am you will be good for me." Absolved, he starts to pace again, smoking with complacent energy.

Addie is thoughtful over his revelation and a bit put off by the self-centeredness of his response—only a bit, though. She's also half amused by it and curious to watch as he comes out. She hasn't seen him in this light.

"Fortunately, I woke up from the spell in time," he goes on. "Father, in all these years, never has. This, in a word, is why Wando Passo is what it is and what you see, which must seem strange to you. I must tell you, Addie, had it been up to me, Jarry would never have been made steward in the first place. It is unwise, most unwise—I can tell you from bitter, personal experience—ever to put oneself in dependent relations with persons of that race. I didn't always feel that way, but time—maturity, if I may say so—has seasoned me. Sadly, though, this water's long since passed the bridge. There are four hundred souls upon this property—from the crop hands to the coopers, gardeners, and smiths—all answerable to Jarry. This plantation is an immense wheel that turns upon its steward as the axle, and if Father were to die while

I'm away, if Jarry were to leave, I honestly don't see how it could turn. The place would go to ruin in a season—nay, a month!"

"I see," says Addie, having finally, with some difficulty, grasped the central point. "You asked your father, then, to break his word."

"Not to break it, Addie, to delay it merely. To wait until the war is done, when I return. There are many in my regiment—even the soberest heads—who think we'll be in Washington by summer."

"Do they? I know so little of military matters."

"You saw how it went at Sumter—judge from that. Even in the worst case, I don't believe the war can last beyond a year. The Yankees hate us, hate our principles, our institutions, our way of life—why would they not let us go? The Union's like a bad old marriage. They may rail at ending it, but will they shed their blood to keep us locked in a relationship they—and we—abhor? I don't believe they will, and so, you see, it's really not that much to ask."

"Of Jarry."

"Of Jarry. How many Negroes in this state, I ask you, can boast of advantages like his?"

"Your father takes a different view. . . ."

"He does. It is his word, you see—he's punctilious upon that point."

What gentleman is not? *Addie thinks, but doesn't bring herself to say. In this area, her upbringing has left no shade of gray. "What happened, Harlan?"*

"It was, madam, as if a hornet's nest had fallen from the eave and burst."

"What did he do?"

"He? They, madam, they! They combined their regiments! I was cast as villain of the house. You may as well know, Addie, this is my accustomed role at Wando Passo—it's been my role for years. They refused to speak to me, to acknowledge my presence in a room. They treated me, in short, as though I were a malodorous substance to be scraped from the bottoms of their shoes."

"But Clarisse relented. . . ."

"Yes, Clarisse, and only she. But I must tell you, Addie, I don't entirely trust her motives."

"What do you think they are?"

"Lord knows! She's a woman, isn't she? If I were to guess, I'd say she may have seen it as an opportunity to play hostess and receive the credit of the event."

"A Negro? Here? In South Carolina?"

"Your incredulity—though shared by me—would be lost upon the other members of this house. In Cuba on a day like this, they would be congratulated and de-

ferred to, Negro blood or no, and it's by this principle that Father has run his house. Rather, it's by this principle that he has let them run it for him. And I'm sick and goddamned tired of it. So, I told her, Addie, I said, 'Clarisse, if you would like to give a party, have away at it, and please accept my thanks. But, I cannot allow you or your mother to mingle with the guests.' "

"What did she say?"

"Not a word," he says. "Not one. Her expression, though, was eloquent. The human capacity for self-deception never ceases to amaze me, Addie. I honestly believe that till that moment, till that very day and hour, Clarisse thought I thought about her . . ." Harlan's gaze returns to that dark corner, as though his train of thought has skipped the track again.

"She thought you thought about her how?"

"Like a sister." Now his eyes come back. "A sister, who is white."

"Oh." Her hand goes to the button on her breast. "Oh, how terrible for her."

"For her?" he says. "It was terrible for me, Addie, for me, to be put in that position."

"Yes, dear, of course," she says. "Of course, it must have been."

"But what was I to do?" he asks, taking out his handkerchief again. "Present her and Paloma to Louisa Elliott, to Miss Blanche Huger, on a footing of equality?"

"No, of course. Of course not, dear," she says, noting how he is perspiring, pacing faster, smoking more, smoking quite furiously, in fact, and accompanying his tale with large, emphatic gestures of his hands. It's as though he stands accused and feels compelled—indignantly compelled—to defend himself, as though, moreover, his accuser is in the room, a ghostly third that he can see and she cannot. Addie can gauge its presence from his actions, though, the way he smiles mockingly in its direction, steps around it or angrily shoulders it aside. And gradually it dawns on her, not certainly, but only as a possibility, that in addition to what he's telling her—which she has no reason to doubt—there is something he is holding back.

"To her credit, though, Clarisse made peace with it and went ahead. It was my father who exploded."

"What did he say?"

"Words that I, as a gentleman, must forbear repeating in your company. I will only tell you that the recent events at Fort Sumter were mild compared to the detonations in this house."

"Dearest!"

"But I granted him no quarter, Addie. I gave it to him straight, no water and no ice! Frankly, the sooner he's gone, the better it will be for everyone. We'll never put

our house in order while he lives. The first thing I'd like to do as soon as he is cool upon the board is put Paloma and Clarisse on a boat to Cuba. It was a mistake ever to have brought her here. Clarisse has never adjusted to the alteration in her status. In South Carolina, she's like a tiger in a cage."

"If she's unhappy, and free, why doesn't she leave?"

"That, madam, is a question you must pose to the philosophers! Father, of course, refused to come out of solidarity with Paloma. For years now, he's refused to attend events where she and they—the 'dark family,' as I believe our well-meaning friends refer to them—were not invited. Which, in short, is why, for years, he's barely left these grounds. By his own choice, he's made himself a pariah, infamous throughout the county and the state, and he's made me one, too, Addie, willy-nilly."

"I had no idea how this had affected you."

"The thing has tainted my whole life, Addie," he says earnestly, "and it is hardly too much to say that it has poisoned it." Harlan now applies himself to his cigar, puffing single-mindedly like a disgruntled infant at a sugar-tit, till Addie sees a glaze form in his eyes. "This is how we live, my dear. It's why Wando Passo is not a proper house. To make it one, you and I have a Herculean task ahead of us. Not to put too fine a point on it, Father treats these half-breed niggers in all respects as he treats me, his legitimate son, as though there were no differences of quality or degree, and I'll go further and tell you he actually prefers their company to mine. That, my dear, is why Jarry was made steward, while I was sent away—exiled is not too strong a term—to Cuba. It's a rare evening, madam, let me tell you, when you don't hear them in the library, Jarry and Father, holding forth, their voices raised over some project or some book. They were at it last night, too—so help me God, they were, with the party looming and Father at death's door, supposedly! They were parsing Wordsworth—I could hear them through the floor. 'It is not now as it hath been of yore. . . .' Grant me patience, Lord! And a quarter of an hour later on to Thucydides! 'The strong do what they can while the weak suffer what they must.' They kept me up to all hours shouting and laughing over cigars and port the way men only shout and laugh when they're aroused. Father, I can tell you, has never deigned to discuss such things with me. I lack sufficient intelligence, you see, to comprehend great English poetry, and the Greeks . . . oh, certainly not."

Addie's eyes are wide, her aspect reminiscent of Blanche's, in the Nina's *bow, under stress from the hot wind.* "And what was the upshot?"

"The upshot of what?" he asks with a brusque note.

"Of your disagreement with your father."

"On what subject, madam? They are multiple and myriad."

"The subject of Jarry's manumission."

"Ah, that! He told me, Addie, to remove my hind parts by the proximate, or nearest, door—and that, madam, is not a paraphrase, but a quote. And from that moment until now, I have not exchanged a word with him or had the pleasure of his beneficent, paternal smile. Now, therefore, let us gird our loins and go to face the dragon in his lair!"

ELEVEN

laire saw them from across the room—the kids in masks of chocolate Soft-Serve and Ran in his white hat and jeans with muddy knees. She rushed downfield to intercept.

"What happened? Are you all right?"

"What?" Ran said. "We're fine."

"Hi, Mommy!"

"Hi, Mama!"

"Hi, sweet girl! Hi, sweet boy! Come give Mama a big hug!" She knelt and took her messy kisses fearlessly. She patted them like pears in tissue, checking for bruises. She gazed deep into their eyes for signs of trauma. None were apparent, even to her X-ray vision. Ran's expression said, *See, I handled it,* and was proud.

"You gave them ice cream?"

"They were hungry."

"I'm sure they were. It's almost suppertime."

"What was I supposed to do—hand them each a crusty loaf and drop them in the woods? You asked us to be here, here we are, per madame's request." He bowed across his hat and, rising, looked at her with melting eyes Claire really couldn't deal with then.

"You're late."

"I had a busy afternoon. Here, check this out." He showed her the blue vial.

"What's this?"

"You tell me. I found it in a pot in the backyard."

"What pot?"

"A black one buried in the periwinkle patch."

"You found a buried pot in our backyard?"

"It was upside down and wrapped with chains."

"Wrapped with chains?" She leaned close and sniffed. "Have you been drinking?"

"What? I had a glass of wine," he said with wounded innocence.

"A glass . . . As in a glass bottle?"

"Hey, excuse me," he said, "if I'm not mistaken, you're working on a wee bit of a Chardonnay flush yourself. And isn't everybody drinking here? It's a cocktail party—so what if I had one before I came? Relax!"

"Oh, Ran," she said with disappointed eyes. "Goddamn it, this is my first day. You promised."

"What!" he said. "*What!* I'm being good. Aren't I being good? Don't I have on my white hat?"

"Daddy's being good, Mommy," Hope explained with gravity that stopped just shy of a chastisement.

"Ice *keem!*" Cresting on his sugar rush, Charlie, spying more, headed off toward the desserts.

"Dute, come back!" said Ransom, laughing. "Where's Cell? I want to see the man and shake his hand! It's time to institute the plan and make peace in the land!"

And Claire was really worried now.

Deanna, overhearing strident whispers, made haste to interpose. "Are these your children, Claire?"

"Oh, hello, Deanna . . . Yes, this is Hope and . . . that's Charlie over there. Hope, say hi to Professor Holmes."

"Hi, Professor Homes."

"Hello," Deanna said, careful not to touch and risk infection.

Ransom smiled and raised his hand. "I'm the houseboy."

Claire frowned. "Deanna, this is Ransom Hill, my husband."

"I used to listen to you all the time at Smith." Deanna, suddenly, turned girlish. "You had a kind of cult."

"No kidding," Ransom said. "A cult at Smith. Tell me more."

"That's it. It wasn't all that big."

"Well, no, it wouldn't be, would it?"

Claire, from the scorers' table, had to give the old man 10 for this.

"We were exclusive, though." Deanna's grin revealed that there were hot springs percolating in the permafrost and also told the world she could be sly, but Claire already knew.

Ransom laughed. "I like this girl . . . excuse me, woman! It's woman, isn't it? Sometimes I forget what decade I'm in—all that sex, you know, Deanna, all those drugs and rock and roll."

And stern Deanna, in her severe black specs and vampire gabardines, actually laughed, and laughed quite volubly, at what seemed to Claire a tired and somewhat marginal attempt.

She watched this with the Tiresian eyes of one who, both as wife and onetime girlfriend, had seen it all before, seen the chilly, hip Deannas melt like ice cubes on the stove as the blaze came up in Ransom's eyes, the sexual one, the power thing, little different now than it had been at twenty-five. Claire wondered if she'd been a bit of a Deannatype herself way back once upon a time, and if so, when she'd stopped liking it . . . or was it only when it wasn't turned on her?

"There's something inside." When Ransom shook the vial, it made a liquid *whoosh* and an illiquid *tink*. He took the stopper out. "Here, Dee, take a whiff and tell us what you think."

"I'm sure Deanna doesn't want to smell that, Ran."

"I don't mind, Claire, actually."

Ransom shrugged. "Dee doesn't mind."

"It's kind of musky," said Deanna.

"Musky . . . Hmmm . . ." Ran offered it to Claire.

"No, thanks."

"Humor me."

She took a wuff. "Perfumy . . . kind of sweet."

"Musky? Sweet?" he said. "It smells like Pap Finn's breath on a bad drunk to me. What the hell could this stuff be?"

Before they answered—assuming either could—his eye drifted over their shoulders, up and up. "Dr. J!" Grinning, Ransom swung his hand wide for a soul shake. "Hey, nigga!"

Pod by pod, the room went still around them, starting with Deanna, in whose little starry eyes the starry little stars winked out.

"What?" said Ran. "Oh, sorry, I guess I can't say that either. Wrong decade again!" He looked to Deanna for salvation, but her eyes had turned indifferent as the sea.

"We used to call each other that on tour. He called me nigga, too—right, Cell?"

"Ran?" said Claire.

He looked at her.

"I'd drop it now."

"Yeah, sure, okay," he said. "As long as everybody understands it wasn't, you know, prejudicial . . . I think the roadies started it, didn't they, Marcel? Tyrell and James?"

"I don't remember, actually," Marcel answered, in a level tone.

"I'm pretty sure it was Tyrell and James. . . ."

In the first moment, Claire felt murder in her heart. The moment after homicide came pity, a deep, aching pang. Less for Marcel, though, than for Ran, who befouled himself more with the epithet than he ever could their friend.

They used to love each other, she thought. *What happened?* Was it the money? Claire almost wanted to believe it was, the old dispute over the chorus of "Talking in My Sleep," the rock that RHB came smash against so long ago. But in her heart, she knew the deeper answer wasn't money or the chorus. She faced it now: *The reason is because of me.*

Repeating the same action and expecting a different outcome . . . Her therapist's remark played back, so why the hundredth time Ran asked had she said yes? Was it because she couldn't bear the thought of negotiating where the children would spend Christmases, because she wished the cup to pass? Having left him for a string of valid reasons, none of which had really been addressed, was it reasonable to believe that they still had a fighting chance? As she observed Ran now with his hazed eyes and vinous breath, an answer flashed at Claire from some deep place. She had agreed to let him visit because she wished—not only wished, but needed—to come to clarity about their marriage. It was time, and way past time, for that. And taking in his large and joyous indiscretion, so familiar against the unfamiliar backdrop of Marcel, another thought broke through. With Cell, she played her mother's role, the center of attention: his. Whereas, in her marriage, for nineteen years, she'd been the gardener, while Ransom was the rose. She'd known that going in, though, hadn't she? Claire had chosen willingly, and did she will it still? Do you get to change, and did she want to? Further questions for a rainy day—she had compiled a good long list.

"And they called me redneck," Ran went on, digging his grave deeper as he tried to shovel out. "And Jethro—remember, Cell? Like, 'Hey, Jethro, how's your sister, I mean mama, I mean sister.' " Pushing his charm into overdrive, he did the Faye Dunaway slap slap slap routine from *Chinatown*. He'd tempted fate with "girl" and got away with it, but now, with "nigga," Ran had sealed it tighter than a Pharaoh's tomb.

"I'm bombing here, aren't I?" he said, reading the writing on the wall the way he always did, eventually. "Sorry, guys, I don't get out much these days. Throw me a line?"

"How are you, Ran?" said Marcel, manfully, showing who he was.

Despite the effort, Claire could see the tightness at the corners of his eyes.

"Doing pretty good, man. Thanks for asking. How about you? You put on some weight?"

"A bit."

"Looks good on you. No kidding."

"What have you been up to?"

"Me?" Ran said. "Oh, this and that. Today I wrote a song, took care of the kids, got started on a major house repair, cooked dinner, made a minor archaeological discovery. I was just telling Claire and Dee here . . ."

"Deanna."

"Deanna. I found this buried pot in our backyard. It was wrapped with chain and full of shells and candle stubs and other shit . . . including this. Here, take a sniff and tell us what it is."

Marcel leaned down reluctantly. "I don't smell much of anything. Pond water maybe?"

Ransom laughed. "Pond water, musky musk, perfume, an old drunk's breath . . . I guess truth is in the nose of the beholder. Hey, Charlie?"

Picking the rosettes off the large cake on the table, their son looked up with a snoot full of buttercream.

"Sometimes less is more, big guy."

Charlie grinned and went back down on it.

Ransom shrugged. "Yeah, well, I never believed that maxim either."

Claire started after him, but he touched her arm. "I've got him, babe. Listen, Marcel, I put my foot in it just now, but the fact that I'm a horse's ass can't come as news to you."

The dean did not dispute this, but he smiled.

"The main reason I stopped by," Ran said, smiling back, "the only reason really, was to say, well, here we are, both—all—in the same town, or close enough. Time's passed, none of us are getting any younger. We're all grown-ups, or as close as we're likely going to get. We really ought to get together."

"Sure, Ran," Marcel said. "Sure, why not."

"How about tonight?"

"Tonight?"

"I fried some chicken."

"Ran . . . ," said Claire.

"What?" He turned an innocent look on her. "I can't say fried chicken? You like fried chicken, don't you, Cell?"

"I like it well enough."

"See, Claire, he likes fried chicken. You like fried chicken. I like fried chicken. The kids like fried chicken. We've got fried chicken. What's complicated here? Come out to the house and eat, Marcel. Bring your djembé, you can help me lay down the rhythm track on that new song. Okay, Charlie-boy, here comes Daddy! Better run!" Ran formed his fingers into claws, like Scar, and took off toward his squealing son.

"So that's your husband?" said Deanna.

"Behold the man," said Claire.

"He's charming."

Bitch on wheels. Claire smiled, relying on telepathy to make the point. Deanna's expression, though, as she walked off, did not conclusively suggest she'd meant it as a joke.

"I'm sorry, Cell," Claire said. "I'm really sorry about that."

"Forget it, Claire. It's no big deal, and anyway, it's not your fault."

"It's not?" she said. "But what if it really is?"

He didn't ask her what she meant. They gazed into each other's eyes and knew.

"How does he seem to you?" she asked.

"Like Ransom, only more so."

"It's that more so that has me worried. It always starts like this."

"So you're concerned. . . ."

"I am. I really am. I don't suppose you want to come out, do you?"

Cell did not exactly leap.

"Don't, then. Really, Marcel, don't," she said.
"You want me to?"
"Not if you don't want to."
"Would you feel better if I did?"
"Yes, but it's okay."
"Let me get my keys."
"Thank you!"

TWELVE

ar? What war? There will be no war!"

     As they make their way into the house, Harlan and Addie are diverted by Colonel Allston of the two-l Allstons, who is in his cups and holding several ladies hostage on the porch.

     "The blood shed in this war won't amount to a gill measure," declares the old man, his silver hair as fine as filaments of dandelion, his cheeks the color of raw meat. "It won't fill this glass, by God—I'll drink the blood shed in this war!"

     "Have some more champagne instead, Colonel," suggests Harlan drily, trying to lure the old gentleman away.

     "Take my word, DeLay," says Allston, as content with one victim as the next, "the moment we fix bayonets, the Yankee popinjays will run like rabbits in the woods. After all, we're fighting for home and freedom. What are they fighting for? The nigger slave? What is your view?"

     "My chief hope, Colonel, is that the Confederacy, when it succeeds, will finally free Cuba from the Spanish yoke and annex her as a new slave state."

     "By God, why shouldn't we?" shouts Allston. "There are bonds of natural sympathy between us and the plantation men down there, Spaniards and infidels though they be. Take Gonzales, Beauregard's new aide-de-camp. He seems a decent sort. Hell, take yourself and Percival—haven't we always been thick as thieves?"

     "Colonel," says Harlan stiffly, "I can't speak to my father's beliefs or those of

Don Ambrosio José, but I can tell you, sir, I am, and have always been, an Episcopalian, South Carolina born and bred."

"Damnation, boy, don't get your back up. All I mean to say is that you'll bring
your sugar into Charleston without tariff. We'll send our rice and wheat to feed your
slaves and pay no duty to the monarchy in Spain."

"On that point, we agree. And, God willing, after Cuba, Mexico."

"Mexico, too?" says Addie, to whom Harlan's viewpoint comes as news.

"Depend upon it, Mrs. DeLay," asseverates the Colonel, "one day a Southern
slaveholding empire will stretch from Maryland to the Yucatán."

"And our king?" she says. "Do you think Jeff Davis's head has swelled sufficiently to support a crown?"

Harlan frowns.

"Damn Jeff Davis, madam!" the Colonel shouts. "Our king will be Maximilian,
archduke of Austria and emperor of Mexico! You there, William!" he shouts toward the
butler, who's appeared on the piazza with a tray. "Where are you off to? Fill this glass!"

As he weaves away unsteadily, Louisa Elliott, like an animal that's been held at
bay, takes the opportunity to bolt.

"Excuse me, if you please," she says. "Harlan, if it would not be too great an
imposition, have someone call my groom."

"Certainly, Louisa, I'll go myself," he says. "But won't you stay to cut the cake
with us? We're having fireworks later."

"I've had sufficient fireworks for one afternoon, thank you."

A mortified blush spreads from Harlan's collar to his crown. "Two seconds,
then. Allow me to take Addie in to Father."

"Very well." Louisa's eyes lock on Addie's now. "I wish you great joy in your
new situation, Mrs. DeLay," she says, pursing her lips as tightly upon "situation" as
her black taffeta bonnet is cinched around her face.

"Thank you, Mrs. Elliott," Addie answers, with a mildness no less pointed, and
she can feel Harlan's fury as they enter and start down the hall.

Forty feet away, before the closed doors of the library, two women are in urgent
conference, and Addie, at a single glance, knows who they are. Between them, they're
holding a white plate, each prizing with a hand, as though disputing its possession.
There's something on it—food for the invalid, Addie thinks. Paloma is tall, with
shoulders like a man's, but lean in a way men rarely are past adolescence, with a
litheness like a deer's, and this lends her physique an angularity and creates hollows
under her high cheekbones that make her face look gaunt, severe, and sculptural. Her

skin is not as Addie has imagined—not amber, cinnamon, gold, or any shade of brown—but a rare and striking black, like melted Jew's-pitch in a Charleston roadbed on a day as hot as this. Her complexion is unlined, so wholly fresh she might be forty, even thirty-five, but her hair is grizzled, and there's thirty years' too much experience in her face to pass for that. She's wearing a black silk dress, good but plain, with gathered skirts and waist attached, and on her feet, which are narrow, large, and flat as planks, a pair of silver satin slippers.

Clarisse—whose back is turned—is, like her mother, tall, but more delicate and willowy of frame, and her dress, though also black, is of a different order from Paloma's, the brocade like heavy web on brightblack satin silk. It's as chic and elegant as Addie's own, but in a different way, not that of a Charlestonian, but of a ha-banera. She is holding a closed fan, and her hair—which is lustrous and wavy, as black as a crow's wing—is pinned up in the manner of the day, à la giraffe, held in place by an ornate tortoiseshell-and-sterling comb. A few wisps, as fine as eider, have broken free and curl against her neck, which is the color of parchment or old bone.

"Ahí están," Paloma says, her eyes fixed on Addie's in deep, lugubrious ap-praisal that is without enmity of any sort.

"Anjá!" Clarisse wheels toward them now, her fan pressed dramatically be-tween her breasts. "You startled me. But, Harlan, is this she? ¡Guapa muchacha! ¡Sí, guapa, muy guapa! You are here at last!"

"Clarisse, Paloma," Harlan says, "this is our new mistress."

Clarisse takes Addie's hand and presses it. "We were so worried when the Nina miss the tide."

There's an intensity in her address that makes Addie reflexively draw back. At close view, the strong planes in Clarisse's face recall Paloma's, but they have a Euro-pean cast inherited, no doubt, from her father. She looks Spanish or Sicilian, and Ad-die, who has been called beautiful in her day and tried—with small encouragement from her aunt and their milieu—to mortify her pride in it, has the rare experience of feeling, in this woman's presence, plain. Clarisse is a great and striking beauty, with a widow's peak on her clear, high brow and full, expressive lips. But her cheeks and throat have a mottled flush and, in her eyes—which are a strange, pale brown, almost yellow—there is a glassy, febrile shine.

"We got to see the river in full sun," she says. "I hope the delay hasn't put you out."

"The delay?" Widening her eyes, Clarisse now laughs a loose, lax laugh. "¿Entiende, Mamá? The delay has put us out!"

"Silencio, muchacha," says Paloma, with a grieved expression.

"*Pero, es divertido, ¿no?*"

Paloma puts her hand on Clarisse's arm in a calming or restraining way. "You are welcome, *niña. He aquí su casa.* . . . Consider this your home. We wish you every joy."

"How is Father?" Harlan asks.

"Very weak. The doctor is bleeding him again."

And now Addie notices that on the plate—what she took, before, for food—are leeches, four of them, glistening and plump, somnolent with being fed, amidst scattered drops of watery, pink blood.

"We have been so curious," Clarisse says to Addie, like a child with a new pet she can't let go. "We have heard so much. Harlan tells us poems. Your hair of gold. Your eyes. *Su sangre azul.*"

Paloma spits in her left hand and swift as thought—too swift to be opposed—thumbs a cross on Addie's brow. "Forgive me, *niña,*" she says, her stare so grave and forthright that Addie merely blinks, astonished, and cannot take offense.

Clarisse laughs and laughs at this. "*¿Qué, Mamá?*" she says. "*¿Piensa mal y acertarás?*"

"You're drunk," says Harlan with disgust, at the very moment the thought occurs to Addie.

Opening her fan the slightest bit, Clarisse touches Addie's arm with it, a gesture as precise as a scientist adding reagent to a titer. "He is severe with me," she says, smiling the disciplined smile of a coquette. "This is how we know him, like *un viejo,* an old man, gruff and tired of life, and then, one day this winter, he come back from the race a boy reciting verse again. You are so good for him, I think. We are so glad you are here."

"Thank you," Addie says. "That is a lovely comb."

"This?" She touches it. "My father gave it me."

"Count Villa . . . Urrutia."

"Urrutia," Clarisse corrects, rolling her rs. "Harlan has told you something of my history. I am flattered. Would you . . . ? Allow me. . . ." When she removes the comb, a tress falls across her shoulder like a soft, black lash. "As a wedding gift." As she offers it to Addie, Paloma stops her daughter's hand.

"*¿Por qué no, Mami?*"

"*Porque lo digo yo. Go attend the guests.*"

"Thank you, but your mother's right," says Addie. "It's far too much. The party is your gift to us."

"It is to your liking?"

"*Everything is lovely.*"

"*Except the cake,*" says Harlan. "*I thought I asked for Sumter.*"

Clarisse now frowns for the first time. "*I tried—all day yesterday—but I could not remember. I saw it just that one time from the boat. My hands made what they knew.*"

"*It is the opera in Havana, I believe?*"

Looking back at Addie, Clarisse smiles and her eyes narrow a degree. "*Yes, Tacón's.*"

"*Why did you choose that?*"

Addie's question seems to take her by surprise. Clarisse considers with a quizzical expression as a silent beat elapses. Having no ready answer, she turns to Harlan, as though maybe he might know.

Atop his head, not just seed pearls, but mature ones whose cost would be impossible to estimate, have formed. They are rolling down his temples now, together with the brine of all the oysters and the water of the seas where they were bred. His eyes, his hazy, ginger eyes, for once are clear—clear and furious. Addie has the strange, specific thought that he is someone else, a man she's never seen before. The man she knows—who courted her and whom, last week, she married—is one she's never thought about as handsome, yet this one, standing in the hall beside them, is more than handsome, he's beautiful, radiantly beautiful, with the spiritual beauty of one in pain. And this radiant stranger, without so much as a glance at her, says, "*Excuse me, I must see about Louisa's ride,*" *and turns and walks away.*

Addie looks back at Clarisse. She has no choice. "*It is nothing, niña,*" *she says with jeering sympathy,* "*an old joke between friends.*" *And now the mask has dropped. Clarisse's eyes, her yellow eyes, burn and simmer, they glow like stoked coals that come to life and die and resurrect themselves again. The pain and hatred in them shock Addie to her core, but there's no mistaking what they are.* "*But, Mami, let me have those,*" *she says, reaching for the plate.* "*I'll take them away. They are disgusting, no?*"

"*I will see to it,*" *replies Paloma, holding fast.*

"*Él me pidió que lo hiciera,*" *Clarisse says sharply.* "*He asked me, Mamá, not you. ¿No es cierto?*"

Paloma hesitates and then lets go. "*Disponga de ellas correctamente. Póngalos en el río.*"

"*Sí, Mamita, sé qué hacer.*"

"*Donde hay corriente,*" *Paloma calls as Clarisse walks down the hall,* "*y luz del sol en el banco.*"

"*Sí, entiendo, in the river, on the sunny bank.*"

When she's gone, Paloma turns to Addie. "*Forgive her, niña. She means no harm. She's had too much to drink. We're glad for you, but it is a hard day for her.*"

"*Why, Paloma?*" Addie asks. "*Why is it a hard day for her?*"

Paloma's stare does not retreat. Her expression is that of someone greatly burdened, without subterfuge, powerful, direct, and sad, someone watching a disaster unfold that she is not afraid of but is powerless to stop.

With a swift and unexpected gesture, she puts her hand—which is long and narrow, like her son's—tenderly on Addie's cheek.

"*Pobrecita,*" she says, "*you have come to a dark place.*"

THIRTEEN

*I*n the parking lot, as they strapped the children in, Claire refused to look at Ran.

"What?" he said to her across the luggage rack, when they finally closed the doors.

"Don't ask me what. You *know* what."

"No, really, Claire, what? I quit writing in the middle of a song this morning and took the kids so you could get to work; I found a rotten sill in the kitchen wall and called the excavator—he's coming in the morning, by the way; I made dinner, picked them up at school, came to the party, shook Marcel's hand and went the extra mile and invited him to supper; I did everything you asked and more."

"I'll say. Including getting tanked and calling him a nigger in front of the whole school."

"I didn't call him nigger, I said, 'Hey, nigga.' There's a difference."

"Is there, Ran? I think the semantic subtleties were lost on your audience."

"My audience . . ." Ran's eyes furred like coals. "You know what, Claire? I love you, but sometimes you're so pure of heart and righteous . . ." He bit his tongue.

"What?" she said. "You'd like to rough me up? Give me one in the old piehole? Bang, zoom, to da moon, like your old man did your mom before she bailed?"

"You bitch," he said. "I never touched you. Did I ever touch you?"

"No, you never did, but the apple doesn't fall far from the tree, and even when it does, it has a tendency to roll back eventually." Even as this left her mouth, Claire knew it was unfair. But having allowed herself to hope—again—having listened to his claims he'd changed and had a "come-to-Jesus" with himself, she was bitterly disappointed and spitting mad. More than angry, she felt burned. And now the words were out there in the world and past recall.

"What I was going to say," Ran said, "is that I love you, but sometimes I don't like you very much."

"That blade cuts both ways."

They faced off, in dire country now, a place they'd visited before, which neither had expected to return to. Or had they only hoped? Ransom felt especially bemused. Each step he'd taken through the day had been aimed at reconciliation, the correction of past wrongs; each had seemed innocent and natural—how had they led here?

"Tell me something, Claire," he said. "When you look in the mirror, can you honestly tell yourself that you, Claire DeLay from south of Broad in Charleston, who grew up with a black maid and servants, are one hundred percent politically correct and certified error-free, that there's no lingering trace of racial prejudice in your own heart?"

"Yes, Ran," she answered without hesitation, "I honestly think I can."

"That's interesting," he said. "That's interesting as hell. Because if you and Deanna and all your new pals inside, if every white college-educated liberal in the whole United States is as pristine and enlightened as you are, or think you are, then why is race still tearing us apart?"

"I don't know, Ransom. Maybe you should write an op-ed piece."

"Maybe I will," he said. "All I know is, fifteen, twenty years ago, way back in the bad old days, when it was me and Cell and James and Ty, two black guys, two white, backstage at three thirty in the morning breaking down the mixers and the amps, we called each other 'nigga' this and 'nigga' that and passed a joint, and everyone was laughing, we felt close. Now the word's off limits and everybody minds their p's and q's, but no one's laughing anymore. It's hard for me to see the big advance. Where did everybody's sense of humor go?"

"I don't know, Ran. I think little girls getting blown to bits in church on Sunday mornings might have put a crimp in it—that and black men getting lynched with their cocks stuffed between their teeth. I think the joke lost something in translation across two hundred years of slavery and another hundred of Jim Crow."

"If so, let the Hugers and DeLays pay reparations. I don't know who my grandparents were on my mother's side much less anybody further back, but I think it's a pretty safe bet that no Hills owned any slaves. While you and Marcel were at prep school, I was mopping floors in a black church. But I was someone in New York when you were just another pair of pretty wannabes at music school. I took Cell in the band because of you, and he toured with us two years making better money than he's probably making now. Then when we were on the cusp of breaking out, right when I needed him the most, he quit. Why, I never understood. I didn't want him to. How much more am I supposed to owe the guy?"

"And while you were being such a saint and altruist, you screwed him over 'Talking in My Sleep.'"

Ransom's whole expression dropped. "So that's it!" He slapped his forehead with his palm. "Stupid me—of course! He wants a piece of the RAM action—is that what he said?"

"We've never talked about it."

"Never? Come on, Claire."

"Read my lips, Ran, never, not one word."

"That's what it is, though. It has to be. He's pissed."

"You could hardly blame him if he were."

"How many times do we have to do this, Claire? I wrote that song, all six verses, every line and every word in every line. I came up with the concept, the music. . . ."

"It also has a chorus, as I recall. Yours was 'But all it ever was was talk / And talk is cheap.' Cell and I changed it to 'But all it ever was / Was talking in our sleep.' We made that up from scratch. Whole cloth. It changed the song. You know it did. We wrote it on the F train coming back from Coney Island one day while you were in the city doing . . . whoever you were doing then."

"Hey," he said. "I was at a business meeting, Claire."

She gave him a hard look not wholly lacking in compassion. "Don't try to kid a kidder, sweetie. I know where you were."

Ransom took a beat. "Okay, I made mistakes, Claire. I admit I wasn't perfect. I never said I was. But that was a long time ago, and I'm here to try to rectify. In the end, it was one line. One. And anything I ever made off my music and my book was share and share alike with you, wasn't it? I think Cell got more from RHB than RHB got back—but if I screwed him, bottom line: so did you."

"Or maybe you screwed both of us."

Ransom blinked and shook his head. "Jesus. Jesus Christ. So that's what all this is about."

"Actually, Ransom, what this is about is the fact that you called Marcel 'nigga,' and embarrassed him—and me."

"You know I'm not a racist, though," he said. "At least look me in the face and say you know that in my heart I'm not."

She looked him in the face and said, "I don't know what's in your heart. What I know is that if it has long ears and goes hee-haw most people will feel justified calling it an ass. They won't look any further or really give a shit what's in your heart."

"But you aren't most people. You're my wife. You have to care. Don't you know what's in my heart?"

"Truth?"

He hesitated only slightly. "Truth."

"Once upon a time, I thought I did, but now I'm not so sure."

His expression turned forlorn. "Then who knows, if not you? I thought we were supposed to know that for each other, Claire. I thought that's what this whole thing was about, for you to know what's in my heart like I know what's in yours."

"I'm not sure you know what's in my heart either, Ran," Claire said, speaking what she'd only thought before. "And as for 'supposed to,' we passed that on the fly ten years ago. And not just us. Everybody does. We weren't singled out. You're just late catching on."

A certain look came into Ransom's eyes, the sad and soulful one that always made Claire think of Mel, the time she went to Killdeer right before the wedding. She'd heard so much about him, yet when they finally met, the big bad monster turned out to be a lonely, sick old man with a lost look in his fierce, watery blue eyes, the look of someone whose drunks and rages were just ineffective protests against a sense of beatenness he'd accepted somewhere so far back that he'd forgotten there was any other way to be. And even if Mel glimpsed it sometimes, before he got too deep into that first glass of 20/20 in the front seat of the Thunderbird, he no longer had the energy, and probably not the wish, to change. Ran—whatever else you said of him—had always had that energy and wish, and if he had some Mel in him, he'd fought against it, too. Claire saw him fighting now, and she did not know what she felt, except she didn't want to see him lose.

"Okay," Ran said. "I'm sorry. I apologized to Marcel. I apologize to you. Just don't give up on me, okay?"

The sudden plaintiveness of this, and its sincerity, wrenched her. "I never have."

Seeing her fighting sudden tears, Ran took encouragement like a cornerback who intercepts the ball and heads for the opponent's goal. "Okay, I haven't done too hot so far, but at least I'm trying," he said. "We've still got the evening, and tomorrow is a brand-new day. If I can cut back on my percentage of errors and add to my percentage of success, before long you'll have yourself a model husband, DeLay. Before you know it, I'll be Jesus fucking   walk-on-water-roll-back-the-stone-and-find-the-Bad-Boy-risen Christ!" His grin was the victory dance in the wrong end zone.

Claire's expression was the silent field. "Ransom, did you take your meds?"

His face lost all its muscle tone.

"Ransom . . ."

"Are you kidding? You don't think I'm fucking with the recipe?" His expression was like Charlie's, caught red-handed in the jelly beans.

In Claire's face, experience vied woefully against belief. "That's important, Ran. That's number one on the must-do list."

"Can't it be the to-do list, Claire? The please-do list? You know about my little problem with authority."

"Deal with it."

Ransom's jaw squared, but he managed a salute. "Yes, ma'am, Miss Claire."

And off they went.

FOURTEEN

*T*here's something just beneath the leaves. It shocks you when you touch it with your hand, but at first it's easy to convince yourself that you imagined it. In the interval it takes to blink, your life has changed, but it takes time, inevitably, to realize it, and more time still before you dig it up and find out what it is.

For Addie, the blow is so sudden, swift, and hard she can't be absolutely sure that she's been hit. Only tomorrow, or tonight, will the soreness and the bruise appear as evidence. And in this state, half stunned, like a somnambulist, she follows Paloma through the closed doors to the library, where Percival, attended by his physician, lies on his chaise, as though in state.

Beside him, on a small table draped with a white cloth, several candles burn, their flames reflected in six or seven gilded sherry glasses filled with water. These are arranged around a larger glass—a snifter—in which an iron crucifix is half submerged, and there are white carnations in a bowl and a half dozen tintype portraits.

As they come in, the doctor, rolling down his sleeves, looks up and smiles with pressed lips, the way physicians smile when there is something to be faced. Percival's robe is open on his breast, which is as smooth and white as marble. Against it, several black leeches—recently applied, still small—throb silently at their work against the lapis-colored veins. The patient's face, which is one of great refinement, is lifted toward the ceiling in an attitude of suffering calmly borne, and the slanting sunlight through the window casts shadows in the sockets of his closed eyes, suggesting statu-

ary even more. His head is noble, heavy, overlarge, almost equine in its length and strength of bone, and seems somehow inconsistent with sickness, age, or death, and, in truth, he seems less old than ruined.

"Percival," Paloma whispers.

When he opens his eyes, there's a brief look of vagueness and disorientation, like someone surfacing from a depth. Taking Addie in, he doesn't smile, but there is something kind, relaxed, and deep in Percival's expression that puts her at her ease. It reminds her of the look that Jarry gave her from the docks and emanates from the same agated, dark hazel eyes. Searching for her husband's likeness in his father, Addie finds instead his other son.

" 'He said that, gathering leeches, far and wide,' " he says, pressing the physician's arm,

" 'He traveled, stirring thus about his feet
The waters of the pool where they abide. . . .'

"Do you recognize the poet?"

"I would have to venture Wordsworth," she replies.

"And you would be correct. And you, I think, are Adelaide, our bride. You have met Paloma. Do you know Dr. Sims?"

"How do you do."

"Congratulations," Sims replies. "I wish you every happiness. Percival, I'll leave you now. Paloma, may I have a word?"

As the two withdraw, Percival indicates the chair. "Sit down, my dear, and let us have a visit. They say your outbound journey was more stimulating than you might have wished."

"For my aunt's sake, yes," she answers, sitting. "For my part, I found it curiously exalting."

"Did you?" Addie reads approval like a subtle index in his eyes; warmed thereby, she warms reciprocally toward him. "If this is distasteful"—he indicates his chest—"I can cover them."

"No. They must be painful, though."

"Surprisingly, no. In fact, after the small ache of the bite, I find they have an anesthetic quality. I much prefer them to the lancet and the bleeding bowl. Tell me, though, do you find Wando Passo to your liking?"

"It's . . . extraordinary."

Percival's expression sobers, as though some equivocation has crept into her tone. "Our customs, I expect, are strange to you."

"No, I . . ."

His glance follows hers to the table with the candles and the crucifix. "You may ask, if you're curious."

"Is it a shrine?"

"Of sorts. It's called a bóveda. They're found in many Cuban homes."

"It is Catholic?"

"Some Catholics have them, but they got them from their Negroes. The African, you see, venerates his ancestors in much the way the Cuban nobleman and the white aristocrat of Charleston do."

Addie smiles.

Percival's failure to return it makes clear that he does not intend this as a drollery. "The difference," he goes on, "is that we worship them as the departed, as something dead and gone. To them, though, the dead, the muertos or nfumbi, are no farther off than those people outside in the garden. Listen." He holds a finger up. "Hear the drone of conversation? Sometimes, lying here, I fancy I can hear the dead like that. And if I'm very quiet, very still, I begin to pick out actual words. And there are windows and doors, Addie, by which they can reenter the living world again and show themselves and speak. A bóveda is such a place, and that is what this is to me, a place where I can offer thanks and ask them for their help and they can answer me. . . . But I've often thought there are few things more tedious than unsolicited accounts of others' spiritual convictions, which one does not share oneself." And now, for the first time, he smiles.

"How do they speak, though?" Addie asks, ignoring his disclaimer, not bored in the least.

"In ways you'd recognize, ways you've experienced a thousand times. In dreams. Through what we call 'intuition.' A sudden flash of brilliant understanding, an insoluble problem suddenly solved. When chills run along your spine."

"How curious, look," she says, showing him the gooseflesh on her arm. "Just as you spoke . . ."

"Yes, niña, that is they. That means they are close. And there are other ways, Addie, secret ways of which I cannot speak, except to say that they are more direct and awful, in the old sense of that word."

And the strange thing is that it does not seem strange at all to Addie to have fallen so swiftly into this conversation with Harlan's father, a conversation not quite like any she's had before. "But how did you find your way into such things?"

"*Ah, well,*" *says Percival, and as he gazes toward the window, a look of melancholy settles on his face. It's the expression, Addie thinks, of a man at the end of a long journey, staring back over the wide plain he's crossed, knowing he won't retrace his steps.* "*In Cuba, when I was young—about your age—I went through a period of trouble. A crucial piece of my invention eluded me, and then my young wife, Melissa, Harlan's mother, took suddenly ill. Hoping to cure her, I exhausted every available medical recourse, and then, when nothing worked, I sought . . . different help. That's how I came to know Paloma. I failed to save Melissa, but my efforts led me through a door into a world that's all but unknown here. The experience changed me.*"

"*How?*" *she asks.*

"*If you're curious, we'll speak of it another time. For now, let it suffice to say, I heard what are called the drums of affliction. I didn't understand that it was them, the muertos, persecuting me.*"

"*Why were they persecuting you?*"

"*For the same reason they persecute us all: to make us change our life.*"

Without prelude or apparent reason, Addie starts to weep, and it is less weeping than a single sob that, once got out, is gone. When she looks at Percival, his eyes have gone studious and deep. It's Jarry's look again, the look of one who knows some crucial truth concerning you that you have not yet learned or not yet found the strength to tell yourself.

"*I've upset you,*" *he says, touching her hand.*

"*But you did change?*"

"*Ah, well, Addie, there's the rub. I changed to some degree. But what I encountered there required still deeper changes that I failed to make. That failure has touched everybody here.*" *He briefly holds her stare, then something draws his attention to the window. Turning, Addie sees Clarisse, her black dress sharp against the white sand road. She's carrying the plate, and what strikes Addie in the moment is that Clarisse is walking not toward the river, but away from it, and not to sunlight, as her mother asked, but westward toward the forest, where she presently disappears into the shadows of the trees.*

When she turns back, Percival is studying her. "*But I hadn't meant to be so heavy. If I forget myself, it's because your face is too good to deceive. I'll kiss you. May I kiss you then?*"

She smiles. "*You may.*" *As she leans to him, Addie catches a whiff of age like soured milk, not quite hidden by the clove he chews. To her surprise, she feels her hair stir with intaken breath, as the old man smells her, too.*

"Now let us speak about more cheerful things. . . . You've brought a book, I see. They've told me you are literary."

" 'They'?" She smiles. "I expect 'they' did not intend it as a compliment."

"Well, dear girl, this is South Carolina, after all, where reading for pleasure, much less for instruction, is on a social par with spreading the wet leprosy."

She laughs gratefully at this. "Yes, in Charleston, they say I drove away my beaux with poetry. The young men there regard me as a sort of Hester Prynne, only in lieu of a scarlet letter, I wear a scarlet number on my breast."

"What number might that be?"

She touches the spot. "At the moment, it is thirty-three."

He smiles. "Well, if it's any consolation, from where I sit—or lie—you seem barely whelped to me. And look around you at these heavy shelves. You see where I have come to die, like an old man returning to the nursery, surrounded by the broken toys of youth."

"Not broken, though, surely?" Addie says. "Tell me one does not outgrow one's books."

"Sadly, yes, for me. In my youth, I was a reader. I searched through all these volumes, seeking one that could tell me the one thing I wished to know."

"And what was that?"

"How to live—what other question is there?"

"And you were disappointed?"

"I never found an answer, and eventually reading came to seem another drug, more benign, but not so different finally from laudanum or alcohol, a distraction from the very thing I sought to do: namely, living. And if the great ones—even Wordsworth, even Shakespeare—couldn't tell me how to live, to whom shall I turn now to teach me how to die? That is the lesson I've gone to school to now. Its rigor is so preoccupying and severe that, in comparison, the thought of opening a book seems puny."

Addie, for whom reading has been a kind of personal religion, unquestioned and unquestionable, doesn't quite know how to take this. "Well, I hope when my time comes, I have the courage to face it as a lesson, too."

"I'm sure you shall. Never fear, my dear."

"Aren't you . . . ?"

"Afraid? Of course. Aren't you afraid of what will happen when you and Harlan go upstairs tonight? Of course you are, yet go you will. You know you must. An irresistible power compels you, and the same draws me. I'm afraid and drawn in just that way."

"Death is different, though, isn't it? What I fear is the thought that I may cease."

"Ah, then we are different there," he says. "That, I don't fear in the least. I'm certain there is further life. My sole concern is what that life may be. But enough of this! Enough of me! What volume have you brought?" She hands it to him, and he holds it at arm's length. *"Byron! Madam! Is this fit matter for one newly entered into the married state?"*

"What, must I give him up?" she answers brightly. *"I've loved him so well, though. I don't know if I could."*

"Well, then, here's someone we can ask," he says as the doors swing open. *"Give us your opinion, Jarry. Is Byron proper reading for a bride?"*

"I can't see, offhand," the steward answers, with a suggestion of embarrassment, *"why he shouldn't be. Unless marriage is the death of love—in which case, yes."*

"I agree!" cries Addie. *"I've always thought of him in just that way—as the poet of true love."*

"Well, let me not to the marriage of true minds admit impediments," laughs Percival. *"You both, though, are at an age for him. But, let me see, I knew some verses once. . . .*

'From the wreck of the past, which hath perish'd,
Thus much I at least may recall,
It hath taught me that what I most cherish'd
Deserved to be dearest of all. . . .' "

"I'm not familiar with the poem," she says.

"We'll have to see if we can find it for you. If you admire him, it's one that you should know. And the sentiment? Do you agree that what we most cherish deserves to be dearest of all?"

"It seems inarguable."

"I wish it seemed inarguable to me!" And now, like an old fire that has struck a hidden vein of sap and flared unnaturally, he seems to gutter and sink back upon himself.

"I was thinking of some lines of his today," Addie says, to fill the silence. *" 'Know ye the land where the cypress and myrtle / Are emblems of deeds that are done in their clime?' How very like South Carolina they seem, and in fact the very landscape we passed through on the boat."*

" 'The Bride of Abydos,' is it not?" says Percival.

She confirms it with a smile.

"*And how does it continue?*"

" '*Where the rage of the vulture, the song of the turtle . . .*' *I can't remember now.*"

" '*Now melt into sorrow,*' " *Jarry offers,* " '*now madden to crime.*' "

She smiles at him. "*You know the poem. . . .*"

"*There's a verse in it that I admire.*"

"*May we hear it?*"

"*Perhaps another time.*"

"*Come, now,*" *says Percival.* "*Don't play coy. Do you mean to mystify us?*"

"*Father . . .*"

"*He thinks, because he is a Negro,*" *Percival says to Addie,* "*that I take undue pride in his erudition and put him on unfair display, but what he fails to understand is that if Harlan knew a line of verse, I'd be no less quick to show him off. And it is not for me, Jarry, after all, it is to reveal yourself, the temper of your mind, to one who may turn out to be a friend. Come, then, in a trusting spirit, give it us. '' Tis vain— my tongue cannot impart . . .' Will you help?*"

Jarry stands in conflict, flushing over the request in a way that both elicits Addie's sympathy and makes her curious to see how he'll respond, who he will prove to be. And in this fraction of a second, she thinks of young freedmen she's passed in Charleston on the street, black men soberly dressed, their collars starched, their ties correct and rich. These men—and, on occasion, women, too—have met her eyes and held her stare, not defiantly, the way some servants will, but with intelligent and friendly curiosity, like her own toward them, and perhaps a trace of irony as though to ward off a judgment experience has taught them to expect in a white woman's eyes. Addie has rarely said more than "*Good morning*" *to such persons, but she's watched them disappear around a corner into their own lives and wondered what those lives consisted of, certain only that they were not delimited by the borders of a cotton field, or the clay embankment circling a square of rice.*

" '*'Tis vain—my tongue cannot impart,*' " *Percival prompts once more,* " '*My almost . . .*' "

" '*. . . drunkenness of heart . . .*' " *Now Jarry picks it up.*

" 'When first this liberated eye
Survey'd Earth, Ocean, Sun, and Sky,
As if my spirit pierced them through,
And all their inmost wonders knew;
One word alone can paint to thee
That more than feeling . . .' "

Now there's a slight hitch in his voice. He turns to the window. And Addie, whose face is bright, who is sitting forward in her chair, thinks, Yes? Yes?

" 'I was free.' "

The answer, when it comes, hits her like a soft blow to the chest.

And it is Percival now who looks at Addie, who gazes deep into her eyes, curious to see how she'll respond, who she will prove to be.

"How beautifully you recite," she says.

"And that surprises you?" *Jarry asks.*

Addie smiles and holds his stare. "It does not surprise me in the least."

"Nor me."

They all turn, and there is Harlan frowning in the door. "We've yet to cut the cake, and already you've started your campaign to turn my wife against me. How should I be surprised?"

"No, dear, it's not like that," *says Addie, rushing to his side.*

"Not at all, my boy," *says Percival.* "We're just reciting poetry. Don't let it provoke you."

"But I'm not, Father," *he answers, coming in.* "I'm not angry in the least. In fact, I'm grateful to you, for this conversation is one we need to have, and Addie should be part of it. It concerns her just as closely now as it does everybody here." *He turns to Jarry.* "Our entire spring order is jetsam washing up along a fifty-mile-long stretch of South Carolina beach. I've been called to serve my country, and here at Wando Passo there are four hundred of your people who need new clothes, who have no shoes or stockings, no candles, no salt for their food or animals, and the only thing you can think of is pursuing your own selfish pleasure."

"That is not—"

"No, excuse me," *Harlan cuts him off.* "Let me tell you a little story about 'freedom,' Jarry. I heard it just today." *Harlan reaches into his coat for a cigar.* "Jules Poinsett told a group of us. A week or two ago, this old Negro, Pompey, showed up at the Poinsetts' gate. Jules had no idea who the fellow was. One old woman in the quarters remembered him. It turns out Jules's grandfather—not his father, his grandfather, old Mr. Sam—freed this Pompey at his death. For forty years," *he says, lighting up,* "he's worked . . . as a free smith . . . in Charleston. Do you know why he came back?" *Harlan poses his question to the room triumphantly, waving out his match.* "I'll tell you why. To ask—no, not to ask, to beg—his old marse's grandson to reenslave him. And do you know why Pompey wanted that? In order to acquire his badge so he can pass the roads and ply his trade without being harassed by the constabulary. This is happening everywhere. That's what it's come to for your free brethren *in Charleston, Jarry. The town is an armed camp. Assuming we did let you go, that's what awaits you there."*

"I don't intend to go to Charleston."

"No? Then where do you intend to go? You cannot emigrate. There are eleven Federal ships now riding off the Charleston bar. Unless you mean to hold your breath and swim to Africa, I'm at a loss to understand what you intend to do."

"I am sure there will be difficulties," Jarry answers. "There are difficulties now. Every morning I awake to a fresh crop and deal with them the best I can, as they arise. I'm confident I'll deal with those that freedom brings in the same way. The dif-ference is . . ."

"Yes?" says Harlan. "Give it us."

"The difficulties here and now are yours and undertaken for your sake; then and there, they will be mine."

"Yes, yes, that's well and good," says Harlan mincingly. "That answer sounds quite fine, but it doesn't deal with the reality of what awaits you. You're like a child. You see this flame called freedom. It's beautiful and bright, and you say ooh and ahh. Those who are wiser, who have experience of it, tell you it will burn, but you know better. You will put your hand into the fire no matter what they say, but I'm here to tell you, Jarry, it will burn you, it will hurt."

"Perhaps, but I feel sure that it will never hurt or burn as hot as slavery has."

Impertinent! Addie thinks reflexively. But there's something dignified and even rather sad in Jarry's face and bearing that has weight, and that weight lingers after re-flex fades. She holds her breath and thinks, No, no, you mustn't speak to him like that. You'll only hurt your cause.

"You are ungrateful, Jarry. You are an ungrateful nigger."

"I won't hear you call your brother that," says Percival.

"He's not my brother. It may please you to consider him your son, but a servant and a slave is all he'll ever be to me. If Jarry were white and capable of a brother's loyalty, he'd have long since volunteered to see us through the war. We wouldn't have to ask." *Now Harlan turns to him.* "How many Negroes, Jarry, are there in this state, I wonder, standing, as you stand, in your good suit, discussing—is it Byron?— and the prospect of their manumission with their masters? Not many, I can tell you. You should fall down on your knees and thank Almighty God for the privileges you've received. This family made you what you are."

"What I am," says Jarry, "is a slave. That is what this family made me." *His voice is strong; his eyes are flashing now. The tense hush in the room is like that which follows the detonation of a bomb.*

Harlan's face has taken on a sober and forbidding look, and Addie feels her heartbeat in her throat. "God made you black, not me. You're right, though, Jarry. A slave is what you are, and what Father, practicing a foolish leniency with you these many years, has allowed you to forget you are. What I've long suspected and hesitated to believe, I now see is true. I think you know that if you leave us, we'll be harmed and maybe ruined, and that is not only a matter of indifference, it's what you seek."

Jarry leaves the mantel now. He walks into the center of the room and turns. When he begins to speak, his voice is soft, but he's panting slightly. Addie sees his shirtfront rise and fall. "You're mistaken. I've never wished this family ill. I understand your goal, that it is to preserve this property for your wife and any future children you may have. If I were in your place, I'd feel the same. But I am forty-two years old and have no wife or child. Since I was fifteen—for twenty-seven years—I've worked to make Wando Passo what it is. There's twice the acreage under cultivation now that there was then. I could have worked no harder had it been mine to inherit, yet I knew I never would, and I never coveted it. I knew the day would come when I'd walk away with nothing but my freedom and the chance to start my life, which Father promised me, sitting in this very room. He gave his word, and I gave mine to him. He shook my hand. I've kept my end. Now I ask that he keep his. I have no legal power to compel you, but I believe your honor compels you."

"Now you will lecture me on honor? I don't believe honor can compel a man to break the law and ruin himself and his descendants for the sake of one spoiled, selfish nigger, who's too great a fool to know his own best interest. I'll tell you something, Jarry, when and if you ever get the thing you're seeking, you'll travel far through the wide world before you find another place where you'll be treated better than you have been here, or even half as well."

"I may be treated worse," he says, "but I'll never have to look across the river at those dikes and see the years I put into them, which are lost and which I can't call back."

Harlan narrows his eyes and stares incredulously into Jarry's face. "You hate us, don't you, who've never done you anything but good."

"No, Harlan," Jarry answers, "it's you who hate me. That's what this is about, not the property, which may suffer from my absence, but will still be yours after the war and can always be made right when you return."

"I don't hate you," Harlan says. "What makes you think I do? Why would I?"

"Because I have the presumption, as a Negro, to consider myself a human being and a man, like you, and because Father, in his heart, chose me. Not that I was better, Harlan. But there has always been a sympathy between us, an effect of tempera-

ment that you've resented for as long as I recall. And now you're asking him to make up to you for the love that you did not receive, which you feel was taken from your rightful share by me, and what you're requiring him to do to make this right to you is to betray me, to betray his honor and to break his word. And I believe the man I know is too wise and decent to let you win."

"That's a lie," says Harlan. "All of it is hateful, impertinent lies. This place made a million pounds of rice last year. The nation needs that rice. The army must be fed. Against that and the welfare of this family, what have you to counterpose? Nothing but your selfish wish. In the end, we no more need your leave to keep you than I need Runcipole's permission to climb upon his back and ride or the permission of the dirt to make my crop. Father may consider you a son, Jarry, but make no mistake, that's what you are to me, the equivalent of so much pasture, so much paddy in a square of rice. Obey me, and you'll have your freedom when the war is done. Cross me, and I'll shove a hoe into your hands and put you on the next flat to the fields and work you like a dray until the day you die."

Jarry holds Harlan's stare, then turns to Percival. "Does he speak for you?"

The weight of it is in the old man's face, and all the room attends. Clearly torn, he hesitates, and Addie sees fatigue and age where they have not been fully evident before. "I'm sensible of my promise, Jarry," he says, looking sunken, grayed, and miserable, "but you must know Harlan can contest the will, and in the courts as they are now, you'd have no chance, my boy, no chance at all. And there's also truth in what he says. The roads are full of armed men now. Perhaps it would be safer for you to bide your time at Wando Passo till hostilities conclude, and it would be a comfort to your mother, too. Would you consider staying on if you were freed and paid a wage?"

"That's not what we agreed."

"You see?" shouts Harlan now. "You see, Father?" His look solicits Addie, too. "He doesn't want to reach accommodation with us."

"What I see," says Percival, "is that you're angry at me, both of you, yet you turn it on each other. Let me take it. Give me what is mine. Can't there be peace and common cause between you, at least until the war is done?"

"There can be peace when he accepts his duty to obey," says Harlan.

"Tell me what to do, Jarry," says Percival, with a despairing face. "If I free you, he'll have the will annulled and punish you; if I don't, you'll feel betrayed."

Jarry makes no answer to his father. The expression on his face is one Addie will remember—the failure of surprise, and, more than that, the fatigue, the immense fatigue of an old wound or grievance, resurrected by this interchange, but older in its provenance, which is the thing that makes his eyes both like and, finally, so different

from Percival's. He puts her Byron on the partners desk and walks out without an-
other word.

Harlan turns to them. "You see? This is what they are." There is a smirking,
mean triumphalism in his face.

"What they are?" says Percival, erupting. "I will tell you who he is. When
Jarry was fifteen, he ran away and was brought in by the dogs. Twice, he tried to kill
himself. The second time, I cut him from the rope with my own hands and sat him
in this chair. I told him, 'If you'll work and reconcile yourself to your position, I'll
free you when I die.' So while you played and rode and wasted what he made, Jarry
rose before first light and came home in the dark each night on the last flat with the
last crew. If you have dreams for the future, dreams for your wife and children, Jarry
built them. What dream does he have? What has he to show for twenty-seven years
of work—a cast-off suit of clothes? A better cut of meat? His one dream was free-
dom, which he's long since earned. Now you ask me to go before my maker with a
broken promise on my head. . . ."

"If he's paid his debt, then free him now."

Percival frowns, clearly surprised.

"Why wait?" says Harlan, pressing his advantage. "This is what I resent, Fa-
ther. Knowing Jarry's value to yourself, you never freed him, just as you never did
Paloma. Now you ask of me—of us"—he rests his heavy hand on Addie's
shoulder—"a sacrifice you found too onerous."

In Percival's expression, there is brief affront, but it is swiftly followed by a look
of acknowledgment. With a tired sigh, he collapses on himself. "So," he says in a de-
flated voice. "So. In this at least, I fear you're right." The old man looks at Addie
now. "I wanted amity between them. I thought, if it could start in this one
house . . . It's my fault it has come to this."

"If you wish to rectify it, Father," says Harlan, waxing as the old man wanes,
"you can do so with a single word. Give me the will. We'll burn it now and have the
matter done. You have my solemn promise I'll free Jarry as soon as I return."

Percival hesitates and looks to Addie, lost. "Perhaps that is the way," he sighs.
"Perhaps the war will not last long. . . ."

"Your father is tired, Harlan," she says, standing up. "And we've neglected our
guests too long. We should leave this to a later time."

"Yes," says Percival. "Yes, I'm tired. I can't wrestle with this any more today."

"I need your answer before I go to Moultrie, Father," Harlan says.

"You shall have it. Now, leave me, go." He shoos them with a weak gesture of
the wrist.

Harlan pulls to the library doors and turns to her. "Addie, you undermined me. I had him at the point."

"I'm sorry, Harlan," she replies. "But you saw fit to include me, and I think it's a grave thing you're asking him to do."

"Jarry is a nigger, Addie. He's a slave, our property. We've given him everything."

"But the issue isn't to whom one's word is given, Harlan, is it? I would think it's whom it's given by, when the giver is a gentleman, as your father is, as I believe—and know—you are."

Now Harlan frowns and his brows gather. "Madam, I've been lectured once to-day upon the obligations of honor by a servant; I don't need another lecture from a woman, and particularly not my wife. You must be ruled by me in this."

"Must I, sir?"

"Yes, madam, you must indeed. We are married now. I understand that you are used to independent ways, and you shall continue to enjoy them here, within reason. I shall always welcome your opinions, but, in the end, when I've rendered mine, I expect your unconditional support. I have a right, I think, to nothing less."

Addie's lips are pressed into a line. Yet she doesn't contradict.

"I did this, in large part, for you."

"For me . . ."

"Have you not grasped what is at stake? I don't believe you have. What I'm seeking to prevent, Addie, is returning from the war a season hence, or in a year, and finding our gardens overgrown and you wandering the roads in rags, with matted hair, begging crusts of bread. I assume this outcome would be unwelcome to you, too."

"It is not a charming picture," she concedes.

"We're agreed then. Come now, let's not fight. Will you shake?"

Addie doesn't smile, but neither does she reject his hand.

"All this will work out for the best. You'll see. Now let us smile and join our guests and go to cut the cake."

FIFTEEN

s the motorcade crawled down the strip, Ran saw the CVS approaching and began to sweat. "Pull in, jerkwad," he advised himself, but Claire's car was right there in the mirror. Having lied, on balance, it seemed best to stick it out. *The road of excess leads to the palace of wisdom.* This proposition was one he'd spent the best part of his youth putting to the test. It had not panned out exactly, but maybe he just hadn't traveled far enough—who knew, it still might.

And if he'd left his scrip unfilled for a few days—it couldn't be as much as two weeks already, could it?—hadn't it been partially unselfish, partly for Claire's benefit as well? It was the reunion, don't you see, the thought of making love to her unfettered by the troublous side effects . . . which in Ransom's case—to get down to the grim brass tacks— amounted to an inability to come. True, he could get it up—he was one of the lucky ones in this regard, as his physician never tired of pointing out—but to be unable to come, to ejaculate, to *jouir*—try that for a week sometime, then try it for a year! To Ran, it was a form of punishment, of torture, servitude, which he, in the main, accepted manfully. But when Claire, the hundredth time, said yes, he'd allowed himself to want once more the thing life had apparently decreed that he could never have again: to be himself. He'd thought, *Well, maybe, just this once . . .* Was that so damnable?

And even if he went in now, you see—if he exposed his lie to Claire and gave her further ammo to add to the arsenal she already had—it had taken two weeks to reach this point (not three, surely! Ransom, out of guilt perhaps, had been less than wholly conscientious in keeping count), and it would take another two (or three) to get his levels back to where they'd been. Better to put it off until tomorrow. So there was the decision made, and by then the CVS was far behind them anyway. They'd reached the light, and Ransom, turning, still felt fine. Ran, in fact, felt buoyant.

He was on a journey—the idea suddenly came clear. "Something's leading me," he muttered, "but who, or what? To where?"

Was it toward his True Self?

"That must be it!"

"What, Daddy?"

"Nothing, Pete."

He'd been on this same journey once upon a time. Way back in Killdeer long ago, when he dreamed of Shea and Fillmore East and hitting that impossible riff, art and music had been his fearless path toward uncovering and releasing it. Then something happened. What? Somehow he fell asleep or merely blinked, and when he looked again, half his life had passed. It didn't matter, though. His eyes were open now; he was awake, and here the path was at his feet! Why had he ever left? It was because of other people, wasn't it? And why was it that whenever he reached this state of triple XL happiness and clarity of vision they started having problems? Why was his True Self something others seemed to want him to suppress? Whenever he got close, like now, he saw the look of fear and worry; he saw them start to shuffle backward toward the door. And this was true of Claire especially. How sad this made him. Claire wanted him to take the drugs, but what the drugs did, all they did—this was crystal clear to Ransom now—was to separate him from the brightness in himself, to take him farther from the True Self he wished to find, farther from the place it was his destiny and right to go. It suddenly occurred to him that Claire wasn't free. And why? Why wasn't she?

"Is it because of me?"

Yes! Somehow it had to do with him and something in their history. Was it because, back when, she'd given up her career for his? Was it because his dream had sucked hers down into its undertow? Yes, this was it, and ever since, there'd been an understanding, never stated, that he had to make it up to her, and this was why he had to take the drugs, to protect Claire from his freedom. Or was it to protect her from her own? The bright skein of his logic began to fray, and Ransom wasn't sure. All he knew was that he didn't want to take drugs anymore. What he wanted was for Claire to be free, too, and as his partner and free equal to meet him in a place of strength and joy. Such a simple wish, but it was all he'd ever really wanted. Somehow in all these years he'd failed to make it happen, but maybe it was not too late. Maybe he could make it happen yet.

Deep into the country now, with the children singing in the back, Ransom had begun to think such deep and deeply hopeful thoughts as these.

"Right over here!" he said, herding them toward the periwinkle patch as soon as everyone had parked. "That's where I found the pot. And the rotten sill"—he strode back to the house—"right there."

"Is our house going to break?" asked Hope.

"No, sweetie, absolutely not," said Claire. "You don't need to worry about that."

"That's right," said Ran. "If we left it, we might have a problem. But we aren't going to leave it. Daddy's going to fix the rot. See, Claire, Marcel, see how the yard slopes back this way? What I'm thinking is . . ."

"I need to pee," said Hope, crossing one leg over the other. "Can I go in the grass?"

"Sure, sweetie, sure," said Ran. "Wherever. A swale . . ."

"No, Hope," said Claire. "Come on, let's go in the house."

Hope looked to Dad.

"Right, you go in the house with Mommy. You may want to throw on a pot of water for the rice," he called after Claire as she took the kids and headed in. "Come on, Marcel, I'll show you the ranch. You haven't been here, have you?"

Jones hesitated slightly. "I helped Claire some when she moved in."

"Did you? Damn good of you, man. I appreciate that. Come check out the view."

They proceeded through the park and came out on the Bluffs. Ran pointed. "Those are the old rice dikes over there. They're pretty overgrown, but it's amazing they've held up this long. Can you imagine what it was like to build those things?"

"Not really," said Marcel.

"Standing in cold black water to your knees," said Ransom, helping out, "digging a brick-sized wad of clay out with your hoe, tossing it over your shoulder, clod by clod, until you had a wall six or eight feet high by six or eight feet thick around that whole twenty-acre field. There were over forty fields or 'squares' right here on Wando Passo, including a couple on Beard Island, just down there." Ran pointed south. "Some guy from the College of Charleston, an anthropologist, found a church there a few years ago, all framed out in cypress, steeple and all, and never sided, never used. No one knows what it was doing there. And these fields stretch hundreds of miles—up and down the Pee Dee and the Waccamaw, the Black, the Santee, the Ashley and the Cooper. People compare the effort to the construction of the Pyramids, but if you ask me, it took more. In its heyday before the Civil War, this place produced a million pounds of rice a year. Tara, all that cotton money, tobacco up my way—that was all chump change compared to rice. This was once the richest place in North America."

"You seem to know a lot about it."

Ran couldn't help but preen a bit. "Oh, not really, man. I just heard Clive give this speech so many times I could do it in my sleep. He wanted to make damn sure this redneck cracker from the other, lesser Carolina grasped the undeserved good fortune that had fallen in his lap. But, hey, I don't know, Cell, maybe all this shit makes you feel strange. Can I say that without starting World War III?"

Marcel smiled. "You can say it."

"So, does it?"

"A bit."

"Yeah, me, too," Ransom said. "It's not like the clank of chains or old spirituals drifting on the wind, but there's something on this land." Ran stared over the water, his face contemplative. When he turned, he found Marcel studying him. "You feel it?"

"There's something."

They held each other's eyes, having stepped by accident, through an unapparent door that neither probably could have found again, into a place where the backlog of their grievances did not exist, or simply ceased to matter, where they were just two men, old friends. Arriving, each remembered he had been here many times before.

Ransom was the first to turn away. "See that over there—that thing that looks like a wooden guillotine? That's called a trunk gate. The blade is called a riser board. They raise and lower it to let river water on and off the fields."

"They have them in Madagascar, too."

Ran blinked at him. "No shit. When were you in Madagascar?"

"With Baba Olatunji."

"Right," said Ran. "Claire mentioned that. Nice gig?"

"We had fun. I learned a lot from him."

"You know, man, I really ought to say, I've followed your career from afar with a certain awe."

"Awe?" Jones asked skeptically.

"Well, awe may be overstating it," Ran admitted. "Seriously, though, you've done good. You should be proud. I'm proud of you. Maybe even a little envious. Oh, what the fuck, I'm envious as hell."

Marcel smiled. "Thanks, Ran. I appreciate you saying that."

"So, can I ask you something? I'm dying to know what you think of RAM's song."

" 'Talking'? I like it."

"It's better, isn't it?"

"Than ours?"

Ran's expression hardened involuntarily.

"You know how you feel at the multiplex?" Cell said, moving on. "At the end of some romantic comedy—some pretty good romantic comedy—when the couple finally gets together, and the sound track swells, and you get that little lump in your throat?"

"Yeah?"

"That's how RAM's version makes me feel, Ran. I liked it a lot the first four times. Maybe five? Now it feels pretty much like wallpaper. Yours . . ."

"Ours . . ."

"Whatever . . ."

"I guess we never got that straight."

"I guess we never did. RHB's, to me, has some of what you feel when you go outside in the bright sun and have to face your life without the swelling strings to buoy you along. That's why it's as fresh today as it was then."

"So you don't think the cream always rises?"

Marcel laughed. "Hell, no. Who told you that one?"

"Ponzi Gruber, among others."

Marcel shrugged. "Sure, Ran, the cream rises. Once in a hundred or a hundred thousand times it does. What comes up mostly, though, is whey and skim and one-percent. That's what I think. But, hey, I'm probably prejudiced."

"Hey, you probably are. I won't hold it against you, though."

"Good one," Cell said, smiling back and conceding five when Ran held out his hand.

"But this is getting kind of touchy-feely, isn't it?"

"A bit," said Cell.

"So, trunk gates . . . ," Ransom said. "How the heck do trunk gates get from here to Madagascar?"

"They came the other way," said Marcel, laughing. "Not from Madagascar, but West Africa."

"You're kidding? That's not true, is it?"

"Sure, it is. You think Claire's people brought rice cultivation out of Sussex? County Cork? No, Ran, the Yoruba and Ewe, the Bantu-speaking people from the Congo River delta—they'd been growing rice for hundreds of years. They brought this whole business with them out of Africa—not just the labor, but the know-how, too."

Ran considered. "Damn, so the white man stole that, too?"

Marcel's expression turned wary.

"I swear to God, we're a predatory lot, aren't we?" Ran said. "Somebody should have exterminated the whole lot of us like Norway rats before we spread."

"I'm not trying to piss you off, Ransom. I'm just telling you a simple fact. I'm sorry if it doesn't fit in with your views on white supremacy."

"White supremacy?" He laughed. "It's just like our old dispute over rock 'n' roll, isn't it, Marcel?"

"Let's don't go there, Ransom."

"Okay, let's don't."

"Nobody knows better than you that rock came out of the blues."

Ran laughed happily.

"I remember you sitting there hour after hour, driving everybody crazy with that old piece-of-shit MCI reel-to-reel, playing phrases over and over, back and forth—Leadbelly, Johnson, Son House—breaking them down into fundamental particles, till you could play them lick for lick, even the mistakes. You were like some sort of junior Alan Lomax. Why are we having this conversation?"

"Everything you say is right, Cell. Rock came out of the blues. The blues came out of Africa. African roots, African rhythms, all filtered down through slavery. The blues are black, one hundred percent. One hundred and ten. But rock and blues are not the same. Rock was a response to blues, and it was preponderantly, overwhelmingly a white response, and rock 'n' roll is preponderantly, overwhelmingly a white creation."

Cell sighed heavily.

"To me, the blues is like moonshine, Cell. When you gotta have it, nothing else will do. There's some great moonshine and some legendary shiners, but in the end you can't compare it to a great French wine. The Beatles and the Stones, Dylan, Led Zeppelin—maybe the Who? And Hendrix—I'll give you Hendrix, even if they said he wrote white-boy rock until he died. . . . You can argue over who should make the cut, add or subtract a couple from the list. But, give or take, those are the great rock 'n' roll chateaux, and all of them but maybe one are white. Which is not to disrespect black music or the blues, but just to say that whites added something to it, some crucial ingredient. That ingredient allowed rock to set the world on fire, which the blues never did and never will."

"And maybe it's like Mitch Pike's easy-listening version versus RHB's," Cell said. "Just because rock reached a wider audience doesn't make it better, Ran. If you ask me, it's very goddamn likely people will still be listening to Robert Johnson and Muddy Waters when the Beatles and the Stones are dust."

"You really think so?"

"Yeah, I really do."

"Then you concede my point that rock is overwhelmingly, preponderantly white?"

"I don't concede it. I'm not conceding shit. And here's another thought: what say we just agree to disagree and leave it go."

"But why?" Ran said, his face intense now, and sincere. "I'm not trying to piss you off either, Cell. You gave me your facts about rice cultivation. I'm giving you mine about rock and roll. Why is this incendiary?"

"You know exactly why."

"Well, I know it's one of two reasons: either it's incendiary because it's incorrect and racist, or it's incendiary because it's true and doesn't fit with your notions of white inferiority."

"I think you know which way I lean."

"So you think I'm a racist, too?"

"I'm not sure you want to know what I think in that regard."

"Who knows, Marcel, the truth may set me free. . . ."

"All right," Jones said. "All right. You want it?"

"Give me your best shot."

"I think you were a poor kid from that town up there. . . ."

"Killdeer," Ransom said.

"Killdeer. I think your dad abused you. I think you grew up telling nigger jokes and despising black folks because they were the only people on a lower social rung. I think you pulled yourself out of there on talent and sheer desperation, which is something you deserve some credit for. I think you went to New York and had some great early success. You impressed Christgau and Lester Bangs, you bought a Comme des Garçons suit and went to Le Bernardin because you read somewhere that Jagger went there when he came to town. You figured out which fork and spoon to use and ordered some thousand-dollar wines. But deep inside you never felt like you deserved it, so when you reached a certain level, you always made sure to self-destruct, which is what you're doing now. And it's a shame, Ransom, because, racist or not, asshole or not, you have a certain genius in you. It comes out when you play guitar, and sometimes in your lyrics, too. There are guitarists I like better, but no one plays like you. When you hear a Ran Hill solo on a good night, it can't be anybody else. It stays with you. I still remember some of them, and that's why 'Talking in My Sleep' is still kicking after almost twenty years. And the sadness in the music is what stands out the most.

"But however far you've traveled, you're still that hick kid from that jerkwater town, and when you see me—this black guy who grew up with advantages, who went to boarding school and has a cottage on the Vineyard—you just can't help yourself, it rocks your world. I'm some kind of oddity to you, this Negro Fauntleroy, and you have to pick and jab to see if you can't get a rise, and maybe you just want to make me hurt as much as you do. I think that's why you call me 'nigga,' Ran. I think it's why you did it in the old days, and it's why after eighteen years that has to be the first word from your mouth. And the truth is, you knew I didn't like it then, and you know I don't like it now, just like you know I don't like 'Cell Phone.' "

"Hey," said Ran, "you can't blame me for that."

"I can and do."

"Everybody called you that."

Marcel shook his head. "No one. Ever. Not until I joined your band."

"Tyrell and James . . ."

"Tyrell and James picked it up from you. Why wouldn't they? It was your band. They took their cue from you. And what really pissed me off was that you thought I wasn't smart enough to get the joke."

"This is interesting, Marcel," said Ran. "It's interesting as hell. What joke was it you thought I thought you wouldn't get?"

"Come on, Ran, you called me 'Cell Phone' because I was so much *not* the kind of guy who'd ever have a street name of that kind. I was so much *not* the kind of guy who called his buddies 'homies' or went around bustin' caps or moves. No one in my whole life ever called me 'dog.' You called me 'Cell Phone' to rub my face in that and plant the subtle implication, *Can a guy like Marcel Jones, who comes from what he comes from, be considered a 'real' black man?* If I consider you a racist, it's for that."

"So I guess I can assume you do."

"Correct," he said. "I think you're a racist and a redneck and you have a questing, yearning heart and some great beauties of spirit, and you can also be as mean as hell and lower than a snake. On balance, what I think of you is something you can surmise from the fact that I left RHB eighteen years ago and didn't choose to stay in touch. And, despite your offer earlier, I don't think I'm going to be seeing that much of you now, either."

"Do I get a turn?" said Ran.

"Go ahead."

"As fantasy, this is semi-interesting, but I think it's all about the song. RAM covers 'Talking,' and suddenly Claire and I have money coming in. It's stirring up old bitterness about me stealing your labor and knowledge. You're the black man who grew up with fried chicken as your heritage, and suddenly I'm the Colonel who stole the recipe and is getting rich. And you're pissed off and want your taste. What do you want for that line, Marcel—my heart? My liver? Will you take a lung? Is one enough, or do you want both? Isn't this what's going on?"

"You aren't even in the ballpark, Ran," he said. "Yes, you fucked me over. Claire, too. Yes, I thought we were friends, and what you did is something friends don't do. If our positions had been reversed, I wouldn't have. Yes, I was pissed. For six months or a year, I was. But that was eighteen years ago. I put all that behind me. I'm not in need financially. I don't want for anything. If you and Claire have money coming in, I'm glad. In fact, it's actually a relief."

"A relief," said Ran. "I'm not sure I follow."

"I think you make it awful hard on Claire."

Ran's expression emptied. "I make it hard on Claire. . . ."

Marcel held his stare.

"I make it hard on my wife. . . ."

"That's what I'm saying."

They held each other's eyes, and suddenly they were in a different, darker room, one where words were done and something else seemed possible, if not required to finish the transaction.

"Ransom! Cell!" Claire's cry broke the spell.

Balancing Charlie on a hip and ushering Hope ahead with her free hand, she ran onto the porch. "Come here!" she called. "I need you both. Please come in the house right now!"

SIXTEEN

*T*he rocket streaks skyward, spilling sparks like red confetti, and then it bursts over the river and forms the trailing fronds of a golden willow tree that wink and stay—one second, two, longer than one would expect—before they fade.

Scattered applause and "Ahs" rise from the yard, where the last guests await carriages to bear them off. After a tearful parting with her aunt—who's staying at Chicora Wood tonight—Addie stands with Harlan at the bedroom window, watching, and the fireworks call to mind the twelfth, when the firing awakened her at four thirty in the morning. At five, Harlan's carriage rolled up to the curb downstairs.

"My dear, it is improper!" said her aunt Blanche. "I cannot let you leave!"

But Addie was too excited not to go.

By the time they arrived, the roof of the Mills House was already crowded with cheering spectators. It was a starless evening; over the harbor, a faint mist lay; the sudden flash of arcing shells pulsed in it like sheet lightning in summer clouds, lighting the bay like a false dawn. From James Island, Morris, Sullivans, Mt. Pleasant, over forty cannon opened simultaneously, rattling the windows of the buildings south of Calhoun Street, shaking the very cobbles in the streets. Addie later heard it said that Edmund Ruffin, that strange and terrible old man, yanked the lanyard of the columbiad at Cummings Point, after his fellow Virginian, Roger Pryor, offered the honor, could not bring himself to fire the first shot of the war. When dawn broke and the Stars and Stripes still flew over Sumter, the young Confederate gunners mounted *the parapets, gave three cheers, and threw their hats for Major Anderson and the Union boys, who showed such pluck under fire. Flushed with fatigue and drink, his eyes glassy, strangely deep, Harlan chose that moment to propose, and Addie, swept up in an emotion she believed her own, said yes. Harlan sent the carriage on and they walked home through a town transformed. At every corner, church bells rang. On the battery, crowds of happy, drunken people strolled arm in arm in their best clothes; the harbor filled with the white sails of pleasure boats. The equal of the scene, they say, has not been witnessed since Paris in the Revolution of '48.*

She looks at him and smiles, and he smiles back. "These were my mother's." Harlan touches the handle of a sterling brush, part of a lady's set reflected in the dressing table mirror. "I thought you might like them."

"Thank you, yes, I would." Addie is subdued after the scene downstairs.

A silence falls that neither quite knows how to fill.

"I expect you'd like to see to your toilet," he says.

"Thank you, yes."

He smiles. "You have no idea how I've looked forward to this evening, Addie." Her face, gazing up at his, is grave but forthright. "I hope it will be . . ." Several possibilities suggest themselves. ". . . satisfactory, dear," she chooses. "As you wish."

"I have no doubt it will. And as you wish it, too, my dear. I expect you have anxieties, Addie. But I want to put you at your ease. The bedroom, dear, should be a place of frankness and freedom. And I want, above all . . . But I've made my speeches for the evening. Another isn't what the occasion warrants, is it?"

And this, in its own way, is charming, and Addie, as he withdraws into the bath, focuses her attention on it, wanting to be charmed. Frankness and freedom seem, abstractly, to the good, though what they mean, in the specific context, she can only imagine. "As you wish it, too, my dear." And how does Addie wish it? Strange to say, she has no wish, no fantasy, no tingle of anticipation, not even—as Percival alleged—any fear. Her imagination is disengaged, deader than a stone, and she, in truth, prefers it so. And why is this? Why is stoic resignation what she mainly feels?

Upon consideration, Addie doesn't like the bedroom, which is painted the old color known as bittersweet, a yellow like crumbling Tuscan walls. It's dominated by a tester bed, its reeded posts topped by urns that are severe and somewhat funerary, or strike her so. And when she picks up the brush, Addie is repelled to see a hair, a single long black hair, winding like a serpent through the bristles.

But how can she believe it? Addie can't. She won't! To believe it would be to entertain a grave doubt of his character and would therefore represent, from her, a grave disloyalty to him. And even were it true, clearly it is something in the past.

Clearly. Their anger says as much. Didn't Harlan say he'd like nothing better than to put her and Paloma on the first boat back to Cuba? And he would hardly be the first man Addie knows to fall prey to that particular weakness, to demonstrate that particular penchant. (Like Percival, she thinks—like father, like son!) Addie's pacing back and forth before the window now. And perhaps it is his mother's hair, left all these years. . . . Yet they'd have cleaned it, wouldn't they? But who knew, after all, what sort of housekeeping these Cuban women practiced!

And if I were she, Addie thinks, if I were Clarisse and I believed that Harlan thought about me almost as a sister, if I spent weeks preparing a wedding party, and then discovered he was actually ashamed of me . . . might my eyes not burn and simmer as I looked at his bride, as hers burned and simmered when she looked at me? Addie has stopped before the window now. She's gazing out, yet her stare is caught up in her own reflection, floating, ghostlike, on the pane and fails to penetrate the dark. "That's all it is," Addie tells herself aloud, decisively. "Surely, that is all it is."

Perhaps it's the absence of her maid, but as Addie sets about her preparations—as she releases her corset, as she feels the familiar dropping down, the return of fuller breath, as she changes into the peignoir she chose so carefully, so specifically for this one night, as she sits before the mirror and contemplates her face—Addie feels more like a guest at someone's country house than a new bride, a mistress and a wife. As she brushes out her hair, her thoughts turn to the argument downstairs. . . .

Harlan's comportment, it's true, left something to be desired. (All that bellowing and pacing, all the waving of the hands, the mopping of the brow—and such perspiration! She's never seen the like, yet it's a meanness to think less of him for a physical affliction—a medical condition, possibly—that's beyond his power to control.) What matters is a man's character, his intellect and heart, and isn't there, in point of fact, a great deal to be said for Harlan in this area? For instance . . . Well, even if nothing springs immediately to mind . . . But, no, she's thought of something now. Surely, it would be a shame, a great shame—as Harlan said—for Wando Passo to lapse into decline. When God favors us, the people of our class and race, she thinks, with wealth and property, He entrusts us with a duty—a sacred duty, one might even say—to keep it up. Harlan made that point, and it is true. Very, very true. And, clearly, too, the DeLays have bestowed significant advantages on Jarry. How well he spoke! And his recitation—he seems to have a more than rudimentary grasp of iambic tetrameter, and in fact, if called upon to judge, Addie would have to say she preferred his delivery to Paul's—Paul Hayne, who admired her once and has now achieved a minor fame (she heard him read some patriotic verses at the Agricultural Hall not long ago). And Jarry's tone, the dignified and undemonstrative way he framed his argument—so sympathetic, so much easier to navigate than Harlan's rambling, explosive rant! And his clarity of countenance, Jarry's limpid eyes (somehow it was their expression of fatigue that she found most affecting) . . .

"What this family made me is a slave. . . ."

And what was it, the hush that descended on the room, like church? What was the opening she felt in her spine when Jarry spoke those words, the stinging in her eyes? Were those her own ancestral spirits, the voices of fifty or a hundred Anglo-Saxon generations crying up from the abyss of time? And what message were they trying to impart? Addie has stopped brushing now. She's staring into her reflection in the glass. . . .

"It was the truth, the truth!" She cries the words aloud. She cries them in despair. Her hands are at her mouth. And will she do that violence to herself, to call the truth a lie, and lies, the truth? They made this man a promise—what matter if he's black! "A promise kept, and Hell hath wept"—from Mme Togno's school, the rhyme comes back. "A promise broken, and Hell hath opened." Whom have I married? Addie thinks. I will never love this man. Love will never come. Not if I live a thousand years.

Yet what of it? She's known she didn't love him from the start, hasn't she? And now she starts in brushing again quite vigorously, furiously, in fact. Didn't Blanche know, too, and never bat a lash? And don't people marry all the time for reasons other than true love—for family, children, class alliance, out of simple loneliness? A hundred times, Addie gave herself these reasons and forgave herself on ninety-nine. So what's different now, the hundredth time? Why does she feel on the verge of panic at the thought that, at any moment, the jovial and undistinguished man she's married to will enter through that door, expecting intimacies she will henceforth and forevermore be obligated to provide? (For she's made a promise, too, as grave as Percival De-Lay's, to love and honor Harlan till they are parted by death.) What has turned that flitting, inoffensive sparrow into the large, obstreperous black crow that's cawing in the corner of the room and clearly in no mood to leave? However it is, Addie, who's leapt with gratitude into this marriage, is staring gravely in the mirror, thinking, What in God's name have I done?

And now the knock. Now Harlan enters from the bath in his shirt and stockings. He's blushing like a bridegroom—which, in fact, he is—grinning in a way that seems wicked, boyish, and good-naturedly naive. The subject of his curious humor, which Addie can't fail to perceive, is the erection protruding through his parted shirt-front, jouncing, as he walks, like a joggling board on a Pawleys Island porch.

"This came upon me by surprise," he says. "There I stood behind the door, *cringing, waiting for it to subside, and then I thought, What are we about here? Freedom? Frankness? Where's your courage, man! What is there to hide?" He laughs. "Ho ho."*

Seeing her expression, though, he comes to a dead stop. His northward-pointing member takes a turn toward east.

"But I hope I haven't miscalculated, dear. Have I embarrassed you? You look rather pale. I don't wish this to seem fearful or unclean. . . ."

"No, Harlan, no, it isn't that. . . . I'm only . . ."

"Yes?"

"Well, dear, it's something of a shock."

Deciding how to take this, he blinks his hazy ginger eyes, in which there is that eager, childlike, reckless something that seeks confirmation of its effect in her and appears, upon consideration, to find insufficient grounds for disappointment. He laughs again. "Ho ho ho," says he. "Yes, well, I can tell you, dear, though you have no standard of comparison, I'm considered rather well endowed. Hung like a bull as some . . . But never mind. Come, let me introduce you to my small, strong friend. It's best to be forthright with him, Addie, to shake his hand or shake him whole." He holds his tumid member for her close perusal, twisting it between three fingers and a thumb, the way he holds his Lonsdale to his ear before he lights, listening to the telltale crepitation of the leaf. "Go on now, touch him. He won't bite. Is he not a handsome fellow? But I warn you, his character is suspect! He's a rakish type, a bounder! Now, let us have a look at you." He takes her hands, small and cool and lifeless, now, as a china doll's, in his great, hot, meaty ones. He lifts her to her feet and spreads her robe. "My, my . . . Yes, as I suspected, your bust is small. Shapely, though." He appraises like a connoisseur.

In his grasp, her thin shoulders feel as insubstantial as the wafer of the Eucharist. He runs his hands down her slender arms and up the undersides. He touches her breasts, gently, then not gently, hungrily. He lifts them to look at them; his face changes as he looks; he excites himself in this lifting and looking, and, yes, in Addie, there's a tingle, a slight uptick of arousal. She looks to him, but he does not look back.

"See how white they are!" he says. "Like driven snow, and this charming little pink bit at the nipple! I must confess, dear, I don't like them with the large brown circles. May I touch? A little pinch? A bite?"

He takes her silence as permission, and Harlan's teeth prove sharper than a mink's! Addie startles, winces.

"Oh!" she says, and still he doesn't look. He's like a sailor who's weighed anchor and is off and gone to other parts, other ports, and the other ports and parts are

her. Her body is the sea on which he sails, but after that brief quiver of desire, that single waking tingle, Addie is no longer on the trip.

It's best to be authoritative, though, thinks Harlan. She doesn't know the facts of life, of course. How could she? (And, frankly, if she did, what good would Addie be?) Given her age, the fact that she is somewhat past her hour, a certain gratitude is due him. Not that Harlan would ever allude to this in word or deed. That would be indelicate, ungentlemanly, but it would be equally false to pretend that she is au courant. The notion of an older woman, grateful to him, with the seasoning to look squarely at the facts, once presented—all to the good. Harlan has no intention of forgoing pleasure in the bedroom and must therefore set the tone. No horse, after all, welcomes its own breaking, but they're happier, aren't they, when it's done? And as he falls deeper into delectation over Addie's body, sucking the tender meat on the small bones as though she were a quail in sauce, a memory of Grace Peixotto flits through his head, the great madam, whose brothel on Beresford Street Harlan discovered in his teens. At their first encounter, Grace made him a merry compliment over what she called his "equipage," which gave him the confidence and barnyard matter-of-factness he's carried into such encounters ever since. He used to fall asleep on Grace's ample bosom in those days and paid for the whole night, though his father railed at the expenses he ran up.

And behind this memory surfaces an even older one, of the house in Matanzas, the quinta with its mango avenue, and the maguey hedge, and the red tile roof and glassless windows with their bars, and the smell of melado, thick and sweet, drifting from the batey on days when they were grinding cane. One Sunday—he could not have been more than five—Percival ordered the volante and took them, Harlan and his mother, past fields of cane in violet tassel and others of plantains lined with stones of coral rock on a drive to the Cumbre, the high ridge north of Matanzas, and they ate a picnic of simple country food, jerked fish and plantains, and drank panales, which his mother made for him specially from sugar and the whites of eggs. They stared out at the broad bay of the city with the ships riding at anchor and north to the aqua sea, and south into the beautiful valley of Yumurí, with its sharp peaks and the pea-green color of the cane in the bottomlands through breaks of mist. Harlan lay with his head in his mother's lap and fell asleep, exhausted from too much sun, and she stroked his hair and sang some old English lullaby he's long since forgotten, though snatches of it come to him from time to time, as they do now, with . . . Addie. It takes him a moment to remember where he is, and with whom. And she caught the country fever, his mother, and died that very year, and then there was Paloma, who kept him clothed and fed, who was never harsh with him and always fair, but only fair. It was Jarry, when he came, to whom she sang the night's last song, who received the soothings and encouragements, the almost sexual confidence a loving mother, with her eyes, puts into a son, while to Harlan she was fair. And so he went to Grace, in the big brick house at number 11 Beresford, and sometimes paid for the whole night, and if Percival railed at the expense, then damn him—his father owed him something, didn't he? And Harlan remembers, too, hearing them, his father and Paloma, their animal cries and gruntings through the glassless windows with their bars, and he's waited a long time to be loved again and not to have to pay for it, to see that warm, melting look Paloma reserved for Jarry and his father in some woman's eyes for him, to be on the receiving end and know that it is meant. And at last his time has come.

He's fallen to his knees now, to Addie's great surprise, and is pressing his face into her belly. He kisses, licks, and laps like some hungry animal or like a nursing child. She looks down at the gleam of his bald head and feels the way she remembers feeling as a child, playing with her older cousins, when they ran ahead to get away from her, and Addie wanted to go with them, to be included in their games, but they went on in cruelty or gay indifference, leaving her behind. Being left behind by Harlan now, Addie gently rests her hand atop his head, trying to summon back that tingle of arousal, trying to catch up. She feels the film of oil from the long, hot day outside, like something you might use to oil the mechanism of a watch. Suddenly Harlan touches her, he spreads her open. She feels his tongue touch her in that place. There's a tingle, but it's too intense, like tasting some hot food, a single bite of which takes you the balance of the evening to recover from. The sensation has crossed the border into unpleasantness, a country there's no returning from. The uptick of arousal is slipping irretrievably into the past now, ever farther away. Something is failing, going terribly wrong. Addie will not catch up. Any chance of this is past. Harlan must realize this and stop. He must wait for her, but Harlan has been waiting all his life, he can't wait anymore. This woman is his wife.

He's pushed her back onto the bed. Like a lamb at slaughter, Addie gazes up, imploring with her eyes, but Harlan, slow to entertain the possibility of disappointment, ignores her look or misinterprets what he sees. His weight on top of her is crushing. Addie finds it hard to breathe. And now he's reaching down between them. He finds himself and shoves it in her like the handle in a churn. There's a drumming sound in Addie's ears. She feels burning, tearing. Oh, the size of him. Oh, the hurt . . .

"Harlan, please, please be tender. . . ."

"I will. I am," he whispers in a perfunctory tone, like someone talking in his sleep.

"No, it hurts! Stop. Stop!" Panicking, desperate for air, she shoves him with both hands.

And now he heeds. He lifts away. He looks at her and blinks.

"Please . . ." Her face is anguished; she's wheezing, small pants, not of passion, but of grievous damage. *"I have to catch my . . . breath. . . ."*

And her expression is clearly different, very different from the one he has expected to receive. In Harlan's hazy ginger eyes the spark of play has dimmed. It is, in fact, extinguished. The eager, childlike, reckless something that seeks confirmation of its effect in others and doesn't entertain the possibility of disappointment encounters now, in his new wife, a disappointment it is, finally, all too familiar with.

He pulls out of her, away. He sits, in a null state, on the edge of the bed, staring into vacancy.

"God," he says, *"oh, God . . ."* With both large hands, he covers his large face.

"I'm sorry, Harlan, you must teach me," Addie says. *"Let us try again."* She touches his shoulder.

He pulls away. *"How you must despise me. . . ."*

"No," she says, appalled. *"No, dear . . ."*

"God . . . oh, God." There's such loathing in his voice. Is it for her? For a moment, Addie can't quite tell. But, no, it's for himself.

Harlan rises now. As he starts toward the door, he stumbles and goes down on one knee. Looking crippled, defeated, he pulls upright, using the doorknob as a crutch. He disappears into the darkened bath.

"Harlan?"

He doesn't answer.

In the silence, Addie realizes the drumming is real and coming from outside.

A door opens on the hall. Footsteps, rapid footsteps, pass the door.

"Harlan?"

Gone.

Downstairs, the front door opens. She's at the window as a swath of light falls on the lawn. And there is Harlan, striding off into the park, into the black shadows of the trees, like one of them.

Hurriedly, she puts on her dress and follows.

From the piazza steps, she sees him by the stable, lighting a cigar with nervous hands. Angry at the match, he curses it and waves it out.

A black man with a lantern—is it James?—leads Runcipole out of the barn. The restive stallion tugs backward at the rein, as though resentful to be importuned at such an hour. When the groom tries to soothe him, Harlan pushes the man aside. Cinching the saddle girth himself, he mounts.

"Harlan!" Halfway across the lawn, she cries his name, and Harlan stares toward the shout with a cold concentration in his face, the way a warrior regards his enemy across a plain. As she walks, then runs in his direction, Addie stumbles, and Harlan rides away in the direction of the firelight through the trees.

A hand now firmly takes her arm and helps her from her knees.

"Where has he gone?" she asks, recognizing Jarry, who has come out of his cottage.

"You'd best go in the house," he answers with the look he gave her on the dock, a look of foreknowledge and compassion that Addie understands far better now.

"Please," she begs. "I'm asking for your help. Tell me where he is."

"I'm trying to help you," Jarry answers. Gently, firmly, he leads her to the house.

It is hours later, when she's finally drifted into fitful sleep, that Addie hears footsteps in the hall. They pause outside her door.

"Harlan?"

They move away again. By the time she opens the door, the hall is empty. On the floor lies her book, her Byron in red morocco. Only when Addie lights the lamp does she see the feather and open to the place it marks.

> From the wreck of the past, which hath perish'd,
> Thus much I at least may recall,
> It hath taught me that what I most cherish'd
> Deserved to be dearest of all:
> In the desert a fountain is springing,
> In the wide waste there still is a tree,
> And a bird in the solitude singing,
> Which speaks to my spirit of thee.

Her eye floats upward to the title: "Stanzas to Augusta."

SEVENTEEN

hap. Whap. Whap.

"Mr. Hill?"

Ransom turned and saw the officer staring through the kitchen screen under a shelved hand.

"Finally," he said to Marcel, not inaudibly. "Come in."

"Sergeant Tommy Thomason," said the heavy-gutted country man, whose egregious comb-over seemed somehow out of keeping with the compassionate Weltschmerz in his face. "This here's Officer Johnson." He nodded to a youthful black companion with a military formality of bearing and a weight lifter's build, who regarded Ransom and Marcel as though he hoped this call might blossom into the heroic crisis he'd been training for for years. "Dispatcher said you had some kind of break-in?"

Ransom moved aside to let them see. When she'd brought Hope and Charlie in the house, Claire had found the kitchen a shambles—almost literally so. The chicken, which Ran had left mounded on the platter, was strewn everywhere. Torn hunks had been thrown against the walls and cabinets, leaving shiny tracks of grease. Here and there on the floor, small deposits of meat had been regurgitated together with broken bits of bloody bone.

"Dag," said Thomason, advancing. "Something sure made a mess. Anything stole?"

"Not that we've been able to tell."

"Door locked?"

"We never lock the door."

They all turned as Claire came in.

"This is my wife, Sergeant Thomason."

"Evening, ma'am."

"Are they down?" Ran asked.

Claire gave him the parental squint. "In a manner of speaking."

Thomason gingerly poked a mangled breast with the pen from his pocket protector. "How old's y'all's kids?"

"Four and two."

"Dag!" Thomason's expression sprang into alarming animation. "I got me two grandkids that old. How old are you, Mr. Hill?"

"Forty-five," Ran answered tersely.

"You ain't! *I'm* forty-five—last June the ninth! You don't look no older than Johnson here."

For an instant, Ransom and Thomason faced off like alternate selves encountering each other at the shadowy intersection of the road-less-traveled-by. Shaped by processes only distantly related to what Ransom understood as life, the policeman had let himself go in a manner Ransom never could, yet Thomason seemed comfortable in his skin in ways that Ran could only speculate about. After brief consideration, neither seemed inclined to regret his chosen path.

"Can you tell us what happened here, Sergeant?" Claire asked.

"I got me a theory. Johnson?"

"Animal?"

Claire turned a vindicated stare on Ran. "Isn't that what I said? That's exactly what I said."

"Um-hm. I think you may have nailed it, ma'am." Thomason held Ransom's doubtful stare. "Y'all got a cat?"

"No, we don't," said Ran. "And, frankly, I don't see a cat . . ."

"I ain't saying cat, *necessarily*. Coulda been a possum or raccoon. Squirrel, even."

"A squirrel . . ." Ransom looked at Marcel, making no effort to conceal his mirth.

Thomason shook his head. "Wouldn't rule it out, Mr. Hill. When it comes to demolition power, pound for pound and ounce for ounce, there's few things can compare to a gray squirrel. Y'all know Titus Nevers down the road?"

"I don't believe we've had the pleasure."

"Last summer, Titus took his wife to Myrtle Beach for their anniversary. Played a round of miniature golf, had a nice dinner at the Red Lobster, then turned around and drove back. When they got home, looked like Al Capone and his whole gang had shot up the place with tommy guns. Know what it was?"

"I'm going to guess a squirrel," Ransom said.

"Yes, sir. One itty-bitty little squirrel. Come in through this gap beneath the eave, dug up all the houseplants, toppled a eight-foot Schefflera, then sat looking out the window trying to chew out through the wall. Damn near made it, too, only he bit into a hot one-ten and fried up crisp as that there chicken. Cost the insurance company thirty-seven hundred dollars and took damn near a month to put back what that dag thing done in a half workday with no overtime."

Claire put her hand over her mouth, and Marcel made a low, deep chortle.

"Yes, ma'am," said Thomason, "it's right funny, in a way. But let me tell you, Titus and Francine won't doing that much laughing."

"Do squirrels eat meat?" said Ran.

Thomason frowned. "Which is why I'm leaning toward a possum or raccoon, Mr. Hill. Could've come up from the crawl space. Old place like this, chances are you got a rotted board someplace."

"We do!" Claire said. "Ran found one yesterday. Didn't you, Ran?"

Ransom pointed. "Officer Thomason, do you see this pot?" Looking refreshed after its bath—one might have thought it newly scoured and blacked—Exhibit A now sat on the table. "When I left here this afternoon, that pot was upstairs in the tub. Are you suggesting this squirrel—Super Squirrel we'll call him—picked it up, brought it down the steps, and set it upright on the dining table?"

This finally seemed to give his persecutors pause.

"Or maybe it was a flying squirrel," said Ran, unwisely pressing his advantage. "Maybe he airlifted it down here and did a drop with a top secret self-destructing parachute?"

Thomason looked grieved. "Now, Mr. Hill, there's no need to take that tone. None a'tall. All we're trying to do here is put our heads together to figure out your problem."

"You're right," said Ransom. "You're absolutely right. Sorry."

"Maybe you moved it and forgot," suggested Claire.

Ran met her eyes and read the implication. "Absolutely not. No way. I'm one hundred percent sure, no, *two* hundred percent sure that pot was in the bathtub when I left."

"What was it doing in your bathtub, Mr. Hill, if you don't mind my asking?"

"I put it there to soak. As far as I can figure, the only person who could have moved it is the person who did all this—i.e., the burglar."

Thomason frowned and shook his head. "Problem is, Mr. Hill, we see a fair amount of burglaries, and this ain't really got the feel. I mean, what's your notion? Fella breaks in, burgles your chicken, makes a mess, then runs off, leaving all that silver in the cupboard there, all that stereo equipment in the other room, plus twenty other things in plain sight he could've sold?"

"What about some high school kids?"

"I ain't never seen no high school kids leave scat, have you?" He nodded to one of the half-digested piles. "That looks more like a hairball th'owed up by a cat."

Ransom weighed the point. "So you think it was an animal."

"That's my best guess."

"I'd like to say you've persuaded me, Sergeant."

"But you just ain't sure."

"I'm not."

Thomason regarded him with the resigned, unresentful expression of one whose best work was frequently greeted with disappointment.

"Could you at least dust for fingerprints?"

Thomason and Johnson exchanged long-suffering looks, and the sergeant shook his head regretfully. "I'll be honest with you, Mr. Hill. On the subject of law enforcement, TV's messed with people's minds. We're a little department here. Getting forensics in means calling down a two-man team from Columbia to the tune of two hundred and fifty bucks a hour. That's taxpayer money, Mr. Hill. If it was someone else, would you want us to spend it over six dollars' worth of chicken?"

"I just want to know my wife and kids are safe in our own home."

"I understand that, Mr. Hill, I truly do. My daddy was a auto mechanic, and one thing he always taught me is look for the simple explanation first. I mean, no sense tearing down a engine if all you need's a eighty-nine-cent plug, know what I mean? Simplest explanation here's a animal." He reached into his pocket and handed Ransom a card. "You have any other problems, just give a holler."

"Well, thanks for coming out."

"You're welcome. Come on, Johnson."

"Night," said Johnson.

Ransom let them out and turned around. "Well, guys, I guess chicken wasn't in the cards. What say we order in Chinese?"

Claire and Cell both hooted.

He gave them a sly smirk and allowed the warmth to spread. Then his face turned grave. "That pot was in the bathtub when I left."

EIGHTEEN

*C*harleston is burning, Addie dreams. The smell, which fire releases from
sodden foundation timbers where the sea has crept, is in the bed with
her when she awakes. It's coming from her husband, who is also
there, reeking of woodsmoke, with soured claret on his breath. Lying on his back,
Harlan still has on his breeches, and his tall tan boots have stained the bridal bed a
color little different from the stenciled maple leaf of blood she finds beneath her. His
soot-smutched face is set in a frown of concentrated worry she's never seen him wear
awake. His left shoulder is bare; his right arm, still in the sleeve of his shirt—his
beautiful, ruined shirt of fine Sea Island cotton woven in an English mill—is slung
across his gathered brow, warding something off. It is as though the process of un-
dressing, in the condition in which he undertook it, proved to be too much.

She feels, for a moment, as she reorients, ill and reeling. The moment after, resigned. Now she is furious. Furious! The marriage is over. She will return to
Charleston immediately. Today. This hour. Explanations? She wants none. What explanations could he give? And on her wedding night! But how could she have mis-
judged him so egregiously? The rumors—the ones she dismissed so blithely during
the courtship—come flying back. What gave her the foolish confidence to think that
she could judge with clearer eyes than social Charleston had? The sob surprises Addie, coming now from so far down, the region where those sodden timbers lie. Oh,
such grief. Not tears, not weeping, an animal moan she tries, and fails, to hold back
with both hands.

Yet does she bear some fault in this? Has she not lived honorably? What has God to put to her account to punish her like this?

You married without love. *The voice she used to hear more frequently and hasn't listened to in years speaks up and answers her. (Whose voice is this?) Oh, she has made a terrible mistake, a ruinous, soul-murdering mistake! And what is she to do?*

What else is there, but to accept responsibility, confess her fault, and call it off? Too late, yes, but better now than in a year from now, or ten. Yes, she will tell him. She will wake him now.

Yet to return, disgraced, to Charleston, and after just one day . . . To face the looks and whispers, the pious mouthings of sympathy under eyes that scintillate with glee . . . (Louisa Elliott!) Oh, horrible, horrible. Is there not some way, any way, to stay and salvage it, some way for the cup to pass? Might not love, though absent now, still grow?

Yet the voice says, No, it never will, *and Addie remembers now why she stopped listening to the voice. To wait for Gabriel forever, even should he never come, even should she die, untouched, an old maid like her aunt—this price seemed too severe, inhumanly severe, and she got angry at the voice and shut it out. And what has reawakened it? That look with Jarry on the dock, a momentary glance exchanged over open water with a man she doesn't even know, a Negro. What is God about? But, no, she will lose everything, but not her faith. Not that.*

And look at Harlan in the bed, so fretful after all, so ill. Doesn't she—as the first racking spasm of anger dissipates—owe him the chance to account for his behavior? And what, exactly, has he done? Perhaps his feelings were simply hurt (like hers). Perhaps he simply gave in to an impulse to flee (the same one she feels now). Perhaps he simply drank himself into insensibility—is he the first bridegroom to commit this particular felony against romance? Perhaps he simply had high hopes and saw them dashed like hers—enough to end a marriage over?

You do not love this man.

Yes, yes, there's that, but yesterday, when she admired the rowers and the parakeets, when the sky looked like a crystal bowl that, if you struck it with a mallet, just might ring, love or its absence seemed beside the point. Maybe tomorrow it will seem beside the point again. (Oh, let it pass!)

But, no, impossible—she must go!

The truth is, she does not know what to do. All Addie knows right now is she must flee this room of funerary urns and bittersweet. She must get out of this house and walk.

But the library doors are open, and though she tries to hurry past, she's spied by Percival and cannot honorably withdraw.

"My dear!" he hails her in a tone of mirth, and then he sees her face. "Great God, Addie, what has happened?"

Her blue eyes, which can conceal nothing, are red and harrowed. She shakes her head, trying to stop tears; she fails.

"Please," he says. "Please, my dear, sit down." He pats the chair, and she obeys. "Can I send for something? Do you require a doctor? Are you ill? How can I assist you?"

"You're kind. No, thank you, nothing."

"What is it, Addie? What's the matter?"

"Harlan left me. He was gone all night," she sobs. "I don't know where he went."

"And he has not returned?"

"No, he's upstairs in the bed right now, sound asleep, still in his clothes, still in his filthy, spattered boots."

Behind his hazel eyes, he works the sums. "I'm sorry, Addie, so very sorry, my dear. You've had a wretched night, a horrid night, one that you did not deserve."

She looks up now. Her tone is fierce. "Tell me where he went."

"Ah," says Percival, "ah, my dear, that I cannot do. And I think I know you well enough, I think I've seen enough of you, to know you know I can't."

"Was it you who left the book?"

"What book?"

She studies his expression closely. "My Byron. Someone put it by my door last night."

"I haven't climbed those stairs in two and a half years."

"It was Jarry then," she says, confirmed in her suspicion. "He marked the place at 'Stanzas to Augusta'—why?"

Percival seems at a loss. "Because we spoke about the poem yesterday—that would be my guess."

"Tell me why you quoted it to me."

"My dear! The verses simply popped into my head. I had no ulterior motive. And yet . . ." His gaze goes past her shoulder now and concentrates on something in the distance.

"And yet?"

"You know who she was, of course. . . ."

"Augusta Leigh was Byron's sister."

"His half sister, yes. You're too young to remember, but I vividly recall, Addie, when news of their relations first came out. The throng of his adorers, who'd made Byron a matinee idol, their little poppet and their doll, all turned against him. The

marquises and countesses, who'd showered him with jewels and raised their skirts for him, drove him from sunny England in disgrace. I met him some time after that. . . ."

"You met Byron?"

He nods. "In Italy, at Strà, in '20, I believe it was. He was living with the countess Guiccioli, dabbling in Italian politics, being watched by the police. He was not then, Addie, the man you probably imagine. His famous jet-black hair had grayed. Though only thirty-two, he was fat and had bad teeth. His breath was not entirely fresh, and he had a portion of his breakfast on his coat—a three-minute egg, judging from appearances. He was still a brilliant talker, but he talked like someone repeating old stories he'd long since lost interest in, someone who's afraid to stop. He was a dry husk rattling around the empty core of what he'd been. Yet out of his misery, he wrote:

'It hath taught me that what I most cherish'd
Deserved to be dearest of all.'

And what he most cherished was Augusta Leigh. Yesterday, when I quoted that, you said it seemed inarguable. Does an argument now suggest itself to you?"

"That is a dark story, sir," she answers, in a stern and formal tone.

"It is, indeed. And the question it raises—the one it's always raised for me—is which was it that ruined him: whether it was loving Augusta, or failing to. . . ."

Addie's brows knit on this. "You mean to say . . ."

"I mean to say—to ask, merely—if, in leaving her, he shirked a truer fate assigned to him by God."

"It's hard for me to credit that God—at least the God I know—would assign him—or anyone—a fate like that."

"Perhaps you have a better vantage point from which to judge His mind," he replies. "For where I sit, it seems to me that He, or they"—he nods to the bóveda now—"whatever guiding spirits rule our lives, sometimes assign uncommon spirits uncommon tasks, tasks the world does not know how to evaluate and therefore has no right to judge. Mine, which I railed against and resisted tooth and nail, was to love a woman of a different race, a woman the law considers three-fifths human, whom I own outright the way I own the horses in my stable, and there are horses in my stable for which I paid far more. Yet I loved Paloma, Addie, better than I ever did my wife, and most of what I know of life, the little bit, I learned from her, or through her. I thank God every day for our relationship, yet I failed Paloma in one profound and crucial way, and that failure, as I told you yesterday, touched our children, hers and* mine. What I didn't say, what I thought and was afraid to tell you, was that it might—indeed almost surely would and must—touch you. And now it has. I won't palliate your husband's fault. Harlan has much to answer for. But the misery you feel right now—the root and head of it is me."

"But what is it for which you blame yourself?"

"To answer that, I must be candid. I did not approve your marriage, Addie. Not when Harlan told me of his plans some months ago; nor do I approve it now."

She colors violently. "Meaning, you do not approve of me. . . ."

"The opposite. I disapprove the marriage for your sake as much as for my son's."

"But why? I am confused."

"These matters are difficult to unravel, Addie. They go back more than forty years," he says. "Yesterday, I told you of that time in Cuba when my wife grew ill and died."

"Harlan's mother . . ."

"Harlan's mother, yes, Melissa . . . We were living at La Mella then. Villa-Urrutia had made Paloma available to her as a lady's maid. Paloma was nineteen or twenty then, and striking, but there was no impropriety between us. You understand. When the fever struck Melissa, she tried to help. Once I overheard her praying to San Luis Beltrán and found a cross of woven basil leaves in a water glass beside the bed. I thought little of these things. I took them for harmless folk remedies, at worst, popish superstitions. At Wando Passo there was a woman, Maum Binah—she only died last year—who practiced midwifery in the quarters and was said to conjure. My father scoffed at such notions, but the slaves all went to her, and my mother . . . I clearly remember, as a boy, accompanying her to Binah's cabin, on what errand I know not. But I'm certain she believed. And so, you understand, when Paloma told me there were others at La Mella who might help Melissa, the image in my mind was that of some old woman, queer and temperamental, living in isolation some-where on the fringe of Villa-Urrutia's estates. It was not like that at all. The door, when it finally opened, opened on a church, a great invisible cathedral, Addie, hidden in plain sight not only in the barracoon of La Mella and plantations like La Mella, but in the cabildos of Havana. And its priesthood—they're not like my friend Hilliard in Powatan. These men don't dip their thumbs in the oils of extreme unc-tion, sign the cross upon the forehead of the dying—men like me—and then consign them to their fate. No, they intervene. They are shamans and magicians."

"What does that mean?"

"It means they bring the dead to life. No, let me strive to be exact with you. There is no death, Addie. Those whom we call 'the dead'—they're known as 'muertos' there—don't die at all. They shed their bodies, yes, but their souls, their 'almas,' pass on to new life in a different realm from ours. These teachings, in their principles, are not so different from ours. The difference is, these priests of whom I speak—those who possess the secret, 'el secreto'—have the power to summon them, to call the dead back down into the human realm again to work with us, the living, to cure, protect, and save, and sometimes also to destroy. Do you grasp what I'm saying?"

"This can't be true, though, is it?"

"It can and is. I'm an Episcopalian, Addie. I believe in God the Father Almighty, Maker of Heaven and Earth, and in Jesus Christ his only Son our Lord. . . . I believe in the Holy Ghost, the holy Catholic Church, the Communion of Saints, the Forgiveness of Sins, the Resurrection of the body, and the Life Everlasting. Before I went to Cuba, how many Sundays had I, like you, perhaps, sat patiently in church and said those words? How many Sundays did I kneel and pray and rise and sing and sit again on cue? I thought that was the human lot, Addie, to sit patiently in the family pew Sunday after Sunday, waiting, hoping against hope and praying that the death of the body didn't mean 'cessation,' as you put it yesterday, did not entail the soul's extinction. I'd never dreamed that it was possible to know. To know, Addie."

"But you do?" she asks. "You know this now?"

"I've seen it, Addie. Seen with these two eyes. Not once. A hundred times."

"But how did you . . . How did this happen?"

"The religion is called Palo Mayombe, Addie. It's practiced mainly among the Congo slaves. Paloma introduced me to her godfather, her padrino, an old Congo named Demetrio. Through him, I eventually found my way to Andrés Petit, a free mulatto, one of the most impressive men I've ever met. It's hardly too much to say he is a kind of Cuban Luther or John Calvin. He founded a line of Palo called Kimbisa, La Regla Kimbisa del Santo Cristo del Buen Viaje, the Kimbisa Order of the Holy Christ of the Good Journey. The first time I approached him—in Guanabacoa—he rebuffed me, yet he did so with great warmth and suavity. I tried three or four more times before Petit became convinced of my sincerity. I was among the first whites to be allowed to glimpse the mysteries, and there were those who thought none of la raza blanca, much less a slaveowner like myself, should be allowed into the templo. To this day, some consider Petit a Judas, who sold the secret 'por ochenta onzas,' for eighty pieces of silver. And it was true, he charged me, but money—that was not the reason."

"Why did he admit you?"

"Because he looked into my eyes and saw that I was grieving for my wife, he saw that I was in despair and thirsting for the truth. He admitted me because I was persistent and sincere and willing to humble myself to him, and because, in the end, he was able to see me not simply as a blanco, a white man, but as a human being, 'un profano que anda errante y desea pertenecer,' one wandering lost and wanting to belong. And he pitied me and took me in. My old religion, the faith in which my parents raised me—this came to seem a child's toy, a wooden sword, but Palo, Addie, Palo was a blade of mighty power that cut to heal.

"I was initiated in Havana, in la calle Ancha del Norte, número 115. I made juramento. I took the fourteen vows and sealed them with my blood. For two years, I attended fechas in Havana with Petit, but most of what I learned was at La Mella, from Demetrio, who took me as his godson, too. By day, I worked in the boiler house, by night I danced and sweated side by side with the same men who fed bagasse, cane waste, into the boiler's fires. By day, I gave them orders; by night, I made obeisance to them as my elders in the faith. We looked into each other's eyes and shared the secret silently. I'd lived with Negroes all my life, but, strange to say, I'd never looked into their eyes and seen their characters as men. I learned to do that there, to see them as Petit saw me. Paloma and I fell in love. I fell terribly and utterly. Looking back, those two years were the best of my whole life. And the strange thing was, it was as if I, not they, had been enslaved, and for that time my chains were loosened. There among the least were truths and answers that we, the so-called great and privileged, had forgotten if we ever knew. It was as though I'd stumbled on the thing that all men spend their lives seeking in vain—the certainty that there is life after death, that those we've loved and lost continue to live on, that the soul persists, that it's immortal and imperishable. More than this, Addie, I learned that there are beings more elevated than the dead, our ancestors. They're sometimes called 'santos,' though 'saints,' the Catholic term, is only a blind and barely hints at what they are. Their true name is 'nkisi'; they are spirits of great power and antiquity, who reside in stars and wind, in lightning and the sea. They, too, concern themselves with human fate, and these men—men like Demetrio and Andrés Petit—can summon them to intervene."

"And you see them?" Addie asks, feeling cast adrift. "You actually see these spirits?"

"Not see, Addie. The nkisi are invisible, but I've heard them speak as clearly as you hear me speaking to you now."

"How?"

"They come down, Addie, bajan. . . . They enter one of the faithful and speak por su boca, through his mouth. They give instruction and direct trabajos, works of various sorts. They heal and exorcise bad spirits. They do what all the poets in all the *books I read, all the books you see upon these shelves, could never do for me: they tell us how to live. And, in the end, they tell us how to die. And they lay obligations on us, too. They make demands. Once upon a time, such a demand was made of me. That is where this tale is wending, Addie. I was told to free Paloma. It was at la fecha del Santo Cristo in Havana on September fifth, the month before we sailed for home. Petit himself was the 'caballo,' the medium or 'horse,' mounted by San Luis Bel-trán. He didn't order me to free all my slaves, to ruin my family and myself finan-cially. No, he told me only to do what, in my heart, I already knew I had to do, and I knelt down on the floor in front of him, I touched my forehead to the bricks, I wept and swore I would, and then . . ." Percival looks away now toward the window.*

"And then?"

"And then, I brought Paloma home with me to South Carolina. She bore my son, and forty years went by, and somehow I never could."

"Why not?"

"Is it so hard to guess?"

She doesn't care to try.

"I was afraid that if I freed her, she might leave."

Outside, in a cedar tree, a cardinal sets forth a strangely cheerful trill, and they both turn their heads.

I was afraid that if I freed her, she might leave. *The words set off an echo in her head, and as Addie listens to the bird, they seem among the most terrible she's ever heard a human being speak.*

"The thought of life without her—and, eventually, without Jarry—was un-bearable to me. I decided I could free them at my death and keep the letter of my vow. I told myself this lie. That's what I meant, Addie. When I said I am the head and root and that this all goes back to me—that's why."

The cardinal takes wing and flies away. Watching, she is thoughtful. "I can understand how this must weigh on you. But what has it to do with Harlan, or with me?"

"You'll understand that story more in time, I fear."

"If you won't tell me where he went, then tell me what to do," *she says.*

"Pose the question to your husband," *he replies.* "If you're to have a marriage, that's the sole recourse I can see."

"I don't think we can have a marriage now."

"That's wholly up to you, my dear. Before you leave him, though, don't you owe it to yourself, and him, to find out what he's done?"

"I'm too afraid I know."

"You're too afraid you know. That is only a suspicion."

She holds his gaze, then looks away distractedly. "You're right, it is."

"There's something I must ask you, Addie."

She looks back at him, and Percival reaches into his shirt. On a string around his neck, there is a key. "In that drawer," he tells her, pointing to the partners desk, "you'll find my will, with the provisions for Jarry's and Paloma's manumission. I would be grateful if you'd put it someplace for safekeeping. I can't trust Harlan to honor my wishes in this matter. That I can't is as much my fault as his. What Jarry said last night was true. I've always loved him more. I didn't choose it so. No father does. But even when I denied it to myself, Harlan knew. There was some crucial aspect of myself that I could never give him, however hard I tried, which I shared with Jarry out of simple joy. And it's curious, then, isn't it, that Harlan will have Wando Passo, all this, while Jarry will leave here with nothing but the clothes on his back? Yet my promise to him will be kept. Had I held dearest those I've cherished most, I should have freed him and Paloma both long since. Now death is my last chance to set it right, and what I fear, Addie, is not cessation, but what the coming life may be for me if I do not. May I count on you in this?"

She takes the will. "I think it is the right decision."

"Now, kiss me," the old man says, "and go and have your interview."

Harlan, however, doesn't rise till almost suppertime. She comes back from a walk to find him waiting, tense, on the piazza, a bouquet of Jarry's wilting roses in his hand. "My dear!" he says, leaping to his feet. "I was afraid you'd left me! Addie, I'm appalled at my behavior! I have no excuse!" He mops his brow and reaches into his coat for a cigar.

"Where did you go?"

"Where? They were celebrating in the quarters, Addie. They wanted me to jump the broom—it's a custom here. We drank toasts. I had too much rum, the better part of a cask, judging by the way I feel. Blessedly, I have few memories beyond that point."

"Few memories . . ."

"Practically none, my dear, yet if it's any consolation to you, Addie, I am suffering. If someone put the Purdey to my temple and pulled the triggers now, I'd consider him a friend. Not to put too fine a point on it, my behavior was piggish. And, in short, I am a pig."

"Where did you wake up?" she asks.

Now he stops. Now the look of mortal suffering, of spiritual beauty, reappears. "In the dirt," he says, "beside the blackened fire. My horse, old Runcipole, was nuzzling me. I thought—nay, hoped—it was the loving kiss of my dear wife."

Addie studies his face closely. "I wish I could believe you, Harlan."

"But you must, dear!" he cries. "You must try! There are things, Addie. Things . . ."

"What things?"

"Things you don't yet understand . . ."

"Explain them to me then."

"I can't!"

"Why can't you?"

"Because you won't believe them, Addie. You'll think me not in my right mind, and frankly, dear, sometimes I fear . . . But no, no. You must try, though, Addie, please try to believe that my intentions toward you are honorable. I'll make it right to you. I'll make it right, whatever it costs. I will fight for you, my dear. Fight for me. Please fight for me!"

And Addie, afraid to wholly trust him, but even more afraid to wholly disbelieve and risk a final breach, allows herself to be coaxed upstairs, where she submits and, in a grim, brief episode, becomes his wife in fact.

NINETEEN

I repeat: that pot was in the bathtub when I left."

"Ransom . . ."

"Don't say it," he said. "I already know what you're going to say, so do us both a favor, just say no."

Claire turned a frustrated glance at Marcel, who looked like a man caught in the wrong place at the wrong time but honor-bound to stay.

"Ransom, sweetie, look," she said, and at that unexpected "sweetie," he gentled like a colt. "Story. When you called me from the airport yesterday, I was in the laundry room. I had a load sorted on the floor, I was waiting for the powder to dissolve, the phone rings, I go to get it, we talk, I hang up. You know what I did then? I went upstairs to get the hamper, and I stood there in the hall a sec, completely blank, and then, away off in the house, I heard that noise from the machine, you know that croupy little groan it makes?"

He frowned. "So what's your point?"

"I think you know what my point is. Everybody forgets little things like this."

"Everybody," he repeated. "Not just drunks and crazy people."

"I didn't say that. Is that what I said? No, I didn't, and you've got to stop jumping from some A, like maybe you forgot, to the P or Q of me accusing you of being crazy. *That's* irrational. And you had been drinking—you admitted it yourself."

Ran looked at Cell. "What did I tell you?"

"And since you bring it up . . ."

"Here comes the other shoe," he said.

Claire gave him her Concerned and Earnest look, the one that made Ran feel like a receding object at the wrong end of a telescope. "Cell's been down this road with us before," she went on, "so I'm not going to mince words—I do think it might be a good idea for you to get your levels checked. Ever since you got here, you've seemed overwrought."

Busted!

"Marcel thinks so, too."

Ransom looked, and Marcel held his stare. Cell's face was open; there was no trace of meanness, no gloating—of course not! When had there ever been? Yet Cell, too, seemed to be looking down on him from an eminence, like some god on Mt. Olympus regarding a poor mortal lost in the dark woods of middle life. And the worst part was, Ran knew that this very feeling—of their exaltation and his comparative debasement—was evidence that they were telling him the truth: he was in trouble, or flirting too close to the edge. Yet, guilty as he was, he still had to fight the impulse to regard them as his enemies and to tell them both to go to hell.

"Fine," he said. "You know what, Claire? If it'll make you feel better, I'll go in tomorrow. But I'm telling you right now, I can get my levels checked till kingdom come and join AA and get a frontal lobotomy while I'm at it"—he could not resist tossing in this helpful shot—"but it's never going to get that pot from upstairs in the bathtub where I left it, down those stairs and up the hallway to this table. And what if, just for kicks, as a sort of thought experiment, you considered the possibility that what I'm telling you is true, that the pot really was in the tub when I left, and here when we came back, and *I* didn't move it?"

"I think I have to stick with Sergeant Thomason and the simple-explanation theory."

"Cell?" Ran said.

"Somebody moved it," Marcel said. "If it wasn't you, then there was someone in the house."

"Thank you!" said Ran. "Okay. And if there was, wouldn't it stand to reason that that person, whoever he was, did both things: the chicken and the pot?"

"Okay, Ran, fine," said Claire, "but why?"

"That's exactly my question! With all the possible mischief you might make in an old house like this, what sort of burglar or vandal would choose to (a) mess up a plate of chicken and (b) move a black iron pot? I mean, on the burglar-vandal checklist, these have to qualify as pretty arcane choices."

"So what are you saying, Ran?" Cell asked.

"Truthfully, man? I don't know what I'm saying. I'm saying none of it makes sense. It doesn't make sense that an animal moved it, because an animal couldn't; it doesn't make sense that a burglar moved it, because a burglar wouldn't. And it doesn't make sense that I moved it in some sort of drunken fugue state, because whatever you may think of me, I've never been that bent."

"So what's left, Ran?" Claire asked. "That pot certainly didn't walk downstairs on its three stubby little legs."

Ran's brow gathered, and he didn't answer.

"Ransom?"

"What?"

"Please tell me you aren't suggesting that."

"No," he answered, in a somewhat grudging tone, "I'm not. Of course I'm not. But I will say this. . . ." He turned to her with a reviving animation. "Since you already think I'm crazy, I may as well tell you that yesterday, and again this afternoon, when I touched that thing, I got a shock."

"A shock . . ."

"So help me, Claire. The thing felt hot. That's why I thought I'd hit a buried power line."

"Oh, Ran," she said. "Sweetie."

"I know, I know," he said, "fine, whatever. Call the funny farm—you know the number—but before you tell the guys in the white coats to unfurl their nets, do me a favor: touch it."

Claire hesitated briefly, then went to the table and complied. "Okay, what?"

"Nothing?"

She shook her head. "Nothing, Ransom. Not a thing."

Ran, for once, could think of no response.

"Maybe the sun had been shining on it," Marcel offered. "I mean, it's black. It was pretty hot out there today."

Ransom looked at him and felt a swell of love. "It was under six inches of periwinkle, Cell. Thanks, though. I don't suppose you'd try it, just to humor me. . . ."

He laid his hand where Claire's had been, and Ransom arched his brows, but Marcel pursed his lips and shook his head.

"Okay," Ran said, "once more we've proved that I'm a jerk, as if more proof were necessary."

"You know, though . . ." As Marcel removed his hand, he brushed it as though rubbing something off and looked at Claire. "At the risk of adding darkness to obscurity, you know what suddenly occurred to me?"

"What?"

"Ben's story. Didn't you tell me that when the minister came out here to look for them, he found the table set and a chicken dinner scattered in the dining room?"

"Whoa," said Ransom. "Who's Ben? What story? What's all this?"

"Ben Jessup," Marcel said. "Our librarian."

"This morning he was telling us about my great-great-great-grandparents, Ran," Claire said. "You know the portrait in the library? That's Adelaide DeLay. She disappeared from Wando Passo right after the Civil War."

"Not the blonde?"

Claire nodded. "Her husband, Harlan, was a Confederate prisoner of war. He came back from up north somewhere, bought some shot in Powatan, and started walking out here, and that was the last anybody ever saw of them."

Ransom pointed down the hall. "Her?" As though drawn by his own hand, he went to the library door and looked back. "White dress? Botticelli hair?"

"Yes, I'm fairly sure," Claire said as she and Marcel followed. "I'm going to call Aunt Tildy in the morning."

"Let's call her now."

"It's too late."

Ran checked his watch. "It's eight fifteen!"

"She's eighty-eight years old. I'll call her in the morning." She turned to Cell. "So what are you implying?"

"I'm not implying anything. It just popped into my head. It's probably a coincidence."

"Unless the *pot* made you think of it."

They both turned sober stares on Ran.

"Joke! J-o-k-e. Jesus, folks . . . Hey!" Ran slapped his forehead. "The tub! Let's go see what came out in the wash!"

They followed him upstairs, where Ran switched on the bathroom light. The water had drained out and left a snaking spill of gray alluvium, like lava covering the remains of a small town. Ran turned on the hand-held, and several stones appeared out of the rinse: a pointed black one rayed with white, a translucent piece of pink quartz crystal, one of cuprous red, shaped like a heart, a fourth which proved to be a lodestone—there were several rusty pins attached. Ran lifted a rectangle of moldy, dripping wood with fittings of corroded copper wire. Preserved in its anaerobic state, traces of stamped blue writing were still visible. "Looks like some kind of antique mousetrap," he said. "And what do you suppose these are?" He held up a pair of rusty rings connected by a length of chain.

"Handcuffs?" Claire ventured.

"Manacles," said Cell.

There was a horseshoe, what appeared to be a railroad spike, the head of a small doll, an ivory ring, and several shells—a lightning whelk and several smaller striped ones similar in size and shape to pasta shells. Finally, out of the black mud, the skull of some small animal, perhaps a dog.

They all stared in silence as the water drummed.

"Call me crazy," Ransom said, "call me irresponsible, but this reminds me of the stuff you see in those shops along North Rampart in New Orleans."

Claire looked up. "What shops?"

"The vodou stores."

"Oh, great," she said, "now it's a vodou pot?"

"Hey," he said. "We all know I'm the voice of unreason here. What's your view?"

"What is it? Some rocks and crap. I think you dug into a garbage mound," she said. "That's your big discovery. I mean, they had garbage back then, too; I'm going to venture they didn't have curbside pickup, so what did they do? They buried it. And your vodou cauldron is just some old cook pot they threw away."

"You know, though, Claire . . ." Marcel picked up one of the small shells. "These are cowries. In Africa, they use them for divination. I don't think we even have them here."

"Okay." Claire held up both hands and backed away. "You've freaked me out. *Both* of you. I am now Officially Freaked Out."

"Look, everyone's on edge," Cell said. "Something happened earlier tonight, and here we are in an old house in the country. . . . All we're missing is the thunderstorm. Chances are, this is no more than a bunch of overcaffeinated med students contracting imaginary diseases from the *PDR*. As far as I know, they don't even use black pots in vodou. If they do, I've never heard of it. But if—and I emphasize, *if*— we wanted to look into it a little more, I'll tell you who might know. . . ."

"Who?" said Ran.

"Shanté."

"Shanté," Claire said. *"Shanté Mills?"*

Cell gave her a confirming glance, but saved the balance of his stare for Ran. "She's here, you know."

Ransom's expression emptied, turning as soft and guileless as a newborn lamb's. "Here?" he said, with a small bleat.

"About an hour south of here, on the way to Beaufort, in Alafia." Cell looked at them as though this ought to ring some bells. " 'Authentic African Village As Seen on TV'?"

Ran and Claire both blinked.

"*Sixty Minutes* did a piece on it. It was started by some disaffected urban radicals from Philly in the sixties. They bought a tract of land and moved down here and essentially seceded."

"From what?"

"Everything. America. The West. The state of South Carolina. They went completely African—tribal dress, agriculture, everything. They've been down there for over thirty years. The place is famous."

"What's Shanté doing there?"

Cell looked at Ran. "Well, you know, after she stopped singing, she spent several years in Africa. Mostly in Zaire. I don't know the whole story, but I know there was a guy involved, and then there wasn't. After they split, she came home and went to Alafia to take some time and ended staying. But the thing is, while she was in the Congo she was studying to be ordained."

"Ordained as what?" Claire asked. "Please don't say a vodou priestess."

"Well, I don't think they call it vodou over there," Cell said, "but that's the general idea."

Ran and Claire both stared.

"Dag," Ran finally said.

Claire began to laugh. "Oh, yes! *Yes!* Better and better! This is all we need! Shanté Mills up here, drinking chicken blood and tossing goofer dust, shaking the dark twins in Ransom's face! That will clear this *right* on up! Let's call her now!"

Ransom, on another wavelength, looked at Cell. "Do you have her number?"

"At home."

"Ha! Ha! Ha!" said Claire.

"Mommy?"

They all turned, and there was Charlie in the doorway in his red firetruck pj's, screwing a little fist into his eye.

"Oh, sweetie, did Mama wake you up?" Claire knelt and took him in her arms.

"The doggy do it."

"What doggy, Pie?"

"There's a black dog in the hall upstairs." Hope stepped from the shadows now. "I'm scared."

Claire looked at Ran, and Ran looked back. "Sweetie, I don't think there is. Maybe you dreamed it, but let's go make sure, and then I'll tuck you both in bed."

"Doddy do it," Charlie said.

Hope concurred. "We want Daddy."

This clearly took her by surprise. She looked at Ran.

He shrugged. "Hey, I'm new," he said consolingly. "They'll learn. You guys go see what you can scare up for dinner. Maybe Domino's?"

Claire obliged him with a smile.

"What?" Ran said. "They must have Domino's."

But she was wise to his old tricks. "Hill, I swear to God, you do still make me smile sometimes. You really do."

"That's a good thing, right?" He gave her his best sly, sheepish grin, and she returned it, but her eyes were thoughtful, as though her inclination toward him worked against her better judgment.

Ran, however, who'd never considered good judgment a large motivating factor in human affairs—not his, at least—took encouragement.

As Claire headed to the kitchen with Marcel, he turned to the kids. "Okay, dutes, let's clear the premises of canine intruders. But, first, raise your right hands and repeat, 'I pledge allegiance to the dad. . . .'"

TWENTY

*J*urned away from him in bed, Addie awakes from a light sleep as Harlan
goes into the bath. It's the shank of the afternoon now, judging by the
melancholy light that filters through the bedroom window. Returning, he
leans over her, scrutinizing, and Addie continues feigning sleep as he dresses and goes
out. From the window, she watches him cross the lawn and come out of the barn on
Runcipole again. He disappears into the same break in the same wall of trees, and
this time, Addie dresses and sets after him.

The way is wet and low and quickly she is in the swamp, where dusk is more
advanced than on the lawn and has a gloomier timbre. Overhead, the bearded cy-
presses are roped with tangled vines. A large crow flits and disappears. On her left
spreads a broad water meadow full of lily pads and rotting cypress knees. There are
wildflowers and green, tender ferns. Her steps make a wet, quashing sound in the
mud, where Runcipole's prints, already filled with water, show the way. Addie's shoes
are ruined, her hem sopped by the time she enters the pine barren. Under the stand
of old-growth longleaf pines, stillness presides, and as Addie walks over the carpet of
fallen needles, the soughing of wind through the treetops sounds almost human. She
thinks she hears voices, and when she stops to listen, she catches sight of a cottage
through the trees. Surrounded by beds of flowers and herbs—there is pink deer grass
and yellow orchis, tiger lilies with their great brilliant trumpets, and basil, asafetida, and
dock—it's made of squared pine logs with white clay daub, with a rustic porch and a
chimney made of ballast stones. The shake roof is black and scabbed with lichen, like

pale green sores, and she can hear hens brooding and clucking somewhere, though she doesn't see the coop. Addie's eyes and full attention are fixed on the porch, which is hung with braids of drying herbs and flowers, and in whose deep shadow Harlan stands talking to Clarisse.

Clarisse is smiling. The unhealthy, mottled flush, the glassy eyes—these are gone. She's radiant. She offers Harlan something, but he pushes her hand away, and now she frowns and her face darkens, as though a cloud shadow has passed over it. Lighting a cigar, Harlan starts to pace, to make the large, emphatic gestures of the hands.

They're arguing. Addie can make out their angry tone, but not the words. The whole forest has grown still around her. The wind has ceased to blow. They face each other. Clarisse is weeping now. As Addie watches, Harlan reaches out and curls a lock of hair around her ear, and Clarisse, by way of answer, slaps him hard across the mouth. Harlan appears stunned, and then—to Addie's astonishment, her horror— he laughs. His laugh is strong and bold, reverberating in the wood. He lifts Clarisse's hand and takes what she was offering before. A slant ray of sun illuminates the glass. There's something in it, a small red berry floating, suspended, like a drop of blood. He reaches in a finger and a thumb. He takes the granadilla out. Clarisse's face has lost its coldness now. It's come alive. With both her hands, she takes his one and pulls it to her mouth.

Addie watches as the eating of the passion fruit becomes, between them, a hungry kiss. She turns and starts to run.

TWENTY-ONE

ee? No black dogs." Turning from the closet, Ran switched the flashlight off. "Okay?"

"Okay, Doddy."

Nestling them on either side of him in his and Claire's—or only Claire's?—big bed, he opened *The Bad Dream,* one of Mercer Mayer's Critter books, and read to Hope and Charlie about a sweet and fuzzy little creature who dreams he's bad and turns into a sort of Critter Hyde with fangs and spiky hair. He acquires a gorilla sidekick and gets everything he wants, ice cream and pizza pie for breakfast. He gives up bathing, takes the other children's toys, and does, in short, whatever the hell he feels like, only to find out in the end that no one loves him anymore, and then he cries and wants his mommy, but it all turns out to be a dream.

Maybe that's what this is, too, thought Ran as he turned the pages on parental autopilot—mysterious intruders, vodou pots, black dogs, the antagonism between him and Claire—that, most of all. Last night, they seemed to have reached a truce—a place from which negotiation might begin—but here it was again tonight, hardened into old, familiar forms. And his manic depression—even after almost thirty years, it still sometimes seemed to Ran that this, too, was only a bad dream from which he'd presently awake.

As he watched the critter morph into his monster form, Ran remembered the first time it had struck him—alone in New York, not long after Delores closed the door, and Shanté, in the dormer, put her hand against the glass and watched him go; not long after Mel, at the bus station late at night, amid the tired winos and the lonely women sleeping with their handbags clutched and the drone of idling engines and the diesel smell, took a twenty from his wallet and said, "Don't spend it all in one place, hot shot," and left to be the first to go. A kid Ran met in group and never saw again gave him a thumbed paperback of *The Mysterious Stranger,* and Ran read the ending again and again till he had the words by heart. . . . "It's all a dream . . . a God who could make good children as easily as bad, yet preferred to make bad ones; who could have made every one of them happy, yet never made a happy one; who made them prize their bitter life, yet stingily cut it short. . . . You perceive *now,* that these things are all impossible except in a dream. *Nothing exists save empty space—and you!*" How Ran had loved that story! And he believed it, too, what Satan said to Theodor—every word of it rang true.

Yet reading to his children, feeling their small, warm presences leaning in, Ransom felt such solipsism was a luxury he could no longer afford. He wanted the world to offer Hope and Charlie other, better sweetnesses than the despair he'd tasted in that book and been, like Twain, too partial to.

"Doddy, what's a critter?" said Charlie as he closed the book.

"Hmm." Ran studied the illustration. "Good question, buddy. I'm not sure. What do you think?"

"I'n't know."

"Maybe it's a woodchuck."

"It's not a woodchuck, *Dad,*" Hope said, slathering his title with heavy irony.

"A groundhog?"

"Uh-uh." She tossed her locks negatingly.

"Could it be, perhaps," Ran proposed, with a trace of mincery, "a muskrat?"

"No musk cat!" Grinning, Charlie joined the game.

"Guys, you're a tough audience," he said. "A nutria? A capybara? I'm running out of options here."

"Da-ad!"

"What do *you* think, Hope?"

"They're guinea pigs," she said, simply.

"Hmm," said Ransom. "Hmm. Actually, you may be right."

"I *am* right." Her conviction was a cloudless, unwavering blue.

"Hey, Charlie-boy," he said, "is it just me, or is your sister, La Princesa, a bit full of herself? A bit big for her cat pajama britches?"

"Hmph." Hope shrugged up a shoulder and looked away, like a snooty princess on TV.

"What do you think, Charlie—does she need a tickle?"

"Yesssssssss!"

"Little or big?"

"Little . . . No, big!"

Ran made threatening claws at Hope, whose deadpan showed no signs of cracking under stress.

He went straight for the pits.

"Daddy! Daddy, *stop!*"

When Ransom did, she gave it up and squealed, "Again, Da-dee, a-*gain!*"

He arched a brow. "What, more?"

"Again!" said Charlie.

"Again! Again! Again!"

"What are you," he asked her, laughing, too, "a guiner pig?"

Behind her eyes, the little cogwheels stopped. Then, like a starfish straddling a clam, she broke the seal and sucked the tender meat. "A guiner pig! A guiner pig! Oh, Dad! Da-*dee!*" Ransom's heart went bump, as though he'd watched a tiny acrobat do her first flip on the trapeze.

"Lie down with me," she said as Ransom carried her from Charlie's room and laid her in her bed.

"Hope, it's late."

"Please, Daddy! *Please?* Just for a minute."

"One." He lay down beside her and clasped his hands behind his head.

"Daddy?"

"Go to sleep."

"I have to ask you something."

"What?"

"What happens when we die?"

Oh, Jesus, Ransom thought. "I don't know, Pete. Some people say we have a soul inside us, and when we die it leaves and goes to live with God."

"Do our bodies go, too?"

"No, we leave those here. Just our souls or spirits go."

"What's a spirit?"

Ransom sighed. "It's hard to explain, Hope. You see this lamp? If the lightbulb is your body, then your spirit's sort of like the light that shines out through the glass." He tapped the bulb. "Even when the bulb wears out or breaks, the light goes on and on. Some people believe it goes to heaven and stays there. Others think it goes to a sort of waiting place, then gets reborn into another, different body. When we come back to earth, we don't remember who we were before. Some very special people may, but not most of us."

"Do you remember, Daddy?"

"No, sweetheart, I don't."

"Will you die, Daddy?"

He hesitated. "Someday, sweetie. Hopefully, not for a long time."

"I don't want you to."

He turned and looked at her small face on the pillow. "I don't want to go. But by then I expect you'll be a grown woman as old as Mommy and Daddy are now with children of your own. You don't need to worry about this, okay? I'll stay as long as I can."

"You promise?"

"I promise," Ransom said, and his voice was suddenly husky.

"Daddy?"

"What?"

"I know a joke."

"Let's hear it."

"Knock, knock."

"Who's there?"

"Orange."

"Orange, who?"

"Orange you glad to see me?"

Ran laughed foolishly at this.

"Daddy?"

"*What?*"

And just that quickly, she was gone. As he reached across and turned the lamp off, he remembered Abner Gant coming up at his father's funeral.

"He never missed a day of work," he said, and that was it, the one ray of light that escaped the black hole of Mel's life. Lying there, Ran suddenly wondered what his little girl would say of him. What would Charlie? Claire?

Downstairs, she laughed a laugh he hadn't heard in longer than he cared to think about, and Ran thought about the time she'd come to Killdeer right before the wedding. Mel, dying then and drinking harder than ever, asked her if she wanted one—like the leper in *Papillon* offering his cigar to Steve McQueen—and Claire DeLay from Charleston, in her sleeveless linen dress, with her yellow cashmere sweater tied around her neck, said, "Sure, why not?" and tossed back a shot of Chateau Shotgun Shack, said, *"Ahhh,"* and wiped her hand across her mouth. Mel's eyes moistened like an old hound's when its master walks into the room, slain by the same thing that slew his son. Mel opened up and told her about the farm where he grew up, about suckering and tobacco worms and riding a canvas drag of primed leaves to the barn behind Commander, his daddy's mule, and Ransom, who had never heard these stories, never heard his father speak twenty consecutive words, listened from the kitchen, amazed, and finally hurt. He went out on the kitchen steps to smoke and stared at the old Thunderbird, still up on blocks, and when Mel fell asleep, Claire found him there.

"So," he said, "I guess you're going to tell me he's not that bad after all."

"No, he's pretty bad."

"So now you know."

"Now I know."

"It's not too late to call it off."

Claire laughed and Ransom studied her with his sad, soulful stare and understood she thought he was joking.

He'd always wanted to give his old man the kind of compassion Claire showed that afternoon, but the best Ran had been able to come up with was to write a check to have the Thunderbird restored. When he pulled it to the curb, the whole block had turned out to look, and Ran was nursing fantasies of Mel like a kid with a new bike, kicking the tires, dying to take her for a spin. Instead, his father walked around the car without a word, picked a fleck of paste wax the detailer had missed off the Continental spare, stared at it on his fingertip, then turned that haunted stare on Ran, not only without gratitude, but with more resentment than before. It took him a long time to understand that Mel, by then, was past the point of wanting the car fixed, if indeed he ever had, and that its brokenness was part, perhaps the most part, of what he loved, and Ran had taken that away. So Mel died, and the sort of simple interchange Claire had with him that day never passed between him and his son.

Remembering this, Ran realized that in the same way he'd forgotten or lost touch with his True Self, he'd also forgotten Claire's, who she'd been that day without even trying. *I think you make it awful hard on Claire*—Cell's words came back, and Ransom, with a heavy pang of ownership, realized it was true. And as he lay beside his sleeping daughter in her narrow bed, it came home to him, not as a thought, but as a stabbing pang in his left side, that what Claire and Cell had told him, the other thing, was also true: *I am a racist,* he thought. Somewhere, in some deep corner of himself, never fully challenged or expunged, he was, and having loved Shanté first, and maybe even best, did not exonerate him.

Yet it seemed to Ran that he could take this on as well, that along with all the rest, he could find a way to be a friend to Cell again as well as the father Hope and Charlie needed and the husband Claire deserved. Maybe it was not too late to be that other, better man he'd always believed he could be and had never actually been. And in the process, maybe he could write that hit song, too. As he lay there, Ransom's heart was full, and he realized this was the answer to Claire's question, the one she'd asked last night, *Why are you here?*

And he wanted to tell her this; it seemed important to do it now and not to wait. The first step was to come clean about his meds. He was on the landing, starting down, when he caught sight of them in the gilded foyer mirror. Claire and Cell were in the library. He was seated at the partners desk, reading from a book. Claire stood behind him, and as Ransom watched, she raised her hand and rested it lightly on his shoulder, just lightly, familiarly lifted it and left it there. There was nothing untoward in the gesture, yet Ransom tried to swallow and suddenly could not. And at that moment, the laundry hamper, the one from her story, caught his eye. For some reason, his glance was drawn to it like iron filings to a magnet. The wicker creel was full, and in the top of it were Claire's hot pink underpants, the bold new lingerie upgrade he'd assumed was meant for him.

The floor began to desolidify beneath his feet, and when Claire laughed again, it was a laugh he didn't know, from some place so old and deep he'd never been admitted there at all, and when Cell looked up at her and smiled, it was no longer Cell, and the woman who smiled back, whose hair shone blond in the deceiving portrait lights, was no longer Ransom's wife.

TWENTY-TWO

*A*ddie *runs and stumbles, stumbles, runs. Her hem is drenched. Her hair is all about her face.* What has Harlan done? *She speaks the thought aloud.* "What has Harlan done to me?" *She's sobbing now; her hands are at her mouth. She shakes her head, and then her eyes are dry, and he's as absent from her thoughts as he was three months ago before she even knew his name. It's a long time before she thinks about the path. By the time she looks, it's lost. The path is lost, and so is Addie, irretrievably, and dark is falling fast.*

She comes into a clearing, into different air. It's warmer here—there's a little rise of ground—but suddenly she feels cold. There's gooseflesh on her arms. Rubbing up and down, she has a sudden flash of Percival—"That means they are close, niña"— but quickly shoves it down. A faint, wet quashing accompanies Addie as she goes, a sound she takes for her wet shoes. There's a blackened circle from some old fire and the fallen carcass of a tree—is it a cypress?—so large that four people holding hands might encompass it, but only just. Insects and rot have mined a cavity in the trunk, and as the slant rays of the setting sun fall into the black cave, something glitters on the floor, winking amber, green, and blue. Peering cautiously in—her hand is on her breast now, her finger at the button—she sees bits of broken bottle glass, unfamiliar coins, and what look like horehound candies, the little ones in paper twists her aunt throws by the handful every Christmas morning to the eager children in the yard. On the floor of the cave is a design in chalk and streaks and smears of some orange

substance like the fat that rises in a pot of cooling soup. There are candles and brimming goblets, as there were on Percival's bóveda, but there are other things as well,
things she did not see there—a rusty knife, a cigar, half smoked, a bottle of dark
rum—and Paloma's plate, the good bone-china one she held when Addie first caught
sight of her in urgent conference with Clarisse. The leeches are still there—still,
there—arranged in the pattern of an X. Each has been penetrated, one by a nail, another by an animal's curved, sharpened bone, a third by a needle and thread; they
loom like soft islands in the lake of Percival's black blood, which leaks its smell into
the air, a smell like rotting meat and copper, along with something thick and sickly
sweet like roses. On the margin of this lake, a single blowsy fly sits, rubbing its
hands. The feeling here is not like Percival's bóveda in the least.

And now her eye is drawn to the deep interior, to something hulking near the
rear wall of the cave. It looks, briefly, almost like a human form, but as her eyes ad-
just, she realizes she's staring at a cloth, a black cloth draped on something underneath. From its upper edge, a branch protrudes, a mottled green and white, like
sycamore. On it is a single twig, and on that twig a single, shriveled leaf. Lower, she
sees the ribbed tip of an ivory horn, and at the level of the floor, a metal foot, animal
in shape—like some large jungle cat, a jaguar or a leopard—and the round black
belly of what appears to be an iron pot . . . one might say a cauldron.

Fear is raging like a wildfire through her senses, but Addie tells herself it's just
some Negro thing, something put here by the slaves, some superstition, like the broom
at weddings. . . . But then she gazes into a depression in the wood as deep as her
cupped hands and sees her own face staring back—not a reflection. Harlan's is there,
too. It's the miniature she commissioned of the two of them, in tempera on ivory, and
gave as an engagement gift. It's been submerged in water, and the rusty knife has
been stabbed into the hinge, cleaving them apart. Clarisse, she thinks, Clarisse did
this, and she feels something stealing over her like madness. In some part of herself,
she half wonders if this is a dream but knows it's not. And it's only now that Addie
notices that the sound she heard before is coming from within the cave, behind the
cloth, and the curious thing is, she isn't moving now. Addie's standing still, dead still,
listening with every fiber, and the sound seems less like footsteps on a muddy path
than something eating, like Sultan, Harlan's bloodhound, off in the corner of the
pen, gnawing his wet bone. And as the hound, sensing an intruder, might stop and
look up from its paws, so this thing now, inside the pot, senses her and stops. She can
feel its alien awareness fixed on her, and it is dour, old, and strong, unspeakably. A
taste she can't identify, a bad taste, fills her mouth, and suddenly she's sweating, not
perspiring, sweating rivers. The whole forest has grown still. No wind blows. No bird

sings. There's only the drowsy buzzing of the fly on the plate rim. As she looks down at her arm, a mosquito lights, and Addie, thinking she should swat it, merely watches as it does its business and flies off into the gloom with a thin whine. Standing here, she has the sudden visceral conviction that the life around her, all the green life of the swamp and of the world itself, including hers, is like a thin skim floating on a deep black pond, and the pond is death. And death is old and fathomlessly deep and life is new and tenuous and thin, and anything—a tossed stone, a breath of wind— could rouse those still black waters, and life, beneath that wave of blood, would cease.

This is evil. *The voice speaks in Addie's mind, and she becomes aware there's something watching her. It's in the tree above her head. For a moment, Addie can't tell what it is. It's like nothing she's ever seen, but then it moves, its feathers give off oily gleams, and Addie sees it is a large black crow. It turns its head, regarding her severely from its polished obsidian eye; then, with an angry caw, it spreads its wings and flies off, croaking, through the trees.*

Addie starts to run again. The last light leaves. She runs and runs until she can't run anymore and then falls, panting, to her knees. She lies, facedown, where she falls, her cheek against the ground. Somehow this position eases her. She's afraid to move, afraid that motion might reawaken her distress. Her heartbeat lifts her up and down, a little less each time. She falls asleep and dreams she's arguing with Harlan. It's a bitter fight. "What have you done to me?"

Her own cry awakens her, and she sits bolt upright, thinking of Clarisse, her manner on the porch. What is between them—this is crystal clear to Addie now—is something old, not new. And the others—Paloma, Jarry, Percival—they all know. Of course they do. "Stanzas to Augusta," Jarry's look—this is what it meant. When she stepped off the gangway onto shore, he knew what she was stepping into. The Negro brother pitied her, but Harlan, the good white son, smiled and let her come. And why? Why, she thinks, did Harlan marry me? Addie cannot answer it. All she knows is that no human being, no enemy, has given her as hard and cruel a blow as her new husband, who vowed to love and honor her, who was supposed to cherish her and hold her dear. In the moment, Addie doesn't know if she can bear up under it and live.

Night has fallen now. The old moon, like a hard mint that has been sucked thin, is setting over the trees, where cicadas chirr their long, uninterrupted note, and mole crickets, their broken, intermittent ones. Addie is wet and starts to shiver. The April night is cold, and cold becomes an agony she can barely stand. And yet she does stand it, and gradually the shivering stops, and she no longer feels the cold, feels almost warm, in fact. Something in her—not the self she mostly knows—something she remembers, though not from where, makes peace with the cold on her behalf. And now here, in the dark, trilling forest, as the old moon sinks, the voice begins to speak again, more clearly. It doesn't say, You've been betrayed. It doesn't answer why or what it means. It says, You married without love. *And unlike yesterday, when the voice seemed an imposition, a sparrow to be shooed out of the house, now, as Addie's thoughts slow down, as anger cools, she listens and replies. You're right. She says the words aloud. "You're right, I did." And then the next phrase in the conversation comes. "I'm lost. I have forgotten how to live." Addie thought she came to Wando Passo for a new life to begin, but now it seems that something brought her here for her old life to end. She starts to cry. There's sadness here, and it is deep, but, deeper still, the truth, long feared, upon arrival, proves a relief. "I'm lost. I have forgotten how to live." She repeats it like a prayer, to what or whom she doesn't know. What Addie knows, and all she knows, is it's the one true prayer that's ever passed her lips.*

Compared to it, the words she spoke in church, the vows that she exchanged with Harlan at the altar at St. Michael's, "I take her . . . him . . . for richer and for poorer, in sickness and in health, till death do us part," are like something muttered in a dream. It comes to her that, once upon a time, someone who believed as she believes right now made up those words and then told others to believe and speak them, too. But those words were true just once, for that one person in the crucial, stinging hour of belief—not anymore. Now those words are dead, and when she and Harlan sleepwalked down the aisle and spoke them at the altar, they were just talking in their sleep. The only words that are fully wakeful and alive for Addie now are those she's learned and ceaselessly repeats. And then she asks the question, "Will you help me?" and the voice she knows but doesn't know from where says, Yes.

This is where Addie is when the first cock crows, and, hours later, when the gray light in the east turns celadon and silhouettes the trees. She's on the edge of the water meadow she passed last night, or another like it. It's carpeted with lily pads, sending up their celery-green stalks, hundreds of vertical brushstrokes, each culminating in a flag of yellow flower, all inclining the same way on the same breeze. There are wild roses on the bank, and scarlet lobelia. There are ferns and pink saltatia, and birds flitting over the water, streaks of canary yellow, blue, and red, and all around her on the ground is a dark green vine she's never seen before, with tiny white flowers whose scent is that of orange blossoms. And it's as if the world Addie knew has been destroyed, and, overnight, another, fresh, has been created to replace it, or as if Addie herself has been destroyed, and her destruction has allowed her to see the world that always was, only this is deeper than seeing. She beholds.

Addie has no wish to leave, or ever to return to that other, prior world, but then she hears them start to call for her. She hears the deep note of the horn, and in the distance, dogs begin to bark. It isn't long before Sultan and another hound appear out of the trees, their sad old heads—like something time has both compressed and stretched—looking oddly out of place on their lithe bodies. They're followed shortly by a man on horseback. It's Jarry. She is not surprised, but Jarry clearly is. Dismounting with his horse in stride, he lets it stop itself and runs to her.

"Are you all right?"

"Yes, I'm all right."

"Thank God." He goes down on his hams in front of her. "We were afraid you'd drowned. Did you not hear us call?"

"I heard."

He pauses at her tone. The hounds, with swifter intuition, begin to wag their tails. They make a happy rush and lap her face, and she, enduring it, closes her eyes and lifts her chin. "Such charity," she says, gently pushing them away.

"Have you been here all night?"

"Much of it."

"You must be freezing."

She shakes her head, but Jarry drapes his coat across her shoulders nonetheless. "We should let them know."

"Not yet," she says, and Addie's cold, smooth face, for the first time, looks haggard. Fatigue swirls up into her eyes, like mud in a clear pool. "Please?"

He reaches out and lays a hand—not his whole hand, just a finger, the middle one, and just the tip of that—on her shoulder. Its pressure is so light that Addie might not be aware of it unless she saw it there. Yet her body, which is clenched from the long night against the cold, opens like a bud to flower, sensing kindness with an intuition like the hounds'. Slowly, softly, she begins to cry.

Jarry's whole face concentrates. His eyes fill with sympathy.

"I saw them," Addie says. "I followed him to the cottage. You told me not to, but I did."

His look is grave. He rests his whole hand on her shoulder now. He doesn't look away. "I'm sorry. I'm so sorry. I'm afraid you may have taken fever."

She shakes her head, but Jarry reaches out, and Addie sees the old scar on the underside of his left wrist. Her eyes go somber over it. They seek his out, but from some innate delicacy, he turns his hand, as though to hide what she already sees. With the back of his wrist, he touches her brow, a gesture brief and wholly circumspect, yet no man has ever touched her there. A conversation occurs between them, with troubled implication given and troubling inference received, in a single wordless glance.

"Why did he marry me?"

"To save himself." Now Jarry sits.

Addie, who does not expect an answer, certainly not one so sure and swift as this, gazes into his eyes and weighs the truth of it.

"From her?"

He nods just once.

"That's why you gave me the poem. . . ."

"I gave it you because you were innocent and deserved the truth."

Her eyes brim, showing him the gratitude she doesn't speak. "There's something I must tell you. . . ."

"There's something I must tell you, too," *he says.* "Father died last night."

"What? Jarry, no!" *Her hand goes to his arm.* "Oh, Jarry, I'm so sorry. And here you are, out chasing me. We should go back."

"Yes," *he agrees, yet neither makes a move to leave.* "Mother found him a little while ago. He had this strange expression on his face, as though something had come into the room, and whatever it was, it wasn't what he was expecting."

As the news settles, she lets her hand rest where it was. "I think he was ready, Jarry. He spoke to me about it. He seemed more curious than afraid. I hope, when my time comes, I can be half as brave."

He makes no answer, gazing out over the water meadow, arms circling his knees. A time passes in silence there's no need to relieve. "There's a verse," *he says eventually.* "It's been playing through my head for weeks. . . .

" 'The old man still stood talking by my side,
But now his words to me were like a stream
Scarce heard; nor word from word could I divide.
And the whole body of the man did seem . . .' "

Briefly, emotion overcomes him, and Addie allows her grip to tighten on his arm till it subsides.

" 'And the whole body of the man did seem
Like one whom I had met with in a dream,
Or like a man from some far region sent
To give me human strength. . . .' "

"It's all right, Jarry. . . ."

He shakes his head and cannot finish it.

"What is the poem?" she asks him, when a decent interval has passed.

" 'Resolution and Independence.' That was the first poem he ever read to me."

"How old were you?"

"Fifteen."

"You were close. . . ."

He shakes his head and wipes his eyes. "I hated him. Our friendship began over that poem."

This is the moment Addie will remember, when she beholds who Jarry is, and it is not as a black man, not even as a man, that she recognizes him, but as a being like herself in a way no one has been before. Like a tuning fork that has lain inert till now, something in her rings responsively, as it hears, for the first time, the true, specific note that it was forged to answer. Her expression as she looks at him is no longer wan and drained. Her eyes have regained their depths. She nods to the snippet of green vine he's plucked and is unconsciously twirling in his hand. "All morning I've breathed the scent of that and wondered what it was."

"It's partridgeberry. The old folks call it lovers' vine."

Addie blushes, but holds his stare. "Why do they call it that?"

He lifts the two white blooms. "When these flowers drop, they form a single berry with two eyes."

The fatigue in him, Addie realizes now, is beautiful.

Jarry hands the snip to her. "What is it you wished to tell me?"

Now her expression drops as she recalls. "Last night I saw something, Jarry. In the swamp, as I was running. It was hidden in the hollow of a tree. It frightened me."

"What did you see?"

"It was a pot, I think. It was partly covered, but I think it was an iron pot. And there were things in it."

"What things?" His tone is suddenly grave.

"Horns," she says. "The horns of some animal, a ram, perhaps. Links of chain. The limbs of certain trees. Harlan's locket, too—the one I gave him as a wedding gift. A knife was driven through the hinge."

He frowns and ponders. "Could you find the place again?"

"I don't know. It was dark. I think I came from there." She points, and Jarry searches till he finds her prints in the wet ground. Leading the horse, they backtrack, walking silently. After fifteen minutes, they reach the rise of ground, the fallen tree.

"There," says Addie solemnly, pointing to the hollow.

Jarry peers inside and blinks. He shelves his eyes to see, then turns to her with a blank expression.

"What?"

"There's nothing here."

"That can't be." She joins him now to look. *"It was here last night, Jarry. I know it was."*

With the nail of his index finger, Jarry picks up something small and shiny from the floor. He holds it to the light. It's a dime, a silver dime, incised with Seated Liberty.

"I don't understand," she says. *"I'm sure this was the place."*

"Come," he says. *"We need to tell my mother this."* Mounting, he reaches her a hand and swings her up behind.

For a moment, Addie feels the awkwardness of where to put her hands, but when the horse starts off, the motion throws her toward him and she puts her arms around his waist. As they ride in silence, the voice she knows but doesn't know from where, the one she asked for help, which whispered yes, now tells her, as she lets her tired head fall on Jarry's back, This is the help you're to receive.

"But, Jarry," she says as they reach the drive and slow down to a walk. *"Jarry! It's just occurred to me—you're free!"*

"No," he says, *"the will is gone. Mother searched the desk this morning. It isn't there."*

"No, but, listen," Addie says excitedly. *"Listen, Jarry . . ."*

He turns partway to face her in the saddle.

"Addie!"

At this moment, Harlan's cry breaks in on them, and they turn toward the house as he steps onto the piazza. Seeing his glassy eyes and brooding face—he appears to have been waiting for some time—Addie never gets the chance to speak.

TWENTY-THREE

*M*arcel saw the silhouette reflected in the gleaming oils of Addie's portrait and was the first to turn his head. "Hey, Ran."

Ransom, from the doorway, answered, "Hey."

Claire looked around. "The kids asleep?"

"Yeah, they are."

"Is something the matter?"

"Actually, I don't know."

She studied him. "Well, are you going to stand there speaking koans, or are you coming in? We're looking at this poem you found."

"You guys go ahead."

He turned away, but she came after him and caught his arm. "Ransom, come sit down. What's wrong with you?"

"Nothing," he said. "I'm just going to take a walk."

"Where's the Purdey? I saw it isn't on the wall."

This took him by surprise. His morning outing seemed like something from a prior era now. "I guess I left it in the yard."

"What were you doing with it in the yard?"

"I wanted to see if it still worked."

Claire frowned. "And does it?"

"Yeah," he said. "Actually, it works quite well."

With that, he left the pair of them to puzzle out the terms of the old text and took the back way out. The air was like a humid, faintly cool caress. In no mood to be touched, Ran walked away from the illuminated house into a hoarse euphony of katydids and peepers, beneath a black sky smeared with stars.

Retracing his steps, he made a perfunctory search and failed to find the shotgun. But it was dark, and he was too disturbed to try that hard.

A waning gibbous moon was rising over the swamp. As he approached the hole he'd dug that afternoon, a coal-black silhouette materialized against a screen of shimmering light. It took Ran barely a second, maybe only half, to realize it was his reflection in a pool the thunderstorm had left, but for that second, that half of one, the figure staring up resembled someone else.

And what if it doesn't happen, Hill? What if that happy future you've imagined doesn't come to pass?

The questions were his own—Ran knew full well they were—yet it almost seemed the figure in the pool whispered or somehow insinuated them into his mind. His thoughts were becoming more and more abnormal—Ransom watched and knew the warning signs: chief among them, the fact that the further they deviated from normality the truer they began to seem, not in the common way, but with some harder, higher truth difficult to achieve, and once achieved, more difficult to stand. This dark other in the pool was not a stranger, nor a friend. He and Ransom were acquainted from way back, and Ran had been on the run from this encounter for some time.

And what happens when you find me?

"Sorry, bub," Ran said aloud, "but what I'm interested in finding isn't you."

So what are you interested in finding—your "True Self"? the voice asked with a trace of hurtful scorn. *Would you even know the thing to see it? And who's to say that I'm not he?*

"I guess I'll have to go with my gut hunch."

That's really stood you in good stead so far.

"Fuck off," said Ran halfheartedly, suddenly having trouble remembering which voice in the conversation was his own, and why it mattered, if indeed it did.

Entering the graveyard by the creaking gate, he sat down on a crypt, demoralized and out of gas. And now his sadness and his fears washed over him, and Ransom let them come. What if he lost Claire and the children? What if that sense of throbbing vividness she'd radiated at the airport yesterday came not from happiness at seeing him, not from being mistress of her own demesne again, but from loving someone else? What if however much he wanted it to work, however hard he was prepared to try no longer mattered? What if Claire was out of reach? The thought that she might give her heart to someone else had somehow not occurred to him in all these months—much less that she might give it to Marcel. And why? Because Marcel was black? Whether this had weighed with Claire at seventeen, Ran didn't know; yet its deterrent value on the woman she was now, at forty-two, was clear to him: the answer being none at all, and maybe somewhat less.

And what would Ransom do if it was true? Return to New York City and the cab? Pick up his dinner at the Korean deli salad bar on the way back from the garage each night? Take it home to the empty apartment? Drink too much wine while Maria Callas sang "Vissi d'arte" in the background, or listen to CDs—Neutral Milk Hotel and Manitoba, Cannibal Ox, the Wrens, this month's crop of hot young bands, kids with talent, prepared to bleed, knowing in his heart that they were now where he and RHB were then, thinking they were going to be the Beatles or the Stones, knowing, unlike them, that it would never happen. To return to that small, bitter life without the dream of love and family that had sustained him through the last few months . . . Ransom didn't know how he could face it, if he would.

Deep inside him, something Ran had never felt before, or not in a long time, began to stir. It was like a seismic tremor, like a trembling in the rails, like the coils of a great snake thrashing awake after a long sleep, and all these things—snake, volcano, locomotive—were one thing: rage, the rage of one who, all his life, had tried to give his best—to his music, his marriage, his family and, not least, his wife—only to find his best was not enough. Wasn't good enough.

Gripping the edge of the cold slab, Ran looked down at the chisel marks the slantlight of the moon had filled with fresh black ink. . . .

CAPT. HARLAN P. DELAY
21ST SOUTH CAROLINA, C.S.A.
b. Dec. 8, 1820 d. September 1, 1863
Fallen in Defense of Home and Country
Resting Now in Patient Hope
Of Resurrection

Wasn't he the one—the name tugged at Ransom's memory—the one from Claire's story, who came home from the war and disappeared with Adelaide, his wife? How, then, did he come to be here? Ran's first thought was that there was some mix-up. Then the answer dawned. There was no one here, nobody in this tomb. No body. Adelaide had buried him—must have—when he was listed killed in action. Then he came home, and . . . what? Walked into the park one afternoon, into the dappled light that fell through the old oaks and magnolias, and found his own name on the new tombstone in the family plot. And what would that be like, Ran wondered, to come home from some Northern prison, after years of suffering and privation, to find your wife has grieved and buried you and moved on with her life?

At the sound of footsteps, a faint, wet quashing on the rain-soaked ground, he turned, but there was nobody there. No body.

The kitchen screen slammed at the house, and suddenly there were voices, real ones, on the porch.

"Ransom? Oh, *Ran*-som?"

He recognized the tipsy humor in her voice and started to answer, then didn't as Marcel came out.

"Where do you suppose he is?"

"No idea."

"Out giving his new broomstick a spin?"

"I wouldn't rule it out."

"Maybe he and Nightmare, his trusty steed, are taking a midnight gambol around the fence lines."

"Also possible," said Cell, following her down the steps into the drive.

"I hate it when you humor me."

"Is that what I'm doing?"

"Yes," she said, turning toward him at his car, "it is. After thirty years, I ought to know."

"I guess you should." Cell left a silent beat before he asked, "Will you be okay?"

"Yeah, I think so. Thanks for coming. I really appreciate it, Cell."

"I had a nice time."

"Vodou pots and all?"

"Vodou pots and all."

"Well, you're a liar, but a pretty nice one."

"I'm glad you think so. It was interesting."

"Interesting . . . Uh-huh."

Ran expected them to laugh, but neither did. He took the moment hard, the next one even harder. . . .

"I guess I'll see you in the morning then." Marcel stood, expectantly, beside his open door, as though their business remained to be concluded.

"I guess you will." Looking up at him, Claire cradled her arms across her front, something she did when she was cold. The gesture somehow made her young.

Ransom watched this like a dream, a spell, a hologram of people long dead or not yet born sent forward or back through time to enact some fateful moment long concluded or still to come. Then Claire rocked up on her tiptoes and simply kissed his cheek.

"Good night," she said, and he climbed in.

She watched his brake lights flash and dim in the allée and went inside, and Ran got up and followed her; through the door, down the hall, up the grand staircase, beneath the chandelier on its fifty pounds of sterling links. The portraits of the ancestors looked down on him, unsmiling, a jury, not of his peers.

What are you going to do? the voice inside him asked.

"Just talk," he said, annoyed at its disingenuous alarm. As if there were any question of something other, something more.

The dead DeLays regarded his upward progress with suspicion and did not seem reassured.

The upstairs hall was dark, and the bathroom door was parted. Standing just outside, Ransom listened to the iron ring of rain in the old tub, then pushed the door. A cloud of warm mist billowed toward him, then he saw her through the bloom of condensation on the transparent shower curtain. Her body was white, but not really—really, there were shades of ivory, pinks, soft yellows, brown hair up and down. Her nipples and her lips were different strokes of the same brush, a slash less red than umber, a period stabbed home, and twisted.

"Claire?"

She didn't hear.

"Claire?"

Still nothing.

"Claire!"

She jumped. "Shit, Ransom!" She poked her face though the curtain. "Who are you, the midnight rambler? Where did you go?"

Out for a midnight gambol with Nightmare, my trusty steed, the voice suggested. He vetoed the proposal. "I took a walk," he said. "I think we need to talk. . . ."

TWENTY-FOUR

*W*hat is there to say?" she asks him in the bedroom. "I saw you kiss her mouth. I saw Clarisse kiss you. Unless you can persuade me to disregard the evidence of my own senses, my two eyes . . ."

"I can't," says Harlan. "I don't intend to try. You saw what you saw, and I regret what you saw. I regret the pain I've caused. But I must tell you, Addie, you don't understand what you saw. You don't begin to understand. . . ."

"What don't I understand?" she interrupts. "Is it your intention to have a Negro mistress in the cottage and a white wife at the house? Did you expect me to consent to such arrangements?"

"That is not my intention, madam. It has never been my intention. You are groping in the dark. You are miles from a true understanding of the case. If you'll attempt to calm yourself and let me speak, I will explain. If, when I conclude, you wish to leave, I won't stand in your way. My hope, though, Addie, my fervent hope, is otherwise. My hope is that you'll stand by me and fight for me, as I intend to stand and fight for you. Despite appearances, I'm fighting for you now."

Her laugh is sharp. "You are right! You are so right! Spending the night—our wedding night—in another woman's bed does not give the appearance that you are fighting for your wife!"

"I didn't spend it there by choice."

"I see," she says. "Her charms, then, her Cuban charms, are simply such that you were helpless to resist. . . ."

"I am bewitched."

Addie's eyes widen. She starts to laugh again. Her mouth actually falls open to emit the laugh, but something in Harlan's sobriety stops her. He isn't sweating now, isn't making the large, emphatic gestures of the hands. Some new self-possession has stolen over him. Is it his father's death? Whether that or something else, his hazy ginger eyes, for once, are clear. His expression is that of a man in contemplation of a peril, not panicked before it, but serious, alert. A thought flies through Addie's mind—the clearing in the woods and what she saw inside the hollow of the tree . . . The small, clawed feet of fear skitter up her spine like mice. Yet she can't take his assertion without contest.

"You are bewitched," she repeats with scorn.

"You smile, madam. But it's no laughing matter, I assure you. Will you hear me?"

Addie won't give him the satisfaction of an answer. Her heart is set against him now. Yet what choice does she have except to listen, and Harlan reads her face and sees she has no choice.

"For you to grasp this matter . . . I must take you back," he says, lighting his cigar, ". . . to the beginning. I ask you to remember, Addie, that my memory of Clarisse, my sole childhood memory, is of a swaddled bundle in Paloma's arms, a voice that, at the quinta, sometimes woke me in the night. I was six the day we sailed for Charleston. Father and Paloma were both there. The bundle wasn't. There was no more crying in the night. I didn't see Clarisse again till I was thirty-three.

"She was raised at La Mella, in Villa-Urrutia's household. I've told you this before, but what is crucial for you to understand is that Paloma was pregnant when Father won her, but the child, by law and right, belonged to Wenceslao. The Count, as you may readily imagine, wasn't pleased to lose his slave and favorite mistress and was certainly in no mood, no mood at all, to toss Clarisse, as further lagniappe, into Father's pile. So Paloma came with Father, but Clarisse, when she was born, went back to Wenceslao, and the old Count found her charming, by reports. She is beautiful, I think you can agree. . . ."

"Yes," says Addie, clipped.

"And charming, when she has a mind. And the Conde, you see, was old, Addie. His other children were all grown. So she became his pet. He raised her as his own, sent her to the Franciscans in Guanabacoa, spoiled her, allowed her to dress like a marquise, and at his death, he set her free and left her little but her wardrobe and her jewels. I knew nothing of this situation, Addie. The day I sailed for Cuba to apprentice, on the very wharf, Father took me aside and pressed an envelope into my hand. In it were a name and an address, a sum of cash. He told me the story in no

*greater detail than I'm telling you right now. A good deal less, in fact. He asked me
to seek her out, to settle the sum upon her, to help her if I could. Understand, Addie,
at that point in time, eight years ago, Clarisse was no more than a name to me, the
Negro daughter of my father's Negro concubine.*

*"But Cuba is different, Addie, as I said before. I began to feel the change some
miles in the offing, while still at sea. The warm south wind off the island brought
a smell of spice, of poinciana. I felt a kind of spell steal over me. At the docks, my
first moment there, I was almost run down by a quitrín. The Negro coachman, the
calesero, in his top hat and silver spurs, made some rude call in Spanish and raised
his whip to frighten me. Me, a white man. Through the window, Addie, as the carriage clattered past, I saw a dark-faced woman, a mulatto or quadroon. She was
wearing silks and jewels, sitting regally on the upholstered bench. She gazed at me
with cutting eyes, as though I deserved to be run down for having the temerity to
interrupt her progress. In Charleston, she and her coachman would have been
taken out and whipped. There, it was a wholly unremarkable event for them to
treat a white man as an object of contempt. I did not know where I was. I felt my
moorings slip.*

*"I wrote Clarisse and asked to meet. She suggested the opera. She said I'd
know her by the flower in her hair, so there I was, Addie, in the street before Tacón's
at eight o'clock at night. The volantes rolled up as before, filled with elegant, well-
dressed men and women. There was hardly a face without some shade of brown,
whether of Spain or Africa—how was one to know? No one seemed to care but me.
And the girls . . . There were scores of them, perhaps some hundreds, all dressed in
the identical style, in white dresses, with lace mantillas on their shoulders, and each
and every one of them, Addie, without exception, wore a flower in her hair. Madam,
I was in a swivet! I turned this way and that. I was perspiring. Not to put too fine a
point on it, I was sweating like a hog! Women picked up their skirts and hurried
past, casting poisoned looks at me. Officers seemed prepared to draw their swords and
run the madman through! And then I saw her, Addie. . . . No, no, at first I didn't
know it was Clarisse. You saw her—would you guess she had a drop of Negro
blood? She was standing in the shadow of a pier, by torchlight, laughing, Addie, this
beautiful, elegant young woman dressed in evening dress, laughing at my frantic exercise. I went up to her, and I was fuming. Do you understand? I meant to give it to
her straight, no water and no ice! Yet she couldn't stop. She tried to stop. She'd hold
her breath for ten or fifteen seconds, but then she'd look at me and that would set her
off again. And I don't know what it was, Addie, even now, I truly don't, but after
two or three such volleys, I started laughing, too. We stood there shaking, literally*

shaking in the street before Tacón's, as the glittering crowd flowed past, giving us wide berth. We were racked with laughter for five minutes, five minutes and a half, before we introduced ourselves or spoke a single word. And what am I to tell you—I'd never had such an encounter with a woman in my life, nor have I since. And when we finally recovered and began to speak, it was not in the diffident and tentative way of new acquaintances; it was as though we'd known each other all our lives. I spoke to her about my mother, Addie, whom I never speak about. . . ."

"Certainly not to me . . ."

"No, Addie, you're right, not to you or anyone, and hardly to myself. Yet, with Clarisse, in the first quarter of an hour, I told the story of her illness and death. I felt some permission, and as I spoke, her eyes brimmed with tears. I saw she understood what that had been to me, a boy of five. We were still there in the gallery, walking up and down, at intermission, and when the final curtain fell. It was as if no time had passed at all. It seemed innocent, Addie. I didn't call it love. It was weeks before I called it that. I only knew a sense of buoyancy had stolen over me. It was as if, finally, I'd discovered what living was, and I was grateful and didn't ask its name. . . ."

"And can you possibly imagine I wish to hear this?" she asks him wretchedly. "Is it your intention to torture me?"

"No, my dear. No, Addie, not at all." He sits beside her on the bed and tries to take her hands, but she refuses. "My sole intention is to make you understand what happened, how it's led to the predicament we're in. May I go on?"

"Yes, yes," she says. "Yes, if I must hear it, and I suppose I must."

There is tenderness in his expression now, tenderness, compassion, and regret. "You see, Addie, when I look into your eyes," he says, "I see suspicion and distaste. I see a person I don't like or want to be, yet fear I am, have always feared I was. I've helped to put that image there, I know. But, in Clarisse's eyes, I saw someone strong and capable, someone generous and full of life, who made her laugh. With her, I saw a person I've never been but always wanted to believe I might become. Perhaps you've never had such feelings, Addie. If you have, I don't deceive myself they were for me."

This is the help you're to receive. . . . *The voice she heard with Jarry on the horse ride through the swamp comes back, and now the nerve is struck. And so, as Harlan speaks, she listens with a double mind.*

"It was the most shattering thing that's ever happened in my life," he continues. "And this went on. Day by day, it grew. And there came a point when it appeared to me that there was no way back. I decided to forgo my inheritance and stay with her in Cuba, and I was happy in the contemplation of that life. I asked Clarisse to be my wife. It never dawned on me that she might hesitate, and yet she did. She said, 'I love you, Harlan, but there are things I haven't shared with you, important things, things I've been afraid to say. I see that you must know them now.'

" 'Tell me, then,' I said. 'For God's sake, tell me now.'

"But she shook her head and put her finger to my lips. She whispered, 'Shhh. There are some things you can speak, and others you can only show.'

"That weekend, we traveled to Matanzas, out to the plantation. Her half brother had inherited La Mella and ran it as an absentee, so there was no one in the house but us. To be clear, Addie, we'd been chaste until that time, and this was by Clarisse's choice, not mine. That night we slept in separate rooms in separate wings. On Sunday morning, the sound of drumming awakened me a little past first light. Shortly after, Clarisse knocked on my door. Understand, Addie, in all the time I'd known her, she'd dressed the way she had that first night at Tacón's, like an unmarried Cuban girl of good descent. That morning she was someone else. She had a printed headscarf on, a red and green one of the sort they call vayajá, hoop earrings and a full skirt with petticoats. There were collares, strings of beads, around her neck and bangles on her arms. Her feet were bare.

"She led me down into the barracoon. I was the sole white person there, and the scene is one I can hardly describe to you. Addie, it was like the end of days. There were people moiling in the streets, dancing, selling jerked beef and plantains, playing games, all to the rhythm of those drums. Right out in the open, as women and children jeered and hooted, men put their cocks—forgive me—grown men put their cocks into great clay jugs to see if they could reach a layer of ash in the bottom and leave a mark. People stared and made way as we passed. I thought it was because of my white face, but then I noticed how they averted their eyes from her, as though Clarisse were some sort of royalty.

"Deeper and deeper we went, till we arrived at a small house, better than the other houses. The door was studded with cut nails and rivets in the Spanish fashion, and a design had been drawn on it in pembe, chalk, what they call a firma, a hieroglyph—I didn't know that then. We passed through into the courtyard where the drummers were, three of them, playing on the caja, the mula, and the small one with the high tone, which is called cachimbo. The dancing was almost at a frenzy. Women with their arms akimbo made thrusting motions with their hips, advancing in a line, while others spread their arms like wings and banked and wheeled like flying birds. Clarisse introduced me to her godparents, Demetrio and Esperanza, two old Congos dressed in white. When Demetrio raised his hand, the drumming stopped.

" 'Padrino, Madrina . . . ,' Clarisse said in the silence, 'Godfather, God-mother, this is Harlan, who has asked me to become his wife. I come to seek your blessing and the blessing of this munanso on our marriage.'

"Demetrio lit a cigar from the candela at his feet and, without warning, puffed *the smoke directly in my face. I flinched, Addie, and several people laughed, but it was kindly laughter. I did not feel ridiculed. And then I heard a bleat and turned to see a young man leading a goat onto the patio. Demetrio unsheathed a knife and dripped the wax from a black candle in lines along the blade, each side. People began to wash the goat's feet and its mouth, and Demetrio chanted, 'Kiao lumbo! Kiao lumbo!' And then he pressed the goat's head to my genitals, to Clarisse's breasts, and began to speak in a loud, demanding voice, Spanish mixed with words I didn't know, 'We are here today to ask the blessing of this rama, both the living and the dead, upon this marriage. And we invoke the nkisi, and above all, Zarabanda, by the power of these firmas, that our sister, Clarisse, may be blessed in her union with this man.'*

"And then, Addie, he showed the knife to the goat, which was pulling and shitting, rolling its eyes as if it knew, and he said, 'Buen meme, y a lesa kwame,' 'Good goat, you will go into a sleep.' He sang this and then whispered something in its ears and nose, and it grew calm, Addie. It grew tame. It was the strangest thing. And then the crowd drew back, and I saw, for the first time, in the center of the patio, what the dancers had obscured, a pot, a black iron pot."

Now the small hairs stand on Addie's back.

"In it were the limbs of trees, many different kinds, and the horns of animals, deer, a ram; there was a machete, there were bones. Animal bones, some of them, but not all. In the center was a human skull."

The clearing in the woods, the fallen tree, and what she saw inside . . . All this returns to Addie as he speaks, and she feels chilled, though these are not the sorts of chills that come from cold. And it's curious, isn't it, how swiftly she—who's often smiled at "Negro superstition," at the ax head under the mattress to cure the rheumatism, at fence-grass tea and the hurried shoving of the poker in the fire when the hoot owl cries outdoors; Addie, who all her life has encouraged her aunt's servants' reason, their belief in Christ—how swiftly magic, presented in this light, reenters her life as a real possibility and wipes away the mistress's smile of condescending knowledge, leaving, in its stead, the sober stare of a small girl contemplating a dark wood at dusk.

"Demetrio presented the knife to this pot, Addie," he goes on, "with the deference of a vassal to his lord, as though it, too, were sentient, or as though some sentient thing resided there, and the people began to sing,

"'Ahora sí menga va corre, como corre,
Ahora sí menga va corre, sí seño,
Ahora sí menga va corre!'

"I understood the Spanish, Addie, all but that one word, 'menga,' which is from an older tongue, but when Demetrio plunged the knife in the goat's throat, I understood. The word was blood, sacrificial blood, and they were singing, 'Now the blood will flow, surely it will flow, surely now the blood will flow.' Demetrio collected it, as it spurted, hot, into a plate of salt and poured it on the skull, which they called 'kiyumba.' He was singing, 'Fogoro yarifo, menga corre menga sangra sala lai la lai la,' and he cut the goat's head off with a sawing, slicing motion. Terrible, terrible. He placed it in the pot, atop the skull, and the drums exploded, Addie, all around, people chanted, prayed, and wailed, it was a Babel pierced with shrieks and moans of ecstasy. They threw themselves into the dance, they whirled and lost themselves, and after some time, one woman screamed and fell. People caught her arms. They supported her as her limbs jerked and quivered. Then she grew still. The tension left her face. She looked, briefly, like someone who was drunk, so drunk she couldn't keep her eyelids open. Only a thin white sliver remained visible, and a rim of iris like a sun, a black sun creeping up over a hill. But there was something else there, too, Addie, not drunkenness, some awareness, still and old and deeply self-possessed. And then she stood and opened her eyes, and I was terrified for the first time. Because I saw her fall, Addie. I saw her close her eyes. When she opened them again, she was someone else. Her eyes were like eternity, two black lakes of thunder in which I saw the lightning flash. I'm forty-five years old, I've looked into my share of faces, but I've never seen a human being look like that. And when she began to speak, it was in a different voice, a man's, commanding, deep. She picked people from the crowd and upbraided them. She told one man to give up alcohol for forty days, another to stop eating shrimp.

"Then suddenly she turned to me and something happened. My head began to swim. I felt light-headed, ill, and then my body caught on fire. I looked into her pupils, and there were what looked like sparks or fireflies swarming there, constellations of swirling stars, and they flew close, and I realized they were spirits, Addie, angels, ghosts, I did not know what they were, but I wasn't frightened anymore. They were clothed in radiant white, clapping their hands and singing. I realized they were welcoming me. And I looked down and saw the courtyard where the dancers were, I saw Demetrio and Esperanza. I saw Clarisse kneeling beside a writhing body. Mine. I was lying on the stones. I'd left my body, Addie. It had fallen down, and I had left it, and these radiant presences, these beings of light, I wanted to go to them, to stay. I didn't see my mother, but I knew she would be there, and these others, they would show the way. And I knew, too, that I would have to die to go. I knew that I was dying even then. I don't know how I knew, Addie, many things were clear to me, and I will tell you, I was not afraid of dying, no, I wanted to, death seemed no more than

opening a door and walking into the next room. And like that"—he snaps his fingers now—"they scattered. I fell to earth.

"I came to on the riverbank. The drumming went on, but it was in the distance
now. I was naked to the waist. I was wet. Clarisse was washing me with something,
some liquid—there was rum in it, and spice, albahaca . . . what is it called? Basil,
basil, yes, of course, and pepper—the same thing they used to wash the goat. It's
called chamba, and it is to them like chrism is to us. She was weeping. I took her
hand and asked her what was wrong. She told me the nkisi, the spirit that had
mounted the woman and then passed into me, had said, through my own lips, that
we could never marry, must not, that to be together would be a pollution. I was
stunned. I asked her why. She shook her head. 'The spirits don't always give us reasons.' 'And you accept it?' I asked. 'You accept the end of everything we've felt and
been to each other, just like that?' She took my hands in hers. 'Harlan,' she said,
'this is my faith. This house, this rama, is my house. It is my church. Demetrio and
Esperanza are its priests. They are my mother and father. I've taken vows to them
and to the nfumbi, the muertos of this line. To break them would invite their wrath.'
I couldn't understand, Addie, I was hurt and reeling. I said, 'The dead? What have
they to do with us, the living? I've given up the life I would have had for you. What
we feel, I've never felt before. Have you? Look me in the face and tell me it is not the
same for you. Look me in the face and tell me you accept that it is wrong to love like
this.' But she couldn't, Addie. She could not. Clarisse just looked at me with those
dark eyes, and said, 'Do you have any notion what you're asking me to do? Do you
have any notion of the price it would require not just of me, but of you?' I said, 'No,
I don't, none at all, I only know, whatever it may be, I'm prepared to pay.' She
gazed at me for a long time, Addie, and then she said, 'Pues, que así sea'—'So be
it'—and she stood up and took my hand and led me into the grass beneath the willow trees." He pauses now. His gaze trains over her left shoulder.

"It is a story, Harlan," Addie whispers, and she is weeping now. "You should
have married her, not me."

"So I intended, Addie. Clarisse accepted me that day. We were lovers for three
years, almost four. We became engaged. Weighing our situation, we both felt we had
to tell Paloma and my father face-to-face. So, we booked passage home to
Charleston. We boarded the Nina there, as did you, dear. We took the same upriver
trip. This was all four years ago. They met us at the landing, just as we met you. Understand, Addie, Paloma hadn't seen her daughter since she was that swaddled bundle either. We came down the gangway, smiling, arm in arm. They were smiling, too.
At first. Then Paloma's expression sobered. She turned absolutely gray. 'Mamá!'

Clarisse cried, grinning with all that light and life up in her eyes. And then, 'Mamá? Mami?' with concern, and her face fell, too. 'What is it, Paloma?' Father asked, but she covered her mouth with both hands and shook her head. I thought I knew, Addie. I thought the fact that we were lovers—which she could hardly fail to glean— had shocked her. I thought that when we announced the purpose of our visit, when she saw that my intentions were honorable, Paloma would be pacified. But it wasn't that. It had nothing to do with that. Do you know what it was?"

"Tell me," Addie whispers, though she's afraid she knows, and her hand has crept to her breast, her fingertip is at the button, circling and circling the polished shell.

"Father didn't see. Nor I. It took a mother's eyes. Paloma took Clarisse's hands in hers. She stared at them, the backs, and then the palms. Then she turned to Father. 'Do you not see whose hands these are? Do you not see whose grin?' "

Harlan leaves the question there to hang. The room is hushed.

"She is your sister after all," Addie says.

"She is my sister after all."

"Oh, Harlan! Oh! But how . . ."

"She'd been with him, with Father, before the faro game."

"And with her old master, too."

"With Wenceslao, too," he says. "And Paloma never knew until she saw my father's grin in her grown daughter's face."

"My God! My God, Harlan!"

"You begin to see the predicament in which I found myself."

"And what did you do? What did you do then?"

"Exactly, Addie. What does one do then? Briefly, each of us went mad. Mad. We wept and raged. We fought. We reconciled. We asked ourselves if we could live with it. We answered yes. We tried. I tried. Repeatedly. Each time, I failed. The notion filled me with revulsion in some deep way that I was powerless to change. How can I reproach myself for feeling the same horror felt by all mankind?"

"No, my dear," she says, "of course you can't. I understand. I understand!"

Now Harlan takes her hands, and she surrenders them. He bows his head and kisses them.

"And Clarisse?" she says.

He shakes his head. "Clarisse felt differently. So, little by little, Addie, we, who'd loved each other more than anything on earth, came to be bitter, silent enemies. I did all I could to make the parting amiable, to make it kind. But she'd given everything, you see. Everything. Even her religion. She'd damned herself for me, and there was no way back—or so she felt. And so she took my withdrawal as a betrayal, Ad-

die. I had to be strenuous with her, strenuous and stern, in order to escape. And this is where I came to see the difference in our characters, Addie, this is where I came to see my fault and my mistake. It was when I crossed the line of race. Cuba cast its spell on me, and I forgot the truths of my own faith, where it's written, 'Of the children of the strangers that do sojourn among you, of them shall ye buy, and ye shall take them as an inheritance for your children after you, to inherit them for a possession and they shall be your bond-men forever.' My compass was struck by lightning and degaussed. I wandered, Addie. I wandered as my father had and almost lost myself, like him. I came so near, so near. Do you see? But I put this sorry episode behind me and set out to reform myself and live a proper life."

"And you met me."

"And I met you. Understand, Addie, my intentions toward you were honorable from the start. And are. For a year before we met, I hadn't been with her, not until . . ."

"Our wedding night."

"Our wedding night."

"Our wedding night, Harlan! Tell me how I am to bear it?"

"By understanding what only dawned on me today. I thought Clarisse had accepted it, Addie. I thought she'd set me free. But that is not the case. My sister has begun to throw on me."

"To throw . . ."

"Don't you see? All the pain and discord of the last two days—this is her doing, Addie. It's *brujería, witchcraft.*"

"Witchcraft, Harlan? Witchcraft? Tell me how I am to understand that. Help me to believe."

"You must trust me, Addie. You must understand I've traveled in a world that you know nothing of and make a leap of faith toward me. If you can't, then I release you from your vows. Because I need you, Addie, I need your strength, your love, your courage. I need you to fight for me, as I intend to fight for you."

"I will try! I will try!" she says, almost in despair. "But, Harlan, if such things are possible, if they're true, how is one to fight them? What is one to do?"

"Truthfully?" he answers. "I don't know. Through faith in God and in each other—those are the only weapons we possess."

And they fall silent now. They gaze into each other's eyes and weigh what has been said. But something has been left unsaid, too, and Addie says it now.

"I saw something in the woods last night, a pot, I think. It was covered with a cloth, but I think it was the same as the one you described."

His eyes smolder. "You believe me then?"

"I don't know what I believe. I'm trying to. But, Harlan, do you think . . . ?"

"Yes, my dear?"

What happened in the swamp, the voice she heard, and what she felt toward Jarry when he came . . . All this passes now through Addie's mind, and was it not, in some way, like a dream, a spell? And what if the voice with whom she conversed wasn't that of God, or from God, not that of some good angel? What if it was tempting her, as the serpent once did Eve in such a place? Would this not explain so much that is confusing now? For her, a woman of her class and station, a white woman, to feel such feelings for a slave . . . Could this have a natural cause? What if . . . oh, what if!

"Do you think it could affect me, too?"

Harlan blinks. "Of course . . . Of course it could! But has something happened, Addie? Have you felt . . . ?"

"No," she says. "No, nothing, I just . . . I . . . ."

He takes her hand and presses it. "I understand, my dear. I understand. It's natural to be afraid."

"What is it she expects, though, Harlan? What is it she wants?"

"Everything, Addie. Don't you see? Me. This. Wando Passo. She wants it for herself and for her children to inherit. Our children. Hers and mine."

"Ah," says Addie. "Yes, I see."

"I left her and came to you by choice," he says. "It was you to whom I chose to wed my future, to be the mother of my children. I love you, Addie. Love me back. Believe in me, and we will win."

"I don't know if I can love you now."

"Can you not try?"

His expression queries and implores her. He touches her, tries to kiss her, but she pulls away. Yet his eyes linger, questioning and unconvinced. He tries again, and this time she does not reject his hand. And it is unlike before, when he went on ahead and left her by herself. Now, seeking to recover what he's lost, he is with her. Harlan is completely with her now.

TWENTY-FIVE

I think we need to talk," he said.

"I have a better idea," said Claire.

Leaving the water running, she climbed out, dripping extravagantly on the tile. Her upper body was flushed, and she came toward him, grinning, like a confident madwoman who meant to do him harm. Grabbing a fistful of his hair, she kissed him violently, opening her mouth wide and sending her tongue probing. Ransom instantly went hard and felt some old, familiar disappointment at his cock's lack of character. It was rare, though not unprecedented, for him to feel objectified by female lust, yet tonight was such a time. Having waited for this moment, dreamed of it, he had mixed feelings when it arrived, and, really, shouldn't he demur? Claire had last night. Right when they'd been at the tipping point, she'd had the guts and self-regard to pull away and say, "How is this supposed to work?" And did he have any less? The answer, the sad answer, apparently, was yes.

"Do you love me for my heart and character, or only for my bod?" he asked her in a feeble effort to preserve some shred of dignity.

"Only for your bod," she said, popping his shirt buttons as she rolled it off his back.

"Well," Ran said, watching as she seized the zipper of his pants. "At least we've got that straight."

Claire laughed, and he did, too, despite concerns that it was not a joke.

He hadn't seen her this uninhibited in quite some time, if ever. She seemed right there, completely without shame or subterfuge. And it would be wrong to say that her address lacked tenderness; it didn't. He had to wonder why she was suddenly so turned on; not enough to ask, though. Even as they began, Ransom knew he would be mulling that question for some time. Right now, sacrificing any vestiges of self-respect, he was content to fuck his wife till they were raw.

With her hand on his cock, like a rosy infant both muscular and soft, Claire stepped into his boxers, which were hung up at his knees, and pushed them to his ankles, stamped on them, before dropping to her knees and going down on him. She took him whole into her mouth, and let her lips cling like half-moist crepe as she drew back and stood. Her tits, small and full, still hot from the bath, grazed his chest. Grasping his shoulders, she pushed him to his knees and put both hands behind his head and pulled him into her bush. Looking down greedily, she made little thrusts into his face, turned on not just by what he did, but by watching herself act. (Ran surmised this from fragmentary glimpses, as she let him up, occasionally, for air.) Too aroused to stick with one approach, she turned away and leaned across the vanity. Like an orphan who has stumbled on the factory where all the love and chocolate in the universe are made, Ransom stood and screwed his fists into his eyes, then wiped the wet that had spread around his mouth like lipstick on a drunk Parisian whore. Her eyes were waiting for him in the mirror, her grin, the happy predator's. Reaching back, she guided him in, and as he fucked her from behind, her eyes in the mirror never left his face. Ransom watched the heartblood migrate to her face, saw the veins form and plump—throat, temple, brow.

"No," she said, "lower, hold it, harder, there, like that." Pushing from above, she forced his cock to mash her clitoris with every stroke, and then she pushed too hard and he washed out on a wave of secretory ointments. Looking down, Ransom saw the puckered circle of her anus and nudged experimentally.

"Is that what you want?" Undeterred, Claire fumbled the drawer open, took out the K-Y, and uncapped it with the same hand she used to smear them both.

"Oh, oh, gently, buddy, gently," she said as he shoved in, but Ran felt madness coming over him, something careless and unstoppable, and he pushed hard, harder, with no gentleness at all. In the mirror now, her eyes were closed, teeth gritting, and her tits, her full little tits, jerked and whiplashed forward with each backthrust she made. His own face, when he glanced at it, seemed vivid, too, relaxed and clarified, but almost lugubrious in the midst of fucking that exceeded fantasy, exceeded his highest anticipated good. Then, like a swimmer who's held her breath as long as she can stand, Claire made a gasping cry and shoved him, hard, away. Turning, she took his cock, and Ransom picked her up as Claire raised both knees shoulder-high, and they went at it that way, face-to-face, at jackhammer speed and rhythm, and she stared, open-eyed, with something in her face he didn't like, almost defiance, as though daring him to miss a beat. He didn't. They went on, perfectly matched, like oarsmen to the coxswain's cadence, and finally her face softened, sadness colored it, and she groaned, "Ohhh," she put her lips against his ear and whispered, "Come on, fuck me, fuck me, don't you, don't you think, don't you think of . . ." Ran began to come now, too. "Stopping," she whisper-cried, "ohhh . . . OHHH, FUCK . . . OHH, FUCK . . . OH, FUCK . . . don't you, don't you fuck me, don't you stop, oh, don't you, don't you, stop."

Lost in lush and irresistible mixed messages, they fell back, spineless, boneless, against the countertop, then spineless, boneless, to the floor, where they lay naked, sweating against cold tile. Like a patient on the table as the anesthesiologist applies the mask, Ransom drifted out, and when he came to, Claire was kissing his cheek.

"How was that for sexual healing?"

Smiling with besotted happiness, he watched her beautiful bare shoulders disappearing, one by one, into her robe. As she closed it, though, something stopped her. Claire looked down and wiped her inner thigh, stared at what was on her fingertip.

"You came?" Her face, as she turned and asked, was wondering and pleased. "How . . ."

Ransom sat up quickly. "Claire . . ."

Now everything in her expression began to run downhill.

"This was it, this was all I wanted, Claire," he whispered desperately. "Just this one time to be with you the way we used to be. Don't be mad, okay? Please."

"You're off your meds?"

"I'm going to the pharmacy tomorrow, okay? First thing. *First* thing."

She simply stared at him, and her eyes filled.

"Claire . . ."

She broke eye contact now, gazed at the wall for perhaps three seconds as though something in the distance had come into focus; then she sashed her robe and left without a word or another glance at him.

Still in the grip of postcoital fatigue, Ran lay back on the floor and closed his eyes. Having died of the operation, he experienced difficulty deciding to come back from the white light in the tunnel where the ancestors await. And the conversation he should have had with Claire he now had with himself. Though it was true he'd flirted with the edge, he hadn't jumped, had he? He hadn't gone over into the abyss. Nothing really bad had happened. Things were still retrievable. All he'd wanted was to reclaim his manhood with his wife—Claire could understand and forgive that, surely. After all, she had in the past.

Taking the hard road back to life, Ran got up feeling arthritic, stumbled, used the doorknob as a crutch. Following her to bed to talk, he found Claire fast asleep.

Ransom looked at her, and happiness crept over him, followed by a twinge of sudden doubt. Was she breathing? For a moment, Claire looked almost dead. Her face seemed relaxed and younger in the way the faces of the dead are said to shed their cares and to approximate a stage of youth. Even when he put his ear close to her lips and heard her breathe, touched her skin and felt its warmth, Ran wasn't fully reassured. A wave of grief washed over him, as though he himself had caused her premature demise. Yet she wasn't dead—he knew she wasn't—but the grief came, nonetheless, on and on—such grief, oh! Oh, such remorse! Ran actually began to weep. And why? For what? Wasn't what had just happened in the bathroom good? Wasn't their closeness the plausible beginning of that new beginning he had hoped for? Why, then, did it feel like something else? Why this sudden dark foreboding? Premonition somehow mingled with the smell of sex. And the strange thing was, the grief didn't really feel like it belonged to him. It felt like it belonged to *someone else.*

With tears still streaming down his face, he walked into the hall, and there the hamper lay in wait. On top of the soiled heap, Claire's pink panties, exactly as before. Ran stopped. His grief vanished as suddenly as it had arisen. Around him, the house went still.

Another clue . . .

The voice whispered, and Ransom felt the zing of fear. What if? he thought . . . What if the journey wasn't leading someplace good, wasn't leading him toward his True Self, but someplace . . . else? . . .

Oh, go on, check them out, you know you want to.

The voice had a certain point. And if he picked them up and looked them over, if he checked for signs—suspect seepage, crust—what harm? Who would ever be the wiser? If there was something to discover, better to learn it now and face facts. If not, better to know that, too, surely, and spare Claire further unjust doubts. A spot check might exonerate her, mightn't it? Well, no, not really—it might only prove that she was being careful. Ran suddenly grasped the crucial fact: the only definitive evidence the panties could provide was of a damning sort, the evidence to convict. And if he examined them now, would that, too, constitute a crime of sorts? Would it mark, in effect, the end of marital trust? Would it mean the end of his ambition to be the husband she wanted and deserved? It would, wouldn't it? And if he ever meant to be that different, better man he'd always believed he could be but had never actually been, wasn't it also true that Ransom had to start the process somewhere? Didn't he, in fact, have to start right here, right now, and walk away?

But the voice said, *Relax, you lox, it's human nature, take a peek, it'll be over in a second and a half.*

Ran actually reached out and touched them, before he stopped himself. Suddenly something opened in his head; awareness rushed back like air into a pierced vacuum. Like a sleepwalker who comes to on the edge of a precipice, Ran found himself in the upstairs hallway, glomming the dirty-clothes hamper, drawn to a pair of Claire's new underpants, fixated like the Millennium Falcon in the Death Star's tractor-beam.

"What am I doing?" he said aloud, and fled.

Taking refuge in the library, he sat down at the partners desk and took his head between his hands. "This is Claire," he said. *"Claire."* Whatever image she projected, had she ever been casual about sex? No, never. (Oh, many—including *him,* early on—had made that sad and bad mistake!) Nor, so far as Ransom knew, had she ever been unfaithful to him. And to say, to imply, "so far as he knew" wasn't fully honest either. In his heart, Ran was certain, one hundred percent sure, that whatever their troubles, Claire had kept faith with him there. The only way he could imagine Claire cheating on him was if it was for keeps, if the marriage, for her, was truly over. And if it was for keeps, wouldn't she tell him? Wouldn't Claire—*Claire!*—have the decency, the respect, to look him in the face and honor their years to-gether with the truth? Of course she would! And Cell was a straight shooter, too. He always had been. The notion of the two of them humping in a motel room somewhere, getting their jollies over Ransom's credulous-ness, his pathetic hope that the marriage might yet work—preposterous! It was like a dream, some horrible dream from which he'd suddenly awak-ened, and once more the strange thing was, it wasn't like *his* dream. It was as if, for an hour, two, he'd fallen into someone else's nightmare like a swimmer in a riptide, and it had almost carried him away to sea. Sitting there, Ran had the sense he'd made the thinnest and narrowest of narrow, thin escapes. But whose dream was it, if it wasn't his? What was all this strangeness?

Disturbed, he took a reading-glasses case that had no reading glasses in it from the top drawer of the partners desk. Secreted there, in a cloudy Bag-gie the yellow of old Scotch tape, a few brittle tops and flowers shifted amid a plenitude of seeds. As Ran rolled the joint, an elephant trumpeted, lumbering across the black ground of the computer screen. Firing up, he held the toke and threw the window up and exhaled into the night.

When he turned back to the room, he noticed the blue bottle on the corner of the desk. Giving it a swirl, he heard the liquid *whoosh* and the illiquid *tink*. Holding it to the light, he promptly fumbled it and watched it burst into a hundred fragments at his feet.

"Shit," he said as the puddle spread.

In the center was a small gray lump that looked like nothing more than mud. When he picked it up, he felt hardness at the center. It was nickel-sized and round, with a hasp or fitting on one side. Something was em-bossed on the surface, and when Ran wiped away the sediment, he saw writing. He read and blinked, and blinked and read again.

OshKosh, it said, in burnished letters that seemed newly pressed into the tin.

"OshKosh," he said aloud. When he looked up, Addie was waiting for him in the portrait, her blue eyes heavy with some information she seemed anxious to impart.

TWENTY-SIX

When it began, nobody can remember
No doubt at the beginning: one fine day
The surface world collapsed around his longing
The deep world yawned and took his love away

And he dove after it with righteous ~~passion~~ ~~indignation~~
passion . . .
And after ~~nineteen~~ twenty years he knew. . . .

an woke up, heavy-headed, at the partners desk and found
these lines. They seemed alien at first, but slowly, as he read, the
details of his late-night session returned. The first verse had
come in its entirety in fifteen seconds. He'd struggled with the second for
an hour and a half. Was Nemo's mission undertaken out of love or anger?
Should Ran use nineteen years, like his marriage, or the thin disguise of
twenty? And whether nineteen or twenty, what, after all that time beneath
the sea, had Nemo learned? Here, the process finally broke down. Ransom
put his head down on the desk, and woke up hours later with a stiff neck
and the imprint of tooled leather on his cheek.

It was almost seven. The windows had been left open and the room was
cold. Under the high ceilings, everything was shadowed, gray. On the

buckram spine of a nearby book, he noticed mildew, and then he looked at all the books there were—so many of the titles obscure, forgotten. He thought of all that effort, all the self-important striving, moldering away, and it came home that the odds of his success on this song, or a future one, were very long. A twinge of fear seized in, and it struck Ransom that his dereliction with his meds might not be so easily forgivable as he'd assumed; camels' backs were broken, after all, with straws, not bricks. His project to become a different, better man—was it fully realistic at his age? To change, at any time, is hard, but forty-five? To become someone other than you've been? Come on . . . And then he heard a thud above him on the ceiling, the tattoo of little footsteps running down the hall.

Into his dark mood ran Charlie, shouting, "Doddy! Doddy! Wake up! Bi'truck!"

Charlie ran to the window and looked back with his fresh, excited face. "Dere! Come see!" Ransom joined him as the excavator's dump truck pulled into the frame, hauling a trailer with a yellow Caterpillar loader chained on top.

"Bi'truck?"

Ransom shook his head. "Excavator."

"Escavator?"

"Yep."

"No bi'truck?"

"No fire truck."

"Wha's exsavator do?"

"He's going to dig a hole."

"A hole?"

"Let's go talk to him."

"Talk to him?"

"Come on."

"Okay, Doddy."

Charlie offered his hand, no bigger than a silver dollar, and Ransom, as he took it, saw in one clear flash how his day would have gone without this interruption. His stiffness left him, the engine began to gather speed.

Outside, he showed the man the rotten sill, explained his idea for a swale.

"Sounds good to me."

"So how long do you think all this will take?"

"No more'n a couple hundred hours."

Ran gave him a narrow smile. "So you'll be done by lunch."

"Most likely, if I skip my doughnut break."

"Doesn't look like it would do you major harm."

"You sound like my wife."

"Tell me about it, brother." Ran grinned and held his palm out, and the man conceded a reluctant but good-natured five. "I have to drop my kids at school in Powatan and run a couple errands. I should be back before you leave."

"I guess I'll be here till you pay me."

"Good, then I'll catch up with you."

Claire, sipping coffee, ran out the back door, her hair wet from the shower.

"I've got to run," she said. "Give Mama a kiss." She knelt and took it. "Later, dute."

"Bye, Mama."

"And you . . ."

Ran searched her face, but found no evidence of condemnation in the look she gave him, which was full of coded messages suspended in a medium of suppressed hilarity. "You were in rare form last night, Hill."

"So were you, madame."

She made a pleasant little smirk, and Ran felt his whole day turn the corner. He went in and made the children breakfast; he got them in the car and drove them into town. The process went more smoothly than before, except for the logistics of the T-Bird. Remembering Claire's complaint, he pulled into a used-car lot.

An aged salesman with an unapologetic see-through silver pompadour strolled out and whistled. "Nice car—a '55?"

"Fifty-six."

"Always wanted one of them," he said as he did the walkaround. Dressed in the manner of an old-fashioned country dandy, in madras slacks, he had the air of one who'd been a ladies' man and was under no interior compulsion to get over it. "I don't suppose you want to sell her."

"I was thinking of a trade," said Ran. "Something for the wife and kids."

"There's your vehicle right there." Old Silver pointed to a Honda Odyssey two shades darker than his mane.

"A minivan?" Ran asked skeptically. "I don't know, padre. I'm not sure my self-esteem and a minivan could coexist in the same universe."

"That ain't your father's minivan, my friend," said the dealer, taking a quick read of the customer and demonstrating no mean grasp of human nature. "It's got leather, two automatic sliding doors"—he prompted one, and Ran looked in—"fold-down seats for cargo. And check this out." He flipped down a rooftop screen.

"A TV, too?" said Ransom, warming.

"That ain't just a TV, brother. That's a DVD."

"No kidding?" Knowing it was wiser to play coy, Ran, unable to, smiled and stroked his chin.

"She's sweet, my brother. Plus, I'll throw in five free DVDs."

Ransom laughed. "Like that's really gonna seal the deal."

"It has before," the old man said.

"Does that include *The Lion King?*"

The salesman looked nonplussed, but only temporarily. "If it ain't, we'll put it on the list."

Ran held out his hand and grinned.

Afterward, he picked up his prescription, bought a Coke and downed his pills right there, then let the nurse at Claire's OB draw blood. By the time he started back to Wando Passo, surrounded by the new-car smell, Ran felt righteous, he felt good. His former mood had vanished like the shadow of a cloud that touches you and passes on. As he drove the Odyssey, Ran began to feel himself settling in, becoming grounded. Through the windshield, he saw the day he would have had in New York in his cab; saw, beside it, the day he now had ahead of him to live . . . thanks to Charlie's little interruption, thanks to Claire's remark and pleasant smirk. Selling his father's T-Bird somehow capped the deal, like surrendering some old baggage he didn't have to carry anymore. In New York his depression would have gone on, gathering momentum as it went; here that hadn't happened. And *that* had been what Nemo lost, what made him a vengeful monster, scarcely human anymore—Captain Nemo lost his family and his wife. Now Ran saw it all. By the time he got back to Wando Passo, the sun was peeking through the overcast. It seemed worth fighting after all.

When he pulled into the allée, however, there beside the excavator's dump truck and trailer were six police cars parked haphazardly with flashing lights. As he pulled into the gravel turnaround in back, he could see the yellow backhoe idling, a tangle of roots and mounded earth in the toothed bucket. Under it stood Sergeant Thomason, conferring with the excavator.

They both turned and watched as Ransom parked and got out of the car.

"Mr. Hill," said Thomason.

"We meet again," said Ran. "What's going on?"

Thomason nodded down into the grave-shaped trench, which had appeared where the former periwinkle patch had been.

Looking up at Ran as though his long-awaited hour had finally come, Officer Johnson lifted a blue plastic tarp. Beneath it, an intact skeleton lay beside a second set of remains the backhoe had disturbed. Ran recognized a pelvis, a string of vertebrae, what looked like a human femur bone.

"Doc?" Thomason called to a gray-haired man in an unkempt suit, squatting on his hams at the far end of the trench, studying something Ransom couldn't see. "Doc Sneeden?"

"Umm," the ME said perfunctorily. Only as he turned did Ransom see the second, larger skull he held. In it was a dime-sized hole with fracture lines radiating out like rays from a black sun. He shook it by his ear and something rattled.

"What the hell is that?" said Ran.

"Let's take a look," said the ME. Unhinging the jaw, he reached into the mouth and took out a small black pellet. "Birdshot. Looks like number 8."

"This here's Mr. Hill, Doc," Thomason said. "The homeowner?"

Remembering his manners, Sneeden hurriedly removed the cigarette and smiled. "How do," he said, and his gray eyes narrowed down on Ransom like the shutter of a lens.

Part II

A CHECKERED SUN

TWENTY-SEVEN

*A*ddie awakens to the sound of shovels making unhurried cuts in sandy soil—chuck . . . chuck . . . chuck—and to the raining plop *of turned, soft earth on turned, soft earth.*

"Hu eh eh, dey yiz," says a voice outside; another laughs. Hearing this, smelling river air, not salt, she remembers where she is and what happened in this bed last night. There's something different, something new in her self-sense, and in her body Addie feels the weighty peace that follows pleasant strife. Is this it, she wonders, the mystery she waited for, was so long vigilant against? She almost feels an urge to laugh. But there's another current, at cross-purposes with her happiness.

And there is Harlan at the window, already dressed—in uniform, with a black silk sash and his dress sword at his knee. He's staring toward the black pond and the cypress, where the Gullah men are making Percival his place.

"Good morning."

He turns, and there's a lightness in his face, not grief, the look of one who's been released. "You're awake."

"I am," she says.

He sits beside her on the bed and takes her hands. "How I regret that I must go, Addie, especially now," he tells her tenderly. "Especially now."

She strokes his cheek. "You'll be home soon. Washington in a month?" She smiles, and he smiles back.

As she offers him this reassurance, though, the sparrow once more flits into the room, making her aware she's not entirely hopeful this is true. And if it isn't? If she's less than fully hopeful of his swift return . . . ? "I was thinking, Harlan," she says, energetically recoiling from the thought and sitting up. "About the shortages? If a few women could help me sew, we could make the crop hands' clothes ourselves. And if there's wool, we could spin and knit their stockings, too. I believe it could be managed," says Addie, who's often knitted baby things, first for friends, and then, increasingly, for young mothers who were little girls in pinafores when she came out.

He pats her hand. "My mother used to say that being a plantation mistress is to be the slave of slaves. I knew you'd do well. Speak to Paloma. She'll get you what you need." Now he rises and begins to pace. "I have to tell you, though. . . . It's a great weight off my shoulders, Addie—this business with Clarisse—to have it out and in the clear. I've wanted to discuss it with you for the longest time."

"I can understand," she says, noting the swift change of subject to himself. And why didn't you? she thinks. What would have happened if he had? Her mind ranges as he speaks. If he'd come to her in Charleston, sober-faced and penitent, if he'd said, "There is this situation, Addie, this event that happened in my past. . . . I fell in love with someone without knowing fully who she was." What could she have done except forgive? No, she thinks, it would have changed nothing—she'd still be where she is. But that he didn't come, sober-faced or otherwise—that is where the trouble lies. That he went ahead and married her, leaving her ignorant of a truth fateful to her happiness, that he took upon himself the risk of ruining her life . . . This is who you are, she thinks, as Harlan smiles and speaks. She sees him, in this moment, clear, yet clarity does not defeat her tenderness. In light of what occurred between them, here, last night, it seems today they have a marriage after all, and Addie, for her part, came into it expecting to make allowances, didn't she? Here, in the cool, sober light of morning, it dawns on her that this is the allowance she must make.

". . . came to his senses in the end," Harlan is saying. "This is the only conclusion I can draw."

"I'm sorry," Addie says. "My thoughts were drifting. Who?"

"Father. We've searched high and low, Paloma and I both, and it's simply nowhere to be found."

She sits up straight against the headboard now. "You're speaking of the will?"

"He must have burned it in the night. Who would think, after all this time, that the old man would finally . . . But, Addie, what . . . ? You're ashen, dear."

"Harlan, I'm afraid to tell you this. . . ."

His face goes sober.

"He gave it to me."

"He what?" he asks, with harsh surprise.

Addie blinks; her glance slides involuntarily to the nightstand. His follows hers. They reach at the same time. Each grasps the corner of the page.

"Do you mind?" he asks, pressing his lips into a prim line they seem ill-meant to convey. Addie can conceive of no response except to let it go.

Harlan scans the page and turns it with a brusque, loud flap. He scans again, and then finds what he seeks. *"Goddamn,"* he says. *"Goddamn him. So there are no surprises after all."* With that, he tears the will in half.

"Harlan, in heaven's name . . ."

Halving the halves, he halves those yet again, then throws them in the hearth. *"What are you doing, Harlan? Stop."*

He strikes a match. Holding it between his middle finger and his thumb, he raises the index finger of that hand. *"Not another word, do you hear me, Addie? Not one. We've had all the discussion I intend to have upon this matter. I'm leaving here today for God knows how long. As soon as Father's in the ground, I'm gone, and I have neither time nor stomach to commence a tedious legal wrangle, which, in any case, would only arrive at this same place."* And now he puts the flame to paper.

"But, Harlan, it was his last wish. . . ."

"I don't know that," he answers, brushing his hands. *"I don't know that at all. The last wish he expressed in my hearing was, in fact, the opposite. Had you not in-terfered . . . But, no, I don't intend to fight. We've fought enough. I think we can agree, at least, on that."*

"Can you not think of Jarry and Paloma, though?"

"Paloma may do as she pleases."

"And Jarry? What of him? Put yourself in his position, Harlan—what if it were you?"

"But it was me, Addie," he replies with a pathetic note. *"It is. It has been all my life. This is where it stops. There comes a time when you must cease to put your faith in others' help and act to help yourself."* The paper now is ash. He smears it underneath his boot and grinds it down into the blackened brick. *"This will never leave this room."*

She maintains a grim silence.

"I must have your promise."

"I don't know if I can give you that."

"You will, though, Addie," he informs her, with a cold assurance she finds threaten-ing. *"You certainly will if Jarry's feelings are of concern to you. This is better for him, too."*

"How?" she answers. "Better how?"

"If it were you," he says, "which would be the bitterer—to stay and work in accordance with your father's wish to keep you safe, or to feel compelled to it by a brother whom you hate?"

She frowns and makes no answer.

"Come now, Addie," he says, gaining confidence, "we may disagree, but it's beneath you, when you know I'm right, to withhold an answer out of pique."

"Perhaps," she says, "but you're wrong upon the larger point."

"That is your opinion. Think what you will. I can't help what you think. But keep your thinking to yourself. I won't have this raised with Jarry or Paloma—do you understand me? This is my family, Addie, mine—my father, my property, my slaves. These matters go back forty years and more, and you've not yet been here three whole days. I am master now, and your husband, too. A week ago today, in church, you made a vow not just to love and honor me, but also to obey. If you intend to keep it, I must have your word."

"All right, Harlan," she says, mortified by the whole conversation and capitulating to escape. "All right, then, all right."

"I have it?"

"Did you not just hear me say you do?"

"Very well, then. Good," he says, and now he risks a smile. "Come, Addie, we've had rough sailing for a day or two, but we've come through. Let's not mar our last few hours. You get dressed and speak to Paloma about your notion while I see if they're ready for us at the cemetery." He bends to kiss her mouth, but Addie gives a cheek instead.

After he leaves, she dresses briskly and sits down at the dressing table. She looks for the black hair in Harlan's mother's brush, but it's gone, and Addie, angry at Harlan, but still angrier at her own concession, wonders if it was ever there at all. Falling into contemplation of her frowning face, she becomes aware she's waiting for something. Since opening her eyes, she has been waiting half consciously, half in fear, for the voice to speak. It hasn't, though; nor does it now. This is a blessing, though. Maybe now, she thinks, life, real life, suspended for these last two days, can recommence. Yes, decides Addie, as she sets in brushing vigorously—brushing quite furiously, in fact—the silence of the voice is a relief.

TWENTY-EIGHT

ell, correct me if I'm wrong, gentlemen," said Ransom, pacing, pacing furiously before the partners desk, "but you don't need a degree in forensic pathology to tell that Yorrick out there with the BB in his brain has been in the ground a hell of a long time."

He nodded to the window and the excavation site beyond, where the remains were being photographed and bagged.

"Well, you are wrong," said Sneeden, the ME, "so I will correct you. Once a body's been in the ground a certain time, Mr. Hill, the bones oxidize, they turn this sort of dingy ivory-yellow, and it's virtually impossible to tell with the naked eye—at least, for me, and I've been doing this twenty-five years—whether they've been there one year or a hundred."

"Is that so?"

"It is."

Ransom, now, came to a stop. "So what are you implying?"

Floating his question, he looked from Sneeden to Sergeant Thomason, who stood holding his doffed cap, watching Ran with soulful, put-upon, clinically dispassionate, unblinkingly observant eyes, like a poor boy on his first trip to the circus, studying the pacing tiger in its cage.

"I mean, based on your years of experience," Ran continued, getting a fresh wind, "tracking criminal masterminds and so forth, do I strike you—

and please be honest, don't hold back for fear of hurting my feelings—as the sort of guy who goes around murdering people for kicks, depositing their remains in shallow graves around his property like a hound dog burying bones? Is that the kind of face I have?"

"Hard to tell what's in a person's heart by looking in their face, Mr. Hill. Awful hard," said Thomason. "Take that fella Ted Bundy, now. . . . Personally, you strike me as a nice-enough sort—a bit excitable, maybe, a little sarcastic on occasion. . . ."

"And from sarcasm it's a short, slippery downhill slope to mass murder, right?" said Ran. "I'm sure that's on page one of the police procedural handbook."

Giving the marked-up page of "Nemo's Submarine" a quarter turn, Sneeden scanned it briefly, sending Ran to Defcon 6, then walked to the window, pulled back the curtain, and appeared to begin triangulating their position relative to the site. "Why are you so touchy, Mr. Hill?" he said, turning back. "That would be my question."

"*That* would be your question," said Ran, "why I'm so touchy? Why I'm touchy, Mr. Sneeden—"

"Dr. Sneeden."

"Dr. Sneeden, is because two dead bodies just turned up on our property, and I seem to be under interrogation, and I'm asking if you think I have anything to do with those bodies being here, and you aren't saying no. I'm a sensitive guy, Dr. Sneeden, an artist, and I find that implication very hurtful, very wounding—see me tearing up? It also gets my back up just a weensy bit."

"Perfectly natural, Mr. Hill, perfectly natural," said Thomason. "I'd feel the same way in your place. Anybody would."

"Has anyone accused you of anything?" said Sneeden. "Has one single word been said to that effect?"

"Oh, wait," said Ran, "I get it now. The sergeant here's the good cop. You're the bad. Correct?"

"I'm the county medical examiner, Mr. Hill," said Sneeden. "I don't know who these people are, what happened to them, how long they've been buried there, whether they died of foul play, natural cause, or what. . . ."

"Well, Yorrick has birdshot rattling in his brainpan," Ransom said, "so for starters, I'd rule out natural cause."

"Could have been a hunting accident, a soldier killed at war, suicide—

there's a dozen reasons I can think of shy of murder why people end up getting shot."

"Can you think of a dozen reasons why they end up in unmarked three-foot graves?"

Sneeden's jaw took a prognathous jut.

"He's onto something there, Doc," said Thomason. "You're on my wavelength now, Mr. Hill. There's a story here, and it don't look to be a good one, but the truth is, we don't know what the story is, and it's our job to find out. That's all we're trying to do here, and the reason we're asking you is because they turned up on your property. It don't go no fu'ther than that. Any information or assistance you can give us in a helpful spirit, we'd most appreciate."

"Well, I know who they are," said Ran. "Would that qualify as helpful information?"

The officers both blinked.

"I seem to have your attention now," said Ran, making a transparently insincere effort to conceal his glee. "They're Harlan and Adelaide DeLay, gentlemen, my wife's great-great something-something grandparents. That's Adelaide right there." He pointed to the portrait.

"What makes you think it's them?" asked Thomason.

"He came back from the war in 1865, showed up in downtown Powatan, started here on foot, and neither he nor Adelaide was ever seen again. They've been missing in action for, what, a hundred and forty years, give or take? As chance or fate would have it, I heard the story of their disappearance for the first time yesterday, not long after I . . ." *Found the pot,* he was about to say, but the voice said, *I wouldn't go into that if I were you,* and Ran, for once, agreed. "So who else is it going to be?"

"Well, he's right on one thing," Sneeden said to Thomason. "The second set's a woman."

"The second set of what?" asked Ran.

"Remains," the sergeant said.

"How did she die?"

"We'll have to wait for the state ME to weigh in on that, Mr. Hill," Sneeden answered. "I did note a shattered rib on her left side, which would also be consistent with a gunshot."

"They'll do osteometrics and carbon dating up there in Columbia, Mr. Hill," said Thomason, "which should tell us if them dates check out. What's your theory anyhow? Somebody murdered 'em?"

Ran shrugged. "I'd put my money on a murder-suicide."

"Shot her, then killed himself?"

"Or maybe she shot him," Ran said.

"Usually works the other way," said Sneeden. "Nine times out of ten."

"Hey, let's not be sexist," Ransom said. "This is the twenty-first century, as people keep reminding me."

"What you figuring for motive?"

"Maybe he was too sarcastic for her tastes." Ran gave his watch an aggressive glance. "And on that note, gentlemen, I've given you all I have, both fact and speculation. Now, unless you plan to arrest me and put me on the chain gang breaking rocks, I have someplace I need to be."

"You ain't going out of town, are you, Mr. Hill?" asked Thomason. "Reason I ask is just in case we think of any fu'ther questions."

"I'm going to pick up my kids at preschool in Powatan. Do you want me to surrender my passport?"

"That won't be necessary, Mr. Hill," said Sneeden drily.

"Then I'll let you show yourselves out. I believe you know the way."

"B'lieve I do," said Thomason, and smoothing down his comb-over, he reapplied his hat.

"Bastards," Ran said as soon as they had left. "*Rat* bastards!"

And he'd known, hadn't he? He'd *known*! That morning things were simply going too damn well. The universe, apparently, had gotten wind: Ransom Hill, for once, was on the verge of happiness; he'd actually had sex with his wife! Call in the Doom Patrol! Let the Harpies shit some droppings in his Frosted Flakes! Let's restore some freaking order, for the love of Mike, before this poor loser starts thinking he's actually *entitled* to a break. . . .

Feeling a little sorry for ourselves? the voice piped up.

"Fuck you, too!" Ran shouted, loudly, in the empty room. "Fuck you and the horse you rode in on! Whose side are you on, anyway?"

Yours, of course. But, really, Ransom, what's the big deal? You know you're innocent, right?

"Hell, yes, I'm innocent! I'm innocent as hell!"

All this happened a long time ago.

"Way to hell and gone back when!"

The story—whatever it is—has nothing to do with you, correct?

"Damn straight!"

So why are you so hot and bothered?

"Hey," said Ransom, "I'm not sure I like where you're going with this."

All I'm saying is, Sneeden makes a certain point. From the way you're acting, you'd almost think this touched a nerve.

"Bullshit!" said Ran. "Bull*shit!* I have no such nerve. This is me, for Chrissakes—*me!* I'm a freaking pacifist. I dodged the draft, or would have, if it hadn't ended three months before I became eligible. Hell, I was once a vegetarian—for thirteen years, I didn't even break an egg!"

Oy, don't remind me.

"Who are you, the Joker? This is serious business."

You're right, it is. Which is why it seems a little strange that you didn't give them everything.

"What do you mean? I gave them everything except a pint of blood."

How about the gun?

Stopping in the middle of the room, Ran glanced toward the vacant hooks above the door where the Purdey had formerly hung. "What do you me— Oh, wait. Wait, I get it. If that's the murder weapon, maybe they could . . ."

Match it to the shot?

"Right, right. Excellent. Good thinking. That never dawned on me."

It didn't?

"Absolutely not."

Oh, sorry, then. My mistake. I thought there was an instant there. . . .

"What instant? There was no instant."

You know, when you were pacing back and forth maniacally, waving your arms, protesting your innocence, expressing your righteous indignation that the officers might consider you—you, of all people, the son of Melvin Hill—capable of violence . . . I thought there was a fleeting moment when you thought, What if it's the Purdey? but didn't say it.

"Well, you're wrong. You're wrong as hell. I don't recall any such thought."

Yes, well it was very subtle, very easy to forget. . . .

"Hey," said Ransom, "hey, screw you! Actually, if you want to get technical, what I remember thinking was, How can I give them the gun when I don't know where the fucker is?"

You don't know?

"Hell, no, I don't know! Do you?"

Hmm, the voice said, in a musing tone. *Nope, sorry. Nothing comes to mind.*

"All right, wiseass, want me to show you? I'll find the thing and turn it in."

You do that, Ran.

"You think I won't? Just watch me. I'll prove it to your faithless, sorry ass."

And, with that, he stalked off down the hallway with that slapping sole.

"Me!" he muttered. *"Me!"* indignantly. Exiting into the yard, he slammed the door so hard he almost broke the hinge.

TWENTY-NINE

*T*here is a pungent smell of herbs, the sound of dripping water, then the louder sound of something being wrung—a cloth or sponge—into a basin or a pail.

Addie follows these into the formal parlor to the right of the curved stairs and finds Paloma silently washing the deceased. Percival is laid out on a door the carpenters have set on sawhorses. Except for a cloth across his loins, he's naked, and his body is almost shocking in its whiteness, shocking and impressive in its size and strength, above all in its seeming youth. Except for the unnatural pallor and a deflated slackness in the lower belly, he does not look old. Addie thinks about Achilles on his shield, she thinks about a painting of the Deposition she once saw. Lifting one slack arm—which seems to condescend to its manipulation with tender indifference—Paloma swabs it with a sponge, moving from the shoulder to the wrist. She washes each finger individually and turns and does the palm, stroking from the heel toward the fingertip. And as she works, the water drips onto the cooling board and onto towels on the floor.

The scene is as intimate as that between two aged lovers in the bath, a husband and a wife. As quietly as possible, Addie starts to leave, but a floorboard creaks.

"What is it, niña?" Paloma's voice is calm and self-possessed, but her face, when Addie turns, is terrible, a mask of bitter, angry grief. She isn't crying now, but her eyes are red and sunken and her cheeks are streaked.

"I'm sorry, Paloma. It's nothing. We'll speak of it another time."

The old woman makes no answer. She stands, in a brown study, staring into space.

In Addie, a pang of sympathy vies against an urge to flee. "Paloma, can I help you?"

"No, you cannot help me. What is it you think to do?"

Addie hesitates, but it is brief. Crossing to Paloma now, she gently wrests the sponge away and leads her toward a chair. "Come," she says. "Come, and rest yourself a bit."

"He must be washed and dressed."

"I know. I know he must. But you sit here and tell me what to do."

The old woman neither consents nor actively resists. Sitting in the rocker, she takes a white candle from the stand and holds it at arm's length, widening her eyes. To Addie's distress, Paloma strikes a match and starts to light the bottom.

"Can I do that for you?"

"No."

"But, Paloma, you're lighting the wrong end."

"I'm lighting what I mean to light," she says. "If you want to help me, do this other the same way. Scrape the wick up with your nail. There, like that. Now, place them to either side of him, and, niña, when you wash him, wash downward, to his feet, not up. Up is to draw. Down, to take away."

Disturbed by these instructions, Addie nonetheless complies and doesn't ask. The coolness of the body is unnerving and the way the flesh, when touched, retains the impress and does not spring back. What unnerves her even more is that Percival, at close quarters, does not seem dead. His eyes are closed exactly as they were when she first saw him on the chaise, as though that moment were premonitory of this. His expression, though, suggests a suffering no longer calmly borne. He looks like someone ill from poisoning or drink, who's closed his eyes to take a miserable rest but cannot sleep.

"Paloma, if I haven't said so, I'm sorry for your loss."

"No, you haven't said so. But I thank you. You, too, have had a blow."

Addie looks up now, and Paloma simply holds her stare, her old eyes fearsome, not with enmity, but with long experience of life.

"How are you, niña?"

"It's in the past, Paloma," Addie says. "How can I blame them for what they didn't know?"

"No, niña, it is how they acted when they learned—that is what there is to blame them for."

This swift, cutting intuition, Addie thinks, Jarry got that from her.

"What is it you came to ask?"

"I was thinking of the clothes we lost. We can speak of it another time."

"What about them?"

"I wondered if we might not do some sewing here. I can knit, and I thought that we—or I—could perhaps begin with a new set of stockings for the crop hands, then—"

"Yes," Paloma cuts her off, "in the old days, not so many years ago, before the cloth from England and the Northern mills got cheap, we did that on the place. But, niña, there are four hundred people here. That is eight hundred stockings, eight hundred feet."

"But it cannot take so long, can it?" says Addie. "A single sock?"

"I don't know. Perhaps." Paloma seems unable, after all, to keep her concentration fixed on this, and they are silent as the water finds the channeled ribs, rills along the door edge, drips onto the floor.

Dipping the sponge, Addie feels something on the bottom of the basin and lifts out a length of dripping chain. She meets Paloma's gaze and blinks.

"Do you know why the top and bottom links are broken?" the old woman asks.

"Why?"

"To unloose, niña. You break the chain to set them free."

"And the herbs?"

"The rue is what you smell. There's agrimony in it. Other things."

"It is Cuban?"

"Cuban? No, I learned it on this place, right here, when I was just about your age—no, even younger. When I first came, I knew no one but Percival. Everything was strange to me. I was grieving for my country and my child. An old woman, Binah, taught me things. There's hyssop in it, too. 'Purge me with hyssop, and I shall be whiter than snow.' "

"That's from the Psalms."

"Yes, Fifty-one. That is what you say when you've brought evil on yourself through your own acts, or for another who has done so. Thirty-seven, if you're innocently wronged. Binah taught me this, and that you put the broken chain into the bath and stroke the body downward toward the feet and burn the candles upside down. All of it is to clean, to wash away, to protect and to reverse."

"To reverse what?"

Paloma's solemn face goes still more solemn now. "That, niña . . . that is what I do not know. There is something, though." She juts her chin toward the corpse. "Look at him. Can you not see the trouble in his face? He's troubled in his spirit, too. He has not gone. I feel him somewhere close."

There is gooseflesh, suddenly, on Addie's arms.

"He's in a dark place, calling out. He's trying to tell me where he is, and I want to help him—that's why I set these lights and made the wash. But I'm angry, too. So angry, niña. I don't know whether he's betrayed us, or if we've been deceived."

The older woman's scrutiny is now so close and fierce that Addie feels the blood rush to her cheeks.

"It is hard, niña," *Paloma says,* "very hard, at such a time as this, not to know the truth. And what is hard for me, for Jarry is harder still. You yourself, I think, know something about this."

It is all Addie can do to hold Paloma's stare and pray that her eyes, ill-suited to concealment, do not betray her. "How is he?" *she asks, subdued.*

"He's not himself. But God sends him busy-ness to spare him grief."

Addie wrings the sponge and stares down at the corpse, feeling wrung and twisted up herself. In such matters, her background has left no area of gray. But she has left the sunny path. She's in the woods. This is the moment Addie recognizes she has lost her way. "You're free, Paloma. Harlan told me so upstairs just now."

"And my son?"

"We can't do without him, Paloma. But Harlan thinks the war may well be done by summertime."

"And if it lasts ten years?"

"What am I to do?" *asks Addie in frustration.* "Do you expect me to step off the boat and start to tell my husband what to do?"

"No, niña, that is not what I expect of you."

"Even if there were a will," *says Addie,* "even if it freed him now, today, as you desire, it would make no difference. Harlan would oppose it in the courts, and he'd still have to stay. So, you see, it really makes no difference . . . You do see this, don't you?"

Paloma shakes her head. "It doesn't matter how long the war lasts, niña—if it lasts till all of us are dead or just one day. What matters to Jarry is what his father said to him in his last act. The worst thing about slavery, do you know what it is? I will tell you, niña. When you put a man in chains, you not only steal his body, you steal from him the truth of who he is."

"How does slavery do that?" *asks Addie, with a trace of heat.* "No, I don't see that, Paloma. It seems to me, you've both been treated fairly, and, in fact, quite well."

"I will tell you how," *she says.* "If you have two children, two sons, and say to one, 'You are my child, you are a human being, when you grow up you will be a man like me,' and to the other you say, 'You are an animal, when you grow up I will put *the bit into your mouth and hitch you to the cart and make you pull.' . . . The first thing that will happen is that second child, if he is strong like Jarry, will resist you, he'll rebel. But if his own father tells him this, the person he loves most and most respects, then that child's heart will break, he'll be destroyed, all but the strongest, and sometimes even they. This is how, niña, do you see? First you steal his body, then you steal the truth of who he is, that he is human, and when you've taken that, he cannot love himself. And when he cannot love himself, he cannot love you either, cannot love others or another, and when that's done, then you have taken his humanity. Then he becomes an animal, in truth, and worse, far worse. Because an animal, even a wolf, is innocent, but a man who's lost this no longer has a human soul, and when the soul is gone, then he is capable of any evil. He is capable of anything. I fought to keep my son from this, and I succeeded all these years. Now Percival has broken his last promise, and I'm afraid for Jarry, but who I fear for still more is Clarisse. Percival has brought this down on all of us, and even more so on himself."*

"You're hard on him, Paloma," Addie says, "too hard, I think. He loved you, loved you deeply. When I saw him yesterday, he told me so himself. Practically the last thing he said was that he loved you better than he had his wife."

Paloma is thoughtful over this. "There was a time, perhaps, when that was true—a few months or weeks in the beginning. . . . It was all so long ago. I remember it, but not how long it lasts. What I remember best is Percival sitting by the bed where we had been, reading poetry to me in English. I didn't understand the words, but I loved the music of his voice and how his face would change. One minute he would frown, and then a smile would break, he'd hold a finger up like this as if to warn or promise what the coming line would be. It was like sunlight, niña, the way it filters through the branches of a tree. . . . Jarry got this from his father. And he is still beautiful." *She gazes, frowning, at the corpse.* "He is still beautiful, isn't he?"

"He is, Paloma," *Addie says with sympathy.*

"But this all ended, you see."

"When he didn't free you . . ."

Paloma shakes her head. "No, it wasn't that. We never spoke of freedom. It seems naive and foolish now, but I felt already free. I felt that, in his heart, Percival had already granted this to me, and, more than that, I felt that I had granted it to him, the same. And, by this, I mean a different, higher sort of freedom, niña, one that neither of us possessed until we found it through each other. We were equal, Percival in need like me, and we both gave and both received. And so, to speak about this other freedom, niña, to speak about the legal thing, the fact that he still held my deed, this would have felt like an embarrassment. We were here." *Paloma holds her hand at the level of her brow. "And to speak about the other . . ." She drops it to the level of her breast. "Do you see? It would be like church, if you were discussing your wedding with the priest, talking of your joy and future happiness in life. . . . To then stop and ask him, how much, Padre, is this going to cost? This would be a smallness, no? So it seemed to me." She stops and looks away.*

"Now there were others in the templo who felt differently. Percival, then, you understand was more Kimbisa than the Kimbiseros—he was on fire with Palo. And if he was sincere, they felt, this blanco, then he ought to free his woman, oughtn't he? Demetrio, our padrino, spoke to him of it, and Percival heard him out respectfully, but then he went his way and nothing changed. Finally it was the santos who placed him under this command. It was San Luis Beltrán speaking through Andrés Petit. But, me, niña, I never asked for freedom. The only thing I ever asked for was Clarisse."

Addie's expression slackens. "Clarisse . . ."

"This is what you haven't grasped. I asked him for my child. Clarisse was three months old, niña, three months, when she was taken from my breast."

"But it was Villa-Urrutia, I thought. Didn't Villa-Urrutia do that?"

"Wenceslao asked for her, but it was Percival who enforced his claim. I begged him not to give her back. What difference did it make to that old man? He only wanted her to punish us."

"For what?"

"For what? Because he lost the game. Because Percival won. Because he wanted me, and I was gone."

"But that wasn't your fault. It wasn't even by your choice."

Paloma laughs. "What of that? Are you shocked that Wenceslao was cruel? That he was unjust? So what if he was, the Conde was still angry and someone had to pay. He couldn't punish Percival, and who was left? So he punished me by taking the one thing I wanted most, and Percival—this man who you say loved me better than his wife—allowed it. That was what I asked him for, not freedom. What is freedom? A word. The only freedom that meant anything to me was to be a mother to my child."

"Oh, Paloma. I didn't see."

"No, you didn't see. Nor did Percival. But it is just this seeing, niña—this, to me, is what love is, the greater part of it. There is in each of us one deep, last place. To truly love another is to see him there, to see him as he sees himself, and hold him, hold his differentness in the same tender care with which you hold yourself. Had Percival seen and loved me in that way, how could he have done this? Had I been white like you, all Cuba would have risen to defend me. The ministers would have thundered from the pulpits. Armies would have marched into the field. But for a pardo

*slave to lose a child—this happened fifty times a day. Who was there to grieve but
me? Binah was the only one."*

"I'm shocked that Percival allowed this."

"He tried to buy her back—I give him that—but to Wenceslao, the meanness
was sweeter than the price. When he refused, that was the end of it."

"But what else could Percival have done?"

"What else? We could simply have climbed aboard the ship and sailed away
with her, and what could Wenceslao have done? He would have stamped and fumed
and been over it by nightfall. Would a man not do this for a woman that he loved, a
husband for his wife? But, no, niña, Percival was a gentleman. To welsh on a gam-
bling debt to another caballero? Unthinkable. So, being true to honor, he took my
daughter—his own child—away from me. Would he have done this to Melissa?
Never, niña. Never in a thousand years. No, if he had loved me as he said, Clarisse
would have come with us to South Carolina. She'd have grown up in this house
with her two brothers. She and Harlan would have looked into each other's eyes a
hundred times a day. And if this had happened, niña . . . do you see? You
wouldn't suffer what you suffer now. Nor would Jarry. Percival would have married
me, and Jarry would have grown up free. But these things, they were not to be, no,
por donde salta la madre, salta la hija. . . . Where the mother leads, the daughter
follow—so in my old country it is said—and hijo de gato ratón caza, the cat's son
chase the rat. You see how it turns out. For Clarisse with Harlan, it is just the same
as Percival and me. Now it has touched you, too. It is all fruit, fruit of the poison
tree. And it isn't over yet. No, I look into your eyes this morning, I look into this
old man's face and see the trouble there, and fear that we have not seen the beginning
of the worst."

"Do you mean to frighten me?"

"It isn't me you need to fear."

"Do I need to fear Clarisse?"

Paloma's face takes an obstreperous set.

"Harlan thinks we've been bewitched."

"What is it to me what Harlan thinks?"

"Did Jarry tell you what I saw?"

"He told me what you said you saw."

"You don't believe me?"

Paloma looks toward the window now. "I don't know what I believe. I only
know there cannot be a prenda here. It makes no sense."

"I don't know what a prenda is."

"And you don't need to know."

"But my locket, Paloma," she protests, "the one I gave Harlan for our engagement—I saw it there. A knife was driven through the hinge. And the plate that had the leeches on it. Who else could have put them there except Clarisse?"

Paloma's eyes are furred and hot. "Do you understand what you are saying? You're telling me she is a bruja, niña. You're telling me my daughter is a witch. I've looked into her eyes, I've asked, and she says she knows nothing of these things. Whose word am I to take—yours, or my own child's?"

"Then whose else could it be? I know what I saw, Paloma."

"I only know it cannot be Clarisse's. For her to do this, to make a prenda—even if she knew how, and where would she have learned?—for any woman not yet past the change to do this would be to risk her life, and more than that. Much more than her life. It would be to damn herself. Why, niña? Why would she do this? No, this I will not believe. Clarisse would not break regla."

"What is regla?"

"Regla, niña? Regla is order, proper order. There is regla in a house, a land, between two people, you and me, a mistress and a slave, between parents and children, between a woman and a man. There is also regla between us and them"—she points her chin toward Percival—"between the living and the dead. When it's broken, niña, nothing can go right. The nfumbis and nkisis give us a chance to make repair, sometimes only hours. Percival was given years and never did make right. Now he's died and left us with his mess. And it's not just Percival. This war that's coming—that is what I think it is. Long ago, in Africa and Europe, regla was broken by our kings, who sold their people, and yours, who bought the slaves. Many of my people have lost faith along the way. They think slavery is proof our gods are weak and lower than your God, but what I think, niña, what in my heart I believe, is the nkisis left it up to us, and now the time is past. Now they are tired and angry. We have failed to make regla, and they are coming to administer it, they are on us even now. Because, you see, niña, we have one chance, however long or brief, to make repair in love and gentleness, but if we let it pass, they come in blood and fire. . . . Now when I hear that there are armies raised to north and south, I fear the spirits are coming to make regla in this nation. I hear you've seen a prenda in the woods and fear they're coming to make regla in this house."

"What do you want from me, Paloma? I mean no harm to you or yours, but I can do only what's in my power."

"The truth is in your power, isn't it? That is what I want from you, niña, and all I want. Before you accuse my daughter, look into your own heart. If Percival is innocent and you know the truth, don't let us put him in the grave, accused. If Harlan's lie hurt you, spare me and Jarry what was done to you. We're human, too. Help us, niña. If you will, then I'll help you."

And whom do I betray? thinks Addie. Do I tell her and betray my husband? Or do I keep the secret and betray Paloma, Jarry, Percival, myself? It's strange to her how clear the answer is. . . .

"I understand your disappointments, Paloma," she says, wringing out the sponge and putting it beside the body on the board. Her face has taken on the melancholy cast it wore as she watched the oarsmen and the parakeets vanish in the Nina's wake. "I wish I could give you what you want and all you want, but I've told you everything I can. All I can do now is strive to be as good a mistress as I can. To that end, I intend to start right now, today, to make arrangements for new clothes so people in the quarters can be comfortable, at least."

Paloma studies her for a long beat. "Bueno, child, que así sea," she says, and as Addie makes her way toward the door, the old woman grips her wrist. "Just remember, niña, there is also regla in the self."

Addie merely blinks and makes no answer, and in this moment it is as if the older woman has receded behind a wall of glass.

Reverend Hilliard is a thin, bald man with an ascetic face and steel-rimmed spectacles that seem at odds with lavish vestments. From the Book of Common Prayer, he reads the Burial of the Dead to those lately assembled on the shore of the black pond, under the cypress, and to those already here, beneath the mossy stones, who've heard the words before.

" 'Thou knowest, Lord, the secrets of our hearts. Shut not thy merciful ears to our prayer. . . .' "

As he reads, Addie's gaze drifts over the small crowd to Paloma, and to Jarry at her side. Clarisse is absent, and Addie wonders at this briefly, but it's Jarry's face that occupies her thoughts. His head is bowed, and he looks fretful and intense. His collar and clothes are disarranged, as if he's slept in them, if he has slept at all. His eyes are red, and he looks drunk or slightly mad.

" 'Lord most holy, O God most mighty, O holy and most merciful Savior, thou most worthy Judge eternal, suffer us not, at our last hour, for any pains of death, to fall from thee.' "

Moving in a kind of dream, she watches Harlan throw his clod of earth and throws her own. In a kind of dream, she takes the white musk rose he breaks from Jarry's climber, holds the stem as Harlan kisses her, and mounts his horse.

"I'm sorry, Addie, at how poorly this began."

The sun is behind him; looking up, she has to shade her eyes. "Godspeed, my dear."

"I wish I could stay," he says, but even with the sun behind him, Addie sees his eyes stray to the tree line and the road. In them is a sheen she's seen in dogs before the hunt, and she can tell that, even as he speaks the words he thinks he means, he's eager to be gone.

"Go," she tells him. "And know that I'll pray always for your swift and safe return."

He leans down and kisses her, and then, at a soft canter, he rides away down the white road, toward the vanishing point where the lines of trees converge in the allée.

Watching, Addie feels a subtle sense of letdown, and the clear thought comes to her, That wasn't it. . . . Marriage hasn't proved to be the plausible beginning of the beginning she had hoped. But under disappointment looms the sudden sense of possibility, the same she felt three days ago, standing in the Nina's bows, as though perhaps now it, true life, can start.

Harlan is gone now, and when she turns, the park opens like the green world of a fairy tale, and coming toward her through it, also moving in a kind of dream, is Jarry. As she waits, Addie's heart is beating out a heavy klaxon in her chest, and she does not know why, or ask, or what will happen when he comes.

When he arrives, she smiles, but he does not.

"Yesterday, when we came back from the swamp," he says, direct, without preliminaries, "you were about to tell me something. . . ."

Addie blinks. She holds her smile, but it grows fixed and out of touch with the false incomprehension in her eyes. "Was I? I was so confused then, Jarry, I hardly remember where I was. I'm afraid it's slipped my mind."

He studies her doubtfully.

"I'm sorry how it's turned out," she says. "I know it must be a disappointment to you."

He continues to regard her searchingly. "It's not your fault," he says, and as he walks away, she waits for the voice to speak, to thunder from the depths and tell her what this means. It doesn't, though, and it occurs to Addie now it won't. The voice, silent for so many years, has gone to ground again. And, after all, isn't it a great relief? Why, then, does Addie feel bereft? The cup has passed, as Addie wished and prayed it would—why, then, the sudden, violent need to drink?

THIRTY

J'm thirsty, Daddy!" Hope whined from the backseat.

"Me, too, Doddy—I firsty, too!"

"We'll get some water in a minute."

"I want *juice!*"

"*Quiet!*" As the yellow light turned red on Meeting Street, Ran gunned it through the intersection. The driver of an eastbound car leaned on his horn, Dopplering angrily away down Broad, and Ransom, rattled by the Charleston traffic, watched him in the rearview and had to swerve to miss a tourist carriage. Jamming on the brake, he felt the ABS engage, stuttering underfoot. The passenger-side wheel scraped the curb and the Odyssey lurched forward, then rocked stiffly back to rest.

"Are you all right?"

From the back, the children regarded him in shocked and sober silence.

As the hansom pulled around, the driver raised an open hand and stood up in the seat to glare. Ransom, feeling like a criminal, sat there with a pounding heart and told himself to breathe.

"Who you trying to kill—yourself or someone else?" An elderly basket lady, who'd spread her wares on quilts before the courthouse, posed this question. It had, for Ransom, an ominously prophetic ring he knew well from prior episodes and well knew to distrust.

Despite the dose of lithium he'd downed at Claire's OB, he was deep in the dark tunnel now and days away from any hope of light. The profound unwisdom of his course struck home, as usual, in retrospect. Last night with Claire, he got his wish; today, he got the price. And here he was—and here they were. Again.

"Let me get back to you on that," he told the basket lady now. "We're having a minor family meltdown here."

She shook her head and tsked, returning to the weaving in her lap.

"I want ice keem, Doddy!" Charlie cried, demanding compensatory damages as he emerged from trance.

"Well, you aren't getting any," Ransom said, "and that's the end of that. It's almost suppertime. I got you ice cream yesterday, and look where we are now."

That's right, said the voice. *It's all the children's fault for wanting ice cream yesterday, isn't it? If not for that, you'd be sipping hurricanes on Easy Street and there'd be naked women fanning you with ostrich plumes and feeding you peeled grapes.*

If he'd known how, Ran would have plunged a karate knife-hand into his chest, grabbed the speaker by his ugly throat, and throttled him, or it. He lacked those skills, however, and it occurred to Ransom as a glancing thought that, whatever colorful and gruesome side effects he'd experienced when he'd gone off the reservation in the past, he'd never heard a voice—not one like this. So what was that about?

The exigencies of parenthood allowed no leisure to contemplate the fine points of his medical and spiritual condition.

"Can we at least listen to another *song*?" said Hope.

"What's wrong with this one?" On the deck, Robert Johnson was wailing "Hell Hound on My Trail." "I thought you liked my music."

"Not twenty *times*," Hope said. "Not twenty times, I don't."

"It's helping me," said Ran with a quaver, feeling assailed from every side, within as well as without. Then he lost it. "Is that okay? I know I'm the grown-up here, and I'm supposed to be omniscient and omnipotent, but is it okay for me, for once, to need and maybe even get a little *goddamn help*?" This rose to a crescendo, and the last two words escaped him at a roar that shook the Odyssey like a tornado rattling a Kansas cellar door.

His Master's Voice, the nemesis piped up, and Ransom didn't need to ask it what it meant.

Hope's blue eyes were filled with the same doubt Mel, once upon a time, had put in his, the doubt that Ran, coming here, had made it his business to remove. Worse, he knew from personal experience that the shout had made her doubt not him, the shouter, but herself. "What's wrong, Daddy?" she asked in a much younger voice. "Did we do something wrong?"

"No, it's me," he answered in a husky whisper. "It's me, not you, okay?"

At his confession, they both went to pieces, and Ransom, overwhelmed with guilt, felt his eyes brim and dropped his head against the wheel.

"I firsty, Doddy!"

"All right," he said. "All right."

"You there, mister . . ." The basket lady snapped her fingers at the car, and Ransom frowned and turned, prepared to take her on.

"There's water in this cooler." She jerked her chin toward the Igloo Playmate at her knee.

Expecting conflict, Ransom blinked and made no move.

"Get out of that car," she said, "and get some water for that child."

Resentful of her tone, but inwardly relieved to follow orders, Ran got out and fetched a pony from the ice. "Thanks. How much?"

She pressed her lips and shook her head, refusing to look at him.

"Let me buy a basket then. How much is this?" He picked one up.

"Twenty dollars."

"The tag says twenty-two."

"I reckon I can charge you twenty if I want to, can't I?"

Cheered by her irascibility, Ran took out his pocket roll and peeled a bill. "Here you go, Alberta." He read the name from a cloth tag sewn cunningly into the reeds.

She tucked it in her apron pocket, then visored her eyes and squinted up at him. "You in trouble, ain't you?"

"A small spot."

"You look like you in a whole heap."

"You're an astute woman," he said unresentfully.

"Whatever it is, it ain't worth that," she said. "It ain't worth yelling at your children. You know that, don't you?"

"Yes," he said after a beat, "yes, actually I do."

"Sometime you got to step away," she said. "Every parent ever lived had to do that some. Me, seem like I had to once or twice a day myself. Ain't no shame to it."

A crack occurred to him—"Thanks for the lecture"—but he found the lecture steadying and held it back.

"Do you mind if I let them stretch their legs?" he asked instead.

"I don't own the street," Alberta said. "Much time as I spend out here, I ought to. They ought to named it after me at least, but they ain't done it yet. That sign still says Meeting, don't it?"

Ransom smiled and nodded.

"Not Alberta Johns?"

"Not Alberta Johns."

"What's your name, son?"

"Ransom."

"Ransom what?"

"Ransom Hill."

"Ransom, let your children get a drink."

He prompted the side door.

"What's your name, Miss Blue Eyes?" Alberta asked, giving her a bottle.

Hope looked at him, and Ransom nodded.

"Hope," she said.

"Know what this is?" Alberta nodded to the basket in her lap, a round shallow one three-quarters done, with the unwoven fibers radiating out like variegated spokes around a wheel. "What the old folks call a fanner. Used to winnow rice."

"What's 'winnow'?"

"That means dividing the good part, what you eat, off from the chaff you give the hogs. I don't reckon you ever fed no hogs, have you? Probably never even saw one."

"On TV."

"On TV. Come over here and let me show you how to weave. Want to try?"

"I'd like to," Hope said, "but I'm not allowed to talk to strangers."

"It's okay, Hope," said Ran.

"And you there, little man," Alberta said. "What's your name?"

"Cholly?"

"Can you count, Charlie?"

"One, two, free!" he said, breaking out in his sweet grin.

"You see them baskets? Run down there to the end and put 'em in a stack for me. I got to leave here soon. Big on the bottom, little ones on top."

"Okay."

"Okay's okay," Alberta said, "but can you say 'Yes, ma'am'?"

"Yes, ma'am!"

Charlie ran off happily engaged, and Ransom thought once more about the universal primer course on parenting—Alberta Johns had clearly taken an advanced degree. Despite his problem with authority, he was grateful to surrender team command, grateful to step back into the ranks and be a PFC. Staring south down the block, his eye lit on a big Georgian double house across the street, and Ransom, granted the opportunity to breathe and gladly taking it, contemplated his next move. . . .

Having failed—despite a second, more exhaustive daylight search—to find the Purdey, he'd driven straight downtown intending to come clean with Sergeant Thomason. As he passed the station with the children, though, a young cop on the steps had shot a dark, suspicious glance his way, and Ransom suddenly worried that, without the gun in hand, a confession might raise more questions than it answered and increase suspicions he'd thereby hoped to quell. On balance, it seemed best to keep moving, keep moving, like Robert Johnson's ghost was singing in the Odyssey right now. There was a story here, as Thomason had pointed out, and even if it happened a long time ago, before he was even born, Ran had begun to wonder and to worry—prompted by that little voice that, as time went on, seemed less and less familiar—that maybe that old story had something to do with him after all, something to do with all of them. To make that determination, first he had to find out what the story was. His gaze homed in on the second-story window of what Ran felt fairly confident was the Music Room, and he prayed Aunt Tildy would be home.

"This here's bulrush, and this one's sweetgrass," Alberta said to Hope, running a supple strand between her fingers to arm's length. "Smell that, ain't it nice? My mama used to smell of that, and that was just about her color, too. Me, I'm like this dark here in the coil. That's pine straw, and this one . . . who you reckon this one is?" Alberta laid a pale frond, ribbon-width, against Hope's arm and smiled.

"Me?"

"Um-hm. That's palmetto, sugar. The rush and grass what make it strong, but the palmetto holds it all together. That's the thread you use to sew the coil. And this here, see? This is your needle. Ain't nothing but a old spoon you cut the bowl off and file flat. Now lookahere. You tuck it in and pull it through, and then you tuck it back and pull it out, in and out, and back and through. . . . See how I do? You try it now."

Alberta gave the spoon to Hope, and Ransom watched his daughter weaving brown with white and white with brown and brown with white again. As the old woman turned the basket clockwise in her lap by slow degrees, the spiral mesmerized him, and the different-colored strands rayed out around the central disk no longer seemed like spokes so much as sunbeams, checkered sunbeams radiating from a checkered sun, and it was not completed yet . . . It was being woven still, by this old woman and this girl, hands black and white, but it was far along and had to be completed at all costs.

Something had seized hold of Ran. He felt the small hairs stand along his back and remembered now what he always forgot, the deeper reason why he strayed from his chemical regime. Sex was the least part of it; the real reason was because there always came a point where what he had no longer felt like a disease. There came a point when he contacted something in himself he trusted more than medicines or doctors, more, even, than he trusted Claire, his wife. Standing on the west side of Meeting Street in Charleston, before the courthouse, opposite the church, Ran had reached that point again, and he smelled the sea air now and caught the *clop* of hooves receding on the cobblestones. The *shhhh* of traffic sounded like breath exhaled, and he noticed the light now, that special September light you find only in Charleston, on late afternoons, from four p.m. and on. Ran, at least, had seen it nowhere else, still broad day away up there, so blue and high, rinsed clean, where seagulls wheeled, while down here, closer to the ground, shadows had begun to fall.

Hard to tell what's in a person's heart by looking in their face, Mr. Hill. Awful hard. Sergeant Thomason's objection surfaced, and Ransom, looking at Alberta, gave it due consideration before putting it aside. That lesson was from the basic course; Ransom, now, had moved on to advanced.

"Alberta?"

She looked up and frowned, as though remembering him unwillingly.

"I've got to speak to someone down the street. You see that house?" He pointed, and she turned her head.

"That's Miss Tildy DeLay's," she said. "What you want with her? You ain't going to knock her in the haid and take her jew'ry, are you?"

"She's my aunt," said Ran.

"Your aunt?" Alberta studied him. "Git on out from here, boy! You ain't got the bones to come from that!"

Ransom frowned. "You're a discerning woman, Alberta—we've established that. I need your help. Can you watch the children while I go?"

"Watch your children . . ."

"For ten minutes. Fifteen, tops."

"What's wrong with you?" she said indignantly. "You don't know me, boy. I could be the devil in blue suede shoes."

Ran stared deep into Alberta's deep experienced old eyes and shook his head. "No, uh-uh, I don't think so. No one who weaves lines that straight can have a crooked heart. You know I'm right."

"You wrong is what I think. You most seriously wrong."

"It's important, Alberta."

"Take 'em with you then."

Ransom shook his head. "I can't. If I was on fire, Tildy wouldn't piss on me to put it out, but this trouble I'm in, Alberta? Tildy's the only hope of help I've got. I can't handle the children and her both. I'll pay you a hundred dollars."

"A hundred dollars?"

"Make it two," he said. "A hundred now and another hundred when I come back out."

"Lord have mercy." Alberta clucked her tongue and looked away. "I hope you ain't the devil come to tempt me."

"I hope so, too," said Ran. "I'm pretty sure I'm not."

"Pretty sure ain't all that comforting."

"That's why I'm leaving them with you. Is it a deal or not?"

"Ten minutes."

"Fifteen, tops." He held out the bill, and she hesitated, then snatched it. "Fifteen means fifteen," she said. "It don't mean fifteen and a half."

"Thank you, Alberta. Thank you very much. You see that window? I'll be standing there the whole time looking down. If you need me, just wave and I'll come running. And if they disappear, Alberta, if my children disap-

pear even for a second and a half . . ." He turned the basket and nodded to
the tag. "Just remember, I know where you live."

"Don't start threatening," she said. "I ain't going to take 'em. What I
want to take 'em for?"

"Here's her number." Ran handed her the card he'd lifted from Claire's
Rolodex, together with his cell phone. "Call me if you need me, and listen,
Alberta, if anything goes wrong . . . and I mean seriously wrong, I mean an
emergency . . . See this? You hit this key—number 2—and hold it down,
and it'll dial their mother. Her name is Claire. Don't call her unless you really
have to, Alberta, hear me? But if you have to, don't even blink. These children are everyth—" Suddenly Ransom had to suck his breath and look away.

"Well, don't start bawling in the middle of the street," she said. "I
watched plenty of children in my time and never lost one yet. I reckon I
can watch two more for fifteen minutes."

"Okay, Hope," Ran said to his daughter, who'd been attending to
this negotiation with an expression of profound misgiving. "Charlie,
bring it in. Listen, guys, Alberta's going to look after you for a few minutes while I run down the block. I won't be long, okay? You mind your
manners, do what she says, and don't go near the street."

"Daddy," Hope said, lowering her voice, "I don't think Mommy—"

"Mommy's not here," he cut her off. "I have to make this call. Alberta's
all right. She'll take good care of you."

Hope looked unconvinced, and Charlie, picking up the vibe, began to
cry. Ran looked back and forth between them. "Look, guys," he said, deciding to come clean, "I won't lie to you. Something is a little wrong, but
I'm on top of it. Daddy's going to get it fixed, but I need your help for ten
or fifteen minutes. Can you give me that?"

Charlie, snuffling up his tears, merely nodded, prepared to charge whatever hill. "I want ice keem, Doddy."

"When I get back, I'll get you some."

"Promise?"

Ransom crossed his heart.

Hope, however, didn't let him off the hook. The look she gave Ransom
seared him. It was the look of someone who's defended you against all
comers, who's called day night for you, and black, white, in the moment she
first realizes your detractors were all right.

"I have to do this, Pete," he said. And Ransom turned his back.

THIRTY-ONE

S o Addie works.

Her first morning alone at Wando Passo, she hurries down-stairs, thinking to throw herself into her project, only to find fifteen people waiting on the porch.

"Good morning. Is there something . . ."

"We yeah fuh git de day tas, miss." The gardener, Peter, looks at her expectantly, holding his doffed cap.

Her brow creases like a press, attempting to extract essential oil from this. "For-get" is the one word she thinks she gets. "Perhaps you should speak to Jarry. . . ."

"'E wif de bud mindas cross de ribbah, mistis." Peter points toward the fields on the far side of the Pee Dee. "Shum, enty?"

"I'm sorry . . ."

"Dey, mistis. Yeddy 'im?" He points to his ear. "Dey dey!" He thrusts his hand in frustrated emphasis.

Fortunately, at this moment Paloma appears from the trees with two young girls carrying the shallow sweetgrass baskets known as fanners. Normally used to winnow rice, these are presently filled with a silvery-white eider Addie can't identify.

"Day tasks" turns out to be the operative phrase, and Addie listens carefully, understanding little, as the old woman sets them all about their work. There is Minda, the head cook, and the gardener, Peter, and Peter's boy, and the butler, William, and Ancrum, the coachman, and Tenah and Annie, the up- and downstairs maids, and the laundress, Hattie, and two seamstresses, and Jas, the second dining room man, and the scullion, Lem, and Peck and John and Tilly, whose duties Addie fails to grasp, and several others whose names escape on this first pass. Addie can't comprehend who they all are, or why so many servants are required. And spoken Gullah is a far cry from the version she's heard Harlan and other Georgetown planters imitate at parties, charming laughing audiences, which frequently included her, with anecdotes about old Quash—frustrated in love and offering the "retort cuddius" to some rival for his sharp-tongued paramour's affections—at St. Cecelia's Balls, between the German and the waltz.

In an effort to make up for the candles they've lost—Wando Passo uses thirty dozen every month—Paloma sets the girls to spinning wicks from milkweed down collected in the swamp, and then she turns to Addie with a cool appraisal that calls to mind the word she spoke in private— "regla"—which forevermore will form part of Addie's core understanding of the world.

Intimidated by the older woman, Addie keeps their exchange polite, but to a minimum. Feeling isolated and superfluous in her new home, the new mistress throws herself into her stocking project, but the maxim from her Mme Togno days creeps back.

"A promise broken, hell hath opened. . . . A promise kept, and hell hath wept. . . ."

Addie knits in rhythm to the words, a maddening refrain she can't purge from her thoughts. To make it stop, she counts. There are two hundred stitches to the row. Somewhere shy of two thousand, in the one thousand nine hundred nineties, Addie loses count and must begin again. By lunch on the first day, she—who's knitted no few infant caps for pregnant Charleston friends—has managed fifty rows; by suppertime, a hundred. Twenty thousand stitches in a single day to make a piece of fabric not quite large enough to cover half her hand. That night, with blurred vision, she reads Mrs. Hamilton on education, wanting to fill her mind with self-improving thoughts, turning the pages with her cramped right hand. On the second day, she picks up her pace and manages a hundred and fifty rows. The first stocking, when it's done, contains nine hundred rows and has taken seven days of constant work. Like a traveler on a mountain she's thought to climb with ease, Addie feels the shadow of the peak fall over her and, looking up, begins to grasp how high it truly is. Seven hundred ninety-nine to go. On day thirteen, in mingled triumph and despair, she finishes the mate. Now only three hundred ninety-nine more pairs.

And it's on this thirteenth day, toward suppertime, that Addie feels a chill—particularly noticeable in her hands and feet—which she at first writes off to overwork. When Tenah comes to summon her to table, the maid finds Addie wrapped in coverlets and blankets, prostrate on the chaise, her teeth chattering uncontrollably.

Paloma comes and lays a warm, dry hand on Addie's brow, checks the inner lining of her lower eyelid.

"El paludismo," she tells her son, and Addie sees the gravity of it in Jarry's face.

Sending everybody from the room, Paloma lifts Addie's nightclothes and loops a string around her waist. This has been dipped in some astringent liquid that smells like turpentine. In it, Paloma ties a knot.

"What is this for?" asks Addie.

"It will help," is all she says.

The old woman prescribes a tea of branch elder twigs and dogwood berries. Addie finds this soothing, but despite the remedy, within an hour and a half, her chill has passed into a fever that rages through the night. Every inch of Addie's flesh feels scalded; she writhes and twists, comfortable in no position. She throws the covers off and calls to have the windows raised, though they're already up. Nor can she quench her thirst, however much she drinks. Finally, toward dawn, the fever breaks. She sweats so heavily, Tenah and Paloma have to change the linen twice. As the crews, still sullen-faced with sleep, board flats to cross the Pee Dee to the fields, Addie finally falls into a torpid sleep.

When she awakes, it's late the following afternoon and Dr. Sims is holding her left wrist and staring at his watch. "I understand you spent an evening wandering the swamps two weeks ago, Mrs. DeLay," he says in a mock-stern tone that instantly braces her. "I strongly disapprove. Most strongly. Your peregrinations have bought you a case of the remittent fever."

"Do you mean . . . ?"

"I mean the ague, madam," he says, snapping shut the lid and slipping his watch into his waistcoat. "I mean, the country fever. That is what the Negroes and the old folks call it, or used to in the days when people still believed that it was caused by miasmal exudations from the swamp. The most advanced opinion nowadays— here and on the Continent—holds paludal fever to be caused by the spores of nox- ious plants, which breed from putrefying matter in the swamps. When the vapors rise at dusk, these deadly influences are carried to us and inhaled into the lungs. Our sys- tems can tolerate a certain amount—a man's more than a woman's, a Negro's more than a white's, a native's more than a visitor's. You, regrettably, are susceptible on all three counts. The only known palliative—and, note, I do not say a cure—is sulfate of quinia. Unfortunately, Jarry informs me that Wando Passo's quinine stores were lost at sea during your outbound trip. I myself, due to the damned blockade—and please excuse my French—have been unable, for a month and more, to procure it for my patients or myself at any price. There may still be some stores in Charleston, but, assuming you can find them, they are sure to cost their weight in gold, and are, in

fact, more likely to cost their weight in precious stones. Your aunt, however, given her position, might be able to prevail on her connections. . . ."

"I'm sorry," Addie says, alarmed, "are you suggesting I repair to Charleston?"

"I'm suggesting nothing of the kind, madam. I'm suggesting—I am strictly ordering you, in fact—to remain exactly where you are, in bed. If it comes to that, you'll have to send someone, though I must tell you, the idea of Jarry here, or any Negro, on the roads—which are presently filled with brigands—with a large sum of cash, is a recipe for misadventure."

"I'm prepared to go," he volunteers.

"It may not come to that," says Sims. "The disease has several manifestations, not all of which are equally concerning."

"Actually, I feel much better now," she says, gamely sitting up.

"That, my dear," says Sims, "is wholly immaterial. The illness follows an invariable pattern—from chills, to fever, to diaphoresis, sometimes called the hot-wet phase, followed, lastly, by a period of remission before the cycle starts again. The key question is the interval. If you go until this time tomorrow without relapse, then you have the less virulent form of the disease, and we can confidently hope to expel the materia morbi from your system with the means at hand, namely emetics, purgatives, and phlebotomy."

"And if it recurs before that time?"

"We shall cross that bridge, my dear, when, and if, we arrive at it. The subtertian or malignant form of the remittent fever is far less common in these parts."

"But if it is . . . what you said."

Sims holds her stare. "Then Jarry will set out for Charleston on your fastest horse."

"You're suggesting I might die?"

"In my experience," Sims says, "the subtertian or malignant fever, if untreated with quinine, is fatal in four cases out of five."

It's a moment before she fully takes this in. "Thank you," she says, in a clear tone, with dignity.

For the first time in the interview, there is a flash of emotion in the physician's eyes. "I'll be back in the morning."

"You should rest now," Jarry tells her, after Sims departs.

"Yes, I know I should. But Jarry . . . ?"

At the door already, he looks back. "I'll sit with you," he says, with the ready intuition she remembers from the swamp. "Shall I read to you?"

"Would you?"

He reaches for her Byron on the stand.

"Not that, though. Not him. You choose for me. I'm so weary of my preferences."

He briefly mulls, then leaves the room. As she waits, the male cardinal alights on a stout limb of the oak outside, and Addie watches as he sings.

" 'There was a roaring in the wind all night,' " Jarry begins,

" 'The rain came heavily and fell in floods;
But now the sun is rising calm and bright;
The birds are singing in the distant woods.' "

"This is familiar," she says at the conclusion of the verse. "Is it Wordsworth?"

" 'Resolution and Independence.' "

" 'We poets in our youth,' " she says, " 'begin in gladness, / But thereof comes . . .' Remind me what it is that comes thereof."

" 'But thereof in the end come despondency and madness'. . . . Yes, those are the lines everyone remembers, but to me, they're just the fruit on the low branches of the tree."

"The low branches . . ." She gives a languid laugh. "Do you know I found Wordsworth dull at school?"

"I'd rate him over Byron—by a wide margin, too."

At the challenge, Addie smiles. "This is the poem your father read you."

"Yes."

"And if you hated Percival," she says, "how did that occur?"

A shadow crosses Jarry's brow. "I'm not sure you'd find it a diverting story."

"Then tell me an undiverting one. . . ."

Closing his finger in the book, he rests it on his knee and sits back in his chair. "That was the year I ran away with Thomas."

"Who was he?"

"The smith. He was more a father to me then than Father was."

"How did you come to leave?"

"I was the scullion," Jarry says, "the same position Lem holds now. Every morning I hauled sand from the river to the kitchen house and scraped the burned muck from the bottom of the pots. Because I was the master's son, the people in the quarters had a hard time accepting me, while Father himself had barely ever looked at me, except to bid me fetch him this or that. The only place I felt at home was at the forge. Thomas was forty-two, the same age I am now. He used to tell us stories. . . ." And now, it is as if a ray of sun has touched his brow, and Addie's face, in its reflection, lightens, too. The door that shut upon the memory of their morning

in the swamp swings open, and what has come to seem almost a dream to her is not a dream at all.

"What stories did he tell?"

"Animal tales, mostly. Brother Rabbit and Brother Wolf."

"Do you mean Brer Rabbit and Brer Fox? Lucius used to tell those stories in my aunt's yard in Charleston."

"Up in Cheraw and that way, they tell it with a fox. When my mother was a girl in Cuba, an old Jamaican woman told her the same tales with a spider and a tiger. But the way Thomas always told it, the way it was told here, was with a rabbit and a wolf."

"And what did Thomas say?"

" 'Well, Brother Wolf and Brother Rabbit, they were neighbors. . . .' "

"No," she says, "as it was told to you."

"In Gullah?" There is something sharp in Jarry's hesitation, before he decides in her favor. " 'Buh Wolf and Buh Rabbit, dem bin lib nabur,' " he begins. " 'De dry drout come. Water scase. Buh Wolf dig one spring fuh him fuh git water. Buh Rabbit, him too lazy and too scheemy fuh wuk fuh isself. 'E pen pon lib off tarrah people.' "

"He . . . depended upon . . . ?"

" 'Lib off tarrah people.' "

"Living off . . . other people?"

"That's it," he says. " 'Ebry day, wen Buh Wolf yent duh watch um,' e slip to Buh Wolf spring, an 'e full him calabash long water and cah um to 'e house fuh cook long and fuh drink. Buh Wolf see Buh Rabbit track, but 'e couldn ketch um, de tief de water—' "[1]

"Wait," she says, sitting up. "This is the tar baby story, isn't it?"

Jarry smiles. "You've heard it."

"Not this way, though. Go on. Please."

As Jarry tells the story, Addie thinks about Paul Hayne, who, long ago, used to read to her in French on the upstairs piazza—love poems usually—courting her secretly, as Blanche sat in the music room over her own book, listening through the open window. Jarry, speaking Gullah, is like Paul, but less like him than like the suitor Paul never quite turned out to be, the one whom Addie dreamed about at Mme Togno's when she read "Evangeline," who never really came. Yet as likeness is a mil-

[1]As told by Col. C. C. Jones, in *The Black Border* by Ambrose E. Gonzales, A Firebird Press Book / Pelican Publishing Company, Gretna, LA, 1998.

lion miles from being, so Addie is a million miles from the girl who read that poem and dreamed those dreams. She's grown and married now, and Jarry is, after all, a Negro and could never be her suitor. There's a period this evening, though, perhaps fifteen or twenty minutes, when Addie ceases to denominate him in this way—as a "Negro," a "black man"—any more than she denominates herself as "white" in her own thoughts. The notion of their difference evaporates, and she finds herself listening as she once did to Paul, only Jarry is more beautiful than Paul Hayne ever was. There's something warmer, more nuanced in his intelligence, and the fatigue that occasionally shows in his expression is exquisite to her, like something painted by a Rembrandt or a Michelangelo. That fatigue has something final in it, that makes her think of how beautiful the world will appear in our last glimpse as we take leave of it. It speaks to a similar fatigue in her that comes from soberly and honestly bearing up the weight of life. Paul, like Harlan, was in flight from that—French poetry, cigars, and Colonel Lay's rum punch—these were just their chosen stimulants and props. This was the reason, finally, that Addie couldn't give herself to Paul and hasn't, now, to Harlan, the way she might, if . . .

"That's one of my happiest memories," Jarry eventually concludes, "sitting at the forge with Thomas. He'd clang some piece of hot iron with the maul, then sip a dipperful of water, and I especially loved the end, when Thomas said, 'De minnit Buh Rabbit drap in de brier patch, 'e cock up 'e tail, 'e jump, an holler back to Buh Wolf: "Good bye, Budder! Dis de place me mammy fotch me up—dis de place me mammy fotch me up." An 'e gone befo Buh Wolf kin ketch um.'" Thomas would always wink at me and say, 'An, Buh Jarry, where yuh mammy fotch you up?' and my part was to answer, 'Ri'cheer in de swamp, Thomas,' and he'd say, 'Me, too, Buddah, ri'cheer, an one day, we gon drap back in the briar-patch, too, enty? Sho nuf, Budder, bof we two gon drap right back.' He told me that for years. And then, one day, we did."

"You went," she says.

"We almost made it, too."

Having drawn him to this point, Addie almost asks, "What happened? Why didn't you?" then, catching sight of the cardinal across his shoulder, doesn't. A heaviness steals over her from no apparent source. Watching the bird sing on the branch, it occurs to Addie that the wall of glass that arose between Paloma and herself has now arisen between her and Jarry, too, and he is singing on the other side, and his song, though not inaudible, has become muted, now, in a way it wasn't then, that morning in the swamp. And it's clear to her that Jarry has no chance to penetrate the wall because he cannot see it. Only Addie can. Her secret confers this power over him. To surrender it might shatter the glass wall, and Addie cannot break the wall be-

cause . . . because . . . But suddenly she can't remember why this would be wrong, and heaviness gives way to an electric pang of fear.

"Did Clarisse do this to me?" she asks, with sudden, seeming inconsequence.

The question takes him by surprise. "I don't know," he says eventually. "I don't think so, but I honestly don't know."

"Then it's possible."

"There are unnatural illnesses, yes. And there are also natural illnesses that are caused unnaturally."

"That thing I saw in the swamp . . . Your mother said it's called a prenda. Tell me what that is."

Something veils itself in his expression now. He gets up and paces to the window. "I'm hesitant to speak of that."

"Paloma didn't believe it was there at all."

"You're mistaken," Jarry says, and now he turns to her, grave-faced. "What's hard for Mother is to accept what it would mean."

"And you?"

"I don't believe a lie is in your character."

Addie blushes now. "Don't think me better than I am."

"I'll think well of you until you give me reason to do otherwise. And even if you had some motive to deceive, how would you know what a prenda is, even to describe one? You could never make up such a thing. Mother knows that just as well as I."

"It is some implement of witchcraft. . . ."

"No," he answers, frowning. "No, it would be a mistake to think of it that way. Father told you something about Palo."

"He said it's used for good, for healings and exorcisms."

"If you're good, the prenda works for good. If not . . ." He leaves her to draw the inference. "A prenda, in some ways, is like a gun. On this river there are, what, a hundred families? Each one owns a gun. The husband uses it to puts food on the table, to protect his children and his wife. It's a tool for life. But if there is just one, one angry man with bad intentions in his heart, he points that gun at you and pulls the trigger, you are dead. That's how a prenda is. It's exactly like a gun, in itself neither good nor bad. What makes it so is what is in the Palero's heart."

Addie reaches out and grips his arm. "And Clarisse's heart? She hates me, doesn't she?"

"You have everything she thinks should be hers by right."

"But I don't even want it, Jarry—don't you see?"

"So you have, for nothing, everything she wants and will never have at any price? Do you imagine that absolves you in her sight?"

They stare into each other's eyes with an openness that's like the swamp, only what was sweet that morning is now an agony to her. The secret she holds over him is like a thorn in Addie's flesh; she wants nothing more than to pluck it out, but can't.

"But your story," she says. "You were telling me about when you and Thomas left."

"Our adventure failed."

"So I gathered. What happened?"

He measures her and sits back in the chair. "We took a piragua from the boathouse—two, actually. The first we set adrift and let the current carry it downstream for them to find. The second, we paddled upriver all night past Society Hill. At dawn, we pulled to the bank and broke the bottom out with stones and sank it. We heard the dogs barking that day, but it was far off and confused. There was no scent for them to find. So we hid and slept till nightfall and set out again.

"We traveled for six nights up past Cheraw and into North Carolina, where the Pee Dee turns into the Yadkin, and we both felt this quiet excitement growing. We thought we'd made it, and it was on the seventh morning, right at dawn, as we were standing in the shallows, washing up, that they found us. We never heard them come. They were just there, on the embankment above us, two bearded men in hats, on mules, with rifles scabbarded. For a moment, I thought maybe they were just chance travelers, but then one of them said, 'Looks like you boys have had your fun. . . . It's time to head on home.' He smiled and spat tobacco juice, and the other one unsleeved his gun. Thomas shoved me toward the shore and started backing out toward deeper water, and the man said, 'Nigger, stop right where you at,' and Thomas looked at me—he was smiling—and he said, 'Whah our mammy fotch us up?' And he let out a yell and turned and dove. 'Goddamn, stupid nigger,' the man said, and then I heard the gun echo off the bluff. The first shot caught him in his shoulder blade, and Thomas kept on swimming, weakly, with one arm. The second bullet hit him in the head. He stopped then, and the current rolled him over. His eyes were open, and his mouth filled up with water, and he sank."

"Oh, Jarry." Addie reaches out and puts her hand on his balled fist. Though he doesn't unclench it, for this moment the abyss between them shrinks to the distance between her bed and the chair. But as she looks into his face, at Jarry's honest pain, the falsity of her position looms.

"They brought me home behind the mules," he continues, "trotting with a rope around my neck. In the infirmary, I broke a water glass and cut my wrists"—he shows her now the scars he hid before—"but Mother found me and stanched the bleeding. The second time, I strung a rope from the library chandelier and stepped off the partners desk. I wanted Father to be the one to find me. I wanted to fix that image in his mind. That time, he cut me down himself. When I came to, I found him pacing. That was when he finally looked at me. 'Tell me why you want to do this to your mother,' he said. 'Tell me why you want to do this to yourself.'

" 'Because a man like you can take the life of one like Thomas and then sit down to supper as though nothing happened and God allows it,' I said.

" 'I didn't authorize those men to do what they did, Jarry,' Father said. 'They said they gave him every chance to surrender, but he turned and swam.'

" 'He turned and swam because he was a man.' I shouted it. 'A man. That's what they killed him for. His blood is on your hands. And I'll never forgive you for it. Never.' Those bastards," Jarry says, no longer repeating what he told his father now, but speaking straight to her. "They should have fallen to their knees and worshipped him for what he did, for showing them such courage and humanity. Instead they shot h——" He bites down hard on what he feels. "Instead, they shot him in the head and watched him sink."

"So Percival saw who you were."

Jarry frowns and looks away. "I don't know what he saw."

"No, he could not have failed to see. I know, because I see the same thing now myself."

He holds her stare and doesn't contradict. "What is it?" he asks suddenly. "What's wrong?"

"I don't . . . know," she answers, panting. Her eyes are round and large, too large for her face; she's trembling, too—hands, shoulders, her whole body now.

THIRTY-TWO

hrough an open window, Ran could hear the buzzer's persecuting whine, mosquitolike, upstairs in Tildy's old white house. As he cast a backward glance toward Alberta and the kids, he thought, despairingly, she might be out. But then the curtain moved, and soon he heard the tread of crepe-soled feet. The door opened and Della— the maid Claire called her "dah"—stared out.

"Mister Ransom," she said, with no suggestion of surprise, no affect of any kind. . . . *Mustuh Ransom,* in that drawling voice he'd always loved, slow, lugubrious, yet droll.

"Hello, Della," he said, smiling despite everything. "Aunt Tildy home?"

"Miss Tildy's upstairs in the parlor." The *pollah,* Della said, incidentally correcting him and giving him a subtle warning. "Aunt" had never been conceded to the upstart North Carolina boy who'd married Miss Claire. Ransom failed to take the hint.

"Step this way."

Opening the big black brass-knobbed door, Della led him down the piazza to the entry in the middle of the ground-floor porch. Inside, in sepia light, they passed beneath the old gas chandelier in the front hall—a Philadelphia piece of bronze and ormolu, as convoluted and baroque, Ran had always thought, as the pipe organ in Nemo's antechamber. He especially loved the globes of frosted glass etched with sheaves of rice, betoken-

ing what, once upon a time, had paid for it. Past Piranesi engravings of Italian scenes—brought back by dead ancestors from grand tours long
forgotten—they proceeded up the stairs to the West Parlor, also called the
Music Room, which contained the pianoforte on which Adelaide Huger
once entertained her future husband, accompanying herself, as she sang
Thomas More's rendition of "She Walks in Beauty Like the Night," the
sheet music of which lay, yellowed but otherwise undisturbed, in the compartment of the bench.

Outfitted in the ceremonial dress and coif of a prior era, Miss Matilda
sat between this instrument and an eighteenth-century harp, constructed in
London by Sebastian Erard, a wizened Euterpe, her palsied hands resting on
a silver-headed cane.

"Long time, no see, Aunt T," said Ran as Della softly closed the pocket
doors and vanished. "Good to see you."

Tildy appraised him with a rheumy eye as cold and dark as the
bull's-eye mirror in the girandole above the mantelpiece. "I wish I could
reciprocate yo' sentiment."

Ran, in light of history, was not expecting a parade; nonetheless, this
greeting stung. "Okay, no light banter. I get it. Ground rules established."
He allowed himself to smile.

Tildy, pointedly, did not. "No news in years has heartened me mo'
than hearing Claire had finally left you and come home to Clive's," she
said, in her gloomy, sonorous old drawl, "where she belongs; nor any dis-
heartened me as much as hearing you'd returned to suck that poor child's
lifeblood once again. When do you intend to let her go? Not, I suppose,
till you've extracted the last dram and left her nothing but a husk."

"Come on, Aunt Tildy, that's a little harsh, don't you think?" he said,
preserving his smile with effort—refusing, rather, to give her the satisfaction of defeating it. But it was dire, and as Ran direly smiled, he thought,
*You hateful, shriveled-up old witch, what do you know about marriage—mine, ours,
anyone's?*

"And I am not yo' aunt," Tildy added, giving the knife an extra twist.

Gravity now prevailed in Ransom's face. Crossing, uninvited, to the
window, he pulled back the curtain and looked.

Wearing a sweetgrass helmet, Charlie was in animated conversation
with Alberta, who stood, arms akimbo, clearly charmed. Hope, meanwhile,
held apart, gazing up at the window, puzzling out the terms. They were

both okay. They were who they were. The problem was the situation he had placed them in. The problem, Ransom realized, was him.

A minstrel . . . The phrase popped suddenly into his head. "We've had lawyers, planters, governors, diplomats," Clive had said to Ran at their first meeting, not long after the engagement was announced, "but it's taken our people a long time to rate a minstrel in the family." And his eyes—his bright, narrow, happy, entitled, avian old eyes—gloated on their small, mean victory, before Clive turned away, putting Ran to death. He'd been at the zenith then—Ran hadn't recognized it as the top, of course, but, looking back, it was. "Talking in My Sleep" was winning airtime in every major urban market in the country; they'd been nominated for a Grammy. Growing up in Bagtown, being Mel Hill's son—he'd put all that behind him, or thought he had, till Clive, in a single second, with a single word, sent him plummeting right back. Like his sister Tildy seemed intent on doing now.

"Don't let her get to you," he whispered to himself, aloud. But the voice said, *Oh, go ahead and let the old bitch have it—it might even do her good. You know damn well if she'd ever gotten fucked, if she'd loosened up that much, just once, she wouldn't have turned into such a spiteful, raisin-faced old judge and monster. Give her a dose of her own meds—a bog-Irish car bomb with a lithium chaser on the side.*

"Shut up," Ran said, no longer fully sotto voce. Across the street from Hope, a man came out of a house and reached into his pocket. . . . *Beep, beep.* It was only a remote, thank God. Thank God! The trunk of a Mercedes popped.

"What?" Tildy demanded as he muttered to himself. "What did you say to me?"

When he turned, Ran's expression had left the artificial country of goodwill. "Look, Tildy, Miss DeLay, whatever I'm supposed to call you after nineteen years, I'm not here to fight."

"Why are you here?" she demanded, imperious and unmoved.

"Because this morning two dead bodies turned up at Wando Passo, buried in shallow graves."

Tildy blinked and blinked again. "So they've finally found them."

"Found who?"

"Harlan and Adelaide DeLay."

His jaw flexed. "We're on the same wavelength, then. He died from a gunshot to the head. She may have been shot, too. They're taking the remains to Columbia to examine them."

"God, rest them. God, rest their souls." Tildy, for the first time, looked away. "Claire should be telling me this, not you. Why isn't she?"

"She was at school when it happened. She still doesn't know. I drove straight here after I talked to the police."

"Why?" Tildy demanded.

"*Why?* Because I want to know what happened to them. I want to know what you know."

"Then you've driven a long way for nothing. The records from Wando Passo were destroyed when Grandfather's law office burned in the Great Earthquake."

"There must be stories. . . ."

"Very few. Mother believed they went to Cuba. She said Harlan came back from the war"—*waw*, she said—"destitute and broken. They couldn't make a go, so they ran away, like Keats's lovers. *'Aye, ages long ago, These lovers fled away into the storm.'* I don't suppose you know 'St. Agnes.'"

"No, but I'd say we can rule that theory out."

"Mother's temperament ran to the romantic. Daddy"—*Deaddy*, she said—"believed the nigras did it."

"The 'nigras'?" Ran couldn't help himself.

Tildy glared. "I suppose you find it ironic, the way I refer to the colo'eds. I am a product of my time and place, as are you, Ransom Hill, whether or not you have the wit to recognize the fact. What you've said turns my suspicions toward the husband."

"Harlan."

"Harlan. Though he came from money, he was the upstart in that marriage—not unlike yourself."

"You aren't going to give up, are you?" Ransom said. "You're hell-bent and determined to get a rise from me."

"I'm determined to say what I believe," she answered. "If I were a man, and younger, I'd rise out of this chair right now and thrash you within an inch of your life for what you've done to Claire and those poor children. I'd send you back to North Carolina with your tail between your legs and make you crawl back under whatever ill-favored rock it was that you were spawned beneath. So help me God, if I were a man, and young, I would."

"If you were a man, and young," said Ran, his shirtfront rising and falling, as he panted shallowly, "I guess we'd see."

She got him, though, with the allusion to the kids. Pulling back the paper cambric sheer, he checked again. The man with the remote was loading a suitcase into the Benz. A Charleston type, in his midthirties, he had thick, dark hair, perfectly groomed, with a first distinguished touch of frost at the temples, and wore a black cashmere sweater with gray flannel pants and shoes of some gleaming, welted skin. They were tassel-loafers—Ran had always hated tassel-loafers. *That's who they wanted,* Ransom thought, *that's who they wanted for Miss Claire. This guy was supposed to be Hope and Charlie's father.*

"Why?" he asked, and then he turned. "Why would he have killed her, Tildy?"

"Why?" she fumed. "Why do husbands ever terrorize and kill their wives? Since when was an excuse required? They do so because they poison the well from which love springs and then expect the water to be pure. They expect women to love them like their mamas did—or didn't—then test that love with outrageous behavior till they succeed in driving it away; when they have, they then set out to wreak vengeance on their 'betrayal'— isn't that the way of it? *You,* I should think, would have consid'able insight into the phenomenon."

An ominous calm stole over Ransom. "I know you never approved our marriage, Tildy."

"I made no secret of the fact."

"You never thought I was good enough for Claire."

"In a word, no, I did not. And do not now."

Ran stared and began to nod. "You know what, Tildy? At my worst, when I was sick, I've feared that, too. Standing here right now, I fear it still. But at my best, and not even that—when I was just my normal weekday self—I've always believed I was good enough for Claire, and, in fact, I think she did right well by me. And if I'm good enough for her, I'm plenty good enough for you and Clive and anybody else. And if you don't think so, frankly, I don't give a shit. I always liked the fact that you were a straight shooter, but, beyond that, I never liked you that much either. I find you tight-assed, punitive, and colder than the winter wind in Buffalo. Most of all, I think you're puffed up with specious pride over something you did nothing for, and what does it amount to, Tildy? A name, a houseful of nineteenth-century antiques . . . Who really gives a shit but you?"

"What I've done, Ransom Hill," she said, "that I'm proud of, is to bear that name, honorably, for almost ninety years. And there are no—or precious few—nineteenth-century antiques here, sir. That chair, for example—the one you're presently soiling with your hand—is English Chippendale, from the third quarter of the eighteenth century. It—or its identical mate—may be viewed in *The Gentleman and Cabinet Maker's Director*. Among the few nineteenth-century pieces I own is the gasolier downstairs, which was installed when the house was piped for gas in 1846. I've heard you wax lyrical about the rice sheaves on the globes a dozen times, but to me it is an abomination, a crass allusion to the family wealth. My people were capable of such a lapse in taste, but they were gentlemen and ladies, nonetheless, even then. Where were yours in 1846?"

Tildy left a pause, but not enough of one for him to answer—if he'd had an answer.

"You don't know, do you? I do, though. In sod houses in the west of Ireland, eating potatoes, with their smutch-faced children running around with lank hair, runny noses, and bare feet, beating each other on the head with sticks. Let me tell you something, Ransom Hill, something you don't know, because you can't. It takes three generations, if not four, to make a name, another three or four to make it matter, and three or four from there to get to where I am and where your wife and children are. You, sir, are at the low and sad beginning of that trip. Your father—what was he? A common mill hand. Nothing. And you, in my opinion, have not appreciably advanced. It's my hope and fervent prayer that your son will be as unlike your side and as much like Claire's and mine as possible."

"And I hope he grows up," Ran said, "both him and Hope, and never do to another human being what you and yours have done to me for nineteen years, which was to judge me, sight unseen, before I ever walked into the room. In all that time, you never had the imagination—or the respect for Claire—to wonder who I really was and what she loved in me, much less the generosity to support her choice. I hope our children grow up and listen to my songs and think, Hey, once upon a time, my dad wrote that, and some kids who were struggling and lost and mad as hell, weighed down by a lot of bullshit piled on top of them in homes like this, listened to his words and took permission to go out and free themselves, or, at least, encouragement to shoot for it. You may not see it, Tildy, but I pray Hope and Charlie do, and I believe they will. I'll put what I've done beside you and your whole line, and let my children weigh them in the scales and then decide. And you know what else? I think that's what Claire did, too, and what you really can't forgive me for. She had all this, all the Charleston pride and antecedents, and she walked into a dingy New York City club one night and heard me playing rock and roll and threw it all away. She scraped it off the bottoms of her shoes like so much dogshit, which is really what it is."

"Your language is disgusting," Tildy said. "Claire acted out of youthful folly, and now, from the perspective of maturer years, she sees the cost."

"That's your opinion," Ran replied. "Mine is: Claire was the best she ever was with me, the truest to herself, and I believe, deep down—even from the perspective of 'maturer years'—she knows it, too, which is why we're going to make it, whether you like it or not."

"If you mean to make your marriage work, why aren't you up there with Claire and your two children, instead of down here harrying me?"

Ransom frowned and turned away. "Because I have to find out what happened to them," he said, suddenly struggling to hold his train of thought.

"Why?" persisted Tildy. "What do Harlan and Adelaide DeLay have to do with you and Claire? What conceivable connection could there be?"

She's right, you know, the voice piped up from the peanut gallery.

"Shut up," said Ransom, clutching his temples.

"Whom are you addressing?" she demanded.

Now Ransom looked at her with his red, harried eyes, and she looked back.

"You're not in your right mind," she said.

"Just help me, Tildy," Ran implored. "I don't know why it's important, I just know it is. Help me figure out what happened, and I'll leave."

"What happened is, he shot her and then turned the gun back on himself from simple shame and self-disgust."

"And then?"

"What do you mean, 'and then'?"

"I mean, if Harlan killed her and then blew his own brains out, he could hardly proceed to get up, dig a hole, and bury himself and Addie *after* he was dead."

"Spare me yo' irony," Tildy said. "Obviously, someone else buried them."

"Who? The nigras?"

"For heaven's sake, anybody could have! What difference does it make?"

"Quite a bit," said Ran. "Let's say you're invited to someone's home for Sunday dinner. You knock and no one answers. You go in and find the wife and husband dead of gunshot wounds. Wouldn't you call someone? Notify the sheriff? Wouldn't it stand to reason they'd be buried in the family plot, in coffins, not fifty yards away in unmarked, shallow graves? Wouldn't some word have come down to us? I mean, word came down they'd disappeared. If they'd been murdered, wouldn't it have come down all the more?"

"All this is idle speculation," she said, and her fierce eyes strayed from his for the first time. "Maybe no one knew."

"But someone had to know. Whoever buried them knew and chose to keep it secret. And if you were the murderer, wouldn't that count as a pretty good incentive for you to shut your trap?"

"I won't abet your obsessions by engaging further in this pointless exercise."

"But it isn't pointless, Tildy. The point is, maybe Harlan didn't kill her after all. Maybe he didn't off himself. Maybe someone else murdered both of them and buried their remains. The questions being, who, and why."

Tildy sat, lips pursed in a recalcitrant way, and Ransom noticed that her spotted hands had turned white on the head of her cane. "You know something, don't you?"

"What do you mean? I've told you everything I know."

"Look at you, you're blushing!"

"You're mad. Stark raving."

"Call it madman's intuition, then. Tildy, for the love of God, if you know something, don't hold out on me. It's not just me, it's Claire and Hope and Charlie, too."

She sat there, fuming, undecided; then with her cane's trembling rubber tip, she tapped—tapped unerringly—a sterling frame, hidden far back in the thickets of family photos on the piano. "There is this. I don't think it will tell you much."

Ransom picked it up. Though her face was slightly out of focus, he recognized Addie right away. She was standing on the piazza at Wando Passo, leaning on the point of a closed parasol. She looked tireder, more prosaic than the woman in the portrait, but more real and solid, too, and as Ran squinted at her, Addie squinted back, as though she could almost make him out, as though Ran were the figure in her dream, or fantasy. After the first moment, though, it wasn't Addie but the handsome black man standing beside her in the shadow of the overhang that drew Ran's attention. With his solemn stare and coat of good but slightly worn black gabardine, he looked familiar somehow, though Ransom couldn't immediately say how.

"Who's this?" he asked.

"Open it," she said.

Turning the frame, he struggled with the fittings, but all he found, when the blue velvet back came off, was a single line in antique cursive: "A. H. D. with J., Wando Passo, Aug., 1865."

"'A. H. D.,'" said Ran.

"Adelaide Huger DeLay. She married my great-grandfather, Harlan. He was the son of Percival there." She pointed to a young man's portrait on the wall. "Adelaide and Harlan had a son named James. The property passed through him to my father."

"Yours and Clive's?"

"Mine and Clive's."

"And 'J.'?"

"A slave named Jarry. I know little about him except that he was plantation steward."

"Why was this picture taken?"

"What do you mean?"

"Why would the mistress—Addie—pose for a picture with a slave?"

Tildy frowned and tightened her grip on her cane. "Happenstance, I expect."

"And you showed me this because . . . ?"

She glared at him, recalcitrant, and the doors slid back.

"Oh, what?" said Tildy, with annoyance.

Della merely blinked and didn't go away.

"All right, all right," she said, struggling to rise.

As Tildy hobbled off, Ran's eye lit once more on the portrait. At second glance, something in Percival DeLay's expression seemed familiar, too. Ran gazed into his agated, dark hazel eyes, then back down at the black man in the photo.

"Who the hell are you?" he said, addressing "J." "Who the *hell* are you?"

The mystery engrossed him deeply, so deeply that it took Charlie's tearful "Doddy! Doddy!" to pull Ran from the undertow.

"What's the matter, buddy?" Ran knelt and took him in his arms. Over Charlie's shoulder, Percival and J. gazed on. . . . Ran blinked at them, blinked down at his son's unhappy face, his agated, dark hazel eyes. Like a boulder on a mountaintop, something in Ran's mind began to teeter.

Before it had a chance to roll, Hope filed in, followed in short order by Alberta Johns, Tildy, Della, and a frowning, blue-clad female representative of the Charleston police. From the doorway, they glared at him as though he were, in fact, what Ran, in his worst nightmare, had feared he was and, till this moment, hesitated to believe.

Alberta was holding something out to him—a gun? Sadly, no. Not that, nor a remote. It was, in fact, his cell phone. The dial was lit. The basket lady looked at him with dour eyes. "Someone wants to speak to you," she said.

THIRTY-THREE

s the fever advances, it grows more regular, and, with each repetition, worse. Every second night, between five and eight, Addie's chills be-gin, succeeding rapidly to fever, which rages through the night, all the following day, worsening toward evening. Addie's pulse accelerates to the point where Sims can no longer accurately count it. Her mouth fills with a foul, viscous phlegm. Lapsing into delirium, she lies whimpering and gnashing her teeth, and as she strug-gles to breathe, her chest heaves like a panting animal's on a summer day. Toward dawn, the fever breaks and she passes into a debilitated rest. The reprieve lasts be-tween ten and twelve hours. Then, as the shadows lengthen toward dusk, it starts again. From onset to onset, the cycle lasts forty-eight hours, and with each onset, Paloma ties another knot.

There's one knot in the string when Jarry leaves for Charleston. Using cedar bark and pitch to caulk the seams of Wando Passo's lighter—the oakum, too, has been a casualty of the Nina's encounter with the Niagara—Jarry loads the boat with rice and sets out with an eight-man crew. The freshet is running, and the men must bight a line to trees along the riverbank and warp themselves upstream by the capstan. It takes ten backbreaking hours to reach the railroad bridge at Mars Bluff and most of the night to unload the lighter and get the cargo up the steep embank-ment to the train. There are two hundred tierces of rice. Each weighs six hundred pounds. This is sixty tons of rice, more than a tenth of Wando Passo's annual pro-duction. In Charleston—where every public space, from Washington Race Course to

White Point Garden, is filled with tents—Jarry sells the lighter load for three cents a pound, $3,600. Despite this sum, despite Blanche Huger's fervent, and at times hysterical, exertions, Jarry succeeds in procuring only fifty grains of quinine. There is no more to be had at any price.

There are four knots in the string the morning he returns. He has ridden all night, and his eyes are red and glassy. His pants are soaked with his horse's sweat, his boots flecked with lather.

"It's half of what I hoped," Sims says, "but more than what we had."

He prescribes three grains the first day, four the second, and so on, up to six on the fourth day. On the fifth and sixth, he gives Addie eight grains at twelve-hour intervals. By the afternoon of the seventh day, she's had no recurrence in forty-eight hours. She's sitting up in bed and showing evidence of life. Jarry brings her gifts from the garden—fragole Alpine, and sugar snaps, and salsify, and the season's first small cimbelines, which is what Peter calls his yellow crook-necked squash.

"These taste like summer," she tells Jarry, breaking a snap with a crisp report and offering him the second half. "I never knew food could taste like this."

Jarry smiles at her elation.

"So my fears were groundless after all. I wronged Clarisse in thinking ill of her."

He doesn't contradict, but something narrows in his eyes.

"Jarry, thank you." She takes his hand from his lap and presses it. Their access to each other—exciting, fearful, without apparent cause—seems unimpaired. Addie can almost forget her guilty secret, gazing into his eyes, which reflect her in a way no eyes ever have. It's as if she's suddenly the person she was always meant to be, who has eluded every effort on her part, but now, with none at all, in Jarry's beholding, she has suddenly become.

"Shall I read to you?" he asks.

"Unless you purpose Wordsworth . . ."

"No, I doubt you're yet strong enough for that."

She allows her eyes to widen at the slyness in his tone. "You have a spark of evil in you, don't you, Jarry? Impertinent, purest evil. I never noticed that till now."

He colors, smiles, and makes no effort to refute her charge.

"You know what I should like far better, though? A walk," she says. "No, no, don't deny me. Please. I've been cooped up here so long. A breath of fresh air and a few stray beams of sunlight on my face—that would do me more good than all the poetry on earth. May we? Just to the Bluffs and back?"

"Are you sure it's not too soon?"

"If I fall over, you may say, 'I told you so.' You may even bring your Wordsworth. I'll steel myself to suffer through a verse."

"It may prove better medicine than you expect."

"Its medicinal properties are not in doubt."

So off they go, this fine June morning, down the white sand road. As they pass the barn, the sound of female laughter draws them.

Inside, a group of long-legged teenage girls, with shimmies showing and skirts hiked halfway up their thighs, are treading barefoot in a soup of dark gray mud. An older man named Jonadab sloshes this from a piggin he fills at a barrel of river water mixed with clay. Conscious of his attention—and that of several older male admirers standing by—the girls dance a kind of sensual minuet, half slip and slide, laughing and shouting protests when a bombardier, hidden in the loft, releases a drift of well-aimed seed that lodges in their headcloths and their hair, before they brush it off and tramp it down.

"What on earth?" asks Addie.

"They're claying the seed for tomorrow's planting," Jarry tells her. "Have you never seen it done?"

"You can't pretend it's any kind of work?"

Though Addie laughs to show how much she cares, one girl takes umbrage at the charge. "Yes, ma'am, it is. If it ain't clayed, the seed'll float up when you put water on de fiel', and then the buds duh et it up."

"The birds?"

"Yes'm, de buds, like I said."

"Well, you've taught me something I didn't know."

"Iss awright, miss," she says, extending charity.

"They almost," she says to Jarry as they continue, "make me remember what it was to be that young and that untroubled. You'd never think that there are hostile armies in the field."

"Children will still play, though there be war."

"Is that a proverb?"

"I think you take some pleasure in twitting me."

"It's not my most attractive quality, I'm sure," she answers with a high color in her cheeks. "Yet it does me far more good than Wordsworth ever could. You wouldn't deny me it, surely?"

And he is flustered now.

"Have I embarrassed you? I have! Oh, Jarry, I didn't mean . . ."

"You didn't."

She studies him, her hand upon her breast, and they are at the river now.

"Look how beautiful it is!" Giving him an intentional reprieve from her atten-

tion, she turns away and finds charm in the blue and yellow jessamine in riot on the banks. There's an egret, poised on one leg, fishing in the shallows on the opposite shore, and a row of turtles—nine of them, lined up shell to shell upon a log—black against the water's dazzle. "Why does the sky seem so much bigger here?"

Recovered now, Jarry shakes his head.

"What does it mean, though, Jarry?" she says, thinking of a question that has several times occurred to her. "Wando Passo? Is it Spanish?"

"No."

"Indian?"

"There was a tribe, the Wando, hereabouts. The creek there"—now he points—"cuts between the Pee Dee and the Waccamaw, and they may have used it to reach the English trading post that once sat on these bluffs. Father thought it might have been a kind of pidgin that arose between two peoples who didn't share a common tongue. Wando Passo . . ."

"A place the Wando passed?"

He nods. "That's just a guess, though. The truth is, no one knows."

"How strange," she says. "To think that once upon a time it meant enough to them to name their land for it, but now it's lost, and those who knew the meaning are all gone."

"I've always rather liked it."

"So do I. It's like the past, isn't it?" She gazes at him, wondering. "Something you can't quite grasp, however hard you try, that lives on nonetheless and casts its spell on us."

Jarry smiles, and briefly, as he holds her stare, there is a kind of spell between them, too.

"Truly, though," says Addie, breaking it, "the people here—are they not worried by the war?"

"Of course they are."

"I suppose they hope for our defeat. You do, don't you?" She casts a glance at him.

"I've made no secret of my views. But, no, not everybody in the quarters shares them."

"How do they feel?"

"The older people worry what will happen to their homes if the South loses. They ask me about their spring and winter cloth allotments, their firewood—will this continue as before."

"And what do you tell them?"

"That when and if they're freed, they'll own themselves and they may sell their

labor and buy these things themselves. They don't entirely trust the notion of a future different from the past."

"How will this place work, Jarry, if we lose?"

He walks to the edge and stares over the prospect, hands clasped behind his back. "Not as it does now. That's the only answer I'm certain of. All of this is predicated on slave labor. If you must begin to pay for what you've always had for free, the question becomes, how much will the labor cost? More than the profit the rice returns? If that's so, what will happen to Wando Passo and places like it? Will they be abandoned to go back to the swamp? And what will happen to the people in the quarters and thousands like them across the South? What will happen to you, the owners?" He turns back now. "Your primary asset has always been the land. If you must sell off parcels to purchase labor to farm the rest—and if all the other landowners are in the same position—how much will the land be worth? Not much, in my view."

"You take a dark view of the future, then."

"I think there are solutions, but they require a shift in thinking I'm not sure either side, the slaves or masters, is prepared to make."

"Tell me what you mean."

"It's long been my view that Wando Passo could produce a third more than it does."

"A million and a half pounds a year?"

"Or thereabouts."

"How?"

He sits beside her on the bench and turns with hands clasped and elbows on his knees. "I could show you, I believe. Tim and Silas have the rice drills on Beard Island this morning. Tomorrow, once the seed has soaked, we'll plant. The two squares there yielded—I'd have to check—but twenty-six or -seven bushels, I would guess, last year. If I said to Tim tonight, 'This year you're going to rent Beard Island from the mistress. . . . You will pay her . . .' I haven't thought this out, you understand?"

"No, of course," says Addie, watching his intensity and not wanting to break the train.

"Let's say ten bushels to the acre." He gets up and starts to pace. "For the sake of argument, ten. If they throw the seed onto the ground tomorrow and go home and stay drunk until September, they'll make ten. But if they have advantage of the weather and work the land as they know how, they'll make forty bushels on those fields."

"Forty!"

"If not forty-five. If you take your ten and half of the additional thirty or thirty-five, you'll do as well or better than you did last year."

"Why not ask that they make forty-five for me?"

He laughs. "It can't be done! Tell me how to do it. I've tried everything—exhortation, shaming, punishment. I've appealed to pride and manhood. None of it has ever worked. The one thing I haven't tried—because I've never had authority—is to let them share the profits. If you want excellence from them, that's what you must do. Then, what I believe you'll see is this: a hand like Tim, who now hoes out his half acre by ten thirty or eleven in the morning and goes home to tend his peas and shoats, then you'll see him in the field till five or six. Instead of one task, he'll do three or four, and because every third hand is capable of this, if you extend this over the whole plantation, you make your million and a half where you only have a million now. If I'm wrong, if they shirk and malinger, all you stand to lose is a few bushels on two fields out of almost fifty. Wouldn't it be worth it to find out?"

"I think it would," says Addie, swept up in his excitement.

"Then I have your permission to propose this to them?"

"Yes, you do," she says. "Only, not tonight. Hold off for a few days. I must write to Harlan first."

"Ah," says Jarry, deflating as though punctured by a pin. "Ah, well then, never mind."

"But why never mind?" she protests. "You think he won't agree?"

"I know it."

"How?" she challenges. "How do you know? Perhaps you do him an injustice."

"I know because I've asked. I made a similar proposal to Father once, and Harlan would have none of it."

"What was his objection?"

"Can't you guess? Wando Passo presently produces a million pounds that he has all the profit of. So why should he change everything to produce an additional half million to profit someone else."

"Is that not a fair point?"

"Don't you see the answer, though? The reason you risk changing everything is to save yourself. In the event the South loses, to preserve the million you have now, you must make the million and a half and give the overage to those who presently own nothing. If you don't, you'll lose the million, and once you lose the million, you stand to lose the land as well."

"Did you explain this to my husband?"

"Harlan understands it. But to lift them into a prosperity that, however modest, he considers undeserved galls him more than the thought of ruining himself, and you."

"I find that hard to credit, Jarry," she says, with a trace of coolness.

"Do you? I think his view is fairly common. If it weren't, slavery could have been ended in this country long ago according to the principle I've laid out. But it's a rare man who'll voluntarily surrender power over another, even when it's in his ultimate best interest. Harlan, whatever his qualities, isn't such a man."

It's true! It's true! thinks Addie with despair. Everything that Jarry says is true. So what is this strange compunction she feels stealing over her, the one that makes her stiffen and inquire, "And you thought I would consent to what my husband has expressly forbidden?"

Jarry weighs her tone and answers quietly. "I thought you might recognize that preserving the privileges you have, which are considerable, would be preferable to losing them."

"I think you know," she says, "I think you full well know I can't make changes, radical changes, on my husband's property without seeking his consent."

"I see," he says. "I would have thought that you, as mistress, in his absence, could do pretty much what you have a mind to do."

"Then we disagree on this. I see no point in continuing in this vein."

"I agree," says Jarry, sitting straight now, backing away from her. "This conversation is a waste of breath."

"Will you read to me?"

"I have no stomach for it now. If you'll excuse me, I have work to do." He gets up and walks away from her, and she is on the verge, on the very cusp, of saying to him, "I should like it very much if you would read."

She doesn't, though.

Later, sitting at her dressing table mirror, she'll reflect on how close she came to doing this, to giving him an order, in effect, that he'd have been in no position to refuse.

And what if I'm like that, too? she wonders, staring at her image in the glass. What if I'm like Harlan in this way? Isn't this, at bottom, why she hasn't surrendered the secret of the will? Because it gives her power over Jarry? Isn't she as reluctant to surrender that as Harlan would be to give away the profit on a half million pounds of rice? Yet her secret power also has a poisoned quality that makes her queasy. Or is the queasiness something else?

Suddenly Addie notices her eyes. Her pupils have dilated to the size of dimes. And there's something else. Leaning close, she sees, at her temple, where her hair is fairest— almost colorless, like fronds of dandelion—a coarse black hair. Was it there before? How could she have never noticed it? And as she reaches up to touch it, to spread it between her fingers for a closer look, Addie startles when she sees it twitch.

THIRTY-FOUR

his lady here, Ms. Johns," said the blue-clad female representative of the PD, "says you offered her a hundred bucks to take your kids."

The officer, Alberta, Tildy, Della, and Hope—yes, Hope as well—representing a pretty fair cross section of female Charleston, Southern womanhood, *das Ewig-Weibliche* itself, regarded Ran with unanimously grim looks, a hanging jury itching to convict.

"To *watch* them," Ransom qualified. "To watch them for fifteen. What's the big deal? They're okay, aren't they? Aren't you okay, guys?" He addressed the children now.

"Charlie has a poopy diaper, Dad," Hope said, in an accusing tone she'd heretofore reserved for Claire.

"I wet, Doddy," said Charlie, with eyes like rain-sheeted windowpanes. His bottom lip—which was full, like Claire's (somehow Ran had never noticed this till now)—was trembling.

"Okay, buddy," Ran said, stricken. "Okay, we'll get you changed."

Ransom!

"Shut up," he said under his breath, smiling at his posse of accusers—who clearly heard him speak—like the honoree at a black-tie benefit who's farted, loudly, in the middle of his speech. Belatedly, Ran realized the tinny voice he heard was Claire's.

"Hello?" he said into the phone.

"Ransom, what the hell is going on?" she said. "Why are you in Charleston?"

"They found the bodies, Claire."

"What?" she said. "What bodies? Who found them? What are you talking about?"

"Harlan and Adelaide."

Dead air, a sound like distant surf.

"Let me speak to Aunt Tildy," Claire said, measured now. "No, never mind. Tell her I'm coming down there. Don't move. I'll be there in an hour, forty-five."

"It isn't necessary, Claire," he said. "I'm on the case. We've got it under control, don't we, kids?"

Hope and Charlie looked at him with tombstone eyes.

"We'll be home by suppertime," he said.

"Don't *move*," said Claire. "Don't you fucking move an *inch*. You hear me, Ransom Hill?"

"Sure, sweetie, absolutely. Understood." Like a harried first executive in the presidential bunker, Ran contemplated the red button and then pressed it, inviting unknown consequences—the end of civilization as we know it, of life on earth. "Call ended," said the LCD. A little check mark wrote and then erased itself. Ran turned back to the hanging jury with a smile. "Okay, dutes, Mommy's on her way. She'll be here in an hour. Everything's copacetic. Come on, bud. . . ." When he reached for Charlie's hand, however, the officer stepped between.

"What? I can't take my own son to the bathroom?" He allowed a note of parental righteousness into his tone. "You're welcome to come with us."

The policewoman frowned. "When you're done, there's some things we need to straighten out."

"Absolutely. I'd like to straighten out a couple things myself. We'll have a straightening convention." He hoisted Charlie with one arm and cut a glance toward Alberta. "You could've cut me a bit more slack, Bert."

"It ain't about you. It's about these babies. You take care of 'em, hear me? Remember what we said." She gripped him, and Ransom, with a thickening in his throat, a stinging at his eyes, looked down at her black hand on his white arm.

"I guess you want your other hundred."

Alberta tsked impatiently and disengaged.

"Hope?" Ran reached her his free hand.

"I don't need to go."

"Come on. You haven't used the bathroom since we left."

Her frown was mutinous. She held her ground.

"Don't mess with me," said Ransom, suddenly putting on the face of power and channeling his father's voice.

Hope came then. Downstairs, past the Piranesi scenes, beneath the gasolier . . .

"There's nothing wrong with it," he muttered, staring upward as they passed.

"Who are you talking to?" Hope asked.

"To you, Pete," he replied. "Tell the truth, now, honest Injun: don't you think that chandelier is cool?"

Hope looked at it and blinked, then looked at him and blinked some more. Suddenly, she was Claire. Four years old, she got the thing that Tildy meant, the thing he never got, however many times it was explained. Her expression didn't judge, it pitied him because he never would.

Ransom felt a tremor in his throat. "Come on, Charlie-boy, let's do this thang! Who wants ice cream afterward?"

"I do!" Charlie said. "Me! Me! Me!"

Hope said nothing. Careful not to look at her, Ran felt like a lifeguard as the line that held his little girl slipped, burning, through his hand.

After he changed Charlie's diaper and helped him wash his hands, Ran knelt, face-to-face with them, a hand on each small hip. "Listen, guys, I need your help again. There's been a little change of plan. We're going to take a ride."

"Where we going, Doddy?"

"I'm not sure," said Ran.

"What about Mommy?"

"Don't worry, Pete. We'll see her later."

"Okay, Doddy." Charlie blinked his little mismatched blink and nodded. He was in.

"Hope?" he said, and swallowed.

"Do we have to?"

Ransom took a sighing breath. "No, you can stay, if you want to. But I'd really like it if you came."

Hope just pressed her lips and nodded, giving him a gift that her expression said might be the last.

Ransom leaned and kissed her cheek. "Okay, upsy daisy! Everybody climb!"

With that, he threw the window up, and out they went.

THIRTY–FIVE

uién hizo esto a ella?"

"Tú sabes, Mamá."

"I don't believe it," says Paloma, stretching the skin on Addie's temple, examining what lies between her index finger and her thumb.

"¿Quién podría haberlo hecho?"

The second voice is Jarry's. Addie—wanting only to sleep, to escape into unconsciousness—notes him and his mother in the room, hears their gravity of tone, but notes it only as one detail among others, none of them important. They're talking about her the way people talk about someone who's dying, or in imminent danger thereof. Is she going to? Until a little while ago, the idea would have seemed preposterous—to die before life has begun? Death, though, now, from Addie's vantage, is only a word, another unimportant detail among unimportant details. Her dwindling reserves are wholly vested in the wish to sleep, that and in summoning the strength to take this breath, and the next one after that, when her chest feels so tender, so wounded and so raw, and each breath is like a drought of fire. And the headache. Her head is ringing like an anvil hammered by a maul. The vibration shivers down into the pit of her stomach, making her feel she may vomit at any time.

"No lo creeré."

"Don't believe it, then," says Jarry. "Just help her."

"Why?" the old woman says. "Why should we help her, hijo?"

"Because she's innocent."

"She's not. This woman looked into my face and lied to me over your father's corpse."

"I don't believe that. And even if she did, does she deserve to die for it?"

"Everything we bled and sweated for, she steps into possession of it all—how is she innocent?"

"If it were me," he says, touching her shoulder, *"you would not allow this."*

"You are my child," Paloma says, *"my son."*

"If I am, then do for her what you would for me. Do it for me, Mamacita."

Paloma frowns. *"Fetch me albahaca from the garden, and holy water in a vial."*

Reaching into the neck of her dress, she takes out her makuto, the leather amulet she wears, and from the pouch, carefully folded, the prayer to San Luis Beltrán, written in the hand of Tata Quien Vence, the nom de guerre of Andrés Petit. Three times nightly for three nights running they say this prayer over her—*"Criatura de Dios, yo te curo, ensalmo, y bendigo en nombre de la Santísima Trinidad, Padre, Hijo y Espíritu Santo . . ."*—sprinkling her with holy water as they pray and making the sign of the cross with basil leaves. By the fourth dawn, however, the fever is undiminished. There are fourteen knots in the string now, twenty-eight days of illness. Addie, physically, has become a wreck. It's become an almost insuperable battle simply to force herself to breathe.

"The bilongo is not familiar to me," Paloma says. *"It's very strong."*

"Can you set the Fiery Wall?"

She gives Jarry a hard look. *"You expect me to set a black light on my child?"*

"Then don't use graveyard dirt. Throw the candle in the river."

"And have it carry her away? No, I won't work against her."

Jarry takes her hand. *"If she dies, Mama—how can it help Clarisse? It won't. It'll just be something else on her account, something else for which she'll have to pay. And what has Addie done to suffer this?"*

Far down in the dark world where she is—like one at the bottom of the sea, gazing up toward sunlight and the white sand beach—Addie hears him plead for her. It's the first time she's heard him use her given name, and this fills her with pathos—not as something that might be, but what might once have been.

"We'll try angélica," Paloma says, but roots, too, fail, and there are sixteen knots in the string now.

"There must be something else, Mama," Jarry says.

"There is one last thing. If it fails, I don't know. . . ."

"Then try it, Mama, try the one last thing."

Paloma frowns at him. *"Bring her, then,"* she says, and leaves the room.

As Jarry picks her up, Addie, far down in her world, alone and frightened, whispers, "Why? Why are you doing this for me?"

He stares into her eyes, incredulous. "Why? Because you are a human being. Because you'd do the same for me."

Wretched, she closes her eyes and turns her face away. And she is like a shot corsage, crushed against him as he carries her downstairs. His arms are a place of refuge Addie's missed and longed for. So why now? she wonders. Why does the nearness of death grant them a permission denied in life? She can smell dust in his black coat, and sweat, a pleasing sourness like salt. Addie thinks about the blocks in the dairy yard and in the horses' stalls, licked into beautiful grotesqueries by need.

Through a gray pall of dispirited languor, she sees sky passing overhead and hears the creaking of the wagon wheels. She feels the warmth of the blanket Jarry's wrapped her in, and notes, with a brief uptick of interest, that the leaves are full now on the trees. Winking through them, incandescent sunlight vies with inky black to form a filigree. They're carrying her inside again. Is it the cottage? Addie doesn't recognize the place, nor, after a vapid attempt, can she much care. There are other people in the room, speaking in hushed tones, but their faces blur. What is that there? Is it an altar? There are many things upon this altar, but what draws her attention is a figurine, a queer, small bust, coal-black, with eyes and nose and lips of cowrie shells. It's almost silly looking, like a crude statue a child might make of mud. Or like the tar baby . . . This thought drifts through Addie's mind, and she closes her eyes.

"Hey titter, enty you gwine tan one side and lemme git some water? Enty you know me pot duh bun? Enty you know me hurry? Enty you yeddy me tell you fuh mobe?"

Jarry's words come back to her, mixing with Paloma's, who is chanting, "Eshu a ke buru bori ake boye to ri to ru la . . . Ye fi yo' ru a're a la le ku'pa she eyo me'ko . . ."

Something soft brushes her face, and Addie opens her eyes to see the roosters' eyes, tranced and golden, as Paloma, holding them by the feet, their wings relaxed and spread, passes them over her like a soft wind.

"Jarry?"

He takes her hand and presses it. "Don't be frightened," he whispers.

And now, when Addie looks at the black figure, the tar baby, which the others address as Lucero, as Nkuyu, as Eshu, it's regarding her with consciousness in its expression. She is terrified. It suddenly occurs to her that the tar baby stands between her and the spring, and the spring is life.

"You're Death, aren't you?" she asks.

And the tar baby—Lucero, Nkuyu, Eshu, there are many names—laughs at her. "No, I am not Death," *it says,* "I am dead, but I am not Death. I am El Portero. I open the gate."

"Am I going to die?"

"Most certainly."

"But I'm not ready."

"No one ever is, niña. I myself was not. Life is like a child's toy you grip with all your might, and then one day you wake and forget your need for it. You let it go, and then you find it in the toy box later, dusty, soiled, and old, and wonder what it was that made you love it so. I was once alive, and that is how life seems to me, like childhood seems to you, a place you think of fondly but have no wish to return to. It will be the same for you."

"Please," pleads Addie. "Please, not now. I want to live before I die. Let me stay a little more." She clutches Jarry's hand, as though to moor herself by it.

Lucero regards her with compassion, the way an adult regards a child who's tired and doesn't want to go to bed. And suddenly a warm rain is falling. Addie feels a droplet pelt her face. And another. And another. Opening her eyes, Addie sees the roosters twirling overhead. They're like dancing girls, she thinks, girls dancing the mazurka, holding up their dresses and throwing up their cotillions. Paloma's dancing, too, dancing with the roosters, swinging them round and round, wringing their necks, chanting, "Ensuso kabwinda . . . Embele kiamene. . . . Eki menga nkisi . . ." *and blood is raining over Addie, a few light drops, and on the tar baby, too, on Lucero, and Addie sees that he has turned away from her. He's taken them instead of her.*

And around her in the room, the people sing,

> "Ahora sí menga va corre, como corre,
> Ahora sí menga va corre, sí seño,
> Ahora sí menga va corre . . ."

It's like a beautiful old song Addie remembers from somewhere long ago, like a lullaby her mother sang her in her childhood, or another life that Addie put away in the box with all the other broken toys and then forgot. And the blood is falling, menga va corre, como corre, like a soft, warm rain, and it isn't horrible to her. There is no horror here. Addie feels like a young girl at church, the way she felt at St. Michael's long ago, taking first communion, when she walked outside into spring light and the fragrance of gardenias, and Great Michael was pealing overhead, and the day was beautiful and still and filled with peace. The rest that has eluded her these many days steals over her, and Addie sleeps for a time that seems like years, though only seconds pass. The sound of Paloma's voice wakes her.

"Bring the knife."

"The knife?" says Jarry.

"Nkuyu has shown me what to do. . . ."

Reaching under the peignoir that Addie chose so carefully, so specifically, Paloma lifts the silk directly over Addie's heart, and cuts away the button of French nacre— the one that Addie picked out for its deep-sea gleam. Tying the button's hasp to the black hair on Addie's temple, Paloma starts to pull and Addie feels it coming, hank by hank, like a piece of fishing line she's swallowed, up through her bowels, up through her intestines' winding course. Then Paloma drops it in a blue bottle filled with chamba and seals the cork with wax. Picking up the Bible, the old woman sits back in her chair, relaxed, and reads Psalm 51:

> "Deliver me from bloodguiltiness, O God, thou God of my salvation, and my tongue shall sing aloud of thy righteousness.
>
> "For thou desirest not sacrifice, else I would give it; thou delightest not in burnt offering.
>
> "The sacrifices of God are a broken spirit; a broken and a contrite heart, O God, thou wilt not despise."

"Now I've done all I can," Paloma says. "For the rest, we must wait and see." She regards her son, speculatively and close, and Jarry nods his thanks.

It's dusk as he carries Addie out again, dusk as she hears the creaking of the wheels, dusk as he carries her upstairs and tucks her into the fresh linen.

"Thank you, Jarry," Addie whispers hoarsely as he cups her nape and lifts her up to drink.

He smiles and wipes her forehead with a cloth, then lowers her gently, like a rag doll, to the pillow. And Addie waits now for the coldness in her hands and feet. She waits for her teeth to start to chatter. It's six o'clock. Now seven comes and goes. It's a little after eight when Addie falls asleep. And for the first time in weeks, she gets a night's uninterrupted rest. In the morning, she's weak, but Addie knows by subtle signs that the sickness has departed. And all of this will quickly come to seem unreal, her conversation with Lucero or Nkuyu something that happened in a dream, when she was talking in her sleep.

THIRTY-SIX

*T*hrough the secret garden, where the scent of orange blossoms lingered, he led the children past Aunt Tildy's headless nymph, her breasts exposed and lovely, though splotched with acid rain. One svelte arm extended, her finger pointed down into the rippling pool that, always emptying, was always full. When Ransom looked, a goldfish whisked its tail, a brilliant flash amidst the waterweeds. . . . Now the big black brass-knobbed door was parting. Meeting Street and open sky again.

As they emerged, the Charlestonian in black cashmere was hoisting his golf bag into the trunk.

"How's it going, man?" said Ran, affecting normality, but hurrying the children on and lowering his gaze as they passed by.

The man frowned and made no answer. In the windshield of the parked car they were walking toward, Ran saw him step from behind the Benz, saw him place his hands on his lean hips and stare.

"Love those loafers!" Ransom, at the car, could not resist. There was a tremor in his hand as he unlocked the door, and the sound of the golf bag—the specific clank of graphites landing in the trunk—hit him like the sound of a maul on an iron railroad spike, a rattling chain, a lash, and Ransom dropped the keys.

The carabiner he used for a key ring lodged between two bars of a sewer grate, and as Ran knelt to fish them out, the trickle of bright water running far below the street made him think about Shanté, the summer she came home from Northfield, when they fell in love and made their plan to run away. . . .

Ran was working at the New Jerusalem Church then, making a dollar thirty-five an hour, but Shanté's cousin, Wallace, said the Killdeer Country Club was where the good, big money was. So one Sunday morning, early, Ran made the trek to the west side. The golf pro, Tommy Janklow, looking sour and hungover in opaque dark glasses, listened to him lie about his previous experience and didn't really seem to give a shit. He assigned Ran to the first foursome of the day, which, as fate would have it, included Herbert Kincannon, Mel's personal bête noire and capitalist nemesis. When the owner of Dixie Bag asked for his Big Bertha on the tee at number one, Ran handed him a four wood by mistake, then dropped the bag when Kincannon was in the middle of his swing. It went downhill from there.

Two hours later, as they headed up eighteen, Kincannon's face had gone pinker than his Izod shirt, a color closer to the medium-rare roast beef the chef was carving in the club upstairs. Big Herbert hadn't spoken to his caddy for the whole back nine, and Ransom, for his part, looked like he'd been swimming in his clothes. He had open blisters on his heels and a tingling numbness in his shoulder from the bag. Kincannon putted out, then turned and said, in a loud, public voice that made everyone in earshot turn, "What's your name again?" It was the first time he had asked.

Ransom answered, and Kincannon said, "Your daddy's Mel Hill, ain't he?"

The trap was sprung, but Ransom merely blinked a sullen, frightened blink, refusing to step in. Not that it saved him.

"Mel Hill's a sorry, no-count drunk who couldn't sew a straight seam with a ruler," Kincannon said, "and if you live life like you caddy, you're gonna end up like him, if not worse. Now get your peckerwood ass outta here. I never want to see you at the Killdeer Country Club again. No Hill has business on this side of town. Never did, and never will."

Then, peeling two damp ones off his pocket roll, he dropped them on the apron of the green and stalked away.

Upstairs at the big plate-glass windows, people coming straight from church to the buffet had gathered two and three deep to watch the goings-on on number eighteen green. Some boy made a catcall; another laughed.

An older woman shushed them. Humanity expressed itself across its range, or so it seemed to Ransom Hill that day.

What he remembered later, though, what Ran remembered now, in fact, kneeling on the rusty sewer grate—having temporarily forgotten where he was, what he was doing there, his wife, his children, his past success, his hope of future happiness in life, and, in the deepest way, himself—was the girls on their chaises by the pool, separated from him by the railing's iron bars. Sunning on their stomachs, bikini straps undone, they held their polka-dotted tops as they raised up to watch these interesting developments, and one of them—Ran didn't know her name, but he could see her still, in Wayfarers—took a cherry coke in a tall glass that Wallace, in livery now, brought her from the clubhouse on a tray. Pursing her lips around the straw, she sipped and watched to see if the caddy boy beside the row of carts would stoop to take his pay. Ransom, who had earned the money, left it lying where it was and walked away with nothing to show for his morning but hurt feelings and blisters on his heels. For all he knew, those two damp bills were still out there blowing through the universe, still unclaimed, still his.

"Doddy?"

Ran looked up into Charlie's curious stare. Charlie blinked, then stared down into the grate. "What you looking for down dere, Doddy?"

"The keys to the highway," Ransom answered, without hesitation, at Charlie's level, face-to-face and man-to-man.

Charlie extended his small fist and opened.

"And there they are," said Ran. Wiping his sleeve across his eyes, he sat back on the curb, took a gasping breath, and stood. "Ho, shit—hoo-ah! Come on, team, pile in."

As he strapped them in, however, the sounds of a minor fracas drifted up the street.

"There he is!" said someone—it sounded like Alberta Johns.

When he looked back toward Tildy's, the young policewoman had a finger pointed straight between his eyes. "You, there, stop!" she shouted. "You, don't move! Stop that man!" Fumbling her hat on, she started running up the block, gun and nightstick pummeling her sides.

The Charlestonian in cashmere looked at Ran, at her, at Ran again, then set off toward them at a sprint. "You there! Stop!"

"Don't mess with me," Ran warned, opening the driver's door.

"What's going on here?" He grabbed Ransom's shoulder.

Ransom stepped out and knocked him down.

"Daddy! Daddy, don't! Don't, Daddy!" Hope screamed in back, but Ran had zeroed in.

"These are my kids," he said, "*mine,* motherfucker. Not yours. You understand?" Ran stood over him, a big man, crazed and utterly committed. "Nod for yes."

The Charlestonian nodded, surprised, apparently, to find himself afraid.

What surprised him in the moment—Ran, the pacifist, who'd dodged the draft and forgone meat for thirteen years—was the sudden soaring sense he felt, the electric *zing* that shot through his meridians, not a sense of trespass, but command.

The young officer had now arrived, flushed and panting, holding down her hat. "Stop right there," she said, out of breath and frightened, unsnapping the retaining strap on her service .38.

Ran faced her, calm and eagle-eyed. "These are my children," he explained. "I'm their father. I'm taking them for ice cream. If you're going to shoot me, go the fuck ahead."

In the backseat, both kids were crying now. "Doddy! Doddy!"

"Please don't shoot him!"

"Don't shoot Doddy!"

"I can't let you go," she said.

Ransom smiled at her the way a man smiles at a child, then climbed into the Odyssey and pulled, unhurriedly, away.

THIRTY-SEVEN

*H*ealth, as it returns, is like water from a cool, sweet well, and Addie takes measured sips in these first days, savoring it the way she has few things before. But where is Jarry? Sitting dressed beside the window, staring out into the park, she waits and wonders why he doesn't come. Into her green reverie, the voice speaks and says, He is afraid. But she is frightened, too; it's as if the permission her near death extended them has been withdrawn by her return to life. And how are they to find each other now? The answer isn't far to seek: if permission is withdrawn, then she must give it to herself. Addie finds a pretext for a visit in a borrowed volume on her shelf.

So today, for the first time since their conversation at the Bluffs, she dresses and goes down, moving tentatively, gripping the banister as she passes in review before the disapproving ancestors, with Percival's Wordsworth in one hand to steady her.

The May morning is halcyon and still. Walking down the white sand road, she follows voices to the cooper's shop, where she finds Jarry with a half dozen men in elated conference.

"Good morning."

"Mistis." The men stand back, and Jarry—who wears a shirt of clean white homespun with the sleeves rolled past the elbow—smiles and nods her toward an open barrel. "Come look."

Inside is a gray, cloudy substance, like translucent ocean sand, still slightly damp.

"Taste it," he says, with the expression of a man enjoying fresh success.

Addie dips her finger. "Wherever did you get it?"

"We made it."

"How on earth does one make salt?"

"Would you like to see?"

"Very much."

So, while he rigs the sloop, she has the women in the kitchen house prepare a basket lunch, and they set out eastward, running before a light west wind, through the winding thoroughfare of Wando Passo Creek. Before they've gone a hundred yards, they come upon the laundress, Hattie, and her crew of girls, cutting up along the bank as they do wash. Dipping the clothes in kettlefuls of suds, the girls throw them onto wooden stretchers and beat them with wide-bladed paddles known as battling sticks. The thwacks resound, following them for half a mile downstream.

" 'Purge me with hyssop . . . ,' " Addie says under her breath.

"What?" he calls out from the stern.

She smiles and shakes her head. "Do you suppose life uses us that way?" she asks instead. "Beats the dirt and sinfulness away so that, at the last, we shall be clean?"

He smiles, and doesn't answer. There's no need; but it is like the day's motif.

Over the hissing bow wave, the drumming flutter of the edge of the taut sail, talk becomes impracticable, but they converse in looks and smiles, and Jarry occasionally points things out—a great blue heron perched on one leg in the shallows, a row of turtles on a log, the sort called cooters, prized for soup, black and round as salad plates, with heads uplifted toward the sun. Occasionally, he calls the names of birds. They see rufous-sided towhees and indigo buntings, a white ibis, a kingbird's nest with young. There are summer tanagers and flickers, a red-shouldered hawk. And once they see an alligator, twelve or fourteen feet, sunning on the slick clay bank.

When they leave the creek and sail into the Waccamaw, the whole scene opens up. It's like God Almighty, Addie thinks, thrusting out His chest to take a deep lungful of air. The world, from here, seems limitless. Things have the gleam of wet shellac. As they make for the wooded western shore of Pawleys Island, a mile distant over open water, a large side-wheeled steamer—two hundred tons or more and a hundred and fifty feet in length—looms up to port. They take her for a riverboat, but, drawing near, they see the gun ports, jury-rigged to fit her added howitzers and Parrott rifled cannon. Crossing her bow—so close, the shadow of the gunboat falls across the sloop—they read the name, Mendota, and, preceding it, the designation, U.S.S. A Federal gunboat in the Waccamaw! Jarry quickly tacks and hauls the sloop upwind, putting distance between them, but not before a Yankee sailor, pissing off the side, catches sight and hails them. "Hey, nigger, can you swim? Half a minute in the drink, and you can be a free man heaving coal for Uncle Abe."

The encounter and the sailor's taunt depress the mood. Putting the tiller in his armpit, Jarry trims the main, avoiding Addie's glance. Fixing on his navigation point, he stares forward with a doleful face, and Addie wishes he would smile again. And what if she told him and the glass wall broke? If it were gone, then what? It suddenly dawns on her that this is what she fears the most. For if it fell, what would be between them then? Nothing—isn't that the answer? And is that what she came to do? Addie is like one who's stepped unwittingly into an ambush she herself has set, and the voice she hasn't heard in weeks speaks up and tells her, Nothing will be right until you do. *But what of Harlan? What about her marriage?* Your marriage is a lie that everyone believes but you. *Yes, but to see the truth and act on it are different things. A part of her is dying to confess, but to advance a black man's rights against a white man's whim—this would be an act not just of disrespect but of outright sabotage, and not toward Harlan only, but toward her class, toward Charleston, toward the South. . . . She's never contemplated such a drastic action. So, after the pleasant respite of their morning's sail, Addie is plunged into anxiety again. She no longer sees the charming river scene and is grateful for the hissing of the bow wave parting on the keel, grateful for the drumming of the edge of the taut sail, grateful when Jarry guides the boat into a small salt creek and beaches it near an encampment in the woods.*

Here, under a light shed, two enormous copper vats are mounted on brick piers. Under one of them a fire burns, and two slaves—Wando Passo men—are feeding cordwood into it. From a crude chimney, smoke is rising, and from the vat itself, a quivering cloud of steam.

"We took an old boiler from the sugar mill," Jarry tells her as he helps her from the boat, "a prototype that Father fabricated years ago, and cut it in half for the evaporating tanks."

A wooden trough—like a small, slanted aqueduct, buttressed with posts—extends a hundred yards into the adjoining marsh, where a scaffold, twenty feet high, is built. On this rests a platform with a handle mounted in the center like the I-shaped lever of a railroad trolley car. Addie shades her eyes and points. "What's that?"

"There's a pump in the salt creek," Jarry says. "At flood tide, when the water is saltiest and the seepage least, we fill the vats and light the fires."

"So you boil them down."

He nods. "We boil them down and we get this." Taking a scoop out of the cooling, second vat, he lets it slough into her hand.

"It's warm." Addie smiles and puts her tongue to it. "It's almost sweet."

"I prefer it to store-bought."

"However did you think of this?"

He shrugs, clearly pleased.

"We'll have some for our hard-boiled eggs?" She lifts the basket.

"Are you hungry?"

"Almost. I should like to stretch my legs a little first. How far is the beach?"

"No more than half a mile."

"Would you share a walk and dine with me?"

He gives the men instructions, and they strike out east.

"My idea," he tells her as they walk, "is to take the salt to Mars Bluff with our rice and trade for cotton there."

"What do we want cotton for?"

"We don't. We'll run it down to Nassau."

"Through the blockade?"

"Through the blockade. There, the British pay in gold. I've spoken to Father's bankers and advisers, and we all think it's the best way to proceed."

"I leave it in your hands," she says. "Honestly, Jarry, I don't know what we'd do . . . what I would . . ."

There's no need to speak this either. Understanding, Jarry smiles and stares down at the ground, which has turned sandy underfoot. Presently, they hear the boom of surf.

Addie takes her shoes off as they climb the dune. "I swear, I haven't seen the ocean in I can't remember when."

On the east side then, in full view of it, they choose a sheltered spot out of the wind, and Addie spreads the cloth and hands across a cup.

"Coffee is a problem we've yet to solve," he tells her as he pours. "But Mother has devised a substitute from toasted okra seeds. Is there another cup?"

She checks the basket, shakes her head. "We can both drink from that."

She reaches, and he hesitates, then hands the cup to her as he has drunk from it, with the untouched rim toward her. Addie, on an impulse, turns and drinks from the same spot where he has placed his lips. When she looks, his eyes are blurred and hot.

"See what we have," she tells him with a thrilling jolt of confidence, and she lays out their simple feast. There are boiled new potatoes, and slices of cold, thick bacon left from breakfast, hoecake and warm buttermilk together with the eggs, and salt so fresh it tastes of woodsmoke from the fire.

"And look what else . . ." Swaddled in the folds of cloth is Jarry's father's Wordsworth.

"I thought you found him dull."

"I'm hoping you may lift my sights."

"Perhaps you overestimate my abilities."

Addie laughs. "Is that a slur on them or my intelligence?"

For once, her swiftness flusters him. "I didn't mean . . ."

His answer peters out, and Addie leaps into the breach. "You never finished telling me the story of this poem."

His expression settles. "Didn't I?"

She shakes her head, and Jarry looks away. "Where did I leave off?"

"You said you tried to harm yourself. Percival rescued you. You accused him of Thomas's death. What did he say?"

"He told me I was right. Thomas's blood was on his hands. He said, 'Hate me, if you wish, but don't hate life.' He said that there's a beauty in humanity that, if I died, I'd lose the opportunity to see. He asked me what I wanted, and I answered, 'Freedom,' and he told me, 'There are two, Jarry, and the first, the one you seek, is the shallower of the pair. I know, because I have it; I own it as my birthright and feel no freer than you. That first freedom is the only one I can give or take from you, but there's a second, deeper freedom no man can deprive you of, even if he takes your life. I've sought it since I was your age, and it eludes me still, but I've learned something on the way. I at least know more than you. And I'll show you where it lies, and how to look for it, and why, but only if you give your word you won't attempt to take your life again. Will you make that pact with me?' He held out his hand."

"And you took it," Addie says.

"I took it."

"And then?"

He picks up the book. "He took this from the shelf and read the poem to me."

"Read it to me now," she whispers.

Weighing the request, he holds her stare and then begins.

Closing her eyes, Addie sees the poet walking on the moors. It's a beautiful morning. The sun is shining after rain. At first, he feels at one with everything. " 'The air is filled with pleasant noise of waters. . . . The hare is running races in her mirth.' "

On reencounter, Wordsworth pleases her in a way he never did at school. What struck Addie then as dull seems plain with high intention now. And there's something in Jarry's delivery—something quiet, passionate, sure-footed, clear—that's ravishing to watch, like a fine horse running in a field.

But then the mood turns. . . .

" 'But, as it chanceth, from the might
Of joy in minds that can no further go,
As high as we have mounted in delight
In our dejection do we sink as low;
To me that morning did it happen so. . . .' "

As Jarry reads, it comes to her that he's revealing the central moment of his life, and her mood turns as well. For it's his life. Jarry's. It's happening out there. He's opening to her, revealing the best part of himself, while she cowers in the darkened theater, hiding her worst. And Addie thinks, What if I told him? What if I shattered it? What if the foundation stones were shaken, and I let them shake? What might happen then? Might that finally be it, the beginning of her own true life?

She doesn't, though, and as Jarry goes on reading, the poet sees an old man in the distance, staring down into a pool.

" 'At length, himself unsettling, he the pond
Stirred with his staff, and fixedly did look
Upon the muddy water, which he conned
As if he had been reading in a book. . . .' "

"Goodness. You've made the hair stand on my arms," *Addie comments, rubbing them.*

Jarry meets her gaze. "I felt just the same when Father first read it to me."

The poet accosts the old man, and they speak. He's a leech gatherer, seeking the creatures in the pools to sell. Pleasantries are exchanged. The old man shares a few particulars of his profession. Apart from that, the meeting is entirely commonplace. Yet, by the time they part, the poet's mood has turned again.

" '. . . when he ended,
I could have laughed myself to scorn to find
In that decrepit man so firm a mind.
"God," said I, "be my help and stay secure,
I'll think of the leech-gatherer on the lonely moor!' "

"So Percival," *she says when he concludes,* "whom you'd run away from, from whom you were estranged . . ."

"*I hated him.*"

"*Percival, whom you hated, read you this . . . and then?*"

"*He asked me what has changed.*"

Addie blinks.

"*What in this encounter has turned the poet's thoughts from*"—*Jarry seeks the line*—" '*Solitude, pain of heart, distress and poverty,' back to life?*"

"*And what has? Did he explain?*"

"*Father explained nothing,*" *Jarry answers.* "*He shoved the book into my chest and bade me go and find the answer for myself.*"

"*And you did.*"

"*I read this poem for two and a half . . .*" *He looks away.* "*Two and a half years. It's hardly too much to say that it was my whole education. The day I came to him . . . That day, he said, 'You are my son. If you'll work for me, I'll try to be a father and a friend to you, and I will free you when I die.' *" *Jarry's eyes are brimming. He doesn't try to hide them from her now.*

Slipping beside him, Addie rests her hand on his broad back. "*So you came to love him in the end.*"

He looks away over the sea. "*He was that old leech gatherer to me.*"

"*He loved you, too,*" *she says.* "*He told me so before he died. Do you know what he said?*"

Jarry shakes his head.

"*He told me you were his beloved son. He said there was something in himself he was able to give to you without effort, from simple joy, that he could never give to Harlan, however hard he tried, and I see so clearly what it was, and why.*"

"*Father didn't love me,*" *Jarry says.*

"*What?*" *she asks, surprised.* "*Of course he did.*"

Jarry shakes his head. "*He believed he did. There was a time I thought so, too. Not anymore. If he had, he would have set me free.*"

Jarry's self-possession has returned. The look that Addie knows, the one she first saw on the dock, has settled in his eyes. They're like the ocean, serious, comfortless, and deep, and touched with the suggestion of fatigue the waves express when they draw back. "*It took me a long time—years—to see,*" *he says.* "*Really, it's only since the funeral, but what Father did, he held out his two hands to me. . . .*" *He extends his fists and turns one face up and opens it.* "*In the right was freedom, and in the left was poetry, and he said, 'This—poetry—is more valuable, and if you will give me that—your freedom—I will give you this.' And because I was fifteen and didn't see the gambit for what it was, because he was my father and I wanted to believe, I accepted it."*

"But, Jarry, I'm sure, in your father's view, poetry was the most precious gift he had to give, and he shared it with you alone, not Harlan."

"I don't deny its value," he replies, "but it's a secondary good. Without the primary one, how much is it really worth? Harlan was able, every day when he got up, to choose his course."

"But your father put the operation of the family business in your hands and taught you how to run it. What did Harlan learn—to ride to the hounds and go whoring in French Alley?"

"If he didn't put his freedom to constructive uses, he was free nonetheless. If I'd told Father I wished to spend my hours in the library and leave the plantation business to others, do you know what he'd have said? He'd have been shocked and offended, Addie. Father would have felt betrayed by my ingratitude. If I'd persisted, eventually he'd have punished me. I know this as I know the sun will rise tomorrow. And how can that be love? It's not. That Father felt a positive regard for me, I don't deny. That there was fondness, affection, respect for my capacities—all this, I concede. But, love, no. For love is never love that regards the beloved in a lesser light or accords him lesser rights than the lover accords himself. Love is never love that oppresses, that grants the beloved lesser freedoms than the lover grants himself."

And she is weeping now.

"But what . . . ?" With surprised tenderness, he touches her shoulder.

"Do you know, I always feared they didn't love me either." She looks at him with streaming eyes.

"Who?"

"My parents. They died not two miles south of here." She points with her right hand. "One day, when I was four months old, an afternoon as calm as this, they walked into this very sea and did not come back. My aunt always said it was an accident, but look . . . Look there, and tell me how could they have drowned."

"You don't believe they did?"

She shakes her head. "I never have and never will."

"But why . . . ?"

"Because of me. Because I was burdensome to them."

"That can't be true. I'm sure it's not."

"And I'm just as sure that Percival loved you."

Reflected in the mirror of the other, each beholds himself more truly than either has alone. And love is close, so close, for what is it but this, one True Self by another beheld, and, by the power of that beholding, freed to see?

Addie is more beautiful now than when she was that girl of seventeen, who read "Evangeline" and vowed that she would wait for her own Gabriel no matter what, however long it took. And she has waited after all, despite herself. No man but Jarry has beheld her in this state; none ever will. A door has opened, one that Addie never found at Mme Togno's school. For each of them, it is as if the world has only been created this last hour and no one else exists in it but them.

And she must tell him now. Addie knows she must.

Why doesn't she? Why, instead, does she allow her head to drop against his shoulder, allow her eyes to close? In this brief, unexpected sweetness, she luxuriates, listening to the waves come in, and Addie vows to tell him on the walk to camp, and yet she doesn't. Nor on the sail back. She's grateful for the hissing of the bow wave on the keel, for the drumming of the edge of the taut sail.

At home again, she accuses her reflection in the mirror as she brushes out her hair. Love is never love that grants the beloved lesser freedom than the lover grants himself. Isn't that what Jarry said, and isn't it what she has done? And why?

The cardinal lights upon the branch, and Addie hears the words as clear as if the dead man spoke them in her ear: "I was afraid that if I freed them, they might leave."

I must tell him, Addie thinks. "I must tell him now." She says the words aloud, and yet she doesn't rise to go. For shaking the foundations is, after all, a fearful enterprise. She never leaves the room all night, but lies awake and tosses, fretting. She'll tell him in the morning. "I will," she vows. "I will." The necessity has the inevitability of death, and Addie dreads it hardly less. She's unaware of having slept, but apparently she has, for something startles her and she awakes to find a gray light in the room and, coming through the window, muted by the panes, the sound of screams.

THIRTY-EIGHT

*R*ight, then left, then right again. As he made his getaway, there was a lump in Ransom's throat, a thickness. Pride. A song was playing in his head: "Street Fighting Man."

"Why did you hit him, Daddy?" Hope asked, crying in the back. "Why?"

The song veered suddenly off-key. In the rearview, he met her streaming eyes.

"I don't know, Hope. I shouldn't have. It was wrong."

Oh, bullshit, said the voice.

"You made him bleed."

"I know I did. I'm sorry."

What a crock.

"Why? Daddy, why?"

He hit the brakes and turned to her with harried eyes. "I was afraid he was going to take you, Hope, okay? That's why. I shouldn't have done it. I'm sorry I did. Now, let's not talk about it anymore."

"I want ice keem, Doddy," Charlie said.

"I'm going to get you some. But right now, let's put something on. What do you want?" He shuffled jewel cases on the console like the face cards in a deck. "Here's *Kipper,*" he said, dealing, "*Dora* . . . *The Magic School Bus Blows Its Top*—how about that?"

"I want *The Lion King,*" said Hope.

"*The Lion King* it is." Ran shoved in the disc.

Why don't you quit lying to her and yourself, you wuss? the voice proposed as Ran set off again, uncertain where they were. *You aren't sorry. You enjoyed it. Quit pretending to be nice. And you know why you hit him. You didn't like his pants . . . his "trousers"—isn't that what Claire called them that time? Remember when she tried to make you buy a pair?*

"Shut up," he said halfheartedly, feeling tired, demoralized. As he turned again, the memory assailed him . . . the prissy little salesclerk in his bow tie and horn-rims, whose handkerchief—which complemented, but subtly differed from, his tie—spilled from his breast pocket in a way that seemed wholly unpremeditated, but which Ransom, on a thousand subsequent attempts, could never quite get right. As they stood before the three-way mirror, in the calculated and revealing light on the sixth floor at Saks, the little man, who seemed so smooth and confident to be a clerk, knelt down and turned the cuff.

"How much of a break do you prefer?"

"You better give me all the break you've got," said Ransom, turning embarrassment, as usual, into a joke. Pushing thirty then, he'd never owned a pair of fitted pants . . . trousers. By that point in the transaction, he was starting to perspire and also to blame Claire—who was thumbing through the rack behind them, blithely unaware—starting, in fact, to hate her just a bit, and then a little more than that, for putting him in the position, for being unaware.

"The drape is very flattering. This Italian wool has such a lovely hand." The little man went on.

Ransom tried with all his might to avoid his own reflection in the mirror. When he failed, a reanimated corpse stared back, blue and sweating, desperately in need of a shot of human blood or whatever alchemical elixir it might be that would make him finally, fully human like the little clerk, like Claire, his wife, like all the other people flitting through the store, like all the other people flitting through this life.

"Didn't like them?" Claire asked, with a light arch of the brows.

They left Saks holding hands that day, but Ransom's palms were sweating, Claire's as dry and crisp as the autumn sky they walked into on Fifth. A sky like this one outside Charleston, where dusk was creeping from the horizon upward toward the zenith, away up there where it was still day, a profound ceramic blue, with a first star twinkling like Cupid's arrowhead dipped in magic fairy dust. And the new moon was his bow, strung and bent, aimed straight for Ransom's chest. And wasn't that what he had loved in Claire—her blithe unawareness—even if he'd hated her for it as well? Somewhere deep inside, he'd hoped Claire's confident belief that life would bring her all good things would rub off somehow, would compensate his secret shame, the sense that he deserved no better than the shotgun shack where he'd grown up and the swift and unappealable correction of his drunken father's fists. He'd hoped, in short, that Claire might save him from himself. And Ran was forty-five and knew full well that people don't save other people from themselves. Yet in that secret, childlike place, you see, never fully challenged or expunged, he'd still not quite surrendered the hope that, due to extraordinary need or merit, the gods might grant a small exception in his case. Was it too much to ask? Apparently so, because in all these years it hadn't happened. Was it too late to think that it still might?

It was. The verdict suddenly came down.

They were on a bridge now, crossing water. Was that the Ashley or the Cooper? Ran didn't know or really give a shit.

"Life's not fair, is it?" The voice—poisoned, unctuous—was speaking, like a red-garbed demon with a pitchfork and a tail, into Ran's right ear, coming from the speaker of the DVD.

"Who's that?"

Neither Hope nor Charlie answered, their little faces anesthetized as they gazed upward in the rearview, transfixed by what was happening on screen.

"Hope, who's that talking?"

"That's Scar, Daddy. *Shhh!*" She glared and put her finger to her lips.

Well, he's right, isn't he? said the voice. *Life isn't fair.*

"He does make a certain point," conceded Ran, as the development began to thin. There were marshes ahead and to the left. The sun in the rearview was bloodred. They must be headed east, he realized, toward the ocean.

It was that unfairness that he and Shanté, once upon a time, had meant to run away from and leave behind. They were going to New York City, where it didn't matter if your skin was black or if you lived in Bagtown and your name was Hill . . . But in the end, Delores found them out and shut the kitchen door. When push came, finally, to shove, Ran's beloved teacher—who fought for civil rights, who got her daughter a full ride at a good northern prep school, the first person who made Ransom Hill believe that there was something in him worth an effort on another human being's part—Delores could extend Ran her largesse, but accept him as her daughter's lover, she could not.

In the end, you weren't even good enough for them, were you, Ran? the voice proposed, *not even good enough for your nigger girlfriend or her nigger mom.*

"Shut up!" he shouted.

"We didn't say anything, Daddy!" Hope and Charlie cried in protest.

"I'm sorry. I wasn't talking to you."

"Who were you talking to?"

"No one." He avoided Hope's query in the mirror. "Myself."

Do you understand? the voice went on, growing ever bolder now. *Do you begin to see why Harlan did it now?*

There was a new voice coming from the speaker now—Mufasa's. His deep-chested, manly baritone seemed familiar somehow. What was the actor's name? Briefly, Ran tuned in. Mufasa was explaining the Pridelands' extent to little Simba. Everything the eye could see would one day be his to rule. All except for a shadowy region in the farthest distance. That place, Mufasa said, Simba must avoid at all costs.

He's wrong, though, isn't he? the voice said. *Don't you have to go there, too?*

Resistant, Ransom clenched his jaw, but what the voice said now seemed true.

They were crossing another, older bridge onto what appeared to be an island—for all Ran knew, it might have been Sullivan's as easily as Kiawah. Expensive homes on immaculately groomed lots stood side by side by shacks with jungle yards. A hippie girl attired for a night out in Haight-Ashbury in 1968 was talking to a haggard homeless man with a fright wig of silver hair. Surfer dudes in wet suits filed off the beach, where a fabulous party roared beneath a pier. Unusually large numbers of dogs and cats wandered near the public road, like aboriginals on walkabout.

Beside a run-down shack that looked suspiciously like Ran's old house on Bane and Ninth, an ancient lady in a rocking chair sat hunched beneath a crude hand-lettered sign: "Fried Popcorn Shrimp."

Pulling into the dusty lot, Ran got out, leaving the children fixated in back.

"Popcorn shrimp," he said, examining the gray specimens she was heading in her lap. "Bait, in other words . . ."

"You got it," she conceded, cheerfully enough. "Don't let that stop you, though. They're good. Here, try one." She offered him a greasy paper plate.

He picked one off the mound. "You're right."

"Even better hot. Can I fry you up a batch?"

"What I really need is ice cream for my kids."

She wiped her hands and put the basket in the fryer. "There's a shop in town. Or I got some Ben and Jerry's in the house."

"I guess it would be asking too much for you to have some cones . . ."

"Well, you are pushing it a bit," she said. "But, guess what, it's your lucky day."

"I could argue the point," he said. "But I won't. Two double scoops to go. I'll make it worth your while."

The screen door slammed behind her, and he listened to the sizzling of the oil, the whisper of breaking surf.

In the van, Scar was telling Simba that the shadow region was only for the bravest lions.

Scar's right, isn't he? said the voice. *However wise and good Mufasa is, he doesn't really grasp the total picture. You have to go there, too, don't you, Ran—to where the shadows are? Isn't that trip, in fact, the one that really counts?*

"That's where we're going now, isn't it?" asked Ran.

And the voice said, *Already there.*

"Mind if I ask a question," he asked the old woman as he paid.

"Shoot."

"Where exactly am I?"

"Folly Beach."

Ran expelled a shrimp, projectile-style, as he began to laugh. "And I suppose that once you get here, you can never leave."

"I might not be the person you should ask," she said. "Been here forty years myself."

"Okay," said Ran, "okay, the Folly part is evident, so where exactly is the Beach?"

She jerked her head. " 'Bout a hundred yards that way."

"Would you object if I let my children stretch their legs?"

"It's a free country."

"Who told you that one?"

The woman smiled at this, and Ransom, cheered by the exchange, took the cones back to the car to find a herd of wildebeests plunging down a sheer rock scarp with hyenas snapping at their heels. Ahead of the stampede, the little lion, Simba, ran, weaving and slipping.

Ransom, like the children, watched, entranced, as black-maned Scar informed his golden, nobler brother, Mufasa, of the peril in the gorge.

Scar and Mufasa traversing down a rocky mountainside . . . Mufasa plunging into the stampede . . . He runs against the herd and gets knocked down . . . He grunts and struggles up . . . little Simba's clinging to a tree limb . . . Now it breaks, he's flying through the air . . . Mufasa catches him in his mouth . . . He puts Simba, safe, on a high rock. The herd sweeps him away, and Simba screams.

Suddenly Mufasa reappears. He lunges, claws his way up the rock face. Above, Scar waits, looking down at him, strangely calm.

Mufasa whispers, asks for help. Scar lunges, digs his claws into Mufasa's paws. His chartreuse eyes are lit up now; Mufasa's golden ones go shocked and round with awful prescience. "Long live the king!" says Scar.

Mufasa, screaming, falls and falls.

The thunder of hooves abates.

Ashen, Ran reached up and turned the picture off.

"Daddy! It's not over!"

"Yes, it is," he said, unbuckling them brusquely.

"What about the movie?"

"Here's your ice cream," he said, handing them their cones. "Come on." He took their hands and hauled them to the beach.

"Look!" said Charlie, running toward the ocean as it came into view.

Hope, less easily diverted, frowned at Ransom.

"What?"

Warned off by his tone, she followed Charlie. "Wait for me!"

Alone, Ran fell to his seat and pressed his throbbing temples with both hands.

"Scar, help me, brother!"

In the final moment, just before Mufasa fell, Ran recognized the voice. The actor was James Earl Jones, but that wasn't it. The connection was to Cell. Cell was Mufasa. Their voices possessed a similar timbre, similar depth. Hope had recognized it, too.

Guess who that makes you.

"Silly, Scar's my *real* daddy. . . ." Ransom suddenly realized his daughter was defending him against Claire's preference. In Hope's fantasy, the bad lion was supposed to win. And why? Because in real life, her daddy wasn't.

Do you think Mufasa ever struggled before a three-way mirror? said the voice. *Do you think it ever cost him any anguish to buy a pair of pants? Sure, you hit that poor schmo in Charleston, but he was just a stand-in—we know who you'd really like to give the old bangzoom. And if it felt that good with a stranger, Ran, think how good it would feel to give Marcel the TKO, to give both him and Claire a dose of the same hurt they've given you. Think how good it's going to, when you finally do.*

It was night now. The incoming wave broke, white as the evil lion's teeth. *Hsssssssss,* it said, in just Scar's tone of voice.

"A. H. D. with J., Wando Passo, Aug. 1865." The thought popped suddenly into his head, and Ran said, "Holy shit."

Starting to get it?

"Wait . . . You don't mean . . ."

Yep, you're very warm.

"Wait! It isn't him? It isn't Harlan in the grave?"

Took you long enough.

"Holy shit! So he came home after the war . . ."

Destitute and bitter, from a Northern prison . . .

"And found out . . ."

A. H. D. with J.

"She was having an affair?"

And Bingo was his name-o.

"So he caught them, right? Harlan caught them, and then . . . And then . . . What happened then?"

You know what happened then. What had to happen happened, just like it has to happen now, again.

"So he . . . ?"

Say it.

"Wait, no, wait," said Ransom, cradling his splitting head, having this highly animated two-way conversation, solo, on the beach.

Come on, Ransom, say it.

"No!"

You know you have to.

"All right, he killed them! He fucking killed them, okay?"

Huh, Good Got! Say it, say it again! the voice exulted, doing a mean James Brown.

"So what?" said Ransom, crying now. "So fucking what? Just because it happened then doesn't mean it has to happen now."

Of course not! it laughed. *This all happened a long time ago.*

"Over a hundred years!"

A hundred and forty, actually. What does any of it have to do with you? Or Claire? Or Marcel "Cell Phone" Jones?

"We're talking murder here," Ran said, pathetically imploring now. "Murder. This is me. *Me.*"

That's the mistake, though, Ransom, don't you see? the voice said, not without compassion. *People think murder's something high and hard and deep. It isn't. How hard is it to pull the trigger of a gun? Any harder than, say, checking your wife's underpants?*

"Hey, I didn't do that!"

You were close, though, weren't you? All we're talking here is capability. And you did knock down a total stranger because you didn't like his tassel-loafers or his pants. If you ask me, a knuckle sandwich, a fist in someone's face, flesh to flesh and bone to bone, is a good bit more up close and personal than a gun. And braver, too. Give yourself some credit. That was a pretty gutsy move. Your old homeboys at Bane and Depot would certainly approve. And you know why hitting him felt good?

"Why?"

Because it was the first true act you've taken in . . . How long has it been, Ran? Years?

"But it's against everything I believe in."

Come on, Ransom, face it, when you get down to it, you don't really believe in all that much.

"It's uncivilized," he said.

So what? the voice replied. *Civilization isn't where it ends—you at least know that much, don't you? Didn't you just agree with Scar that Simba has to journey to the shadow place?*

"That's true, I did," said Ran, impaled on his own point.

Beyond the border, past the defended gate, there's a whole wild wilderness out there—in here. That's where Simba had to go in order to become king. And you do, too, Ran. That's where you'll finally find the thing you've been seeking all these years.

"What's that?" he asked, suddenly needing help remembering.

Your True Self, the voice obliged, *remember? It's waiting for you there. You know, and I know, you have to take the trip. It's foreordained. You're already on the path. There's no way back, no way out but on.*

"But, murder," Ran protested. "Not murder, though. This can't be where the journey leads. I'm not capable of that."

Remember Chinatown? *"Under the right circumstances, Mr. Gittes, a man is capable of anything."*

"Yeah, I remember. So, what's your point?"

The same one Sneeden made this afternoon—if you're so innocent and squeaky clean, why did it jerk your chain to be treated as a suspect? If you're so confident you're incapable of murder, THEN WHY THE FUCK DID YOU HIDE HARLAN'S GUN?

"I didn't, though!" Ran protested. "Did I?"

Having reached an angry pitch, the voice maintained a contemptuous silence now.

"I really don't remember!"

Yeah, right. And Buh Rabbit doesn't remember the path out of the briar patch.

"You never believed in me," Ran said, with a note of wounded, child-like petulance.

Au contraire. I'm the only one who ever did. It's you who always undermine yourself, and me who has to go behind you cleaning up the mess.

Pondering this statement, Ran came to now, as he previously had before the creel of dirty clothes, and for the first time didn't answer. In the quiet, he could hear his children laughing. Night had fallen on the beach. A wave came in. He stood.

"Who are you?" he said, aloud, but quietly, speaking toward the sea. The sudden bristling along his spine was like the ridge of hair that rises on a dog the moment it first senses an intruder, not yet seen. "Who the fuck are you?"

Me? I'm no one, Ransom. Isn't that who you told Hope you were talking to?

"No one, as in . . ."

Pleased to meet you, can't you guess my name?

"Nemo," Ransom said.

The voice laughed. *You can call me Captain, or mon capitaine. Just remember to salute.*

Ransom, now, did not reply. Looking up, he saw the stars out in their billions, and it struck him that Van Gogh painting *The Starry Night* had not been rendering a visual conceit, but painting what he saw in the night sky over Arles, something that was really there. And Ransom knew because he saw the same thing now, a swirl above the drawn bow of the moon, a vortex spinning slowly in the sky above the South Carolina coast.

"Hope! Charlie! Come on! It's time to go!"

"Just another minute, Dad!"

"Right now!" he roared into the night.

"Again! Again! Again!"

So this is where the journey leads . . . this is where the journey leads. . . .

"I need help," he said aloud then, not to them, or to the voice, but to the painter of the canvas overhead, the author of the world, in Whom, even then, Ran only indifferently believed. Yet he had nowhere else to turn except himself. And his self, Ran realized, was no longer something he could trust.

That was the moment when it finally dawned on Ransom that the little voice, the familiar one that helps out in the morning when you hesitate between the blue shirt and the red, had stopped being his, stopped being him. At some point, it had become the voice of something other, not himself, not aligned with Ransom Hill and not his friend. And what point was that? The moment Ran dug up the pot.

This is where the clues were leading all along. . . . And what do you do then, when you're already on the path, in the moment you finally realize where it leads . . . ?

"What do I do now?"

The first part of the answer—but the first part only—came to Ransom as he carefully (oh, so carefully) strapped the children into the car and started off with them again.

THIRTY-NINE

*T*he first scream registers surprise and grief. It's the second that will wake Addie late at night in her remaining years. There are no screams after that. By the time the cemetery gate swings to, the creaking of the rusty hinge is all there is to interrupt the morning's silence. Paloma is lying faceup in the grass. Except for her left eyelid—which has drooped three-quarters closed and is twitching—the old woman seems composed, staring almost thoughtfully up into the dappled light that filters through the beard of the old cypress.

"Paloma?" Addie slips a hand beneath her head. "Paloma, can you hear me?"

"Escuche, niña. Los periquitos . . . ¿Usted los oye?"

"Paloma, I'm sorry. It's Addie, I can't understand you."

"Han venido para mí."

Paloma smiles with one side of her mouth, and Addie thinks, decisively, *A stroke.* She can't be sure if Paloma recognizes her. The old woman's face is like a mask, half of comedy, half tragedy, and her eye beneath the fallen lid has taken on a terrible opacity, like that of a poached fish, as though some hot explosion in her head has cooked it from within. Like a gunshot, then, the slamming door at Jarry's house breaks the stillness, and only now does Addie see the green cloud rise above the dike and drift uneasily back down into the fields. "Periquitos"—the word comes clear. Half shouldered on, his coat flutters as he runs—like a flag, it strikes her, the black flag of an army charging toward defeat. She feels a futile impulse to cry out, to tell him not to run, and stifles it.

"What's happened? What is this? Is she . . . ?" Falling heavily to his knees in summer grass that looks suddenly, cruelly lush, he looks to her.

"I found her only now."

He leans and whispers, "Mama? Mama, what is it? Talk to me."

"¿Percival, eres tú?"

"No, Mama, it's me, Jarry," he answers with a stricken look.

"You sound so like him. Tienes la voz igual que tu papá."

"What is it, Mama? Are you ill?" He strokes her hair. "Where does it hurt? ¿Dónde le duele?"

"You should go for the doctor," Addie says, willing measure into her tone. "I think you should ride straightaway for Dr. Sims."

He looks at her, his reddened eyes filled with a brief flight of indecision and despair, and she is sick for him. To lose his mother now . . . Let it pass, Lord, Addie thinks, and if that be not possible, give him strength to bear.

"No te preocupes por el doctor," says Paloma. "Ya es demasiado tarde."

"No, Mamá." With a reckless desuetude, he collapses and lifts her head into his lap. "You're going to be all right." He's weeping now, yet Addie notes the way he keeps his voice in a clear, tender register and gently strokes her hair. There's a softness in his jawline as he gazes down, as if Paloma were a child or some unweaned, defenseless animal he's determined to protect. When he looks at Addie, his eyes are full of naked pain and questioning, and she holds his stare as long as necessary, taking what she can, sharing what it's possible to share.

Paloma, who seems far more unconcerned than they, tries to lift her arm. Palm up in the grass, the fingers uncurl slightly, further letting go. With the other, then, she weakly cups his cheek. "¿Tú ves lo que ha hecho tu hermana?"

"What, Mama?" he answers. "What has she done?"

"Mira, niño." Paloma's expression has now clarified. In it, there is some unspeakable surmise. Jarry glances soberly at Addie, then at what she's long since seen. . . . Beside the stone, its name still sharp from the chisel, lies a mound of tumbled yellow earth, abandoned when daylight caught the diggers at their work, rifling the grave of Percival DeLay.

"Ve a traerla," Paloma says.

"Let us get you in the house first, Mama."

"Bring her, now!"

"No hace falta."

At the voice, they turn and find Clarisse, staring impassively through the bars at them like animals in a cage. From her headscarf to her skirts, she's dressed in white homespun, clean, pressed, and virginal, almost blinding in the light. Her feet are bare

and there are strings of colored beads around her neck. She's carrying a staff of var-
nished wood with a leopard's head with staring eyes of somber jet.

"¿Quién es?¿Clarisse, eres tú?"

"Sí, Mamá. Estoy aquí," she answers. Her face is sober, watchful, keen, the
look of someone stepping into an ambush she expects and does not fear in the
least. Her lack of surprise is what strikes Addie, that and the fact that Clarisse
does not seem especially troubled—merely thoughtful—over her mother's plight.
And Addie can't help noticing her vividness, which is like the grass, radiant with
cruel summer health. Her skin has the gauzy freshness of one who's risen from a
pleasant bath, and her expression is as languid as a queen's at a review, all except
her yellow eyes, which seek Addie's pointedly and first, and, finding them, smolder
with hatred that briefly flares into the fire of an exultant and offensive confidence.
If I hate her back, she wins, thinks Addie, falling back upon the platitudes of
youth. But she, who's never truly hated anyone before, is miles deep in that dark
country now.

"¿Qué has hecho muchacha?" Paloma cries out, struggling to rise. "What in
God's name have you done?"

"Nada malo, Mama. No he hecho nada malo," she answers, coming through the
gate. "Sólo busco la justicia. Only justice," she says, inside now, lapsing into English,
making sure that Addie understands. Clarisse's eyes have ceased to gloat, and their so-
briety is more impressive and frightening by far than all her taunting glee.

"¿Justicia?" Paloma says. "¡Ésto no es justicia, niña! Ayúdame a incorporarme."

"Lie still, Mama," Jarry says. "You must rest."

"Help me up, I said!"

Reluctantly, he supports her elbows as she sits.

"They told me you were sick, niña." Clarisse address Addie like an acquain-
tance at a social tea. "You are better, I hope?"

"Much," she answers, clipped.

"Bueno, china." And then, to Jarry, in a dark, commanding tone, "Déjenos.
Llévese a la blanca de aquí. She has no business here."

"Who did this?" he says, ignoring her and pointing to the grave.

"Éso no es asunto suyo."

"He was my father. How is it not my business?"

"Era mi padre, también, hermano. Él y yo lo convenimos."

"¿Qué?" he says. "What was agreed between you?"

"If you don't know, ask Mama. She knows the answer, don't you? Ella sabe
muy bien."

"I won't allow it!" shouts Paloma. "¡Yo no lo permitiré! ¿Me oyes?"

"I hear you, Mama," Clarisse replies, "but this is not your business either."

"Él no sabía lo que hacía."

"He knew more than you think. Who do you think taught me the secret?"

"Muchacha," Paloma wails, "muchacha, what have you done? Ven aquí. Come here to me." She reaches out her one good hand, but Clarisse stays where she is, unmoved. "What has happened to you, child? Have you forgotten Demetrio? ¿Se te ha olvidado lo que él te enseñó?¿Qué, no recuerdas nada?"

"I've forgotten nothing, Mamá. No se me ha olvidado nada. I remember things that you know nothing of. You have no right to judge me. Ninguno de ustedes tiene el derecho de juzgarme."

"And regla, child? What of regla?"

"What of it, Mama? There is no regla here. No hay nadie que nos diga qué hacer. Todo está roto, Mama. Everything is broken. We must make regla for ourselves, like Binah did. Binah hizo lo que ella quería. Haré lo que yo quiera, también."

"Regla doesn't come from your padrino, niña. Viene de los muertos. Los ojos invisibles te están mirando. Verán y sabrán."

"Let them see, then. Let them know. What is it to me?"

"You will suffer, niña. Los dos sufrirán los dolores del infierno."

"¿Los dolores del infierno?" Clarisse laughs bitterly. "What further terrors do you think hell holds for me? Los sufro ya."

Paloma now begins to weep. "Hija, le pido que no hagas esto. Por favor. I beg of you."

"It's too late, Mama. The pact is made. No puede ser deshecho."

"You will deny me my last wish?"

"Sí, Mamá, si éste es su último deseo, entonces mi respuesta debe ser no."

"Go away! ¡Vete!" Paloma collapses against Jarry's chest, and Clarisse, before she goes, turns to the side and rests her hand on her belly in a soft, proprietary way, making sure that Addie sees the slight but unmistakable new bulge. "I, too, niña, have been unwell," she says, "but I'm better now, like you." The outrage Addie feels, the fury and shock, wash over her in an incapacitating wave—and, strange, but no less deep, a pang of shame and grief.

And there they are, the wounded left abandoned in the field, as Clarisse returns the way she came.

"We should get her inside, Jarry, out of this heat," says Addie.

"No, niña, let me be," Paloma says. "I want to die outside, Jarry. Deseo morir debajo del cielo."

"*You aren't going to die, Mama.*"

"*Sí, niño, estoy muriendo.*" His mother looks at him with tender pity now. "*I cannot spare you.*"

"*Not now, Mama. Hoy no. No te vayas.*"

"*Sí, niño, me voy,*" she answers softly. "*No puedo esperar. Déjame ir.*"

Jarry merely nods his head and weeps. "*All right, Mama. All right, then.*"

"*Pobre muchacho, don't be sad for me. I'm tired, Jarry. Estoy tan cansada de vivir. No tengo miedo de morir. I welcome it.*"

"*Go then, Mama.*"

"*Listen, niño. Los periquitos—¿Los oyes? Remember when you were a little boy? Te conté la historia de los periquitos.*"

"*Sí, Mamá, the story of the parakeets. I haven't forgotten.*"

Paloma's features suddenly contract into a rending wince of pain. "*Who was there to tell stories to Clarisse? Clarisse nunca tenía a nadie, Jarry, nadie.*" She grasps his collar with fearful energy and pulls him down into her face. "*Ella es una bruja, Jarry. ¿Entiendes? Your sister is a witch. Encuéntralo y destrúyelo. You must find it and destroy it. Do you understand?*"

"*¿Sí, Mamá, entiendo, ¿pero cómo? Destroy it how?*"

"*Las hormigas, niño. Las hormigas harán el trabajo.*"

With this, she sinks back, exhausted. The pulse in her neck is fitful. It reminds Addie of the wounded parakeet in Jarry's hand, the rapid, frantic respiration that so suddenly and absolutely ceased, as this now ceases, too. One minute, Paloma's brow is fretfully contracted, like someone listening to a dark, demanding overture that only she can hear; the next, an overspreading peace widens there—forehead, cheeks, jaw, lips—moving like a ring from a dropped stone that sinks away to emptiness. A soft breeze rises in the park, rippling the black pond, turning its gleam matte and rustling through the canopies of the old trees. When it passes, everything is still, and Addie now becomes aware of cicadas chirring and, farther off, the splash of water through the gate on the far shore.

"*Vaya, Mamá,*" Jarry whispers. "*Vuele con ellos. You're free.*" He kisses her brow tenderly and covers her eyes with his whole hand, as though shielding them, and when he moves it, they are closed.

"How I wish I could spare you this," says Addie now, with burning eyes.

"That's what she said. She couldn't, nor can you."

"Do you know what I believe? Character is how we stand the pain of life, nothing more than that. I've never admired two people more than I do you and her."

Jarry doesn't answer, but Addie sees he's moved by it, and she stands up and *sweeps her skirts unhurriedly. Unhurriedly, she gazes up into the canopies of the old trees and to the sky beyond, which is blue and where astonishing white clouds move with a majestic slowness that has some aspect of eternity. There is, for once, no hurry, no hurry about anything.*

"There's such peace here. Do you feel it?"

His participating silence is all the answer Jarry gives. Allowing him his privacy, Addie gazes at the river sliding by. From the far shore, she can hear the brooding chitter of the flocks.

"She used to say they come from Guinea," *he says, after a time.*

Addie looks at him. "Guinea?"

"Africa. Mama's mother and before her . . . The old people there believed that when we die, we cross an ocean, so when they were brought here, when they were captured and put into the ships, they thought, some did, that they'd been brought to hell. They thought this was the land of the dead. . . . And when the birds came, Mother's mother told her they came from Guinea, all that way across the ocean. She said they were God's messengers, sent to us as friends, and that they came to eat the Pharaoh's rice. She said they stand for what was before the plantation and will be after the plantation ends. . . . Because here, you see, we are in hell. We are in torment and subjugation, but the birds come to remind us of our true home, across the ocean, tan lejos . . . so far away. . . ."*

"That's why you put the feather in my book," *she says to him, with shining eyes.*

"That's why I put the feather in your book, because you came with the birds, and like them, you reminded me that past hell, past the end of days, there is a world of life, and someday I will be delivered unto it. We both will be. For I now see it is the same for you."

"Yes," *she says,* "it is the same for me. Thank you for seeing that."

"That's what her story meant. She told it to me for the same reason her mother told her, to give me something to believe in and to hope for. And that's why I put the feather in your book, to say, take heart, though you suffer, there is still beauty and beauty is something . . . to say, take heart, there is still life, and life is something. And someday you will return to your true home."

Jarry looks at her. His eyes are still questioning, but they've opened past the pain and grief. They're like windows into something deep, and in that deep place, there's a relaxed, sad strength, heavy with the weight of life, bemused by it, but wondering, too—not in flight from it, not rejecting, not rebelling, not afraid.

"There's something I must tell you, Jarry." *She kneels beside him on the ground, and they are face-to-face.* "You're free."

He merely blinks. "With you, you mean. . . ."

"No," she says. "I mean your father freed you in his will. He gave it to me, Jarry. Harlan took it and destroyed it. He swore me to silence, and I . . . It was against my conscience, but I allowed him to prevail."

He holds her stare for a long beat. Addie sees he's unprepared for this, but his openness to her remains. And then he starts to weigh. A reckoning sets in; the opening begins to narrow. His eyes glaze, and Jarry finally looks away. "I expected something of the sort," he says eventually, in a level tone that makes her start to panic. "Mother said you were involved. She said she'd seen it in your face. I didn't believe her."

"Please forgive me—can't you?"

He doesn't answer, doesn't look at her, and at his silence, his refusal to meet her gaze, Addie feels opened up and gutted, the way a hunter guts a doe.

"Jarry, please, say something." She reaches toward him. "Don't leave me comfortless."

"As you left me?" he says, gazing down at her white hand on his black arm. "As you left her?"

Addie receives this like a slap. Stunned by it, she can't think what to say. And as she watches, speechless, Jarry picks Paloma's body up and starts out of the plot.

She runs after him and stops him by the gate. "I should have spoken, Jarry. If I didn't, it was from fear and weakness. It was because I was confused. I am at fault, and I apologize with all my heart."

Jarry simply looks at her for a long beat, and then, carrying his mother, he turns and walks away.

FORTY

ansom knelt with them on Meeting Street before the big black door. Sweeping Hope's hair from one blue eye, he straightened Charlie's collar, then licked his fingers and took a swipe at the ice cream on his son's cheek. The smell—saliva mixed with chocolate—conjured up a ghostly image of some woman doing this to him. Was it his mom? Another memory to add to the impoverished album Ran possessed, which consisted, really, of just one page, just one clear shot: her sliding down the kitchen wall with blood streaming from her nose, as Mel stood astraddle, drunk and bellowing, "It ain't never enough, is it, bitch? No matter what I do or don't, it ain't never fucking good enough." The kids began to squirm, and Ransom gave the ice cream project up.

"Listen, guys," he said, "Mommy's right upstairs. I'm going to call her, and she's coming down."

"Are you coming in?" Hope asked.

"No, Pete, I have to leave."

"Why?"

"I just do."

"Forever?"

He touched her cheek in sympathy. "No, sweetie. Only for a little while."

"How long?" she asked.

"Where you going, Doddy?"

"I'll be back soon," said Ran, who didn't have the answers to their questions. "Now you wait here," he said, terminating the interview. "She'll be right down."

"Okay, Doddy."

Hope, pointedly, made no reply, and Ran once more bit back the impulse to apologize.

Walking north, he flipped his phone and scanned facades, then chose the church. Stepping into the shadows of the portico of St. Michael's, he hit number 2 and held.

Claire answered halfway through the ring. "Hello?"

"They're right downstairs."

"You left them on the street?"

Never fucking good enough . . .

"I have my eye on them. I'm right nearby." He closed the phone.

The street door opened almost instantly. Claire knelt and kissed them; she hugged them to her, hard; she held them at arm's length and peered into their eyes for signs of hidden trauma. Ransom, now, could no longer confidently aver that she found none. When the ritual was done, Claire ushered them inside, then lingered, peering into the shadows.

His phone rang. "Where are you?"

"Close, I'm watching you. . . ."

Every move you make . . . every breath you take . . . The voice now, doing Sting, was singing in his head.

"Ransom, come inside. You need help. Let us get you some."

"Us?"

The silence on her end made something wallow in his gut.

Tildy's house was all lit up. On the upstairs piazza, Ran saw Della supporting one of Tildy's arms. Marcel held the other.

"I know what's going on," he said, with a quaver in his voice.

"Ran, come home," she said, denying nothing.

"I can't. I better not."

"Why? Why can't you? Why had you better not?"

Because I have this feeling, Claire—this bad, bad feeling—and if I find out it's true, I honestly don't know what I might do.

The voice made its suggestion, but Ransom, weeping, merely closed the phone and dropped it in the trash can as he climbed into the van.

"What do I do now?" he whispered as he turned the key. "What the fuck do I do now?" But neither the author of the universe nor his arch-nemesis, Captain Nemo—the little voice that didn't seem so little anymore—returned an answer. And Ransom didn't have a clue.

Umm-umm-umm, blues falling down, like hail,
Got to keep moving . . .

sang the ghost of Robert Johnson, in the timeless voice of troubled people everywhere. Was that an answer? In the moment—as Ransom, in the darkness, watched his wife pull to the big black door, enclosing herself and their children in the safety of a lighted world—it was all the answer Ransom knew.

. . . keep moving
Got a hell hound on my trail.

FORTY-ONE

s Addie walks along the white sand road, she can hear drumming from the quarters. There are shouts and frenzied laughter. She can see firelight through the trees and leaping silhouettes against the pyre. Since nightfall, there's been a feeling of unrest, of order breaking down and energies unleashed in the wake of Paloma's funeral. For the first time at Wando Passo, she feels afraid, a stranger in a home she only tenuously possesses, yet despite her fear, she continues on her way to Jarry's house.

Those who've gathered to commiserate are mostly house staff and some elder slaves who practice trades. She's made a pound cake from her aunt's recipe—and Blanche's mother's before that. Addie spent a good part of the day on it. The effort helped her nerves. The mourners look up when she knocks and enters with her covered basket. Conversation stops. Jarry looks at her, and in his glassy eyes, there is a brief, hot light she cannot read.

"Where should I put . . . ?"

"Let me take that from you," he says, with rushed politeness, rising and crossing the room.

"If you'll just show me . . ."

"No, let me."

And it is a pathetic comedy, she thinks, this mutual deferral.

She follows him into the small dining room, where the table is laden with other gifts of food. He takes the basket, puts it down, and when he turns to her, she *whispers—for the door is open to the other room—"Jarry, I know this is not the time, but I've been in agony since yesterday. If I may only have a minute of your—"*

"No," he says, "no, I also wish to speak to you. And I have something for you, too. I'll join you on the porch."

And as she proceeds back through the room, Addie notes how studious the other mourners are not to look at her. They know, she thinks. They know. She has weighed anchor and has neither the ability nor the wish to return to port. The seriousness of it is heavy on her mood as she goes outdoors, yet it's freeing, too, and only makes her more determined to say what she has come to say. She gazes at the leaping figures silhouetted by the pyre, and then she hears his step.

"It's strange," she says, "how different the feeling is today than at your father's funeral."

"They respected him. Her, they loved."

And now she turns. "Yes, that's it, isn't it? You have that same thing she had, Jarry, that cutting thing that goes straight to the heart. I love that part of you, and I can't bear to think you're angry with me, Jarry. You have a right to be, but I can't bear it if you are."

"Love"—it's the first time she's used the word, and, strangely, he seems almost pained by it. "I'm not angry, Addie."

"I'm so relieved!" She steps toward him, reaches for his hands and finds them occupied, finds her book, her Byron in red morocco. In the yellow lamplight from the window, she sees his solemn face, and her relief is short-lived.

"Anger isn't what I feel," he says, in a tone that's soft, but firm, and he presses the book into her hands that want only to hold his. As he turns away and walks to the far end of the porch, Addie catches the scent of musk roses from the climber in the yard.

"Then what . . ."

"I've thought about our conversation, too," he says. "The person I believed you were could not have done this. You're someone else. I don't know who you are."

"I don't believe that," Addie says. "I don't believe that in my heart. You do know me. You're the only one who ever has. And if I've hurt your trust, then you must let me earn it back. I will."

"If you'd seen me, Addie, if you had any notion who I truly am, you could not have done this. Had I been in your place, I don't believe I would have to you."

"But I do see you, Jarry," she says, crossing to him, looking fervently into his face, "I do see you. I see you the way no one ever has or ever will."

"Then tell me this," he says. "Had I been white and free, like Harlan is, would you have kept this from me? Would you have kept from him a truth as fateful to his happiness as you knew this one was to me?"

"Oh, Jarry," she says, "I don't know, I don't know! How am I to answer? Perhaps I wouldn't have. Perhaps I would have told him, but—"

"That's what I believe. You certainly would have. Not to have told him would have been a stain upon your honor. Whereas to tell me now . . . isn't it essentially an act of charity? A philanthropic act toward one less fortunate, of lower circumstances than yourself? No, Addie, for you to tell me this is an act of generosity, a grace note in your character, whereas not to have told a white man would have been an inexpungable disgrace. This, Addie, this"—and he is earnest now, and fierce— "is where you cannot see me. This is where I am invisible to you."

"But you're wrong, Jarry. You are so, so wrong! I don't feel generous. Not a day has passed, not an hour, that this hasn't weighed upon my conscience, especially in light of all you and your mother did for me when I was ill. And yes, my silence was disgraceful. I have disgraced myself, but, Jarry, try to understand. . . . If you see me as you wish to be seen, you must grasp that I was silent out of fear and weakness. I felt my loyalties divided. I was confused, my dear. I didn't act with evil in my heart—surely you don't think that? I had no intent to harm. Don't I at least deserve the chance to correct a fault when it is pointed out to me? If I don't see you fully, if I've seen you through a glass darkly, can I not learn to see you face-to-face? Can love not teach me this? Can it not teach us both? Can I not change? Can I not hope that love will make me better than I am? If I've failed you, at least give me the chance to amend my fault. Jarry, Jarry . . . Believeth all things, hopeth all things, endureth all things. . . ."

Addie's weeping now and wild, but the softness she so loves in Jarry is absent from his face tonight. "My mother lies there in the graveyard, Addie, dead of grief," he says. "She went to her death with an accusation in her heart against my father that you and you alone knew to be untrue, and you kept it from her. You kept it from us both, and she died without the consolation of the truth. And if my father's spirit now suffers I know not what torment, if Clarisse has worked some evil against him . . . And all this, because you didn't speak?"

"You blame me for your mother's death?" she answers, shocked. "You hold me responsible for what Clarisse has done? Is this what you believe?"

"What I believe," he answers, "is that it can never work. Mother told me this before she died, and I didn't believe her. I refused. But she was right, Addie. It didn't work for her and Father. He was a decent and honorable man. He loved her, or believed he did, yet he kept her a slave until the day he died. Harlan loved Clarisse, and look what it has brought her to. None of them, none of you, could see us as you see yourselves, and you do not see me. You can't."

"I do," she whispers, passionately. "I do." And now she takes his face between *her hands and kisses him, and the kiss is hard and hot and passionate with longing long suppressed and with the desperate fear of losing him.*

Recklessly given, the kiss is recklessly received, but Jarry, when he pulls away, says, in a despairing voice, "I don't know, Addie. I don't know. . . . I must go back."

"Go back," she tells him, tenderly. "Go back to your guests. We'll speak more of it tomorrow. Will you come? There's so much more I want to say."

This question goes unanswered, too, and Addie will remember, later, that it did. Tonight, she walks home in the dark, and she is troubled, she is sad, but despite this, she's amazed at the size and power of what she feels. So this is what the poets meant by fate, she thinks. All those years, even when she was a girl, she never quite believed. But everything they promised, everything they said—all of it is true, all of it is real! How strange to no longer be afraid, to no longer want for anything she doesn't have. How strange to no longer wish to be other than she is. And this is Addie's thought: So this is what being human truly is.

She isn't tired, but she sleeps, and so it isn't till first light, when she awakes from a dream she briefly recalls, which then slips through her fingers like a thread, that Addie sees her Byron on the stand, and notices the feather, green against the gilded page, and opens to the place it marks.

'Tis vain—my tongue cannot impart
My almost drunkenness of heart,
When first this liberated eye
Survey'd Earth, Ocean, Sun, and Sky,
As if my spirit pierced them through,
And all their inmost wonders knew!
One word alone can paint to thee
That more than feeling—I was Free!

It is "The Bride of Abydos," the verse that Percival prevailed on Jarry to recite to her on that first day, but there are these lines, too:

E'en for thy presence ceased to pine;
The World—nay, Heaven itself was mine. . . .

When Addie reads this, she has a premonition that darkens into certainty when Tenah comes to tell her Jarry's gone.

Part III

THE HOT-WET PHASE

FORTY-TWO

*T*he old man—was it Mel?—was whispering in Ransom's ear. . . . *And now his voice to me was like a stream scarce heard, nor word from word could I divide.* . . . Straining to make it out, Ran, in the driver's seat, jerked awake in time to see the black dog in the head lightbeams. He swerved to miss it, and then he saw the tree. Holy shit! he thought as it loomed up. Holy shit! The oak spread its black arms. This can't be it? he thought. His stomach did a pressure drop, and at the same time, he felt strangely light. When else was death going to strike but when you least expected it? What other rabbit had he thought to pull out of this hat? So this was where the clues had been leading all along, this, the journey he'd been on!

But there's still so much I want to do, he thought. And Nemo said, not without a certain tenderness, *But, really, Ran, like what?* Something in him deflated then. True, he thought, too true. But on the other hand, Fuck you! As the Odyssey took wing, something else in Ran came to. He screamed the words aloud. "Fuck you!" he roared. "I want to see my children grown! At their weddings, I want to dance beneath the tent! I want to see Claire's face when it grows old! I want to hold her wrinkled hand when I go out! The last thing I want to see when I leave this shithole world is those crème caramel eyes I helped to burn and know we made it anyway, know that we outlived it all, even our differences! And on top of that, you mocking prick, I'm going to finish 'Nemo's Submarine'!" Ran, aloud or in his thoughts—

it no longer mattered much—said or would have liked to say all this. And Nemo answered, not without a certain tenderness, a chillier, more ethereal strain, *"You Can't Always Get What You Want,"* singing now, doing not just Mick but the whole London Bach Choir, all the parts in the chorale that stood in Ransom's mind beside the Ninth, an Ode to something, but not Joy. Somehow, that song was in the carousel as it came round, cueing in the changer as it changed, when all the other songs that Ransom Hill had loved, including those he wrote, went down.

The impact, when it came, was hard, but brief—hardly worth mentioning, in light of everything. Maybe, Ran thought, as he bowed his head to it, he'd underestimated God a bit.

"Where the fuck's my airbag, though?" A consumer to the end, the question suddenly occurred to him. "Old Silver! You sonuvabitch! You sold the module on the aftermarket, didn't you?" Ran felt a certain grudging admiration, and then somehow he was outside the car. How? Logic, continuity—neither, now, was a high priority, and Ransom understood they'd ever only seemed to be. He understood a lot of things. Not the main one, though. It was daylight. How suddenly it came! There were people on the road, a stream, like refugees, all headed in the same direction, moving fast and purposefully. Ran felt inclined to join them, felt the lonesome, longing ache you have in autumn, when you hear the honk of geese. But there, again, was Mel . . . was it Mel? And there was someone with him.

"Delores, is that you?" he said. She didn't look quite like herself, taller, with deeper hollows under her high cheekbones. Her eyes were marbled and opaque, like a poached fish's.

Standing at the bottom of the tree in a forbidding pose, she pointed back to where he'd been, looking none too pleased.

"You're dead, though, aren't you?"

Like a specter in a silent film, she moved her lips, and Ransom heard, as through a muffled wad of gauze, a sound, but not a word, and when he turned his head, he saw the Odyssey lying over on its side, with one front wheel still turning, and his own body slumped at the wheel, clearly dead, then, *clap,* he was back inside. . . .

There was the airbag after all, clammily deployed, like a condom engineered for single use. There was something burbling like a stream, and he smelled gas, tasted something sweet and salty on his lips and then his tongue, coming not thinly, in a stream.

Caught in his shoulder harness like a paratrooper in a treetop over St. Mère Église, Ran reached for the driver's door above. With his left hand, he tried to shove it up like the too heavy iron hatch of a too heavy iron submarine, but he lacked the proper angle and, finally, the will to open it. So, Ransom, not quite flying, not quite on the ground, suspended, rather, in his fall and not too terribly alarmed, simply closed his eyes and fell asleep.

When he opened them again, it was morning.

He did a quick internal diagnostic, like an astronaut ticking off the items on his screen. Neck, a little stiff. Hands, check. Feet, still there. Otherwise, all systems green.

With his left hand, he reached right and pressed his seat belt tab. It didn't release.

"Don't guess you should complain, old man," he told himself. "It probably saved your life, and when you get right down to it, you're sort of of that nonreleasing-under-tension mind-set yourself, aren't you?"

This seemed pretty good for one in his condition. Taking heart, Ran did a chin-up toward the roof and freed himself, crashing earthward toward the passenger-side door and making his eventual escape through the sprung rear hatch. And there, on the culprit tree, as if at Ransom's thought-command, was the sign he'd been looking for when he dozed off: Alafia: Authentic African Village As Seen on TV.

"Not bad for a nighttime carrier landing," he said. "Especially given you were fast asleep . . ."

The truth was, despite his neck, despite his general soreness, like a boxer's the day after the fight, Ran felt pretty much all right, even semi-hopeful, as he started down the rutted, sandy two-track into deep pine woods. Like a signal that fades in and out, the sense that he was on a journey came in strong again. So, maybe this wasn't the end. . . . Who knew? The end could be a long way off. A damn long way! Maybe this was, in fact, his elusive, long-sought chance for a fresh start. Right here, right now. Why not?

"Who else gets to make that call but you?" Suddenly last night's hypothesis seemed less far-fetched. Maybe, after all, the gods had granted an exception in his case and he was finally going to get his break. Within a quarter mile, Ran was feeling pretty goddamned great. . . .

"This is how human beings are meant to live, isn't it—going from adventure to adventure, fearlessly?" Eschewing Nemo now, cutting out the middleman, Ran carried on this conversation, mano a mano, with himself. "The modern world, the numbing safety of our days, toiling mindlessly like ants, for what? That's what's got us so fucked up." He was figuring it out, knocking down the major ills like bowling pins, launched upon his bid to roll a straight 300 game. "Self-destruction? Hell, no. *Hale, no!*" said Ran, reverting to the old Killdeer accent. "Marcel Jones can kiss my ass." What need for Nemo now? Ransom Hill was Nemo to himself!

"Are you one hell of a man?" He posed the query to the silent woods. "You are! You da man! You da man!" Addressing himself in the second person, he brayed his chant, ignoring his general soreness, ignoring the mask of crusted blood that lent a sense of immobility to one side of his face, ignoring, in fact, everything that did not accord with his hypothesis, a happy revenant, going down the road of life.

And now he came to an unmarked fork. "Two roads diverged . . . Hmm . . ." Ransom stroked his chin. "You don't think you're going to throw me with that lame trick, do you?" Shouting this, he pumped his fist at God, the Nemesis, whoever his unnamed interlocutor might be, then took the road-less-traveled-by and promptly came to a locked fence.

Only then, as he stopped and took brief stock, did Ran notice the stillness of the wood, the oppressive heat. It was like the sensual embrace of some inhuman force too old and powerful to defeat. *Nature*—the idea struck home in a flash.

"But, hey, goddamn it, aren't I Nature, too?" asked Ransom, with a plaintive note. How had he forgotten this? "So what is this *against?*"

In the trees nearby, a bird he couldn't see answered with a loud ca-*raw*. Wingbeats filled the air, like the sound of a soft helicopter prop, and as they faded, a brooding strangeness descended over everything. Staring up through foliage, he saw turkey vultures—there were three—in sky so blue it made Ran's heart ache with longing for . . . what? eternity?

"What the hell are those things tracking?" he muttered. Then the idea struck. "Jesus! Me? Am I alive or not?" He took a beat. The question was not so obvious as it had once seemed. "I better be," he said. "I better not be lying back there dead under that tree. This better not be some Ambrose Bierce, 'Occurrence at Owl Creek Bridge'–type stunt. It fucking better not." He cast a frowning eye aloft on this.

He did feel a little strange, though, and when you got right down to the brass tacks, Ran wasn't one-hundred-percent convinced he was alive, or even clear on how you tell. And once you lose that basic certainty . . . well, folks, to coin a phrase, it's hard to put the egg back in that shell. But maybe he was treading on a higher plane—was this what the Buddhists meant? "Oh, what the fuck," he said, losing patience with this train, "you have to go on the assumption, right?"

Following his own advice, he ignored the Keep Out sign and climbed the fence, and before too long at all he heard music in the distance: drums. In a junkyard on the left, an old panel station wagon had been abandoned, perhaps the very one the radical founders of Alafia had traveled south from Philly in, wheelless now and rusted out, covered with African graffiti. There were broken farm tools, busted-up appliances, shop jacks, and littered ax- and hammerheads. From a live oak limb, a monster block and tackle hung, trailing heavy chain. And in the midst of this, what made the place seem less a junkyard than a shrine, an enormous iron man, a king of iron surrounded by his iron swag. His head was made from a toothed gear that must have weighed three hundred pounds, and his iron shoes were covered with feath- ers, smeared and glued like the hatchet block in a farmhouse abattoir. His rusted pitchfork hand was raised forbiddingly.

"I come in peace," said Ran, choosing to take the gesture as a welcome. He bowed low to the ground, and when he straightened up, there was a peacock in the tree, regarding him, a calm, impressive presence, and the sun- light touched its feathers, flowing down its wings and back like melted jew- els, like a tumbling blue-green mountain stream.

Ca-*raw,* it said, and then it flew off down the white sand road—ca-*raw,* again. It disappeared around a bend, and at that very moment, from the op- posite direction, an old-style VW van came barreling toward him, its toylike engine whining like something that derived its motive power from tight- ened rubber bands.

It stopped beside him. The driver, a woman, stared out and blinked. Ran blinked, staring in.

At first take, Ran's surmise that he was dead was further reinforced. The driver was Delores Mills, or rather, her unaged body double and dead ringer in a bitambala headscarf, black with a large gold sunflower, and dan- gle earrings.

"Shanté?" he said, taking a gander.

"Ransom?"

"What are you doing?"

"Looking for you," she answered. "What are you doing?"

"Looking for you."

"What the hell happened to you?"

He touched his cheek. "This? Had a little crash. Fell asleep at the wheel . . . Story of my life."

"Are you all right?"

He shrugged. "Either fine or dead—haven't reached a verdict yet." He grinned, but she, looking more than ever like her mom, was in no mood for comedy. "Why were you looking for me anyway?" he asked.

"Because your wife called here, frantic, at midnight and said you'd disappeared and they couldn't think where else you might be. Why are you here?"

Ran blinked. "Now that you mention it, I have no freaking clue. I was driving. I saw the sign for Beaufort. I remembered Cell saying you lived nearby. A little birdie whispered: 'Go see Shanté.'"

"A little birdie . . ."

"Well, I don't mean a literal bird, of course."

"What do you mean?" Shanté was clearly in a literal mood.

"I mean, something said go pay you a visit, and here I am. Don't look at me like I have the lampshade on my head. Don't you ever have impulses and give in to them?"

Giving him a severely doubtful look over glasses that were themselves severe—small, square, and hip, with inner rims of limpid gold—she nodded to the shotgun seat and said, "Get in."

With this terse remark, she executed a three-point reverse, and her wrap—in the same pattern as her headscarf—slipped, showing the black Lycra rim of biking shorts that hugged unfashionably stout but sturdy thighs that flexed impressively as she pressed the clutch with one bare, dusty foot, and, with the other foot, the gas. Her toenails, Ransom noted, were painted a pale shade of pink.

"Damn, Shan," he said. "It's great to see you. You look good. I swear to God, though, when you pulled up—and don't take this wrong, I mean it as a compliment—I thought you were your mom."

"How else would I take it, Ran? I say hello to her in the mirror every morning when I wake up. I'm no spring chicken anymore. Neither are you."

He gave her the opportunity, but she didn't bite. "I look okay, though, right?"

"Actually, you look like shit. . . . Hammered dogshit in the vague shape of a man."

He shook his head and grinned. "You haven't lost those winning ways. . . . So what exactly did Claire tell you?"

"An earful. None good."

"Oh." Fleeting contact with reality put a minor crimp in Ransom's mood, and he sat back like the reprimanded student on the corner stool.

The village, from without, resembled a frontier fort, walled with sharpened palings sheathed in bark. Over the gate, a banner proclaimed, "Harvest Festival Today, Visitors Welcome." Shanté parked in a dusty lot where pickup trucks and farm machines sat cheek by jowl with Mercedeses and Lexuses with license plates from Cobb and DeKalb counties, Georgia, Baltimore, and Washington, D.C.

"So what exactly are you harvesting?" Ran asked.

"Ground nuts." Shanté nodded to a field they passed as they walked in.

Ran squinted at the knee-high foliage. "Soybeans?"

"Peanuts."

"A goober fest!"

She smiled with narrowed eyes. "You showed up right on time. Wait here."

Crossing the courtyard to confer with several colleagues, she left him by the gate. In the shade of a thatch-roofed building, men were drumming, while others danced—a few. More watched or simply milled, ducking into dimly lit temples, where candlelight flickered on lavish altars where gifts of fruit and flowers had been placed. Presiding over one was an iconic man of sculpted ebony, brandishing a two-sided ax; in another, a bare-breasted black Madonna, holding in one hand a dove, in the other, a human heart. Towering above a concrete basin the size of a home swimming pool, though just six inches deep, was a dark-faced Neptune with a trident and a crown. Dripping down his washboard superhero torso, the water, cycling back, set the scales agleam on his blue-green merman tail. He might have been transported from a miniature golf pavilion in Myrtle Beach, thought Ran, wondering where the hell he was, and liking it.

"Who's King Neptune?" he asked Shanté when she returned.

"His name is Olokun. Come on."

In the crowd, as they passed through, Ran saw the occasional fela or dashiki. Many more, though, looked like moms and dads out for a Sunday stroll in chinos and Lands End sweater sets. Ran's was not by any means the sole white face. A rangy kid slouched by with matted dreads stuffed into a tricolored Rasta hat, and there—conferring, bleary-eyed, over a map—were the inevitable Scandinavian students with backpacks, leather clogs, and mussy, slept-on white blond hair.

A relaxed and festive atmosphere prevailed. There were people eating Ethiopian bread and Southern barbecue, salt peanuts in the shell. The scene, Ran thought, was like a street fair, the San Gennaro in New York, or some blue September Sunday in Montmartre, toiling up the hill behind the crowds to Sacré Coeur. It was, in a way, unlike any place he'd ever been, and in another, pretty much like anywhere.

Shanté led him off the beaten path and down a narrow street of shops, all of identical Third World shotgun-shack construction, dirt-floored, with whitewashed plywood hatches propped open to provide awnings over narrow countertops where there was business being done. The necessities were in evidence: cooking oil and kerosene in reused plastic jugs, shrimp and fish on beds of ice, fresh produce and eggs—not just white and brown, but speckled ones and pale blue, too, from Araucana hens—in recycled cardboard crates.

Ran caught a complex smell, sweet like perfume, with astringent notes as well. There were hints of camphor, roses, pepper, wine, Thai lemongrass, and wintergreen, and then he saw the stall: "Crossroads Spiritual Supply and Curio." On the back wall, on shelves of cinder block and pine, were stoppered vials of many shapes and sizes. In different-colored oils—golds, merlots, muddy browns, and fiery orange like Tabasco—were various grasses, seeds, and roots, some of which resembled human body parts.

Shanté started lowering the hatch.

"This is your place?"

She nodded. "I'm going to take you to the house, and then I have to get right back."

"So what is all this stuff—vodou supplies?"

"It has nothing to do with vodou."

Ran waited, but clearly he was going to have to ask. "So what is it?"

"It's hoodoo, for the most part."

He blinked. "So, hoodoo and vodou—these are different?"

"Very." Terse and in no mood to educate her former flame, she conducted him ever deeper into the village, between the canted walls of compounds where Ran heard radios tuned to NPR—the *BBC World News*. There were TVs blaring, mothers scolding kids. In a sun-baked square, boys were playing stickball. They passed an open gate, where a handsome twenty-something man in a white wrap with blue birds on the wing was speaking on a cell. Behind him in the yard, his wife (Ran assumed she was his wife) was hanging batiked cloth on a line as the wind bloused into it. Laughing at something in his conversation, he caught Ran's gaze and smiled with twinkling, good-natured eyes before he softly closed the gate, and Ran walked on, feeling touched by grace.

Shanté's house was cinder block with a tin roof and a swept dirt yard dominated by an enormous tree with a broad, flat crown and a buttressed trunk.

Inside, her clean, spare room smelled like her shop. One whole side was dominated by a plywood worktable, where she clearly made her preparations. There was a bed, a dorm-sized fridge, a bookshelf, a stove, a dining table, and two chairs. There was a small shrine, too, with several stemmed glasses filled with water, a crucifix, a bowl of white carnations, a King James Bible opened to the Psalms. There were numerous photos there, including one of Delores, before which a votive burned.

"All right, listen," she said, in a martial tone that Ran, despite his problem with authority, really didn't mind. "Let's get that cut cleaned up, and then I have to go. This is one of the biggest days in my whole year." She handed him a phone. "Call your wife."

Ran took the receiver dutifully, then stood, paralyzed. "I don't think I can talk to Claire right now."

She regarded him, arms akimbo. "Why not?"

"We're sort of going through a patch, Shanté."

"A patch . . . What kind of patch? A bad patch? A briar patch? What?"

He shrugged and looked away. "Could you just do me a favor and let her know?"

"What's going on here, Ran?"

"I'd tell you if I knew."

"Why don't you know?" she persevered. "If you don't know, who knows?"

"Look, don't give me the third degree," he said, "okay? What did Claire tell you anyway?"

"Where do I start?" She shoved a chair at him and fetched some swabs and alcohol. "That you're manic . . ." A trifle brusque, she started to debride the cut. "That you're off your meds. That yesterday you kidnapped your children, assaulted a stranger in Charleston on the street, and now you're on the run from the police. What else? No, that was pretty much the gist. Of course, she didn't know about your wreck."

"Tune in to *America's Most Wanted,*" Ransom said. "They're featuring me this week."

She pulled away to look. "You think this is funny?"

"No," he said, "but it's a little funny, though. I mean, come on, Shan, there's a fair amount of spin on all of that."

"I've known Claire a long time, Ransom," she replied. "I'm pretty good at compensating for her spin."

"Look," he said, "I admit I let my medication slide a bit, but I took it yesterday. I'm getting back on track, and it isn't like I'm crazy. . . ." He floated this, but she just frowned and let him stew. "I don't seem crazy, do I?"

"I'm making up my mind."

Ransom was the first to blink. "Damn, you remind me of your mom!"

"Say it one more time, you're going to get one in the arm."

"A noogie?" Ransom asked. "Look, you almost smiled—I saw that!"

"Here." She handed him the swab.

"So, enough about me," he said. "Cell said there was some guy?" He glanced toward the bed—single, tightly made as though for camp.

"Simon. That's been over for two years. We split up when I left Zaire."

"You were in Zaire?"

"For four and a half years."

She kept her eyes fixed on his forehead, and Ransom felt the distance loom. "I guess I haven't been too great at keeping in touch."

Acknowledging the understatement, she let her gaze drop to his face.

"What were you doing over there?"

"I was in a kinkimba."

"What's that?"

"A school where they teach kinganga."

"What's kinganga?"

"A science."

"What kind of science?"

"The science of how to be a human being," she replied, "how to live a human life."

Ransom blinked. "Damn, I could use a course in that! So you studied for the priesthood?"

"Actually, I was a cook. That's the only way they let a woman in. Eventually, I learned the traditional practice."

"Meaning, vodou . . . excuse me! Hoodoo?"

"No. Hoodoo is what traditional Congo practice turned into in the U.S., when slaves brought it here in the eighteenth and nineteenth centuries. It was called Conjure then. Vodou is something else—not Congo, Ran, but Fon, okay?"

"What's Fon?"

"The Fon," she said, with modest heat, "are a tribe from West Africa. They went to Haiti and developed vodou, or vodun. Santeria or Ocha is from the Yoruba, another tribe from a different part of West Africa. Olokun—the one you asked about outside?—he's the Yoruba god of the sea. Most of the people in Alafia follow Yoruba traditions. Me, I'm Congo."

"Why?"

"Why? Because when I went over there with Simon, in the little villages near Tsheila and Isangila, among his people, the BaManianga, half the people on the streets looked like my aunts and uncles."

"Sort of like the little birdie?"

"Okay, Ran. Okay. Touché."

"They're all related, though, right, these religions?"

"Sure," she said. "As Southern Baptists are related to Swedish Lutherans are related to the Church of Rome."

"They can all tell you what happened on the cross, though, right?"

She conceded him a grudging smile. "They can all tell you what happened on the cross. At that level of generality, they're related."

"So, nobody since Simon?"

"I'm celibate," she said.

"Celibate?" This came out sharper than he meant. "Why?"

"Religious reasons."

"Meaning . . ."

"Meaning, none of your business . . . Now, look, I won't be gone long. Why don't you shower, fix something to eat, and lie down."

"Hey, Shan . . ."

"What?"

"I was sorry about your mom."

She softened a bit. "Yeah, I know, Ran. Thanks."

"You know I dreamed of her last night?" Leaning toward Dolores's photo, Ran noticed, hanging on her crucifix, on a fine gold chain, a Saint Christopher no larger than a dime. "Hey"—he lifted it—"hey, is this . . . ?"

Shanté smiled a quick, bold smile that brought things back. "You gave me that, didn't you?"

"What, you forgot?"

"No, I remember. Do you?"

"Are you kidding? Hell, yes, I remember. *Hale,* yeah!"

His Killdeer accent finally made her laugh.

"That thing cost me four Saturdays scrubbing down the head at Dixie Bag," he said. "Know where I bought it? Alston-Heller."

"That was a pretty tony place."

"Damn straight," said Ran. "That's where all the rich kids got their sterling baby cups and pinkie signet rings. When I came in the door, the alarm went off automatically. Armed guards in camouflage rappelled down from the roof on ropes. I shit you not. They searched my body cavities three times before they let me pass."

Shan continued smiling as he talked, but her expression had turned thoughtful in a way that Ran, at all costs, had hoped to avoid.

"Come on!" he protested. "This is my best stuff. Why aren't you laughing?"

"Well, to give you credit, you were never cheap."

"Hey, tell that to my wife!" Ran instantly knew this was a tactical mistake. "I swear, Shan," he continued, hurrying on, "it seems like just last week we were on the Ferris wheel at the state fair, gazing over North Raleigh, making plans to run away. And then we blinked, and half our lives are gone. We hardly know each other anymore, but you know what I really feel, Shanté?"

"What?" she asked, with an expression that seemed wistful.

"In another way, it's like no time has passed at all."

"It has, though, Ran," she said. "We aren't the same people we were then."

"I am," he said, with his bright face. "Aren't you?"

She shook her head. "No, I'm not."

"How come you seem the same to me?"

"I don't know," she said. "I guess the answer has to be because you want me to." She reached out and took his hand. "Why are you here?"

"I don't know," he said, fighting sudden tears and angry with himself for them. "Is that okay? Does there always have to be a reason for everything, for every fucking little thing we do? Don't you ever do things without knowing why?"

"Sometimes," she said. "Sometimes I guess I do."

"Don't." Ran held his finger up. "Don't do that to me, okay? Don't look at me like that." He got up and walked away.

"How am I looking at you, Ran?"

"Like that," he answered, turning back. "Like Claire. Did she tell you two dead bodies turned up in our yard yesterday? Was it yesterday? . . . Yesterday. Did she mention anything about a black pot?"

"She said you dug one up and that you seem to think it's having some effect on you."

"I'm asking you flat out," Ran said. "Are they used in vodou . . . hoodoo?"

"No, not in vodou, not in hoodoo. In Palo Mayombe they are."

"What's that?"

"Palo is another form of Congo practice, Ran. It developed in Cuba. The pots are called 'prendas' there. But for a Cuban prenda to turn up on a nineteenth-century South Carolina rice plantation is a stretch."

"But Claire's people had all *sorts* of Cuban ties, Shanté!"

She considered. "Claire thinks it's just a cook pot—I expect she's probably right."

"Are you sure, Shanté? Are you positive? Because one of those bodies was Claire's great-great-great-grandmother, Adelaide DeLay, and the other, I'm pretty sure, was the plantation steward, a slave named Jarry. I think they were having an affair. I think she was pregnant with his child, and Addie's husband came home from the war and murdered them."

"How do you know?"

"I don't know how I know! Because a little birdie told me so, all right? But, really, Shan, it's connected to this pot. It's like the pot, or something in the pot, is telling me. I know it sounds crazy, but it's like it's dropping pebbles in the woods for me to find, and if you really want to know, I think it sent me here to you. I mean, why would a cook pot be buried with manacles and cowrie shells in it? Why would it be wrapped with chain?"

"The pot you found was wrapped with chain?"

"Uh-huh. Does that mean something?"

Her expression now was grave. "Was it buried, by any chance, in the shadow of a tree?"

"A tree?" Ran said. "I don't know, maybe. There are trees around. Actually, it was in an anthill."

"An anthill . . . The pot you found was buried in an anthill?"

Ransom nodded. "Why?"

She didn't answer. "Look," she said, in the martial tone he liked. "Look, I'm listening, okay? But first things first. I really, really have to get back to the shop. You eat and try to rest. As soon as I get back, I'll tell you what I know about black pots."

FORTY-THREE

*W*ith the victories in Virginia, Charleston's mood is gay that winter, 1861, but Addie, on a brief visit to her aunt's, finds herself out of step and put off by the gaiety. At a St. Cecelia's Ball, her cousin, Lavinia Lesesne, shows up in a dress from Paris that cost eight hundred dollars, it is said. It was run in through the blockade on a dark, fast ship with six thousand vintage champagne bottles in the hold. And medicines are lacking for the boys with missing limbs and eyes, arriving daily on the Northern trains, so much soberer than when they marched out in high summer to the sounds of drums. In the Mercury, she reads the names. John Middleton, who got drunk at her wedding and fired off Harlan's gun—dead, at twenty-one, the first in a long, ghastly toll. Against that black-piped column, those sober boys with pinned sleeves and patches on their eyes, the sight of Lavinia on the stair at the Hibernian in that red Parisian dress, with three-quarters of her décolletage exposed, fills Addie with a premonition she can scarcely name. And the Federals have taken Port Royal Sound and Beaufort, only seventy miles south, where she was wont to summer with her aunt. Is that where Jarry went? When she thinks of him, it's as if a lightning bolt had struck the earth directly at her feet, and Addie stands there with a pounding heart, hardly knowing what it was or where it went, wanting only what she cannot have: for it to come again.

It's to distract herself from this that Addie goes to town, and one afternoon at Russell's, her old haunt, she hears George Fitzhugh, the philosopher, holding forth to an enthusiastic crowd:

"Liberty and equality are not timeless human values," he maintains, and it's half a minute by the clock before the clapping, stomping audience can calm themselves sufficiently to take their seats. "They are new under the sun. The free states of antiquity were founded upon chattel slavery. Only France and the Northern states have fully and fairly tried the experiment of a social organization founded upon universal liberty and equality of rights. And what is the result? Let us pose the question to the women and children deep within the bowels of the mines, who drag out their lives in darkness, harnessed like horses to heavy cars loaded with ore. Let us ask the pallid children in the factories, who work fourteen hours a day and go home at night to sleep in damp cellars. The experiment has failed. Riots, trade unions, strikes for higher wages—these are the result. Crime and pauperism have increased up North.

"The apologists of liberty and equality propose to enhance society by encouraging free competition, but it's chiefly this which defeats well-being among men. My evidence? Look to nature, friends, and tell me what you see. . . . A war of competition, the result of which is that the weaker or less healthy are continually displaced and exterminated by the strong. Where men of strong wills and self-control come into competition with the weak and improvident, the latter soon become the inmates of penitentiaries. The employer cheapens his employee's wage; the retail dealer takes advantage of his ignorance, his inability to visit other markets, his want of credit, to charge enormous profits. The free worker is the muzzled ox that treadeth out the straw. Had they been vassals or serfs, they would have been beloved, cherished, and taken care of as our slaves are in the South. Here, we provide for each slave in old age and infancy, in sickness and in health, not according to his labor, but according to his wants. A Southern plantation is the beau ideal of communism." (Addie, caught off guard, laughs aloud at this and ignores the disapproving stares she gets.) "As love for others is the organic law of our society, so is self-love at the North.

"A state of dependence is the only condition in which reciprocal affection can exist among human beings—the only situation in which the war of competition ceases, and peace, amity, and goodwill arise. A state of independence always begets jealous rivalry and hostility. A man loves his wife and children because they are weak and dependent. When they assert their independence, he's apt to transfer his affection. But slaves are always dependent. Hence, though men are often found at variance with wife or child, we never saw one who didn't like his slaves."

A hearty, general laugh attends the line, and this time Addie's is the sole dark face.

"Greece and Rome were indebted to this institution for the leisure to cultivate their heads and hearts," Fitzhugh goes on. "Had they been tied down to Yankee thrift, they might have produced a Franklin, with his 'penny saved is a penny *gained'; they might have invented the spinning jenny, but they never would have produced a Socrates, an Aeschylus. Had the Hebrews believed in freedom and equality, where would be King David and the Psalms?"[1]*

This discourse is interrupted, over and over, by applause, and the women, Addie notes, cheer louder than the men. As she slips out the back, she thinks, How plausible these ideas seemed, and not so long ago, and, now, how wrong.

"And did I not see you? Did I not?" Under her breath, she reproaches Jarry, in his absence, carrying on the conversation in her heart.

And as she hurries south on King that day, passing sights familiar since her birth, among the people, her people, whom she loves, she thinks once more: all this is a lie that everyone believes but me, and Addie feels herself a stranger and a spy in her own home. And what if I am wrong? she thinks. What impudence to put herself in opposition to everything she's known!

To slay "that Death, the Self," to learn to suffer without rebellion, she turns to God in prayer, and why she seeks His help is because rebellion is so strong.

No, Charleston leaves her in a restless, anxious state, and she goes home to Wando Passo and throws herself into her work. They're winnowing the seed rice for next season now, at the little hip-roofed house on stilts beside the barn. Addie watches the rough rice fall through the square hole in the floor, where the wind catches the tailings and carries them over the river in a sifting, golden plume. Under Jonadab, the new steward, the men are bringing in the firewood now, mending fences, mauling roads; the women, picking apples, putting up the pork. For two weeks, they slaughter, and Addie works beside them, holding a glistening sleeve of gut between two fists, shaking hot salt water back and forth, then letting it spill into the great smoking hole, carrying away the smell of shit from what will now be casings for the Christmas sausages. She spends five days sunk to her armpits in corning brine, until the flesh shreds off her palms in sheets. At night she reads, sometimes till one or two. Irving's "Sketchbooks," Gilpin, Cowper, "Lalla Rookh," and Scott, "The Lady of the Lake" and "Marmion," "The Story of Rimini" by Leigh Hunt. She's drawn, especially, to tales of lovers who come to tragic ends. Her Byron, though, sits on the table, unopened, with the green feather at the place; beside it, Percival's old Wordsworth and "Evangeline"—she never touches these, nor lets them far outside her reach.

It's this winter, soon after her return, that the fright begins. One night, alone in the house, brushing out her hair after Tenah and the others have retired, Addie

---

[1] Adapted from Fitzhugh's 1850 essay, "Sociology for the South," by George Fitzhugh, A. Moms, Publisher, Richmond, VA, 1854.

glances up and sees a figure in the mirror—fleetingly there, half glimpsed, then gone. A hand over her pounding heart, she sits there as the cold wind blows outside, tossing the old trees against the moon, and she remembers what hasn't troubled her in all these years.

When she was a little girl in bed upstairs at Blanche's house, sometimes she closed her eyes at night and saw her mother's face—something she'd, no doubt, confabulated from a photograph—but not as she had been in life. The woman Addie saw wore a black wreath of waterweed and came flying like an angel through a current undersea, her torn, drenched clothes rippling and streaming out behind. In the mirror, Addie sometimes glimpsed her pale, drowned face, before her eyes registered what was really there: herself. For the whole of one dark year—was she seven? Six?—she avoided mirrors, would not on any dare gaze down into a puddle in the street. She always fancied it was to tell her why she'd walked into the sea that day that her mother came, and at the bottom of it all, Addie was terrified to receive this confidence. For once you knew . . . what then? What, then, would there be to prevent you— you, too . . . ? Was this it?

And then, when she was eight, as suddenly as it arrived, the vision went away. And from that day to this, not until tonight, has Addie given it a thought. So why this winter, with such good news from Virginia, with Charleston all so gay, why after Jarry leaves, does Addie see the figure in the mirror once again? Why, now as then, does she look up each time a board creaks in the hall? Why does she wait, with bated breath, for silence to redescend?

And one night—not this first one, but the second or the third—the creak is followed by another. There are footsteps.

"Tenah?" she calls, and her heart is like to burst. "Who's there?"

No one answers, but Addie, sitting there in bed, fancies she can feel an awareness, not her own, on the other side, an awareness like that of the hound dog, Sultan, the moment when he looks up from his bone, sensing an intruder, not yet seen.

There is something in the house with her—the thought is very clear. . . . Clear, too, the intuition that it's not her mother. The presence is a man.

FORTY-FOUR

*R*an was far too wired to sleep. After showering, he gave consideration to a shave.

"What, though, would be the point?" Apparently agreeing, his reflection shrugged, and so he kept the growth and snooped discreetly, running his finger down the spines on Shanté's shelf. *Folklore from Adams County* by Harry Middleton Hyatt; *Pow-Wows, or The Long-Lost Friend* by John George Hohman; *El Monte* and *Reglas de Congo* by Lydia Cabrera; *Hoodoo in Theory and Practice* by Catherine Yronwode; *The Master Book of Candle Burning* by Henri Gamache; *The Book on Palo* by Raul Canizares; *Secrets of the Psalms, The Sixth and Seventh Book of Moses, Mules and Men* by Zora Neale Hurston.

On Shanté's worktable, bath crystals, incense, and sachets were being weighed and placed in foil packets with dramatic, retro-looking labels featuring black cats, dice, lightning bolts, and flames. Bundled candles had been sorted by their use and color—green for money, red for love, purple for power, black for evil deeds, and white for opening the way. There were small flannel bags in similar colors in a section labeled "Mojo Hands." There were loose herbs, roots to which the earth still clung, and perfume-sized bottles of anointing oil with scores of different names, the same ones on the packets of incense and sachets: "Van Van Oil," "Do as I Say," "Cast Off Evil," "I Can You Can't," "Come to Me," "Follow Me Girl."

"'Essence of Bendover Oil,'" he read. "Hey, dute, I think someone may have been using that on you—meaning me!" Addressing the interlocutor, he laughed, knowing what he thought he meant.

Outside, he sat propped against one of the buttresses of the great tree and glanced at the Saint Christopher. He'd wanted it inscribed "To Shanté . . . Love, Ran" but the jeweler had said there wasn't room. "Love, Ran," was all it said. *Love, Ran . . .* Fatigue stole over him and he lay down, hands behind his head, feet crossed, gazing up into the tree's broad crown and listening to the rustling leaves. Beyond, great clipper ships of cumulus were sailing east through azure seas. *On a journey, too,* he thought. *But where? Same place as you. Same place as me.* He closed his eyes, and when he opened them again, the light had changed, and Shanté sat beside him with a book.

"Hey," he said. "I didn't hear you come."

"I didn't want to wake you."

"Was I asleep?"

She smiled. "All afternoon."

"Really? Damn . . ." He took a beat. "You know, this is an amazing tree."

"Is Mama Iroko speaking to you?"

He turned his head to her. "Mama Iroko?"

"It's a ceiba, Ran. In Cuba, they're considered sacred. In Palo, the leaves are used to make a tea that's said to open the third eye." She put her finger in her book and leaned against the trunk, gazing up with him.

"You look at this and have to wonder if humans really are the peak of life on earth," Ran said.

"You thought we were?" She smiled. "Think of what it does. It turns sunlight into life. It takes what's dead out of the earth and converts it back to life. It harms nothing, kills nothing."

"It isn't conscious, though."

"Who says? Close your eyes." She put her hand lightly over them. "Don't you feel its awareness of us? We're like this little mosquito whine of energy on its periphery, but what it's mainly conscious of is the sun. It's like a mighty being deep in contemplation of that fundamental source. And it takes that energy and lives on it and turns it into life. Can we do that? No, Ran, we aren't the top."

"That's sounding kind of New Age, Shan."

She laughed. "No, baby, what you hear is Africa. Africa's as Old Age as it gets."

"I'd like to go there. I've always felt some sort of tug."

"Maybe it's ancestral."

Ran smiled, thinking he was supposed to.

She did not smile back.

"You're suggesting I'm part black?" he asked with skeptical amusement.

"I'm not suggesting it; it's true. We all are. The difference is, my ancestors left Africa two hundred fifty, three hundred years ago; yours, sixty thousand, give or take."

"Is that true?"

"Sure, don't you know that? You think white people evolved separately in Europe from white European apes? No, Ran. Humanity evolved one time, in Africa, and then spread out. Geneticists think there was a single migration around sixty-five thousand years ago. A band of hunter-gatherers, probably no more than a couple hundred of them, followed a coastal route to India. They or their descendants spread into Southeast Asia and eventually reached Australia fifty thousand years ago. Offshoots of that wave went northeast to China and Japan, over the land bridge to North America—they became the Indians—and westward into northern Europe. The colder it got, the less sun they saw, the lighter their skins became to absorb vitamin D. Archaeologists think there were multiple migrations, but whether there was one or twenty, if you trace the family tree back far enough, we're all black Africans."

"Damn, I never knew this. How do they know?"

"Genetic markers in the blood of populations on the old migration routes. Everyone alive on earth today has the same piece of mitochondrial DNA, inherited from the same woman."

"The same woman?"

"The same black woman, actually. They call her 'Mitochondrial Eve.' She lived two hundred thousand years ago."

He took this in. "So it's all kind of silly, isn't it, this whole racial business?"

Shanté just looked at him and shook her head and laughed, and it was different now, it was her old, rich, easy laugh with all its different colors, all its different notes.

Ran turned on his side and propped his head. "So, tell the truth, Shanté, this hoodoo stuff, this Congo stuff you're into—is it really real?"

"Naw," she said, reverting to the Killdeer accent now herself. "I left singing, spent five years in Africa, gave up sex for something *unreal*—is that what you think?" Her smile was more incredulous than fazed.

Ransom blinked. "What did your mother think of it?"

"Oh, you know, Ran, Mama had no truck with roots. She and Reverend Satterwhite—you remember Reverend Satterwhite?"

"Sure, I do."

"To them, roots were devil's work, but those ladies in our church, the ones in the big feathered hats? When they got worked up on Sunday morning and fell down in the aisles and spoke in tongues, they were doing exactly what I saw the ngangas in Boma do, only, in Zaire, they were channeling the nkisis, the ancestors; here, it's the Holy Ghost. It's a newer variation on an old theme, though. Forty percent of the slaves who came through Charleston and New Orleans were Congolese. They brought their knowledge and traditions with them, and they spread all over the Americas and the Caribbean. In Jamaica, it turned into Obeah; in Brazil, Umbanda; in Cuba, Palo Monte and Mayombe. Here, in the U.S., it turned into Conjure, and another branch runs straight into the black Spiritual and Pentecostal churches, and Mama was part of that, whether she understood or liked the fact or no, and she passed it to me."

"I wonder why I dreamed of her."

"I'll tell you why. She was telling you to get your shit together."

He lay back down. "It's funny, Shan, when I crashed, I thought I was going to die. It didn't hurt, though. It didn't feel the least bit strange. I used to be afraid of dying; now I'm not. What do you suppose that means?"

"I couldn't say."

"It's good, though, right?"

Shanté didn't answer, and Ran was careful not to look at her, but he could feel her lingering study, a warmth against his face.

"They got your car out of the ditch," she said after a silence. "It's pretty banged up, but it runs. They don't think the frame is bent."

"You know I only bought it yesterday? I sold Daddy's Thunderbird to get the goddamn thing for Claire."

"I called her, Ran."

He let a beat elapse. "And . . . ?"

"She's relieved you're okay."

"Really?"

"Yes, really. Meaning what?"

"Meaning, frankly, Shan, I have a hard time imagining Claire losing sleep worrying how or where I am."

"She said you took a gun out of the house."

Ran pondered this remark. "So, what, she's scared? Is that what she said?"

"Why would Claire be scared?" Shanté's expression challenged him, direct, severe, but Ransom didn't answer. "Truthfully, Ran, I think Claire's more concerned about you doing something to yourself. Is that something you're considering?"

"No." He clenched his jaw and looked away.

"You're sure?"

"I don't have the gun, Shanté."

She held his stare, not cowed, not reassured.

"Sounds like Claire told you quite a bit," he said. "Did she mention she's having an affair?"

"With who?"

"I'll give you three guesses. One should do."

Shanté took this in. "You're sure?"

"Pretty goddamn much."

"And you've asked her?"

"Gee," he said, "I didn't think of that. . . ."

"You have to ask her, Ran."

"I think, under *Robert's Rules,* the burden of disclosure falls to the de-ceiver in the case."

"I'm sorry, honey," Shanté said. "If that's true, I'm very, very sorry for you."

"Fuck it, Shan. Don't be sorry for me. I'm a grown-up. I've had affairs. People do. You don't end a twenty-goddamn-year marriage over them."

"Sometimes people do."

He turned to her and frowned. "What, exactly, did Claire tell you?"

She shook her head. "Nothing, Ransom. Only what I've said. Can I ask you something, though? How is your marriage anyway? Are you sure you aren't just clinging to something that's already dead? Because people do that, too."

Ran felt something roiled and dark rise up in him. "I love her more now than when we met."

"And Claire?"

"You'll have to ask her that."

"You're the one who has to ask. That's what you need to do, and the sooner the better."

"I can't go back right now."

"Why not?"

"I just can't, okay? I need to get my thinking straight. I was hoping maybe I could stay here for a while."

"Here?" The suggestion seemed to take her by surprise.

"Just until the Odyssey is fixed," he said, backpedaling.

"I don't think so, Ran."

"Why not? Because I'm white?"

"That's one reason. This isn't someplace where unhappy white guys get to come and sleep in a grass hut and get some R and R."

"So what about the family tree?" he asked her, with a bitter note.

She just stared at him the way her mother had through the screen that night so long before, with an expression in which sorrow and pity had made peace with something else resigned and hard.

Ran gazed down at the medallion in his hand. He pressed his thumb over the incising, hard. "You know," he said, "those old bastards at the mill, my dad and them . . . In that bathroom I used to clean, they pissed all over the floor and walls."

"Why did they do that?"

"To show how mad they were, I guess."

"You think your dad did it against you?"

Ran stared at the medallion, uncertain of the answer. It didn't take him long to find it, though. "No," he said. "No, actually I don't. I think he did it to get back at Kincannon. And do you think Big Herbert ever set foot in that place? Probably not one time in his whole life. Daddy knew that, too. He knew who was going to have to clean up after him and still pissed on the walls. Do you have any idea what it's like to be that mad, Shanté, so mad you'll hurt yourself and make a cesspool of your head—a place you and your buddies use a dozen times a shift—all in order to inflict a meaningless revenge on a man who'll never even notice? That's what Daddy did. He made it worse on me, on him, on everyone. Because that's all he had to strike: himself. If you understand that, you understand a lot about my dad."

"Is that how mad you are?" she asked.

He gazed at her with burning eyes. "We aren't talking about me."

Shanté held his stare and just said, "Oh . . ."

"You shat on me," he said, sitting up. "You and Delores both."

"How, Ran? Because I didn't run away to Neverland with you? I wanted to explain. You never returned my calls."

"That's right," he said. "Go ahead. Put the blame on me because I didn't stay in touch. You think I don't know the reason why you didn't come? You were the closest thing I ever had to family, and you shut . . ." He looked away. "You shut the door in my fucking face, Shanté. . . . Because I wasn't good enough."

She shook her head. "That wasn't why."

"Don't bullshit me," he said. "You were middle-class and I was poor white trash. I wasn't good enough then, and now I can't even spend the night down here because I'm white? Where am I supposed to go, Shanté? I can't go home; I'm not good enough for Claire. Her aunt Tildy informed me yesterday I'm not good enough for my own kids. You want to know why I came here? Because there's no place left. I don't have anybody else. You were the last card in my deck."

He tried to hand her the Saint Christopher, but she closed his hand back over it. "It was a sweet dream, Ran. It was the sort you're supposed to have at seventeen. I wouldn't trade it, but it was never going to come to pass."

"Why not, Shan? Why the fuck—"

She put a finger on his lips. "Shut up now and listen. I'm going to tell you what I think. I think you're running away. I think you always do. You say Mama and I shut the door, but you're the one who ran. Just like your name. What are you doing here, Ransom? What is this, road trip? Is this your 'Freebird' thing again?"

He put his hand over his heart. "Ouch, Shan, Lynyrd Skynyrd? That really cuts."

"Fuck you," she said, dead sober now. "If you're on vacation from adulthood, Ran, do it someplace else, on someone else's dime. Don't waste my time."

He started to get up, but Shanté pulled him back. "Listen to me, you son of a bitch. Among Simon's people, there's a saying: 'Ku Mpemba kwatekila wa waku ukudila mvutu.' It means, 'In Mpemba, the land of the good Dead, there is one of yours who will assist you in your hour of need.' If you dreamed of Mama, Ransom, that's the reason why. White or not, you were one of hers, and she was one of yours, and so am I, goddamn it. So am I, Ransom." She took his face between her hands. "I'm here for you, right now, today. If you're having problems, spiritual problems, and they're real, I'll help you any way I can. But only if you mean to face them. If you're going to run, the gate's right there. Get the fuck out of my house."

"I can't go home, Shanté," he said, and Ran was weeping now. "I can't."

She put her arms around him. "Why not?"

"Because," he said, "a long time ago, this unhappy white guy just like me came back from the war and caught his wife having an affair with a black man, Shan . . . just like Claire and Cell, you see? And he killed them, Shan, he shot them in cold blood, and their bodies turned up with this pot. And if I go back now . . ."

"You're telling me you're going to hurt Marcel and Claire?"

"I'm telling you, what if it's not me? What if the goddamn pot is causing this, leading me where they all went?"

"Is that what you believe?"

"It is." Ransom didn't hesitate. "It really is."

Shanté took an appraising beat. "Okay," she said. "Okay, Ran, listen. There's evil in the world. I've seen it. In the Congo, there are witches called 'kindoki.' Everybody there believes in them. It's usually someone in the village, next door, down the street, even a member of your family, who flies out at night in dreams and eats your soul. The people that happens to? They die, unless they're helped. Helping them is part of what I learned to do. And there are worse things than witches, Ran, deep-level demonic forces that prey on certain individuals, and I'm here to tell you, there are outcomes far more undesirable than death. In Conjure, people in that state are considered crossed. Crossing is real, but it's also rare. Many people who think they're crossed are really just dealing with garden-variety mental illness, unhappiness, bad luck. There's a chance that's all this is with you. That's clearly what Claire thinks. But the one thing you've said that gives me pause . . . really, there are two. First, what you say you found inside this pot is pretty much what I'd expect to find inside a prenda. It's called the 'carga.' It's what makes it live and work. But let me tell you what a prenda is. . . ."

She opened the volume she was holding, a slim white one, to the place her finger marked. "This book is by Lydia Cabrera. She was a Cuban ethnographer, a student of Ortiz. She's dead now, but she's still regarded as the preeminent academic authority on Palo." She showed him the cover. *La Regla Kimbisa del Santo Cristo del Buen Viaje.* " 'The Kimbisa Order of the Holy Christ of the Good Journey.' It's a study of a line of Palo called Kimbisa. This is what Cabrera says: 'A prenda or nganga'—that's the Bantu term—'is the pot in which dwells . . . el alma de un muerto . . . the soul of a dead person . . .' "

She glanced at him over her rims. " '. . . sometido por su voluntad y mediante un pacto con el individuo que le rinde culto' . . . subject by his will and by means of a pact with the individual who pays him homage . . . and whom the muerto helps . . . con su poder de ultratumba . . . with his supernatural—literally, 'beyond-the-tomb'—power. So: An nganga is the pot in which dwells the soul of a muerto, subject by his will and by means of a pact with the individual who pays him homage—who 'feeds him'— and whom the muerto helps with his supernatural power."

"Wait," said Ran. " 'Feeds'? Who feeds whom?"

"The Palero feeds the muerto."

"Feeds it what?"

"Life-force offerings. Blood, primarily."

The silence now resembled that which follows a hundred-year snowfall.

"What was the other?" Ransom finally said.

"The other what?"

"You said there were two things."

"The one way to dissolve a prenda—the only way, so far as I'm aware— is to bury it in an anthill."

"It's real, isn't it," Ran said. "Holy shit."

"Let me fetch some things out of the house, and we'll go see."

FORTY-FIVE

O *nce a fortnight . . . then once a week . . . then every second night Addie*
senses the presence in the house. She often lies awake in bed till dawn,
then, in the fields, drives herself to exhaustion and far past, dreading the
hour when she must return and light the lamp alone.

And the news is all so terrible . . . Tom Wagner, killed at Fort Moultrie, when
one of his own cannon exploded during a routine inspection. The new battery on Mor-
ris Island, from which Harlan writes, is named for Tom. And Jimmy Pettigru, who had
such a clear, fine face and ringing laugh, and Will Porcher, Addie's cousin, with whom
she danced the German at her first St. Cecelia's, and Thad Middleton, for whom she
never cared (but, oh, his mother, and his sister, Ann), and David Guinn, who had such
pretty curls, such a fine seat on a horse (he made her heart beat once, if only for a week),
and Mitchell Ball, that sad, soft something in his eye that always broke her heart . . .
The roll is called, and those who answered, flushed and laughing, in the bosom of their
families as recently as Christmastide—in the high mood after Fredericksburg, as the
plowmen at Wando Passo broke the squares behind the oxen—are ghosts before the
new rice pips in April, when they let the Sprout Flow off. There is hardly a house in
Charleston without black crepe at the door.

When the Federal shells begin falling, her aunt's house, which escaped the
fire, takes two hits through the roof within a week. Blanche has gone to Addie's
cousin, Delphine, in Cheraw. "And you, my dearest child," she writes, "should
come here, too. You're no longer safe, with Federal gunboats running up the river at

*their pleasure as they do. And the Negro troops, they say, under Higginson and
Wentworth, these Boston men, are pitiless in their revenge against masters who put
the very bread into their mouths and were their former friends. I fear for all of us, but
mostly, Addie, you."*

*There's a day, and not just one, when Addie considers heeding this advice. . . .
When the squares are "flowed," as John, the minder, says, she's careful not to look down,
afraid of what she'll see reflected back. Night, though, is the time she fears the most.
When Addie hears the footsteps now, she tells herself to slay her foolish fear and check the
hall, but she can only lie there, rigid, staring at the ceiling, thanking God the door is
locked. And outside the cold wind blows, the old trees toss against the moon. It's hours before she sleeps, when Addie sleeps at all, and one night she dreams she's swimming with
her mother in the sea. Pulled down toward the black weeds, Addie starts awake to find
she's drowning still. There's something in the bed with her, pressing down like cold, dark
water. Addie fights, but she can't move her arms or legs. When she tries opening her eyes,
her lids flutter and won't obey. Finally, after what seems hours, the thing abruptly leaves,
and Addie sits upright in a full sweat. Steam is rising off her arms. She lights the lamp.
There's nothing here.*

I have seen the wicked in great power, and spreading himself
like a green bay tree.

Yet he passed away and, lo, he was not; yea, I sought him, but he
could not be found. . . .

*Seeking comfort, she turns to the Psalms, and at midnight, from her window, she
perceives an orange glow on the horizon and stands outside for half an hour, not knowing if the Federals have invaded Charleston, if the slaves have risen up, watching the
Great Fire move south from Hassell Street along East Bay, engulfing the market as it
spreads west to Meeting Street, burning, eventually, all the way to the Ashley River
along Tradd, leaving five hundred acres of the city a smoking ruin.*

Back inside, she picks up Percival's Wordsworth for the first time since Jarry left.

But, as it sometimes chanceth, from the might
Of joy in minds that can no further go,
As high as we have mounted in delight
In our dejection do we sink as low;
To me that morning did it happen so;
And fears and fancies thick upon me came;

Dim sadness—and blind thoughts, I knew not, nor could
name. . . .

So what is it that turns the poet's thoughts from "Solitude, pain of heart, dis-
tress and poverty"? Remembering Jarry's question, Addie seeks the answer on the
page tonight and cannot find it there.

In the morning, for the first time in months, she sends the crews to work alone
and takes the path into the swamp.

Clarisse is eight months pregnant now, and changed. Her former animation has
been replaced by a wan languor. Instead of silk, she's dressed in a loose frock of
simple white and purple calico, and her hair is loose and halfway down her back.

"Are you doing this to me?" Addie demands.

Clarisse seems unsurprised. She neither replies nor asks her mistress in, her de-
meanor formal, polite and cold.

"What have I done to you?" asks Addie. "The past is what it is and can't be
changed, Clarisse. I, too, have been wronged, but I hold no grudges. We are two
women here alone. Can we not live in peace?"

Clarisse stares into Addie's eyes with a severe and threatening neutrality. "You
hold no grudges. . . ."

"None. I've borne and bear you no ill will."

"The gun bears no ill will," she answers, "but it kills you nonetheless. You want
peace and bear no grudge, but it's you, nene, you who are the bullet in my head.
Afuera con embuchado, china." Her eyes smolder, and she steps onto the porch. "If
you want peace, there is the road." She points. "Stay, and you will die. This is your
warning. I give you only one. It is a promise, not a threat."

"You hate me, don't you? Why?"

"If you were starving," Clarisse replies, "I would take the final crust of bread
out of your mouth and watch you starve and spit upon your grave and dance for hap-
piness when you were dead. And all this, I would consider justice."

Her hate is like a wind that blows Addie back against the rail. "Justice? To re-
turn deliberate harm for harm unmeant?"

"This was my father's land," says Clarisse, "where you now live. My mother put
her whole life into it; my brother, Jarry, much of his. It belongs to Harlan now, my brother.
If he should die, is it your intention to surrender it to me and to my child, Harlan's child,
what is ours through blood and right, which you've done nothing for?"

"Whatever you've been to him, Clarisse, I'm Harlan's wife. If we have chil-
dren, the property will pass to them."

"There is your answer then. Ask yourself, nene, if you were me, if you had 'been to him' what I have been, and loved as I have loved, and suffered what I felt, if you now carried in your body what I hold in mine, would you not feel what you intend as harm and would not that harm seem 'meant'?"

Addie can muster no reply to this.

"Harlan was like you," Clarisse goes on, *"and, before him, Father. He meant no 'harm' when he took my mother and sailed away with her, leaving me with Wenceslao. Harlan told you something of my history. What he did not tell you was who that old man was to me. From the time I was eight years old, china, Wenceslao came to my room at night, this man I believed to be my father. Do you know what it is, when a man does this? It is as if he puts a knife into your tender place. That place is not made to feel bad feeling, but for one thing only, to feel what is dulce, oloroso . . . sweet . . . And if you put a knife into a place that is meant only for sweetness, what is it you feel? Sweetness, china. This is what he did to me. For years, he put his tired old knife into the place of sweetness, and because I was a child and knew nothing else, I took this for love. For love. You see? I thought this is what fathers do. I thought this is family, this is human life. I wanted him to be with me, and then his wife discovered us, and I was sent away to the Franciscanos en Guanabacoa. And Wenceslao died and left me not a peso. My best hope, then, you see, is for some pardo tradesman, some free Negro man to marry me.*

"Then Harlan came. He brought me money. We looked into each other's eyes and felt love, what I look into your face and do not see. Am I mistaken? No, it isn't there. You don't love him. Look at this."

She steps inside and takes a picture from a shelf. *"Look,"* Clarisse repeats, handing Addie a tintype portrait of herself, seated in a chair with a closed fan pressed against the breast of her black dress. Her straight dark hair is piled, as formerly, à la giraffe, held in place by the roof-tile comb of tortoiseshell and sterling. Behind her, a younger, fresher Harlan stands, stout and prematurely balding, with muttonchops he must have later realized brought out the weakness of his chin. He's dressed in a manner Addie could never have imagined, like a Cuban dandy, in a swallowtail coat, nankeen breeches, flesh-colored hose, with silver buckles on his shoes. His right hand rests on Clarisse's shoulder, his left—or rather two fingers of it—slipped between the buttons of his piqué waistcoat. In his mouth is a cigar.

"Do you know what this is? It's our engagement portrait. We had it made to give to Mama and to him, to Percival. This, you see, this love was the best thing that happened in my life. It changed everything for me. Then we arrived, and it was taken from me, too, by him, by you, and no one, no one meant me any harm! Everyone wants peace, like you!"

"*I didn't fully comprehend what this had been for you,*" says Addie now. "*But,* still . . . *Still, Clarisse, would it not ease you to forgive?*"

Her laugh is furious. "*You mistake me, china. It isn't ease I seek. I want what's mine. I won't be thrown away or left to beg for scraps. I may suffer, I may be destroyed, but if it comes, I'll know that those who did this wrong to me will suffer more. Including you, 'who mean no harm.' No, nene, the only peace there'll ever be between the two of us is when you leave or when you're dead. You decide. Now go.*"

FORTY-SIX

*J*he tires went *tump-tump,* and they were home.

Returning straight from Tildy's, Claire carried Hope upstairs and tucked her in. She took a melancholy read of the frown her daughter wore in sleep. *Daddy's little girl.* Thinking of Gardener and herself as much as Hope and Ran, Claire experienced a heavy pang of doubleness, child and mother both. With a sigh, she pulled the sheet over Hope's bare shoulder and tiptoed down the hall to Charlie's room. Backlit by the hall light, she stood silent in the door and watched, arms crossed and elbows cupped, as Cell unbuttoned Charlie's shirt, then, supporting his nape, lowered him like a rag doll to the pillow and, one by one, untied his little shoes.

"What?" he whispered as he passed her in the door.

"*I* can't even get his clothes off without waking him."

Seeing her furred eyes, his furred, too.

Downstairs, as Claire switched on the portrait lamps, she glanced at the empty hooks above the door, and she and Marcel traded looks.

"Could he have gone to Killdeer, do you think?"

"Why?" she asked him. "Ran has no one in Killdeer anymore."

"He's probably just driving, Claire. I doubt he has a plan."

"Do you think it's too late to call that Sergeant Thomason?"

"I wouldn't. And anyway, the police already know, don't they?"

"I guess they do. It's unbelievable, Marcel. He's forty-five years old and now he's going to fight the law? Who does he suppose is going to win?"

"I'm not sure winning's at the top of Ran's priorities right now."

"Has it ever been? I wish someone could tell me what is at the top of Ran's priorities."

He blinked but didn't look away. "If you want my vote, I say we wait a bit before getting too proactive. He'll probably show up here before too long."

"That's what I'm half afraid of."

He studied her. "Meaning . . ."

"Meaning my husband, who's off his meds and crazy as a shithouse rat, is out there somewhere with a shotgun, and you're telling me he may be coming here? I don't know, Marcel. I honestly can't tell you I'm not a little spooked."

"Well, if it makes you feel any better, I'm not going anywhere."

"Damn straight, you're not. In fact, if you don't mind, I'd like your keys." She held her hand out, and Marcel smiled. Claire, however, didn't. "Let's have a drink. Since you're my captive and all. Do you agree?"

"Oh, yes," he said. "I absolutely second that."

She poured them each three fingers of Clive's old single-barrel sour mash, then sank beside him on the scuffed green leather sofa—not too close together, not too far apart. "Do you know what he told me on the phone? He said, 'I know what's going on, Claire.'"

"Meaning what?"

"I think he thinks we're having an affair."

Claire's face was sober, and Marcel briefly held her stare, then let his head recline against the sofa back. In the quiet, with the windows open, they could hear cicadas chirring in the trees. When he finally spoke, his voice was soft. "So, what exactly are we having?"

"Oh, shit, Cell, don't," she answered, with a husky note. She touched his arm. "Don't do this now, okay? Do we really have to?"

He turned his head to look at her. His face was sad. "I think we do."

Now Claire's expression settled, too.

"All these years, Claire, ever since Mt. Hermon . . ."

"You loved Shanté." She cut him off and wiped her brimming eyes.

"I had a crush on her, but really, it was you. You're why I went to Juilliard. I joined the band because of you. I thought I could take it, but I couldn't. It came to me that day on the F train, coming back from Coney

Island. You had on that little peach-colored dress and Wayfarers, and your nose was burnt. You were eating a cherry ice, and it came to me, 'All it ever was was talking in our sleep, that's all . . . Just talking in my sleep.'"

"I knew that's what it meant," she whispered. Her face was soft now, and her eyes were bright and deep.

"I had to get on with my life. And I did. I got over you, and twenty years went by, and then one day the phone rang and there you were. It was as if no time had passed at all. And to lose you again . . .'"

"I understand," she said. She took his hand in hers and put it in her lap. "You know what it is for me?"

"What?"

"There was this time in my life, Cell, long ago now, at Northfield and those first years in New York, when I felt better than I do now, better than I am. I felt clearer in myself, more confident, in touch with something . . . I almost want to say holy—I know that sounds ridiculous. . . ."

"It doesn't."

"I felt that way when I was in my teens and twenties. I don't even remember where I lost it. I just know I did. I woke up one day and it was gone. And now I'm forty-two. I gave up on ever feeling that again almost twenty years ago. I thought, That's part of growing up, it's just the human lot. Now here I am, and here you are, and suddenly I feel that way again. And it's not that what I felt for Ransom wasn't true, Marcel—it was for a long time. It's just that, after an even longer one, it was over, and I haven't wanted it to be. I kept thinking there had to be some way to coax it back to life. I feel like the condemned person; it's eleven fifty-nine and I'm still waiting for the governor's call. But it isn't going to happen, is it?"

He held her gaze, then his eyes drifted, and hers followed his. The mantel clock said 12:15.

"Shit," she said. "Oh, shit, Marcel. I knew. After all his talk of how he's changed and how hard he means to try, to find out he's been off his meds . . . When he told me that, I felt something just go crack inside me. That was it. I used to love him, now I don't. Now I love you, and you love me. You do, don't you?"

"Yes," he whispered.

"It's just that simple, isn't it?"

"It is."

"Oh," she said, "oh, Cell, I've been so scared of this conversation, so scared. I put it off and put it off for months. I told myself it was because of Hope and Charlie, but what am I teaching them—to go down with the ship? To stick it out even when it's dead? That's not what I want them to remember when they look back at my life. And Ran. I feel so bad for him, Marcel. Now I have you, and you have me, but who does Ransom have? He's out there somewhere with a gun, and if he hurt himself . . . But, the truth is, every time I've ever tried to pull away, he's lured me back by getting sick. For years, I've let myself be held hostage with that threat, and I'm not going to do it anymore. I'm just not."

"It's hard, though, isn't it?"

She squeezed his hands. "So hard. *So* hard. Thank you for seeing that. It's like dying, Cell."

He reached out and wiped her cheek. "Do you know what your boy Faulkner said, the one thing that really made me think he might have been as great as everybody said? He said, 'It takes an awful lot of character to quit anything when you're losing.' "

"Oh," she said, stricken. "Oh, it's true, isn't it? But I'm happy, too, Marcel. I've wanted to say this to you for the longest time. You knew, didn't you?"

"How would I have known, Claire?"

"You're right," she answered, stroking his face and smiling as tears ran down her cheeks. "How would you? I've been denying it for months, haven't I? I am de Queen of de Nile, aren't I?"

"You are," he said, smiling, too, holding her wet face between his hands, "you are de fucking Queen of de fucking Nile."

And now she kisses him, and the kiss is like a book that seizes them and neither can put down. At the end of every chapter, they're compelled to turn the page, into a new adventure, and it goes on and on, and they're lost in it and lose all sense of time, and when it ends, they're refreshed like dreamers who awake and have no idea how long they've slept.

Then Claire stands up and offers him her hand.

Upstairs, in the big bed, which isn't hers and Ransom's anymore, which, as of tonight, is only Claire's, she whispers, "Even if we do this, we can still turn back, right?"

Marcel gazes down, unsmiling, with tender fearlessness, and answers, "I don't think so, Claire." And then he drops his face against her neck, and they begin.

FORTY-SEVEN

*W*alking from Clarisse's back home through the swamp that day, Addie all but decides to leave. She doesn't take Clarisse's threats lightly, doesn't take them lightly in the least. Yet she doesn't go, and why? Addie hardly knows the reason. Deep down, she is angry, too, angry both with Clarisse and like Clarisse. Addie's angry at the war, at the way her marriage has turned out, at life, her life, which is not what she expected, not what she was promised and felt herself entitled to. She's still waiting, waiting somewhere deep inside, for the true thing to start. And it hasn't. There's a part of her, connected to this anger, that won't be driven out—not by Clarisse, or anyone. And so that night, instead of packing to join Blanche and Delphine in Cheraw, Addie leaves the hall door open when she goes to bed. She lies awake and waits, and nothing comes. And the fear passes, as it did when she was eight. She's still shy of mirrors, though, and when the fields are flowed, Addie makes a point to not look down.

She takes satisfaction in the work. By 1863, there's beginning to be hunger everywhere. Fifteen cents before the war, beef, now, in Charleston, is three dollars a pound. . . . A dollar for a cabbage—not even the head, but just the leaves! She must see the crop is made. There's nothing but her will holding things together anymore. Running off in twos and threes since '61, the slaves, emboldened by Emancipation, vanish now in fives and tens and take the boats. A quarter of them, gone. So every morning now this spring, in one of Percival's straw hats, she's on the first flat to the fields. Her face and arms, by May, are long since brown. She wears a dress of white and purple calico sewn by her own hand from the same bolt pilfered from the storehouse by Clarisse. Addie's last good dress—the blue from Mrs. Cummings's shop in the now-dated style called bayadere—went to the Ladies Christian Auxiliary for bandages, to wrap the bloody stump of some poor amputee. The hospitals . . . the suffering is so terrible there. Three-quarters of her crop of rye is flatted to the still in Mars Bluff, made into demijohns of whiskey and shipped out on the train. For what relief have they to give the wounded and the dying now but drunkenness? And Wando Passo's mistress will starve her animals to give it to them, and who shall tell her no?

No, she will stay and do her little part, though some mornings, on the dike, so help her, when the slant sun hits the fields—which are under the Long Water now, as Oliver and Tim wade through and rake away the trash—she wonders how Almighty God can justify such beauty, how He can still allow the sun to shine, the rice to needle up and head, so bountiful and green, out of the mud.

And Chancellorsville, dear God, another victory—and how is she to feel? Her heart cannot but exult for Lee and for his gallant troops. But, oh, the cost. Jackson, lost, oh, Jackson. They shall not soon find his like. For Addie, now, despite the exultation, the notion of young boys with feathers in their caps, running yelling up a hill behind a flag into a withering rain of iron fire, dying with high hearts and cheers upon their lips, no longer seems so fine as once it did. Against the roll, the absent names, the funerals, the mothers dressed in black and clutching handkerchiefs, not to weep in, but to catch some last, brief scent their sons or husbands left in them, the waste, the appalling, simple waste of it, on fine May mornings such as this, makes her want to fall and beat her fists against the earth and cry, What for? What is it for? States' rights? Self-determination? The orators intone in terms like these. "The torch of liberty, passed from the framers' hands, falls now to us to defend against the Northern despots as once our fathers fought the English kings. . . ." Addie hears the fine, high-sounding words, but it's hard for her to think in such abstractions anymore. Watching Oliver and Tim, waist-deep in black water in their swimming shirts, alert for moccasins, Addie thinks, States' rights, self-determination, the torch of liberty . . . it all boils down to this: the right to keep them here, unpaid, against their will, to make the rice for which we shall receive the gain. The framers fought for freedom from oppression; we fight for the freedom to continue to oppress. Is this not so? Is this not the "right" her state has chosen to assert, the path that Southern "self-determination" takes? A spy, a stranger, in her own land, yet Addie stays to make the rice. And will God, Addie wonders, let us win?

The twenty-first of June . . . The Point Flow is off now. The fields are dry and *they're pulling weeds by hand, when word comes up from Hasty Point—Lee has crossed the Potomac and is marching north toward the Susquehanna with 160,000 men! The whole South waits with bated breath. Those whose faces have settled into the long stare look about with timid wonder, as though waking up for the first time in two years. And from Vicksburg—they're saying Grant is dead! That he's retired his forces to Grand Gulf!*

July the first . . . The Army of Northern Virginia has taken York—they're fifteen miles from Harrisburg! On the third, the smuggled papers out of Baltimore speak of a chance skirmish between Lee's force and Meade's, some little place called Gettysburg. . . . On the sixth, they say a major battle has been fought. . . . The result is "indecisive," a Northern code word for a Southern victory . . . By the eighth, the absence of dispatches from Lee's army is creating an uneasy mood. . . . And then the tenth, the tenth, oh, the tenth! Vicksburg, fallen! Pemberton has surrendered his command, his whole command, to Grant, who still lives after all. And Port Hudson, lost . . . The whole Mississippi under Federal control, the Confederacy, cut in half. And Lee, oh, now word comes, a defeat with terrible losses, and the army in full retreat back over the Potomac, under the old man's grieving, stoic gaze . . .

That terrible July, that day of fate, the tenth, as John is opening the trunks with the high tide and letting the Layby water flood the fields, word comes from Charleston, too. . . . Gillmore's forces have crossed Lighthouse Inlet from Folly Beach and overrun the Confederate rifle pits on Morris Island. Wagner, where Harlan is, has held, but three-quarters of the island has been lost. The battery is in desperate straits, under constant enfilading fire from the monitors offshore, which raise their guns and rain killing grape and canister over the fort, as Federal troops dig siege guns into breaching batteries in Wagner's front.

Not till the fifteenth does Addie learn that Harlan has survived. He writes from Fort Moultrie, where he arrived on Saturday, when the garrison was relieved. Tomorrow, Wednesday, under cover of dark, the boats will take them back. "In haste," he writes. "Forgive the appearance of the page. A shell has overturned the inkstand. We are under constant fire from Dalgren's fleet. One can hardly hear to think. The men are tired, but morale is good. The assault on Wagner is expected momently. When I return next week, I shall seek leave. Meet me at the Mills, Tues., inst., at 6 o'clock. I shall only have till midnight. So, my dear, till then . . ."

The grand assault comes the night of the eighteenth. By noon the following day, word comes that the battery has held, yet Addie has no word from Harlan. None the next day, nor the next. On Tuesday, nonetheless, she is at the Mills House at five o'clock. At six, he isn't there. Eight comes. Then ten. Finally, at a quarter past, he walks in. He is so thin, so sunburnt! His full lips look chewed and scabbed. His face and hands are clean, and he's shined his boots, but they're down at heel. His cuffs are frayed and his uniform smells of powder and is only as clean as clothes can be that have been washed in seawater without soap. And even as he takes off his hat and smiles across the room, she can see the terrible somberness that's settled upon him, settled on all of them, the somberness of those who've looked upon a fearful secret they must keep both from and for the rest.

"Forgive me, the boat . . . ." He takes her shoulders in his hands.

She puts three fingers, tenderly, on his chapped lips. "It's nothing. I'm so relieved."

"It's been impossible to write."

"I have champagne. . . ."

He looks at it and smiles. "We have little time. In two hours, I must be at the Laurens Street wharf. Let's take it with us to the room. . . ."

She gazes up at him, forthright, the way she did their wedding night, and goes.

Upstairs, though, things do not proceed as she expects. "Forgive me, dear," he says, "I disgust myself. I should like to take a bath."

"Of course."

"But pour a glass, and sit with me."

"You are so thin, Harlan," she says, running her hand over his bare chest, where she can count the ribs.

"As are you. Look at your hands, Addie!"

"I've learned to work."

"Would that you'd not had to."

"There are worse fates than that."

"So there are." He steps into the tub, leans back, sips his champagne, and puts the glass down on the floor. He closes his eyes. "Such a thing as water, hot water . . . One forgets. . . ." And now he opens them again. "How are you, Addie?"

"I hardly know," she says. "I work and sleep and dread tomorrow's news. Little else. But we shall make a crop."

His eyes study her with a knowing, soft attention she does not remember from before. "You've had a time of it, I think."

"Little enough, compared to yours."

"You see now what Jarry meant to us. . . ."

She holds his gaze, but doesn't answer this.

"You know," he says, after a time, "he's in Beaufort. Or he was. He was seen. I believe he's given them intelligence."

Her heart beats harder still.

"I was certain we would meet upon the parapets. I had such a feeling, Addie, almost a premonition."

"And did . . ."

He shakes his head wearily. "If he was there, I didn't see him. I suspect and pray he's dead and lying in the trench upon the beach with Shaw and all the rest. They killed Cheeves, Addie."

"Langdon!"

"Yes. And Haskell, we think. He's been missing since the tenth. And Johnny Bee. Macbeth . . ." He closes his eyes and shakes his head. "God, such a night . . . I hope to never see its like again. . . . I don't want to speak of it. . . ."

"No, my dear, put it out of your mind." She touches his hand, dangling limp over the rim.

"They were three and four deep in the moat," he says, almost immediately. "The bodies, Addie . . ." He looks at her with that terrible stare, bemused and vulnerable and deep. "In the dark, we didn't know who they were till they were almost on the wall. . . . The cowards, Addie, they sent the niggers in, the Fifty-fourth, to show us their contempt. The Yankees let them take the fire. . . . They came at eight o'clock, a little before, marching in good order up the beach, and we held our fire and watched them come. . . . A hundred yards beyond the moat, they charged, and we fired into them. . . . The whole front of the battery was a streak of fire. It was like tossing pebbles at a cake. . . . They simply melted, a quarter of their number, perhaps half, in a minute and a half. . . . The Yankees didn't even give them scaling ladders. They were left to climb the walls by hand as we rained musket fire down on them. And their boy colonel, Shaw . . . he wasn't forty yards from me . . . he made it to the parapet in the first wave and raised his sword. 'Onward, boys!' I heard him shout. Really, he was rather fine, but it was suicide. A dozen balls hit him in the face and chest and down he fell into our ranks. . . . And still the niggers came. . . . We fought them on the ramparts, Addie, hand to hand, with swords and bayonets. I have to say, they fought like men, but they had no chance. They could not advance, and to retreat was suicide. It put them back under our artillery. . . . When it was done at one o'clock that night, they lay tangled in the moat and on the sea beach, rolling in the swash. . . . There is this new light, Addie, this terrible calcium light they turn upon the walls to blind our gunners. I shall never forget when it was over. . . . They swept the beach with that, and the fiddler crabs, Addie—hundreds, thousands of them—you could see them creeping from their holes toward the dead. . . ." He reaches for his glass and closes his eyes and takes another sip.

"The next morning, under flag of truce, we buried them. Gillmore asked for Shaw, and I felt we should have returned his body, but Graham would not relent. So we pushed him with his niggers into the same common trench. Now their sappers—when I left, they were barely ninety yards outside our wall—must tunnel through the remains of their own dead. Not a shell falls on that beach that doesn't open up a grave. And the very water that we drink, Addie, the very water, brown, as brown as tea . . ."

"Oh, Harlan!"

"I tell you, frankly," he goes on, *"we shall not withstand another such assault. And it's sure to come, Addie, as sure as you are there and I am here."*

He looks at her, and she thinks, What am I to say? What am I to do?

But Harlan does not require an action on her part. He simply slips off his wedding ring and holds it out.

"Harlan, no . . ."

He opens her hand gently and puts it there. *"I couldn't bear it, Addie, to think of some Yankee private taking it as a memento, the way I've seen them do. And ours."*

"I'll keep it then, but only till you return."

"Yes," he says. *"Till then. Should something happen to me, though . . ."*

"Harlan, please—"

"No," he cuts her off. *"There's a time when speaking of such things is morbid, Addie, but that time is past. I've left my will with Father's attorney, Edward Laurens, on Broad Street. I think you know the place. . . ."*

"I do."

"I've left everything to you."

"It's generous of you," she says. *"I hope I shall never have the benefit of it."*

"It is my wish you should. It's little enough, Addie. I've ruined your life."

"You haven't. No."

"Let's speak the truth for once."

She holds his stare, and he stares back, and Addie, now, is moved. *"You've changed,"* she says.

"As have you. The war has changed us all."

"And Clarisse?"

"What about her?"

"What is your wish?"

"Damn Clarisse," he says. *"If I've ruined your life, she's ruined mine. She shall have nothing from me, Addie. Not one dime."*

"You know she has . . ."

"A child. Yes, I know. I pity him. He didn't cause what he is, but he's an abomination to me nonetheless. He shall never have a father's love any more than I had mine." From his pocket, he takes out his watch. *"Look, it's already eleven twenty-five."*

"Should we . . . ?"

He shakes his head. *"There isn't time."*

"You're sure?"

"No, I must go."

From the Mills House, they walk south through the deserted streets, as they walked after Sumter, when the crowds strolled arm in arm in their best clothes, and church bells rang, and the harbor filled with the white sails of pleasure boats. Addie can't get that prior walk, that prior time, out of her mind, yet she says nothing, hoping Harlan may be spared the memory. She's never felt so close to him, but it's tinged with an imponderable regret. Around them, under a brilliant gibbous moon, all is blackened, silent desolation. Weeds grow among the cobbles in Meeting Street, where broken window glass lies thick, as though their way is strewn with jewels. With her key, Addie opens her aunt's door. They pass beneath the Philadelphia gasolier of bronze and ormolu, its globes etched with sheaves she can make out in the moonlight streaming through a gaping hole in the roof. Its beams light a scene that makes her think about Miss Havisham's. All the photographs, Blanche's mother's things, the water-swollen books open and facedown, the furniture in shards and splinters everywhere. Neither of them speaks a word. After one long look, Addie turns away and locks the door, and they go on their way.

At the wharf, she feels his urgency increase. He has begun to pace.

"Can you not sit with me and rest?"

"Addie," he says, as if he hasn't heard, *"I don't know if we shall ever meet again. I regret the sorrow I have caused. . . ."*

"Please, Harlan, please, my dear, don't distress yourself."

"No," he says, *"no, Addie, let me speak. I've spent my life an angry man. I didn't understand this, but these nights upon the wall, waiting in the dark, alone, for death . . . Even in my happiest hours, when I was jolly with my friends, joking and feting them at my expense, I was angry underneath. I've come to see it has to do with Father, the fact that he loved Jarry in a way that I could never gain no matter what I did. Father saw me as unworthy in some way I couldn't understand or change, and so I came to seem—and, to this very moment, feel—unworthy to myself. And I lived forty years, almost forty-five, right up till the day he died, in the expectation that he would recognize his wrong and somehow make it up to me. I felt he*

owed me this, but now, Addie, just lately, pacing on the watch at night, I've come to see that, right or wrong, owed or spent, none of this shall ever be. He's gone, and I've forgiven him. I forgive him everything with all my heart. Yet what I've come to see is that some wounds, though we forgive them, never cease to bleed. . . ."

And now, the signal lantern flashes on the water. Now, they hear the sound of oars.

"I had a dream," he tells her, rushing on. "We were in the bombproof. There were many with me, both the living and the dead, and there was something at the ceiling, Addie, like a cloud, dark blue, a dark blue cloud of swirling steam, and a voice spoke out of that cloud that no one else could hear. There was a spirit in the cloud and it spoke to me as I'm speaking to you now. In the dream, I understood the words, though I lost them when I woke. I only know they angered me, Addie. They were commandments of some sort I didn't wish to keep, and I picked up a hammer and I threw it. It disappeared into the steam and did not fall back to earth again, and others saw, and still, no one believed. . . . No one believed. . . ."

"Captain DeLay?"

"The boat is here," he says. He pulls her to him hard, hard. "Good-bye, good-bye." And he is gone, leaving Addie with a pounding heart. Forgetful of herself, she glances down in the water now and sees a pool of lamplight undulating there, and in that pool, a coal-black silhouette, still, wholly still, upon the softly tossing waves.

"Who are you?"

The figure doesn't answer, and in this moment Addie has a strong, sudden premonition of death. Is it Harlan's? Taking it so, she turns and walks back along the glittering path that leads through desolation and goes she knows not where.

FORTY-EIGHT

cool exhalation from the river further softened the soft light as the car moved up the potholed drive under heavy branches draped with Spanish moss where cicadas whirred. And there—as Ransom pulled the battered Odyssey into the turnaround in back—in gray flannel slacks with a soft drape and tasseled Italian loafers of some gleaming, welted skin, was Marcel Jones, pushing his children—Ransom's children—on the swing.

"Hey, Doddy, hey!" At the zenith, Charlie launched himself into the blue. "To Fininity Amboyon!"

On reflex, Ran made an aborted lunge, like a receiver toward a Hail Mary pass he knew he'd never catch. Charlie, however, touched down without incident and ran on, unaware he'd skirted death. When Ran knelt to receive him, his son pressed the new Buzz Lightyear laser on his wrist instead, painting a red dot between his hapless father's eyes. "Not today, Zurg!" he said, making his voice big and plangent, and his cheeks, Ran noticed, with a pang of helpless love, were strawberries and cream, as flushed and pretty as a girl's. His blink—where was that? Ran had almost started to develop an affection for that blink, but bangzoom, it was outta here, and in a single night! Even a man of stronger psychic constitution than himself would have found it difficult to read these signs and conclude anything but that his absence had been beneficial to his son.

"Hi, Hope!"

She looked up at his hail, noting Shanté's presence with mild curiosity.

"Hi, Daddy . . ." Her voice was both familiar and brand-new, disengaged in a way he'd never heard from Daddy's Little Girl before. Otherwise unmoved by his return, she went on twisting in her swing alone, back and forth, and forth and back, like four-year-old Ophelia plaiting a sad crown of rue. Her lips moved silently as she took a saltless pretzel from her bag and offered it to the unseen creature she was talking to.

A single night, and Ran, once more, had fallen years behind the curve.

A weirding light had fallen in the park, and Claire was out the back door now, moving hurriedly to intercept. Drying her hands on a white cloth, she was wearing her cutoff overalls and a black Lycra tank, and she was barefoot and so beautiful he knew he stood no chance. He'd come prepared to throw himself upon the mercy of the court, but Claire's frown—battle-hardened, weary, ready to march on, however far, however long—showed little sign of leniency, in fact, no leniency at all.

Why did you come home? said Nemo. He hadn't spoken in a while.

Ransom shoved him back into the submarine and slammed the hatch. "Look who I brought." He smiled, making an effort not to grind his teeth.

"I appreciate your doing this," Claire said forthrightly to Shanté. "I wish I could say I'm happy to see you."

"Well, I'll be happy for us both." Shanté spread her arms, and Claire stepped in.

Ransom gave Marcel a look. "Do you need a hug, too?"

Caught off guard, Cell laughed with an attractive, natural surprise. "I think I'll pass, but thanks."

"Don't say I didn't offer."

With this, the conversational momentum ground to an apocalyptic halt.

"Hope," Claire said, falling back upon the children as a social crutch, something she was deeply critical of in others, "come meet Mommy's friend."

"And Daddy's friend," Ran qualified.

"Come meet Shanté," said Claire.

"Hi, Shanté," Hope said. "I have a new dog."

"What's his name?"

"He doesn't have one."

"Where is he?"

"He's imaginary," Claire informed the group.

"No, Mommy," Hope corrected in her parsing and emphatic way. "He's not. You see him, don't you, Daddy?" She held the leash in her left hand, and her right opened slightly wider, following the contour of the head, stroking backward from the snout across the crown.

Ran squatted on his hams. "Sure," he said, "he's white, with a black patch on one eye and ears that fold down at the tops. He's attending to His Master's Voice."

"No," Hope said, impatient with the joke, "he's black, Daddy. All black. And he's hungry."

"Maybe we should feed him."

"I don't know what he wants."

Ran stared into his daughter's grave and slightly worried eyes and glimpsed the sunken anger there.

"Well, take him in the house," Claire intervened as Daddy's smile died on the vine. "We're going to have an early bath."

As Hope moved off, Ran looked at Claire as if to say, *What's this?* But Claire, this time, did not look back.

"What's that?" she asked instead, taking in the Odyssey.

"I bought you a new car," Ran said.

Claire looked some more, then gazed around the group to see if someone might explain the joke. Her eyes arrived, at last, on him.

"It got a little beat-up in the accident," he conceded, "but the body shop can fix that up. It has a DVD."

"Did it come with a handful of magic beans as well?"

In the beat before he found his answer, a surge of rage and grief shot through him, wild and deep, like the first jolt of the electric chair. *Never fucking good enough* . . . "No," he said, turning from the precipice, "but I did get five free movies."

Claire's expression turned perplexed.

"I sold my father's Thunderbird to get you this," he said, aware it sounded childish even as he spoke, but unable to resist. "But no big deal."

"And you expect my thanks. . . ."

"That would be asking a bit much."

She stared at him and then at Cell. It was a look that Ran knew well, as if to say her prophecy had been fulfilled. The expression was one she'd heretofore reserved for him.

"I'm fine, by the way."

Claire's look turned forthright now, and it dawned on Ran that this was all he was going to get. "Are you?"

"Nothing to worry about," he said. "Just a lot of pain, is all." The quote was Henry Fonda—*On Golden Pond*. In days gone by, they'd watched that movie many times, eating popcorn, holding hands, passing back and forth the Kleenex box. They'd seen themselves, their fretted love, in it and thought—or Ransom had—they'd end up old like Kate and Hank, and Ran, the first to go, would meet his maker staring into these crème caramel eyes which would have forgiven him—surely would have done by then—for the burn he more than anyone had helped to put in them.

There was no forgiveness in them now. If the allusion to the movie registered, Claire gave no indication.

And Ransom had to contemplate the possibility that Claire might not be there to grieve him when he went, that he might be denied the consolation of knowing he'd been wholly loved one time, one time at least, by one other human being on this earth, even if he couldn't love himself. And was that—being loved once in this life—just another sentimental dream of youth, like playing Shea and Fillmore East? Where, finally, do you make your stand? And is there any bedrock in this world? Ran was getting down to that point now, down to bedrock, down through flesh to bone and wholly unprepared to yield his point. He'd begun to contemplate the sanctity of vows. . . . *In sickness and in health, for better and for worse* . . . Deep inside, something he'd always felt, felt as long as he remembered, felt as long as he could stand—then ceased to feel, or ceased to know he felt—began to stir toward consciousness again. And it was like the coils of a great snake thrashing awake after a long sleep, like a seismic tremor, like the trembling in the rails you feel before you see the train. . . . Then suddenly there it is, barreling toward the crowded station, no sign of slowing down. . . .

Then Claire reached out and lifted up his hair. Her gaze was clinical, nurselike, but at her touch, every joint in Ransom's body turned to liquid.

"Okay," he said, feeling something in his chest, hope or panic, he couldn't tell. "Okay," he said, panting slightly, "so it isn't going to be *The Big Chill*. We can still be grown-ups, can't we? I think we can manage that at least."

"Who wants a drink?" said Claire, with foxhole gaiety, driving home another long, sweet nail.

"Excellent idea," he said. "Let's drink some alcohol and burn some meat. What say we fry a chicken? I've still got a hankering for that."

"I wouldn't mind a glass of wine," said Shanté with a look of hard compassion toward them both. "But before we get too far into the night, I'd like to see that pot."

FORTY-NINE

eptember . . . The last water, roiled white and stirred with chaff, mingles with the river's brown. John drops the counterweight and shuts the gate, and on it flows, one thing. It's harvest now, and down the rows they wend, bending over, with their sickles, the small, curved knives called reap-hooks here, cutting always toward themselves, laying the gold heads on the stubble, singing in slow cadence as they go:

In case I never see you anymo' . . .

Where they cut yesterday, the women gather up the sheaves and bind them with a wisp of rice, leaving small cocks in the field to dry until tomorrow, when they'll tote them to the flats. And Addie comes behind them with the children, last of all and singing, too, gleaning unhulled grains out of the mud. She has an apronful and she's perspiring, though the sky has lifted off and there's a difference in the light today. When she climbs the dike, a puff of wind blows back her hair and catches in her dress as in a sail. The sun is striking off the water, and Addie smiles and closes her eyes, feeling its reflected warmth. The goodness of life, she thinks, is mostly little things like this, a breeze as soft as a caress, September light, an apronful of rice.

When she opens them again, Jules Poinsett is standing on the piazza in his uniform, one arm behind his back, the other sleeve folded up and pinned. Below him in the drive, Peter holds his saddled horse. Jules is gazing straight at her, and Addie, across the distance, knows from this . . . She's been expecting this visit for some time now, truly, since that night in Charleston, when Harlan spoke about the blue cloud swirling over him, and Addie gazed into his face and seemed to see its shadow there and knew him marked. Once upon a time, the girl she was, or thought herself to be, would have released the corners of her apron and allowed the rice to spill, unheeded, on the ground, but she resists this now and carefully puts her contribution in the fanner with the others', then wipes her hands and calls Tim to pole her back.

"Jules," she says, holding out her hand, forgetful briefly.

He takes it with his left. "Mrs. DeLay," he says, not Addie, yet there's something personal in the pressure he exerts that makes her know he is no stranger to his task.

She sits in the rocking chair, leaning forward slightly, erect, and folds her hands.

"It's my sad duty . . . ," he begins, and though Addie expects the news and feels herself prepared, she flies away, some part of her, for a time, however long or brief. She becomes aware of the dappled sunlight falling through the old trees in the park, the softness of the air, the September sky with the great ships of cloud that come back every fall. I never loved him, *Addie thinks, watching as they sail away.* How sad . . . how sad that is. . . .

"In the evacuation . . . ," Jules is telling her when she comes back.

"The evacuation . . ."

"Of Wagner, Addie, yes, the night before last. The order came from Charleston. Motte . . . You know my cousin, Motte, I think. . . ."

"Yes, slightly."

"He was able to secure the steamer, Sumter, *to assist in taking off the men. They were primarily of the Twentieth South Carolina and the Twenty-third Georgia, and it was after dark to avoid the Union guns. Captain DeLay volunteered to remain to spike the howitzers. It was dangerous duty. Their sappers, by then, were no more than forty feet outside our ditch, and would've swiftly overrun the fort had they suspected our retreat. The garrison marched up the beach in silence, without light, to Battery Gregg, where the transports took them off. I don't know a great deal more. Captain DeLay was in the final group to board. Motte saw him in the stern, looking back over the rail as the shells arced down on Wagner from the fleet. He asked me to tell you that. Motte then went forward to the pilothouse, and Harlan—Captain DeLay—wasn't seen again. They were almost at Sumter, perhaps a half mile off, when there came a flash from Sullivan's. Motte first thought it was a signal flare, and then here came the ball, he said, skipping through the waves and raising streaks of*

spray. The first shot missed, but then the whole battery opened up. The boat took several fatal hits and rapidly began to sink. There was great confusion, men shouting, running, stripping down to jump into the sea. . . . It's shoal there, no more than shoulder deep, but the tide was running hard to sea. Those who were able waded off to get out of the fire. After fifteen or twenty rounds, the gunners at Moultrie realized their mistake and held fire, but the garrison was stranded there all night in the sea. At dawn, as they were being carried off in boats, they came under Federal fire. Captain DeLay was not among their number when they mustered at the fort."

"What happened? Where . . ."

"I wish I had an answer. The truth is, we don't know. The stern quarter took a direct hit from the Parrott guns. That's where Motte last saw your husband. It's his belief that Captain DeLay was killed by that shell. He was never seen after they entered the water."

"Could he not have swum . . ."

"Some did. Sumter was the nearest point of land, but Captain DeLay wasn't with them, nor was he seen. I know how tempting it can be, Addie, when there's any thread of hope, to cling, but it's Motte's belief and Colonel Graham's, as well as mine, that Harlan perished. The overwhelming likelihood is that he was killed instantly, and though it's no comfort to you now, I believe in time you'll come to see that a swift death is merciful. A brave mission successfully accomplished, the hope of coming home, of seeing you and Wando Passo once again—he had this, I expect, before his mind, as his last thought. That's as good a death as any man can have."

"But to be killed by his own guns!"

Now Poinsett frowns. "It was a mistake."

"A mistake!"

"Would that these things never happened, but in war they do. The gunners at the fort saw a boat proceeding through the harbor without lights and fired, according to their standing orders. Those men at Moultrie knew him, Addie, they were Harlan's friends, many of the Twenty-first. I know they would do anything to call back those shells."

"But they can't."

"No, they can't."

But it can't be, she thinks, surely life can't be as tenuous, as fragile, as contingent upon accident as this. And then, as Jules stands up to take his leave, a momentary panic overtakes her. Oh, don't go, *she thinks.* What do I do now? Tell me what to do! *And then she stares into his eyes, which have the same look she saw in Harlan's at the Mills House in July, when she last saw him—the last time!—the*

*look of one who has beheld a secret he must keep from you and for you, but Addie
knows the secret, too: that it's possible, and not only possible, but easy, to die without
ever having lived. The thought of Percival is so strongly with her now. . . . "I
searched through all these books, and never found an answer. . . ." And this is what
she wants from Jules right now: for him to tell her how to live, and she looks into his
face and thinks,* Poor man, you know no more than I. . . .

"And what will happen now?" she asks. "Will Charleston fall?"

"We'll hold out as long as we can. Our best hope now, I think, is that the
peace party at the North may prevail in the election and sweep Lincoln and his
minions out of power. Then, perhaps, we can make an honorable peace and have our
independence."

"Personally, I shall pray for swift defeat."

"Good afternoon, Mrs. DeLay," he answers, coolly, standing up. "I have other
duty to perform."

Ah, thinks Addie, who?

"Thank you for informing me," she says, like someone speaking rote lines from
a play that she lost interest in long ago.

And Jules is gone, and the air, the lifted sky, the ships of cloud, the September
light—this no longer comforts her. It's like the air at the summit of some high peak,
and it's strange, having never loved her husband, how hard it is, for the next thirty
minutes or an hour, for her to breathe that thin, cold air and want to live. Strange,
too, how swiftly Addie's done with grief.

I must tell Clarisse, she thinks. Resistance boils up in her heart, but breeding
overcomes it, and this is the best part of what she learned in Mme Togno's school and
at Blanche's knee: that, however hard it is, you must never cease to be a human being.

In the barren, under pines, on the soft straw before the cottage, a quilt is spread, and
on the quilt, a child of one sits and plays alone. It's the first time she's seen the boy, and
Addie, at a distance, stops and watches as he puts a block atop another and knocks
both down and makes a crowing noise and claps his hands. Pleased with his success,
he looks up at her with Percival's and Jarry's hazel eyes and the full, bee-stung, almost sybaritic lips that Addie only realizes in this moment Harlan and Clarisse both
share. Both shared. His dark hair forms a cropped cap on his head, and he is neither
black nor white, but somehow both and neither, and finally just himself. His expression sobers when he sees a stranger near, but he seems curious and without fear, and
Addie becomes aware of a constriction in her chest, a hammering under her left ear,
and then Clarisse is there—in her same white and purple calico—to sweep the child
onto her hip and turn, as though to interpose herself between him and a threat.

And what was that brief constriction in her chest? What did Addie feel? Whatever it was, it's faded now. Her expression, like Clarisse's, hardens with dislike.

"They've just come to tell me Harlan's dead."

Clarisse's dark eyes smolder. She makes no reply.

"He was killed in the retreat from Wagner—possibly by an exploding shell, or else he drowned. That's all I know."

Addie waits for a response, but it is only a fraction of a second before she knows there will be none. She starts to walk away and then turns back. "What is his name?"

"James."

"James . . ."

"He is Harlan's son."

Addie briefly holds her stare, then turns her back and goes.

"He's Harlan's son!" Clarisse shouts after her.

The shout fades. Now there's nothing but the sound of Addie's soft tread through the pines.

The effort this has cost steals on her suddenly. Realizing how tightly something in her core is clenched, she tries to breathe and let it go. She leans against a tree and drops her head, and then she sees her hand, so pale and soft against the ridged, dark bark, and they seem part of the same thing. She looks around. She's at the water meadow now. Was this the place? Then it was spring, now it's fall, but there are tender ferns along the ground, and cardinal flowers, and looking down she sees the vine, the partridgeberry Jarry said the old people call lovers' vine. Then, it was covered with white flowers with the scent of orange blossoms. Now, they've succeeded to the fruit. Mixed among the deep green leaves are scarlet berries, like pendant drops of blood. Lifting one, she sees the eyes, two of them, where the small flowers were that dropped and died. Something is upon her now, some lifted sense, and Harlan is clear before her mind, not as she knew him, but as he was on that first afternoon, frowning and blushing in the hall beside Clarisse, when the spiritual beauty of one in mortal pain shone in his face. That is who you were, she thinks, a man I glimpsed just once and barely knew. I loved you not, yet we were bound by marriage, history, class, a heavy iron chain, and what does it mean now? Oh, Harlan. You wanted to reform your life through me and failed against the odds you faced. I wronged you in marrying without love, and you wronged me. In the end, wrong balanced wrong, and you are gone, and I am free, and I have had the better of our fray.

Something is upon her now, some high and lifted sense, and she thinks, God has answered after all. He has answered me. His justice, which we trusted to protect the

South, has defeated us instead. Everything we believed was wrong, and nothing, no one, was more wrong than I. Oh, Jarry. Jarry. I took my husband's side against you. I was given such a gift and felt I had no right to it. I know what Percival meant now, for I, too, have missed my fate. What bound me to you was a breath, a golden breath, a vapor, and I chose the chain instead, against my heart's true cry and what I knew was right. I chose against myself. And that is why you left me, is it not? Is it not?

She looks up at the canopies of the old trees that seem to have a grace and wisdom that surpass human understanding, then down into the water at her feet, where she sees her own reflection against a silhouette of bright blue sky.

And now the words come back. . . .

> At length, himself unsettling, he the pool
> Stirred with his staff and fixedly did look
> Upon the muddy water which he conned
> As if he had been reading in a book. . . .

And what has turned the poet's thoughts to life away from death? As though a ghostly hand has brushed her back, the small hairs rise on Addie's spine. I looked into the pool and saw myself, she thinks; then, stepping in, she doesn't drown, she breaks her image up.

FIFTY

laire handed Shanté the Mini Maglite from the cluttered necessaries drawer, and Shanté turned the beam into the pot, which was keeping vigil on the sideboard as before.

"So, what," said Ran over his shoulder, floating the first breast into the lake of burning oil. "A wash pot, right? For cooking black-eyed peas?"

"Did you see what's in the bottom?"

She stood aside and handed him the light. There, outlined in fresh new rust, was a faint design: a cross within a circle and several smaller marks scratched with a chisel or a nail.

"That must have oxidized," Ran said. "I don't think it was there before. What is it?"

"It's a firma," Shanté said. "In vodou, they're called veves. In other traditions, sygills. This one's Cuban, specific to Palo Mayombe, but in Zaire I've seen BaKongo cosmograms quite similar."

She retrieved her Chardonnay and took a sip as Claire and Marcel filed to look.

"What's it for?" asked Claire.

"It's a religious pictograph. The circle represents the world. In the cross, the horizontal line is the threshold between the living and the dead. The vertical line shows energy rising from their realm into ours. It's the sign of Zarabanda."

"What's that?" asked Claire.

"Who. He's one of the nkisi, a spirit in the Palo pantheon. Honestly, Ran, that was my first thought when you said the pot was wrapped in chains. Zarabanda's cauldrons often are. What I don't get, though, is how a prenda could have gotten here."

"Couldn't the slaves have made it?" Marcel asked.

She shook her head. "What I'd expect to have been practiced here, Cell, as I told Ran, was Conjure. It's Congo, too, but instead of prendas, they'd have made these little flannel sacks called mojo hands or tobies. In Zaire today, priests use something called a futu, which is similar. To anyone familiar with Congo traditions, the technology is more or less the same, meaning a futu or a mojo hand is essentially a miniature prenda, and a prenda is a larger mojo hand. There are differences, but the process that occurs in them is basically the same."

"And what process is that?" Claire demanded soberly.

"Basically, it's a recipe, Claire. There's a list of ingredients—'palos,' sticks from certain sacred trees—palo hueso, malambo, quiebra hacha, and so forth; different earths: from the cemetery, the crossroads, from beneath the jailhouse and the court, river and ocean sand; different minerals, stones, roots, insect and animal remains. You put these all together in the pot and you create an environment—a kind of magical terrarium—into which a muerto, a disincarnate spirit, can materialize, which becomes the Palero's ally and then can be sent out to do his bidding. 'Una Prenda es como el mundo entero en chiquito y con el que usted domina.' . . . That's what Cabrera says: 'A prenda is like the whole world in miniature—in microcosm—which you use to dominate.' "

"To dominate what?" said Claire.

"Whatever you want or need to dominate," said Shan. "In the first instance, whatever's dominating you. Slaves used them for help and protection from their masters. Basically, anything a Christian might pray to God for, a Palero can ask of the nfumbi and nkisi."

"And this is real?" Claire said. "You're telling us you believe all this?"

"Absolutely." Shanté took a heavy sip of wine. "I've been in ceremonies where people are mounted by these spirits, Claire—possessed by them. Someone will say, 'Pruébalo'—'Prove it'—and hand the caballo, the medium, a machete or a knife. I've seen them slice their arms until the blood just pours. I've seen them cut their tongues and eat glass and fire. I've seen them press burning cigars into their cheeks. And I've seen it faked, too. Even in big celebrations in New York, I've seen fake possessions, prendas that aren't alive, just big, ugly, smelly messes someone made out of a book or bought from some fraudulent online Palero. But when the spirits are there, there's no mistaking it."

"So how did this thing get here?" Ransom asked.

"I seriously doubt it was brought over in a boat," she said, "so someone with the knowledge probably made it on the place. Someone Cuban, I'd bet. Someone black—a slave. Probably a man."

"Are you sure of that?"

Claire's sharp tone made everybody look. She traded looks with Cell, then turned to Ran. "Tildy told us something last night after you left, Ran. . . ."

" 'Us'?" he repeated, wretchedly.

"Do you remember Ben Jessup's story?" she said, ignoring this. "The little boy they found after Harlan and Adelaide disappeared?"

"He wasn't Harlan's child, was he?" said Ran, who'd long since arrived. "Addie had the child by someone else."

Claire pressed her lips and shook her head. "It wasn't Addie's child at all."

"What!"

Claire shook her head and slid a photograph across the table, a tintype of a dark-eyed habanera seated in a chair with a closed fan pressed against the breast of her black dress. "Her name was Clarisse. She was the daughter of Percival DeLay and a slave—a Cuban slave—named Paloma." Claire pointed to the young man with muttonchops and a cigar, standing behind Clarisse's chair. "That's Harlan. This is an engagement photograph."

Ran blinked and blinked again. Then he looked up. "His own sister?"

"Half. They didn't know. They met in Cuba as adults and fell in love. Clarisse came here with him. Tildy doesn't know how they found out, but somehow they did, and the wedding was called off."

"And he married Addie."

"He married Addie."

"And the little boy . . . ?"

"Clive and Tildy's grandfather. In his final illness, he told his son that his mother's name was Clarisse."

"And Tildy knew this?"

"Tildy knew," Claire said.

"Goddamn." Ran sat back in his chair, letting it sink in. "God*damn*." He slapped the table with his palm. "I knew she was holding out on me. That old bitch! After all these years, all the social agony your people put me through . . ." He got up and started pacing. "Do you see what this means? She's *passing,* Claire. Miss Tildy I'm-better-than-you-are-it-takes-twelve-generations DeLay is passing. *Clive* was passing. Hell, Claire, *you're* passing! Holy shit!" He slapped his forehead. "Holy, holy shit!"

"If I'm passing, Ran," she replied, "then so are those two children up those stairs."

Ran blinked again. "You're right, they are! It's unbelievable! Am I the only honky in the house? I am! God*damn*. Ransom Hill, come on down! And after all Tildy's social airs and lectures . . ."

"I fail to see how having an African bloodline should affect her pride in who she is in any way," Claire said.

"Yeah, right," Ran said. "That's why they hushed this up for the last hundred and forty years. In Charleston, Claire? Get real! I mean, you know, don't you, in the big scheme of things, this doesn't matter to me in the least?"

"I wouldn't have thought so, Ran. What I find hard to stomach, though, is all this glee."

"Come on, babe," he said, "after you and yours have used me as your social whipping boy for nineteen years, you can at least allow me to gloat for thirty seconds, can't you, before you sic the thought police?"

Her stony face was her reply.

"*Sistah!*"

Ignoring him, Claire turned to Shanté. "Clarisse was Cuban. She was black."

"She fits the bill," Shanté agreed, "except one thing. No woman would have had licencia—permission—to make a prenda. Not even in Cuba to-day, much less in the nineteenth century."

"Do witches ask permission?" Ransom asked.

"Why do you need witchcraft to account for any of this?" Claire asked.

"She wanted to get rid of Addie," he replied. "Don't you see? She wanted to get rid of the white wife."

"How do you know that it was Addie in that hole?" Claire asked.

"She was having an affair," he said. "Harlan came home and caught her."

"And?" Claire challenged.

Ran met her stare and then Marcel's, and for a moment—only one—
they were together in a different, darker room, and it had ceased to be entirely clear that the subject was the past.

Ran broke eye contact first.

"Even if they were," Claire said, "what makes you think they just lay
down for it? How do you know the bodies out there weren't Harlan's and
Clarisse's instead of Jarry's and Addie's?"

This notion bollixed him. Ran had simply never thought of it.

"And, I repeat," Claire continued, on a roll, "why do you need witchcraft to account for any of this? I mean, whoever the murderer was, he—or
she—used a shotgun, right? I don't mean to be obtuse, but spirits don't use
shotguns, do they?"

"My answer to that," said Shanté, "is that when spirits get involved, it
increases the likelihood of shotguns being used. It increases the chance of
people getting hit by buses, falling off cliffs, committing suicide, having
aneurysms, and the like."

"And maybe by Occam's razor," Claire replied, "whoever committed
the murder was simply a murderer and responsible for his acts like every
human being is, like everybody in this room. Why throw the blame on
spirits?"

"Very true, Claire," Shanté said, "but Occam's razor, as I understand it,
is the simplest way to account for all the observed facts, and your explanation doesn't account for the fact that there's a prenda sitting on your sideboard as we speak. You have two dead bodies in a hole. I don't pretend to
know who they were, but it does strike me as, at the very least, curious that
you have title to a South Carolina rice plantation passing to a mixed-race
child in, what—1865?—a time when such a thing was about as likely as a
person of color being elected president or flying to the moon. Even if you
dismiss that as fluke or happenstance, someone with knowledge made this
prenda and drew a Palo firma in the bottom. Clarisse was Cuban, she was
black; based on everything you've said, she certainly had motive. What I'm
still hung up on, though, is why she would have made a cauldron of Zarabanda. Zarabanda is the god of justice. His energy doesn't lend itself to evil
acts. If this had been meant for witchcraft, what I'd expect to see is a
nganga bomba or a sacu-sacu, a kind of prenda made in a burlap bag and
hung in a tree. Instead, you have an iron cauldron with Zarabanda's firma
and the proper carga. Which inclines me back toward Claire's opinion.

Nothing about this really smacks of witchcraft. In Palo Nzambi—'good' or 'legal' Palo—the Palero and the spirit make a pact, a contract. The muerto goes into the pot and serves by choice. 'Sometido por su voluntad.' Remember, Ran? 'Subject by *its* will'? I don't see anything to indicate that it was any different here. What it looks more like to me is that something went wrong. Something led Clarisse—or someone—to bury her prenda in an anthill, upside down, which, for a Palera, would be like burying your mother on her head. Why would she destroy her pot? My guess is, she broke the pact. Whatever promise she made the muerto went unfulfilled. If the spirit is still here, that's why. It wants something, and what it wants now is probably what it wanted and was promised then. I think we have to find out what that is. But, first, we have to find out who the muerto is."

"Wait," said Ran. "You're saying a specific person was put into this pot?"

"Specific, yes," she said. "A person, no. It was a person once upon a time, but who we are in life is not who we become after we die. According to Congo metaphysics, human beings are composed of three interwoven faculties: the nitu, the kini, and the mwela. The nitu is the physical body, or 'death-body,' which we leave behind. The kini and the mwela, together, are the 'life-body.' The kini, which is also called the energy body, looks exactly like the nitu, but it's incorporeal. When you see a ghost, that's what it is, the kini, hanging around. The mwela is the soul, which Africans identify with breath. The mwela is immortal. At death, it goes to Mpemba to live with the ancestors. It's said that the mwela never divorces the kini, they're married eternally, but the kini can be split off, and this is the part a brujo would be most likely to put into a pot. In fact, this part most often becomes the working spirit, the ndoki de la prenda, of any nganga, whether used for good or evil. The ndoki or kini preserves some aspects of its former personality and short-term human memory, but not the real character or soul. It's equivalent to what Jungians call the shadow and is in fact identified with it. My best guess is, we're dealing with the ndoki with whom Clarisse made the pact."

"But if what it wants now is the same thing it wanted then . . ."

Everybody looked at Ran.

"Come on, people, you know what I'm saying. . . ."

"No, Ran," Claire replied. "What are you saying?"

"I'm saying whatever it wanted then led to Addie and Jarry . . . or Harlan and Clarisse . . . or *someone* out there murdered and buried in a hole. What if history's repeating?"

Claire stared him down. "You know what, Ran? You're out of your mind. You're in the middle of a full-blown episode, and I'm sorry, Shan, you're my friend and I know you mean well—I have to believe that—but this vodou bullshit is just egging him on."

"You're my friend, too, Claire," Shan replied evenly, "but this is very serious, and you don't know the first thing about it."

"And I don't want to either." She started to get up, but Marcel held her—not held, just lightly laid his hand across her arm. "What?" Claire said. "You're buying this?"

"If Shanté says it's real, I think we ought to listen."

Claire gazed into his eyes, considering.

Watching this, Ran felt as though he'd been served his liver on a plate.

"So how do you propose to do this, Shan?" said Cell. "How do you propose to get the answers to these questions?"

Shanté shrugged. "I don't have an instruction manual, Cell. Ask, would be my guess."

"Ask who?" said Claire. "The spirit? How do you pose questions to a ghost?"

"We go to the graveyard," Shanté said. "We go to the graveyard in the morning, Claire, and cross our fingers, and hope like hell they'll answer us."

FIFTY-ONE

*T*here are three bedsheets laid out on the forest floor—on the first, pine straw and cones and little ferns lifted, undisturbed, with squares of soil; on the second, paler subsoil; on the third, the grayish-yellow clay, some of which will not go back into the hole that Addie, with Old Peter's help, digs to hide the silver chest. She's meant to do this for some time, and why, suddenly, today? Who knows? Addie woke up to the honk of geese above the house, and it seemed important to delay no further. This is where they are—they've dragged the third sheet to the edge and thrown the clay into the pond (a single clod of this, a grain, can give it all away)—when they hear the low drone of an engine on the river. Sultan, Harlan's hound, begins to bark. There's a distant sound—tat . . . tat . . . ratah . . . tah . . . tat—so toylike, how could it portend anything of consequence?

When they come out on the road, there's great activity in the barnyard. Addie, for a moment, can't make heads or tails. There's something off in the perspective— it's as if she's come to the wrong house—and then she realizes an enormous boat, a ship almost, is moored at her dock, eclipsing her accustomed view of riverfront. U.S.S. Mendota she reads across the bow, and now, for the first time, she's afraid. There are men she doesn't know—black men in blue coats, with bayoneted muskets—moving here and there, striding purposefully, while her people stand and watch with troubled eyes. A small bareheaded man with a revolver stops by the dairy yard and stares in at the bony cows. After a moment's contemplation, he raises his *gun and shoots Patch in the head. Patch, who calved last spring, goes down on her hocks and knees, and then he fires again, and she collapses like a sack of rocks.*

"No," *Addie whispers. Her hand goes to her breast. Now he shoots another.* "No!" *she shouts, and starts to run. Hogs squealing, the sound of breaking glass . . . At the kitchen house, a man pulls Minda from the door and throws her to the ground. Black smoke billows from the window. They're on the house porch, too. The scene is like an anthill that's been overrun by a competing swarm.*

"What are you doing?" *Addie asks the little man, who stares at her with tranced bug eyes, red with sun and drink.* "Those cows are for our children's milk."

As though he doesn't hear, he puts the barrel to her head and pulls the trigger. Click. Click, *and* click *again.*

"Goddamn," *he says.* "Gotdamn." *He backhands her across the mouth and knocks her down, then, cursing all the while, reloads.*

When he raises the gun to fire again, Peter steps between. "You," *he says, pointing his finger in the man's face, his voice trembling with fear and outrage.* "You, I know you. You Musta Aw'ston's from Hasty Point. You let her 'lone, yeddy?"

"I ain't no one's, Daddy," *says the bug-eyed man.* "I free. Free as a frog. Free till I fool. I belong to me."

"Look here—"

Now the tat *is close and loud and big. Blown back against the fence, Peter crumples like a paper thing. Addie sees brain spatter hit the rail and drip onto its owner's cheek, the blood bright against the pale green lichen on the slat, like the scarlet berries on the partridgeberry vine. The little Negro stares at Peter, bug-eyed with wonder at his accomplishment, then, bug-eyed, at his gun, the smoking instrument. A half smile on his lips, he catches Addie's eye as though inviting her to share in the exquisiteness of what he's done, the wonder that he is. Somberly, she waits to die, but he's lost interest, or rather thinks the cows are better sport. Turning to the dairy yard again, he resumes his work, shooting down the great, slow animals, who are lowing now in terror, methodically, one by one.*

Addie, on her feet, runs toward the barn, and when she comes around the side, she finds Oliver and several others rolling tierces down the bank toward the boat. They're being held at gunpoint by Federal Negro troops, while a white officer, a stooped man with a hook nose and a lined and whiskered face, looks on. When she appears before him, frantic and disheveled, he regards her with mild curiosity. There's no surprise at all in his gray eyes. With no change of expression, he goes on observing, hands clasped behind his back as though attending a review.

"For the love of God, help me!" *she cries.* "Are you in charge?"

"I am."

"One of your men just shot my . . ." And, oh, it hits her now . . . Peter, gentle Peter, with his fragole Alpine, Peter with his cymbelines! Bending double, Addie covers her mouth, stifling something half a sob and half a scream. "My gardener. He's back there killing all our cows! Can you not stop him?"

"You'd best keep out of the way," he says, not looking at her now. "You won't be harmed unless you interfere."

"Who are you?" Addie screams. "What is your name? What are you doing with my rice?"

"James Montgomery. Colonel James Montgomery. Second South Carolina Volunteers. We're requisitioning it."

"Stealing it, you mean? How am I to feed my slaves?"

"You have no slaves, madam. We've come to liberate them."

"How, by starving them? Please. Please! I beg you. I have three hundred people here to see to. This is all the bread I have to put into their mouths. This is wrong. I see the guilt of it upon your face."

"You see what isn't there."

"Then look at me!" she shouts. "Will you not look at me? Do you not have a mother or a sister? Do you not have a wife? I am a human being, just as they are. Can you not think of them and pity me?"

And now Montgomery turns on her. "You ask for a consideration you did not extend to whose whom you enslaved. You caused this war, you people here. Do you not know what you are fighting for?"

"I'm fighting to survive!" she cries. "And for my home!"

"You fight for your home only in the second instance," he says, with the cold relish of a rhetorician, who won't deny himself the pleasure of a righteous victory in argument, even in a scene like this, "because in the first you fought to perpetuate the freedom to oppress. This rice, this barn, this house, this land—all was made or purchased with illegally extorted labor and is forfeit as fruit of the poison tree. And, no, to answer your question, I don't see you as human like my mother or my wife. You, the Southern slaveowners, brought this on yourselves and all of us, including many of my comrades, who've drenched Virginia with their blood and won't go home to see their mothers or their children or their grieving wives again. If you want pity, ask it of Almighty God. I have none to give."

"But can you not leave my Negroes something to eat?"

"I suggest you feed them beef."

With this sober quip, he turns and paces off, his hands still clasped behind his back—like a grim prelate, Addie thinks; then, hearing screams, she runs toward the house. In the library, flames are running up the ivied drapes like orange squirrels up a tree. Addie tears them down and stamps on them. Books are scattered on the floor. The partners desk has been ransacked, the drawers all out and broken. Downstairs, she can hear men shouting angrily and battering the cellar door.

Another scream. It's Tenah, from upstairs. . . . Addie finds her in the bedroom, on her bed, skirts raised, legs forced up around a man, a white staff sergeant, with muttonchops like Harlan used to have and a dimple in his chin so deep it looks as if it's been indented by a pencil that deposited its lead. His striped trousers at his ankles, he's humping her with brutal and efficient speed, while Tenah ineffectually beats his chest and bites her lip and weeps. His musket, with the mounted bayonet, leans against the bedpost, and his left fist holds a crocus sack half filled with swag.

"Get off her!" Addie shouts.

"Damn you, bitch!" Startled, he withdraws, stumbling over his dropped trousers as he tries to pull them up. "Ain't you never heard of knocking? I thought y'all was supposed to have such fine manners here."

Recovering his confidence, he laughs, swigging from a bottle of Harlan's good Málaga.

"Come here," Addie says, and Tenah, like a cat, is off the bed.

"Hold on, now, we ain't finished here."

"Tenah, go downstairs."

The sergeant smiles and shakes his head. "You ain't real obedient, are you, dear."

Noticing the sterling lady's set, he tries to put the brush into his sack, but fails to open it with both hands full. "Get over here and help." He gestures loosely with the gun.

"What's this?" With his little finger, he fishes Addie's mother's pearls out of a dish. "These'll look all right on my old woman, don't you guess?"

When Addie makes a grab, the string breaks and they ping on the floor and roll away in all directions.

"Pick 'em up," the sergeant says, in the tone of a reasonable man proffering a reasonable request.

"I won't."

He holds her stare, smiling as he takes her measure. "Put that mirror in my bag." He nods to the dressing table.

Addie picks it up and smashes it on the chair.

The punch is so hard and swift she feels her jaw unhinge, and she is lying on the floor, feeling stunned and thick. She tries to rise, but it's as if her limbs are *bound with tiny threads, like Gulliver. She thinks about the spirit pressing down on her in bed. . . . But that was just a dream. A dream . . . Is this?*

The man is on her now, ripping at her clothes, her white and purple dress. She feels his calloused hand on her bare breast and smells his breath, sweet wine and throw-up.

"What is it you think to get?" she whispers in his tufted ear. "What is it you think to get by this?"

"Shut up," he says calmly, punching her again. "Just shut up, bitch, and spread your legs."

He's in her now, and Addie turns her head away. On her face, her frown is carved as deeply as a mask's. She feels a pang of grief and pity, the sort you feel for someone else. There's a patch of sunlight on the floor, a slanted rectangle, warm and yellow, rich. It's just beyond her fingertips, and in that light, a pearl. She thinks about it, warm against her mother's skin the day she walked into the sea. There's radiance upon the top of it, and down below it casts a shadow on itself. A brilliant, checkered thing that casts a shadow on itself . . . That's what human beings are. This is the thought in Addie's mind. She's gone into a dream, and in this dream, she hears a voice she knows.

"Get off," it says.

"Nigger, wait your turn."

Now the rifle butt comes down, and the sergeant with the dimple in his chin rolls off with a deep groan.

And now, in Addie's dream, it's Jarry looking down at her. His face is large and soft.

"Is it you?" she whispers.

"I looked everywhere for you," he says. "I tried to stop it. I'm sorry. I'm so sorry."

Reaching to cover herself, her hands can't manage it. She flushes hot with shame, and he averts his eyes.

"I should not have left." Squatting on his hams, Jarry lurches forward, then sideways.

"Jarry, what is it? What's wrong?"

Falling over on his seat, he looks down at his breast, and something presses up his coat, like a finger working underneath, and then the blood begins to spread.

"That'll teach you, nig." On his knees, the sergeant withdraws the bayonet with a wet sissh.

Jarry fumbles for his sidearm, but his right arm flops. He looks at Addie with such grief and such apology; then there's a roar. The sergeant flies back against the wall, and there is Tenah with the Purdey in the door.

Jarry sits against the bedpost, with his hand over his breast like a boy making a pledge.

"Jarry?"

He opens his eyes and looks at her. There's a wet gurgling as he pants, like someone with the croup.

"Miss, the Rebs is in the yard," says Tenah.

"Quick, get some of Harlan's things."

There are shouts below, and gunfire, as they change Jarry's pants and shirt. Footsteps on the stair, and Jules Poinsett walks in with a LeMat revolver in his hand.

"They said there was one up here."

"There he lies," says Addie, nodding to the dead man.

"And who's this?"

"My steward, Jarry."

Poinsett frowns at her and then at Tenah. "Come now, it's well known hereabouts your steward ran off years ago and sided with the Yanks."

"He saved my life, Jules. Please. Are you not tired of death?"

Poinsett stares at her with a severe and monumental frown, as if making up his mind. "Your name meant something in this country once," he says, and walks out of the door.

FIFTY-TWO

*R*an's knife, put down too hard, clanked on his plate. "So, what's the plan?" he asked the others, whose chicken lay, like his, wounded, if at all, only in a polite, pro forma way. "Are we going to sit here looking glum all night, or does anybody want to hear my song?" He looked at Claire, but she declined to leap into the breach.

"I'd love to hear it," Shanté said.

Ran turned to Cell.

"Why not?" the big man said. "Let's hear your song."

In the library, he took his vintage Gibson from the thicker case. A J-45 from 1946, it had been purchased long ago in Nashville on the strip and had another life before it came to him, a life that Ransom sometimes, catching fire, fancied he could channel through the strings. With its top of proudly pick-scarred sitka spruce, its mahogany sides, the mother-of-pearl bridge dots on its rosewood frets, it was the first truly fine guitar he'd ever owned, the one he held on to through the years as a dozen others came and went, the one he still loved best. If the electric in the thinner case—a 1960 Les Paul 'Burst—was Ransom's mistress, the old acoustic was the one Claire meant when she called it—half joking . . . but only half—"the wife."

Slipping his pick from between the strings, he turns a nickel peg or two, correcting tune, and plays the first few bars experimentally. Even in his mind, Ran has yet to hear the song this way, unplugged, and has to find the stresses, reinvent the slower rhythm as he goes. After a moment, he puts the pick away and begins to finger in a style he learned from the greatest blues picker of them all, Mississippi John Hurt, whom Ransom, in his youth, paid homage to as devotedly as ever did Palero to the muerto in his pot. The old black man gave him master lessons from beyond, and it is to this heritage, this devotion, that Ransom reaches back tonight, and underneath the madcap surface, his song reveals a sadder, unexpected undertone, a blue-lit gloom like undersea, as Ransom sings:

> *"In the submarine of creation Captain Nemo*
> *can be found kicking ass and taking names.*
> *I ought to know 'cause he impressed me deeply*
> *and I attended boot camp in his brains.*
>
> *It never rains down here; there isn't any weather.*
> *On maneuvers, blind fish osculate our masks.*
> *I'd like to know their taxonomic listings,*
> *but I fear Nemo would torpedo if I asked.*
>
> *It's not that he's a tyrant or a monster—*
> *in fact, he's like a father to us all.*
> *It's just that loneliness has made his heart ferocious,*
> *and he's grown deaf to any softer call.*
>
> *When it began, nobody can remember.*
> *No doubt at the beginning: one fine day*
> *the surface world collapsed around his longing,*
> *the deep world yawned and took his life away.*
>
> *And he dove after it with righteous passion,*
> *But after twenty years he knew it wasn't there.*
> *Then he stopped caring and a change came over him:*
> *he learned to breathe the sunless element like air."*

Under the high ceilings, amid the walls of books, Ransom holds the room, reminding each of them what they all know and frequently forget, that sadness, slightly lifted, slightly shaped, is at the heart of every beauty, and loss the central subject of all art. He speaks both for the living, who are present, and for the dead, those who sat here once—who loved their lives as fervently as these do here tonight, found it as inconceivable that they might end—and they are gone. And is it any truer, is it more plausible, to say that it is intuition, something in himself that Ransom owns, than spirit voices, beings outside Ran and greater than himself, that lift him now and whisper in his ear the next verse of his song?

> *"And though we know he's mad, we don't desert him.*
> *For in a way, he's better than the rest.*
> *For he held fast in his unhappiness*
> *To the injustice we forgave so we could rest."*

However it may be, from whatever source it comes, it comes. And after all the madness of these last days, it's strange how relaxed Ran is right now, how calm, how settled in his stance. Like a marlin that's thrashed on deck and been released, he whisks his tail and vanishes into the deep. And each of them—Shanté, Cell, and Claire, especially Claire—listens with bittersweet emotion, weighing the gift that Ransom has in him against the troubled man he is.

When he's done, he lifts his head. Having done this many, many times over many, many years, Ransom isn't unaware of what their silence means. The expression on his face is that of someone who believes he's finally loved, when he's long since given up the hope of it.

"Best song you ever wrote," said Marcel Jones, the first to speak. "I have one small criticism, though. . . ."

Ransom blinked. "Lay it on me."

" 'Osculate'?"

Ran weighed it for a moment, then laughed out loud and slapped both knees. "I knew you were going to say that! Eighteen years, and I damn well knew you'd give me shit for 'osculate'!"

"I mean, how much would you really lose with 'kiss'?"

"You're right! You're absolutely right!" Ran laid the Gibson tenderly back in its case. "It's that poor-boy part of me, Marcel, the one who never finished high school. He still has to show the world he has a passable vocabulary."

"You proved it long ago," said Claire.

"That proving thing, though, Claire . . . ," Ran said, and the softness in his face was gone. "Is it ever really finished?" When she didn't answer, he flipped the lid closed with his toe. "You don't like it."

"I think it's strange and strong," she said. "There's a wildness in it I haven't heard from you in years."

His heart, that quick, was in his throat. "But—"

She shook her head. "No but. I was just thinking . . . For someone who has so much self-awareness, you can be so fucking blind, so blinded by yourself."

"And that makes me different from anybody in this room?"

"Yes, it does," she answered, clear. "And there's a side of that that's good, and another side that's very hard to live with."

And now, around them in the room, the silence falls like rain.

"I've caused some damage, Claire," he said, "I know I have, but, sitting here—me here, you there, face-to-face—I have to wonder if the person you see in the mirror can tell herself that she's caused any less. I don't see much difference."

"That would be my point."

Claire looked at him with the expression Ran remembered from his first night back, gazing in the lighted window from the yard, when he could tell she couldn't see him through her own reflection in the glass. Her solemnity was that of someone who has no sense of humor left, who's lost the ability or will to smile at pleasantries, to engage in small talk, to gladly suffer fools, someone who no longer cares to save for rainy days or mind her p's and q's, someone for whom the world has become a profoundly serious place. She was as beautiful as Ran had ever seen her, but like a solemn angel God had sent in wrath. This was the secret Claire, the one Ran feared the most and had wooed hardest, tried the hardest to appease. Her judgment, falling in his favor once, had saved him, he believed. Were it to fall against him now, Ran didn't know who, on the other side of judgment, he would be, what piece of him, if any, would be left.

"Listen, I've been thinking . . ." He flicked the case-lock shut. "It's a little late in the day, I know, but I've been going through this, and I think Cell should have a cut of the song royalties."

"How about me?" Claire fired back. There was no hesitation. Not a trace.

Ran smiled, hoping he was supposed to, knowing, deep down, he was not. "It's sort of the same thing, Claire, isn't it?" he said. "What's in my pot—so to speak—is in your pot, too."

She started to retort, but Ransom cut her off before she could. "But okay, okay, whatever, you, too. You guys tell me what you think is fair."

"How about fifty percent for you," Claire said, "twenty-five apiece for Cell and me."

Ran smiled, but it was slow to come. "Gee, Claire," he said, carefully modulating his tone, "from the point of view of strict equity, that seems a little steep."

"All right," she rejoined, "'from the point of view of strict equity,' what do you consider fair?"

"Something more along the lines of ninety percent for me, the two of you split ten."

Claire smiled bitterly. "You think it would be number one if the title was 'Talk Is Cheap'?"

"How about something in between?" Shanté put in. "Ran says ninety, you say fifty. How about seventy-fifteen-fifteen?"

"That's way too much." Having set out to be generous, Ran felt the old resistance rising now.

"I think it's not enough," Claire said. "You wouldn't even have retained mechanicals if I hadn't put Gruber's feet to the fire."

"That's true," said Ran. "You negotiated that. Why don't you take twenty, Cell gets ten."

"Sixty-forty."

"Actually, guys," Cell said, "I don't want anything."

"He'll take it, though." Claire kept her eyes fixed on Ransom's as she put her hand on Marcel's arm. Ran stared at it, Claire's hand, pale, on Cell's black arm, and he could feel it like a brand searing his own skin. His vision blurred. He went away. For a moment, he did not know where he was or who he *is*. When he came back, he said, "Why don't you just take it all?"

"No," Claire said. "You don't get to go there anymore with me. You say you want to be grown-ups. This is what grown-ups do. Sixty-five for you; for us, seventeen point-five apiece."

She held out her hand, and Ransom stared at it. "How much for 'kiss'?"

"Ask Cell. He came up with it."

Ran looked at Cell, and Cell looked back with grave, deep eyes, and just said, "'Kiss' is free."

"Ho, shit . . ." Reclining in his chair, Ran pushed his hair back with both hands. "Where is this all going, guys? I have a real bad feeling. Where is this supposed to end?"

No one answered.

"Daddy?"

They all turned and there was Hope, in cat pajamas, halfway down the stairs. "I'm scared, Daddy," she said. "Will you read a book to me?"

Ransom, with a flight of desperation in his eyes, looked at Claire, at Hope, and back at Claire again.

"Can you handle it?" Claire asked.

He took his daughter in his arms and started up the stairs.

FIFTY-THREE

*I*n the kitchen, as they cleaned the plates, Claire cut the water off and turned. "Go ahead and say it, Shan."

"You're a grown woman, Claire. You don't need advice from me. Ransom is a pain, and life is short."

"All true."

"I'll be on the porch," said Cell.

Claire looked at him, but that was all, so he just went.

"Anything I tell you," Shanté said, "is probably something you've already told yourself. . . ."

"No doubt. But?"

Shanté laid the flatware in a tangled heap. "Okay, what worries me? And this isn't about Ransom, Claire. . . . Right now, I'm thinking about you and Hope and Charlie and your family, all right?"

"What worries you is . . . ," Claire prompted with a stony face.

"I don't know exactly what you're feeling, but I can form an educated guess. I've seen it many times, Claire, I've been in the same place myself. . . ."

"Go on."

"You start out at a pitch so high you think no one else can grasp your feelings. You've stepped through a magic door and found a love that no one else has ever felt before on earth. And maybe it's true. Maybe once or twice in a thousand or a million times those feelings last, and maybe you and Cell are among the blessed. But speaking for me personally, Claire? I've rarely seen it play out that way. In fact, I've never seen it once. What I've seen is people flying, who crash and fall back, burning, to the ground. I've seen the white heat pass into mere warmth. And the light, the brilliant light, Claire, gathers shadows. Sometimes it takes a year, sometimes two, but chances are, you won't die at the peak like Juliet and Romeo. You'll come back down. Most people do. Then they find themselves where you and Ran are now, with 'issues,' in a different marriage to a different person identical to the marriages they left. For most people, Claire, this kind of passion is a dream they wake up from. And when you do, after that year or two, your children will look at you with something broken in them, honey, something you won't live long enough to ever put back right. Your life and theirs will be in pieces, and you'll have wounded the larger Self you truly are, which is not just you, Claire. I don't mean to preach, but there's your ego—it's not a dirty word, and I don't mean it in that way. . . . It has legitimate needs you have a legitimate right to seek, but your Self, Claire, your *Self* is something larger. It includes your children and your family and tribe and your community, and it includes your husband, too. And if you act against that, Claire, if you wound it, my worry is, you'll be diminished, too."

"So you can never leave," Claire said.

Shanté went to her and took her hands. Still holding them, they sat down at the table face-to-face. "People can and do, but the results are always mixed, baby, mixed at best. More generally, they're fucked up. Listen, Claire, I've known you a long time. I know your heart is good and that you're doing what you think is right. But there's one more thing I want to tell you. There's an image in Jung somewhere. It may not mean anything to you, but it's meant a lot to me, and what it is is Jesus on the cross. Jung says the deeper meaning of the crucifixion is that it represents the ego on the tree of Self. It's nailed up there and stretched and racked, and the purpose of that suffering is to make it grow, to make the ego grow to accommodate the larger thing that's underneath, the larger thing we are, and that's what human life is, Claire. That is human life on earth. Try to escape it, try to climb back down, you shirk your fate and end up queer and smaller than you should have been."

"What if it's my Self, though, Shan?" Claire said. "What if it's my Self that's on the tree?"

Shanté gave a sober blink. "Well, baby, that's another matter, then.

That's a wholly different thing. But, Claire, don't make him lose the children, too. Because, if you do . . ."

"If I do, then what? You see where he is. What am I supposed to do?"

Shanté shook her head. "I just don't know what will be left to hold him to the ground. I really don't."

Claire started to reply, but there in the doorway, like a spirit, suddenly was Ran.

"I think you'd better come upstairs," he said.

"What's the matter?"

"Both of you," he said.

In the bedroom, Hope was sitting against her headboard's painted scene: a little girl in yellow mud boots chasing down a windblown kite. Her face was bright, excited. There was a disturbing avidity in her expression that was not like any four-year-old's. "I know what it wants," she said.

"What what wants, Hope?" Claire asked, sitting on the bed.

"The little animal that lives inside me," she replied with her bright face.

"Do you mean your dog?"

"I don't know, Mommy. I can't see it anymore."

Claire closed her daughter—softly, calmly, firmly—in her arms. "What does it want?"

"Meat and grapes," Hope said. "It wants to drink my blood, and when I die it will leave my body. Sometimes it bites me, but it doesn't mean to, it doesn't know it's me."

Ran stood beside the bed with the expression people wear in waiting rooms.

"And do you talk to it?" Claire said.

"No, I can't see it."

"Does it talk to you?" Shanté asked.

"No, it can't see me. But I hear it singing sometimes."

"What does it sing?" said Shan.

"Rarrr-rarr-rarrr," Hope answered, "rarr-ruh-rarr-rarr-rarr . . ."

Claire held her tighter in her arms. "It's going to be all right."

"Will you sleep with me tonight?"

"Yes, sweetie, Mommy will stay. I have to talk to Daddy first."

"Leave it on, Daddy, okay?" Hope said as Ran reached for the light.

"Okay." He brushed her hair back from her forehead and planted a kiss there.

"What happened?" Claire asked, in the hall.

"I don't know," Ran said. "We were just reading."

"I didn't tell you this before," Shan said. "But in prendas of Zarabanda, the muerto always receives an animal helper. . . . A black dog."

Ran and Claire both stared at her, and then Claire said, "Excuse us, Shan, I need to speak to Ran."

"Listen," she said as soon as Shan was gone, "I've had as much of this as I can stand. I'm going to take the kids and leave tonight."

"And go where?"

"I don't know," she said. "To a hotel, I guess. I don't want them exposed to this any further."

"But they've already been exposed. Did you see what just happened?" He pointed to Hope's door.

"What are you saying, Ransom? That our daughter is possessed?"

"I don't *know*, Claire," he replied. "I only know all this is coming from the pot, and we have to put our faith in Shan to tell us what to do."

"Bullshit, Ran. I don't think the pot has anything to do with anything. And there is no 'us.' There's only you. If anything is causing this, it's you, that's who: you, Ransom. You're higher than a kite, and I'm, frankly, scared of you, and scared for Hope and Charlie, too."

He gripped her arm. "You think I'd ever hurt you? You think I'd ever hurt our kids?"

"Let go of me," she said.

He did. "Okay. Go, then, Claire. By all means, go. Teach them their dad's a dangerous lunatic they need to be protected from. Teach them his friends of color—your friend, too—who practices a religion different from the one they taught you at St. Michael's is a freak to be avoided at all costs. They may as well start learning the important lessons early."

"You think they don't already know? Their hearts are broken, Ran. You broke them. You, with all your craziness."

"You bitch," he said, and tears were running down his cheeks. "It's not just me. We're all involved in this. Every goddamn one of us, including Cell and Shan. After everything we've been through, you can't do this one thing for me?"

"What, Ransom? What one thing?"

"Stay and see this through."

She was clearly torn. "If I stay, Cell does, too."

"Where?" asked Ransom. "Where does Cell stay, Claire?"

She hesitated, and her face was firm. "He can stay downstairs in the guest room."

"Are you sure? You don't want to put me there, and have him here up-stairs in the master bedroom?"

"Ransom . . ." Her expression softened. She put her hand on his arm now. "Ransom, listen . . ."

"Are you fucking him?" he said. "Because if you are, Claire, if you are . . ." He held his finger in her face, and Claire stood like a deer gazing up into the crosshairs.

"Then what?" Her voice was soft.

Ransom turned away and didn't walk toward the stairs. He ran.

FIFTY-FOUR

The winter of 1864 is bleak and some say biblical throughout the South. In Charleston, where once there were gay Secession balls and suppers, a Secession something somewhere every night, there are consolation parties now, where people drink and sing the Psalms till dawn, and women there, formerly considered proper, are fast like no place else.

But for Addie, at Wando Passo, it is during this time—as Jarry slowly convalesces from his punctured lung, as he lies in Percival's old place, on Percival's old chaise, and listens to her read until he falls asleep (they are on "The Prelude" now, having come, unspokenly, upon this common ground, which is, to them, a kind of Psalm) . . . It's now that Addie has the thought she sometimes whispers to herself, but never speaks aloud: My true life has begun. And why does she not speak? Perhaps because it is with him, her dead husband's brother, a Negro. Perhaps because it is so far from social Charleston and friends she knows would not forgive the feelings she has now, friends whose opinions she once cared about and even feared. Perhaps because it is without the carriages and jewels, the clothes from Mrs. Cummings's shop. Perhaps because it is so small and humble, Addie's life, in this quiet library, beside this fire, by the smoky light of tallow candles Addie made herself from the rendered fat of her own hogs . . . She could never have imagined any of these things, nor how happy she would be. But so she is, and so it has turned out to be. Yet there remains, despite their growing closeness, a reticence on Jarry's part that Addie doesn't fully understand or know how to relieve.

It's the fifteenth of December, a frosty morning, when Jarry rises and accompanies her to the fields for the first time. Oliver and his crew are replacing a broken trunk, washed out by a high sea tide. It's thirty-degree weather at eight o'clock when they arrive, but by eleven, nearing fifty. She and Jarry stand on a board atop the muddy dike and watch the men—waist-deep in cold black water—float the new trunk, a log of hollowed cypress, into place and seat it as the tide ebbs. They've cut three flatloads of fresh, good mud, and it becomes a race to pack the gate and firm it up before the tide comes in. Seeing need and, finally, unable to resist, Jarry grabs a hoe and joins them in the water over Addie's protest. Then, over his, she joins him. All work at a fevered pace while the river rises, rises. They're jubilant when it holds. Around a fire, they eat their midday dinner out of piggins and remove their boots and dry their stockings, and then Addie sends the crew home. She and Jarry walk the fields, where she's had the plowmen turning in the winter rye and oats.

"What did these fields yield this year?" he asks.

"Not quite twenty bushels to the acre."

He turns to her. "Not quite twenty . . ."

"Seventeen, I think," she says reluctantly. "I've often thought about your forty bushels, Jarry. Frankly, I fail to see how it's possible, but I'll do whatever you suggest."

He walks down a row and pulls a weed that doesn't yield. He turns to her. "May I show you something?"

Sweeping aside the new-turned dirt, Jarry shows her a foot-wide swath of rock-hard clay the plow has missed. There's a swath like this on each side of the furrow he points out, as there is, skillfully concealed, on every furrow in the twenty-acre field.

"You see what they've done," he tells her, in a tone that's settled, gentle, unsurprised. "They've plowed half the square—less than that, a third—in a third the time, and done a third the job and covered up the rest to make it look as though they'd done it all."

"I didn't know."

"How would you?" Jarry says. "They're perfectly aware you didn't. They've taken deliberate advantage. It makes me, frankly, angry."

"What are we to do?"

"One option is to punish them. That's what they expect, what they're accustomed to. Do this, and things will go on as before, the way they always have."

"What would you do?"

He frowns and walks away, in conflict.

"Jarry, if I haven't said this, I've often thought, and felt, this land is far more yours than mine. Your father owned it. You worked it almost thirty years, as I have done for not quite three. Even by that measure, you've ten times more right to it than I."

"It's yours in law."

"What is that to you and me?"

They hold each other's eyes across the distance now, as afternoon declines, and she
goes up to him and takes his ice-cold hands. "One day, Jarry, I shall have my aunt's
Charleston house. I shall have her things. I'll be well off, if not rich, and there's a
rightness, an entitlement, I feel to have what's been passed down by my people through
our line. I'd be hurt and disappointed not to receive these things. By that same measure, that same rightness, I feel Wando Passo is and should be yours. You must believe
me. I, too, have given thought to this. Were you to tell me now, 'Addie, there are three
hundred people on this place and each of them, including you, should have the three-
hundredth part,' I'd have the papers drawn."

"I wouldn't accept that for myself."

"What, then, would you accept?"

"All right," he says, and now he paces off. "All right . . ." He's agitated now,
intense, when he turns back. "There are eleven hundred acres, give or take, at Wando
Passo. If it were mine? If it were me?"

"Yes?"

"Beard Island contains four hundred acres. Four hundred and eighteen, I believe.
Except for the two squares on the creek, it's mostly pineland. There's good timber there,
and pasturage. The soil is rich." He paces toward her, and away again, and Addie feels
her heart begin to lift, with what, she hardly knows. "If this place belonged to me?"

"Yes?"

"I'd cede it to the people in the street. No, I'd sell it to them for a dollar, so they
might possess the whole in fee. I'd have it surveyed, Addie. I'd have it platted out in
lots. If there are fifty families in the quarters now . . . ?"

"Something like . . ."

"And perhaps the same number living by themselves?"

"About."

"I'd assign the families five-acre lots, the individuals two or three, however it
works out. These, I'd assign by lottery, so that no one should be unfairly advantaged
over anybody else. Out of this, I should reserve a common area along the riverfront.
The eighteen acres? There would be a wharf, a church, a school, a dry goods store,
whatever may be needful. Those who wish to leave might sell their parcels to those
who choose to stay. I should allow them to remain in present quarters till they're prepared to build their homes. When they move, I should allow them to tear down the
cabins and salvage what they can in terms of boards and doors and fittings for reuse.
What more materials they need, they shall supply themselves with timber from the
land they clear or profit from the sale of it. And all this shall be paid for out of rice."

"Which they shall rent?"

"Exactly. You shall continue to own the squares," he says, *"and they shall do the labor, just as they do now. You'll furnish land and seed rice, tools and teams, which you will also feed, and half the profit shall be yours, the other half to them. Only, Addie, listen. . . . Though you shall have but half of what you have and had before, there'll be no more of this. . . ."* He kicks the turned dirt in the row. *"No more of this subversion, this resistance. Instead of half this field, the third, they'll plow it all. And so, instead of all of seventeen and twenty bushels to the acre, you'll have the half of forty and forty-five, and they'll have a stake in making every field bear every grain of rice it can. Each man's and woman's participation in the profits will be according to the hours they put in, the work they do, and for the first time, they'll have homes on land they own. They'll buy their teams of oxen next, and then a cow, then a horse and buggy. As they prosper, so will you. And those, like Paul and Wishy, with a trade? They'll build homes while the homeowners work the fields, and they'll be paid in bartered rice, and so with all of them—the carpenters for building, the boatmen for hauling freight, the butterers and poultriers for buttering and poultrying, and there will be enough. And Clarisse . . . She's Father's child as much as I."*

"That's so," Addie concedes, but something in her stiffens now.

"If it were me, Addie, I'd give her title to the Cuban property."

"Yes," she says. *"Yes,"* says Addie, with relief.

"That's where she belongs. She can live there handsomely. I have no wish for it."

"Nor I."

"This is the dream I've long had in my heart."

"And us?" she asks. *"What are we to be to each other in this scheme?"*

"I don't know," he answers. *"I suppose you'll own the seven hundred acres that remain. I suppose I'll run it and be paid a wage."*

"That's not acceptable to me," she says. *"I think Wando Passo should be yours."*

"That does not sit right with me."

"What does?"

"Half to you and half to me."

"Then let us have the papers drawn."

"We can't draw papers till the laws have changed. But I'll take your hand on it."

"Then here it is."

And in that frozen, half-plowed field this afternoon, December fifteenth, 1864, while the light is fading, as the sunset comes, bloodred, in a haunting winter sky with *tones of lavender and palest green, they stand face-to-face, with cold-flushed cheeks and watering eyes, and shake with hands like icicles. Then they go. Their boots crackle the thin ice, and Jarry helps her as she leaps the quarter ditch. They climb the dike and paddle home and light the lamp.*

And what Addie did not imagine either, what she could never have anticipated, is that it would be this—not some soulful look exchanged over a book of poems, but a handshake in a field, a contract, honor made and bound, that would sweep away his final reticence, that love would come from this. But so it is.

As they share their quiet supper, Jarry puts aside his fork. "I must tell you something, Addie. . . ."

"Yes?"

"There's a feeling in my heart tonight, a fullness I have never . . ."

"Dearest!" She goes to him and takes the chair beside his own.

"I've never known before," he says. "I've had feelings for you, Addie, almost from the start, and I've felt, or hoped, that you had some for me."

"I have. You know I have."

"But what I didn't know, what I did not believe, deep down, till now, was that there could be justice . . . justice. . . . I can't put in simpler words what that is to me. . . ."

"I know what justice means."

"I know my father loved me, I know he loved as deeply as he could, but he could never give me, Addie, what you've given me today, and a part of me has been in pain and bleeding over it, all this time, all these many years. I can't recall a time that I was ever happy without some sorrow mixed in it, but tonight for the first time . . ."

"Tonight?"

He smiles and shakes his head. "It's gone. If I should only live to see this done, I'll die a happy man."

"Do you know what I feel?" she asks.

"What?"

"All my life, since I was young, I've been waiting for something, Jarry, waiting for my true life to start, and it has, it did long ago. . . . There it was in front of me, and it was you, you, Jarry, all along. . . . All I could think was it was a bewitchment. I'm so sorry for my blindness."

"If you were blind, then so was I," he says. "It doesn't matter now. I love you as I've loved no one, as I shall love only one time."

"And so it is for me."

She holds out her hand—there's no need for more—and they go upstairs to bed. And as Addie blows the candle out tonight, and on the succession of nights that follow this and seem that they will never end, what she comes to in herself is that the wisdom of the girl of seventeen—which said Evangeline must wait for Gabriel however long it takes, no matter what—is finally truer than the wisdom of the bride of thirty-three that said get on with it and live. And no one taught her this—not social Charleston, not her aunt, not Mme Togno's school. Addie learned this lesson for herself.

And Christmas comes. She sits on the piazza, hands folded in her lap, as Jarry talks and tells the people the agreement they have reached. They're solemn as they listen, but that night in the quarters it is Jubilee. . . . And New Year's Day, when they walk the squares after the plowmen leave, there are no weeds left, no unturned earth between the rows. And the ewes lamb in February—there are thirty-six!

And on April thirteenth, a Thursday, finally comes the news—Lee, gallant Lee, has surrendered at Appomattox Court House. At intervals through that sad day, the tidings come—Selma captured . . . Mobile . . . Joe Johnston has surrendered his command. And, then, oh, at breakfast, Lincoln dead, and Seward . . . shot! Rumors spread that every man above the rank of captain in the Confederate army will be hanged, but the smuggled papers out of Baltimore say Beecher pleads for mercy on the South. And as the world outside the gate collapses into ruin, within, the April rice is clayed, the herring run upstream, the dikes erupt in flower—violets, blackberries, the blue and yellow jessamine. The women sow, walking with that lovely swing they have, down the rows, bent over, their skirts hiked, singing as they go.

And in Maytime, when the rice is under the Long Water, coming into milk, in the time of the singing of birds, one morning Addie sees something different in the dressing table mirror, and she looks down, both hands on her stomach, realizing what is there. She's four months pregnant when the harvest starts, and they go through the fields with reap-hooks, tying up the cocks with wisps and leaving them to dry tonight before they tote them to the flats.

Through that spring and summer, the roads are full of men, straggling back home from Virginia, barefooted, some of them, with nothing to eat except a pocketful of parched corn, if that. They're all thin and bearded, scarecrow men with haunted stares, who look as if they've seen too much ever to smile or be put right again. Many make their way up the allée and stand on the piazza, caps doffed, and ask if they can work for food or spend the evening in the barn. They're never turned away. One afternoon, though, one late September afternoon, as Addie walks up from the river with her alpenstock, in her new, loose frock, she sees such a man, and something in his aspect stops her. Bearded, tall and thin, in threadbare clothes and a worn hat, he's no different from the hundred others who've passed this way, but, unlike them, he doesn't wait on the piazza or in the yard, holding his doffed hat. He's in the family graveyard, where a stranger has no business being, staring at the stones a stranger has no business seeing, staring quite specifically, quite fixedly, at one in particular. And though his back is turned, Addie, after telling herself it cannot be, thinks she knows this stranger and what his interest in that gravestone is.

FIFTY-FIVE

*O*pening the book of Wordsworth's poems, the one with the green feather that tumbled from the shelf his first night back, Ran's eye lit on a verse:

> *The old man still stood talking by my side;*
> *But now his voice to me was like a stream*
> *Scarce heard; nor word from word could I divide;*
> *And the whole body of the man did seem*

"Like one whom I had met with in a dream . . ." The words rose up in him from some deep place, and Ran spoke them aloud, eyes closed, and checked the text, and they were right, and he felt gooseflesh on his arms.

How hard is that to guess, though, Nemo pointed out, *that "seem" would lead to "dream"?*

"True," Ran said, deflating.

The button, though, was real.

When he opened the top drawer, however, the object in the pencil-well, though round and nickel-sized, didn't say OshKosh. It wasn't even made of tin, but mother-of-pearl, like the bridge dots on his old guitar.

Poor boy, you wanted so badly to believe, didn't you? You wanted magic to attend. All a dream, Ran, all a dream. Nothing exists but empty space and you. . . .

Too demoralized to contest the point, Ran took the reading-glasses
case without the reading glasses from the drawer. As he rolled the joint, a
chimp, beaned by a falling coconut, let out a screech on the computer
screen and thudded, hard, to earth.

"You and me, my brother," Ran said through clenched teeth as he held
his toke. Throwing up the window, he listened to the sash weights rocket
down their beaten grooves, and blew his smoke into the night.

In the distance, a whippoorwill cried out, and, farther off, a freight.

Only minimally anesthetized by the first hit, he turned on the TV, restlessly surfing till he came to a rerun of *Saturday Night Live*. After a few skits,
Eddie Murphy came on in a preposterous Uncle Remus beard, the old routine about white liberals attending summer camp down south, where they
pay to pick cotton and receive lashes from Negro overseers. Stoned now, finally, Ran began to laugh a bit, and then it built and built, till he was pealing great guffaws, swiping spilled ashes from his thighs.

At this juncture, Marcel appeared from the guest room down the hall.

"Am I keeping you awake?"

"No, I was just looking for—"

"Claire? Sorry, no, it's only me."

"Some towels," Cell said, "actually."

Ran made an exaggerated comic shrug. "Don't have any on me. Come
sit down, though. Smoke this chub with me."

"I think I'll pass."

"Come on, Cell, you're always passing," Ran coaxed, inhaling, speaking
through clenched teeth. "Don't decline my hospitality. You can sit down
and smoke a joint with me, can't you? For old times' sake?" When he released the hit, his smile, if anything, had brightened, but menace flashed
through the hilarity, running none too deep.

Marcel seemed unwilling to decline. "I'll sit for a couple of minutes,
but on the joint, no thanks."

"Fair enough," said Ran. "Pour yourself a drink. There's some of
Clive's sipping whiskey on the cart. Do you know this one?"

"I remember it," Cell said, glancing at the screen.

"Funny as hell, isn't it?"

Cell shrugged and took a sip.

"Come on," Ran said. "If Murphy can laugh at it, why can't you?"

"I guess, after all, we don't all think alike."

Ran's expression sobered now. "So, what, I'm having another cracker flashback? This is racist, too?"

"I don't know that it's racist," Marcel replied. "I just don't find it funny."

"Why not?"

"There's too much pain in it."

"But comedy comes out of pain, Cell—isn't that what they say?"

"Maybe so. But if your mother gets murdered, you don't laugh at murdering-your-mother jokes. If your child gets abducted by a pedophile, dead-baby jokes may not make you roll."

"But your mother wasn't murdered," Ran rejoined. "Your baby wasn't killed. You didn't sweat on a plantation picking cotton. Neither did your parents or your grandparents or theirs or, probably, even theirs. What's the statute of limitations on this, Cell? Where's all this pain coming from in you?"

"That's two questions, Ran. On the first, I guess it's as long—at least as long—as white Southerners regretting the loss of the Civil War. That was a four-year episode in their history they're still carrying remorse about. Slavery went on for two hundred and fifty. I don't see the statute expiring anytime soon. And on the pain question, it's not about me specifically."

"Why not?" Ran asked, sitting straighter in his seat. "When does it get specific, Cell? See, this is where I fall down every time. I don't know how to play the role you want to cast me in, the Abstract Oppressive White Man. I don't know how to treat you as the Abstract Black Man Oppressed. I think political correctness makes people scared and too self-conscious to act naturally, to just behave like human beings to each other. To me, that's where racism ends, when it finally gets specific, down to you and me, right here, right now on this sofa, man-to-man and face-to-face."

Cell put down his drink. "Say what you have to say."

Ran put down the joint and leaned forward, elbows on his knees. "We've known each other a long time, Marcel."

"True."

"We've been something in each other's lives."

"Okay."

"There was a time I believe you cared for me, and I know there was when I did for you."

"I'm not disputing anything you've said so far."

"I don't have the credibility to preach. I'm as flawed a human being as

God probably ever made, Marcel, but I still think relationships come with obligations. If I haven't always been the best at keeping mine, I came down here to turn over a new leaf, and however it may look to anybody else, I'm trying the best way I know how. I have a wife upstairs, Marcel. We've been married nineteen years. I have two small children sleeping in their beds. I'm asking you to put yourself in my shoes, Cell."

"Like you did for me?"

"Didn't I?" said Ran. "If I didn't, I'm sorry. I apologize, Marcel. I'm trying now. And sitting here beside you, trying, I think I see someone who'd be desperately unhappy if another man came between him and his family, between him and his wife. I'm torn up about what's happening, Cell. I'm putting my cards on the table and reaching out to you as an old friend, as another man, as a human being, because in my heart, Cell, I believe that what we have in common is greater than our differences, and I think, in your heart, you know it, too."

"I don't need you to tell me what I know."

"You know," said Ransom, firm.

"So what if I do?" Cell said. "So what if what we have in common, deep down, is greater than our differences, Ran, but it's so deep that, on a daily basis, it has no practical effect, whereas the differences are right there on the surface, hot and vexed? The truth is, I didn't create your problems, the ones you're mired in now, and I don't have a solution to a single one. What you really want is for me to put my happiness aside to rescue you from the unhappiness you've caused yourself, and why should I do that for you, Ran? Why should I do that to Claire or to myself? It isn't going to happen, and I'm not going to sit here and let you bait me into getting involved in more of your bad dramas."

"That's right," said Ransom, sitting back. "I understand, Marcel. You want to withdraw from me, to disentwine and disengage and sever the connection and tell yourself, 'That Ransom Hill, he's so retrograde, such a redneck fuckup, he's not really human in the same way I am or Claire is. So, we don't have to treat him according to that old notion, the Golden Rule'—remember that one?—'as we'd wish to be treated in his place. It doesn't matter how much pain we make him feel.' But isn't that where your hurt comes from, Cell, that once upon a time someone did that very thing to you and yours?"

"Listen, Ransom—"

"No, you listen to me, Marcel. When I'm finished, you can talk. Once upon a time I screwed you. Tonight, Claire asked for your seventeen-point-five apiece, and I agreed. If that's what it takes to make it right, so be it. That's the one specific wrong that I'm aware I ever did you. The year you toured with RHB, you were making seventy-five or eighty grand when that was serious money. You had a nice apartment with a river view. I know you're carrying some hurt around, but you know, Cell, sitting here, face-to-face and man-to-man, you know in your heart of hearts that if we took the sum of all your days on earth and weighed them in the scales beside the sum of mine, it wouldn't even be a contest, you're the happier and more blessed between us two. So what more can I do for you? What more do you want? I think I've gone as far as I can go. I'm not threatening you, I'm just laying down my cards. I think we've reached the line, Marcel. Here it is, right here." And Ransom drew it on the sofa now, down the middle.

"Yes, black people were oppressed, and I regret it, Cell," he said. "If any of my forebears profited from slavery, I don't see how. But I still wish for your sake, and Shan's, and her mother's, and everyone's that history had come down differently. It didn't, though. The Indians were oppressed as well. They went through genocide. So did the Jews and Palestinians. A long time ago, in England, my people, the Saxons, got their asses kicked by the Norman French, who used to draw and quarter them for stealing deer to feed their raggedy-ass kids. The Romans enslaved the tribes in ancient Gaul, and the Visigoths sacked Rome and led them out in chains. History is full of insults and injustice, and it's no comfort to you, but one day being a black man in America won't mean any more to your descendants than being a Saxon means to me. I think that day is coming soon, Marcel. It may not be in your lifetime. Just like one day they'll have a cure for my disease, and I won't live to see it either, Cell, which is why I feel I know, a little bit, what it is to stand inside a black man's shoes. My particular form of slavery is biochemical, it's in my brain."

"It's not the same," said Cell.

"Why not?"

"No one did that to you, Ran. No human being or group of human beings exploited you for their self-interest or deprived you of your liberty or caused your suffering through malice."

"Maybe not," Ran said, "but, sitting here, staring into your eyes, Marcel, I'm going to tell you I think suffering is suffering, whether it's caused by human beings, by God, by nothing at all, or just the fuck because. I think what I've been through, specifically, is as grievous as anything you have to weigh beside it in the scales. But, see, Cell, here's the other thing that I believe. You with your grievances, me with my mine, we both feel singled out and specially fucked, but the truth is we're no different from anybody else. Here's the secret, Cell. I'm stoned and probably crazed, but what I think is this: human life is a condition of oppression, all of it—black, white, red, brown, yellow, all the same. I can't prove it, Cell, but just lately now I've come to think that's why we're here on earth, to experience this condition of oppression and to seek the secret of release—even if we never find it, even if we only get partway. That's why Keith Richards and Mick and John and Paul heard the blues and got the message. They didn't need a black translator to break the code, Marcel, they understood it in their bones, because they'd suffered, too. Their people suffered in the mines and in the mills, like mine, and I'm not saying working-class rage and misery in Liverpool or Bagtown is the same as slavery. It's not. The two do not equate. But there's a common thread. So, when Robert Johnson and the Reverend Gary Davis and Muddy and Son House and all the others played, those skinny white kids in Liverpool and Muscle Shoals heard it, Cell. Deep inside the prison of the twelve-bar blues, they heard that yearning spirit, rattling the cage and seeking to break free, and they brought it to a million, and, after them, to millions more. That's why those little girls on *Sullivan*—remember them?—the ones standing at the barricades in '64 when the Beatles came to town, that's why they wept and tore their clothes. The Beatles showed them, for the first time, what human life might be, which they learned from black people, who brought it out of Africa, and those children underwent conversion, Cell, they had a religious experience by proxy for the rest of white America. Now it's all the fuck mixed up, mixed up in you, mixed up in me, mixed up in my wife and in my children up there sleeping in their beds. And I, for one, am happy, so goddamn happy that it is. That's it, Marcel. That's all I know. Human life is a condition of oppression, and religion is the search for the release. Everyone alive is after the same thing—it's our commonness, and I believe it's greater than our differences. And that's why, however singular it seems to you, your pain is comprehensible to me: because I've felt my own.

"Now you try feeling me. Remembering there was a time when I loved you and you loved me, let's take the race card off the table and level down the playing field and turn the scoreboard back. It's zero to zero, Cell. Now let's make it specific. Once upon a time I stole your line. Tonight I gave you seventeen-point-five to rectify. Now I want back what you stole from me."

"That's a good speech, Ran," Cell said. "There's some of it I agree with, and some I don't. But if you want to make it personal, here goes. I loved Claire all those years—years before you even met. I joined the band because of her, and I never tried to get between you. Never. That's why I left RHB—a fact that, despite all your fellow feeling, never dawned on you. Fuck 'Talking in My Sleep.' I didn't give a shit about the song, and I don't now. It was watching Claire throw herself at you and watching you hurt her, watching you mess up again and again and again, the same way every time, which is what you still don't get. It's what I object to in everything you said. See, Ran, black people will get over slavery when they decide it's done, not you. The Jews will put the Holocaust behind them when they decide it's time, not because you or anybody else is tired of listening to them kvetch. This is like a central thread that runs through all you say. You somehow think it's about you and should be subject to your will and your decision. But it's not. The same is true with Claire. You had nineteen years to get it right, and whatever the statute of limitations is for me, for her it's finally run out. See, Ran, her heart and her affections belong to Claire and Claire alone—not you, not me. So, even if I thought you deserved a second chance, or an eleventh, or a twenty-fifth, she's not mine to give you back. Even if I wanted to, Ransom. And I don't."

Cell left his drink, sweating, where it was and walked out of the room, and Ransom sat there for some time, listening to laughter swell the sound track. He could no longer follow what was going on on-screen. *But now his voice to me was like a stream scarce heard, nor word from word could I divide. . . .* The lines ran through his head as the figures flitted past like ghosts.

Eventually, seeking deeper solace, he went to the stereo. Flipping through CDs, he knocked a stack of jewel cases to the floor. There on top was his most recent effort, *A Stranger to Myself,* already two years old. Cross-legged on the floor, he opened it and read the liner notes:

One day you hear a grinding in the works, a rent opens in the bedrock, you peer down, mesmerized, into the molten stuff. You laugh and scoop

*the magma up. Your hands don't burn. You stomp in it like a bad child in
a puddle in the rain; you wash your face with it and run your fingers
through your hair. Then you collect, you collect in glasses, buckets, Mason
jars. You fill and fill and return over and over to the well.*

He wrote this at the beginning of the bad time in New York. He was
already driving the cab, but it had snowed the night before and Ransom
didn't go to the garage. Instead, he sat up all night writing, not even really
knowing what it was, and then at 6:15 the house began to stir. There was
no milk, no formula for Charlie, who was eight weeks old, and Claire
peeked in and asked him to go, and Ransom, not unwilling, said, "Just let
me finish up," and then the next line came:

*And eventually you start to weary, though it itself, the stuff, is inex-
haustible and boils up still, yet you are only human—you've forgotten
this temporarily, but you remember now. And as you tire, your hands begin to burn, they crisp and blacken like Cajun snapper in a skillet seared
by Paul Prudhomme. Still you collect, more and more, as much as you
can bear, knowing the hour is late and there will be no more.*

The next thing he knew, it was five after seven, and he heard the locks
rattling on the front door, heard Claire say something cross to Hope, heard
them bumping and banging down the stairs of their fourth-floor walkup,
saw them emerge on the unshoveled sidewalk. Claire glared up toward the
window as she wrestled the double stroller up the steps and put the children,
bundled in their snowsuits, into it, and set out for Gristede's, plowing virgin
trail. And Ransom, in his T-shirt and his boxers, knew he ought to rush
downstairs and take his part, but the image was right there, right there. . . .

*And eventually you fall down, dumbfounded, and gaze at the sky in a
bereft, demoralized exhaustion, and where your hands and arms were are
now only smoking cauterized stumps. And as you gaze your vacant gaze,
the grinding in the works recurs, the rent that opened in the bedrock closes
back. And this is all there is.*

*The next day or the day after or the following year when you come out
of your torpor, you gaze at it on your bedside table. The magma has cooled
now, it's clear like moonshine in a jar. You raise it to your lips, you taste,*

*and, yes, you think, there's something wild and strange in it. A little star-
burst winks at you. This is all there is. You pass the jar to others who will
tell you, too much tannin! Too much fruit! Too dry! Too sweet! Too sweet
and dry! But if you're lucky, someone, or some few, will look you in the eye
and smile and nod and sip again. And in that hope, I pass the jar to you.*

By the time it was done, he couldn't see his wife and children anymore,
but he imagined them . . . Claire locking the stroller to the meter, hoisting
Charlie on a hip, commanding Hope not to run, afraid she'd disappear
around an aisle and get snatched and they'd never see her anymore. And if
only Ran had overcome his selfishness that one time, and a thousand times
like it . . . For all this he blamed himself tonight, because long ago he'd
made a commitment to his art he had no power to reverse. And then she
left him one day in the spring. He came home with her coffee and her
muffin in a bag and found the letter, and the voice that spoke to him that
snowy night, that had spoken to Ransom Hill since he was young . . . that
went, too, in the middle of a song, like God deserting David. Ran stopped
sleeping, he sat up in the rocking chair all night where he'd rocked Hope,
then Charlie, and he smoked and screened the tape, staring out the window,
talking to himself, befriending the little voice that helps you choose between the blue shirt and the red, when there was no one else. And in the
morning he showered and went to the garage, and then he stopped showering. Then he stopped going to the garage. And the one taste of happiness
he'd known, the one taste of joy, was when Claire, the hundredth time, relented and said yes, when he saw her at the airport, barefoot on the Astroturf, when he saw his children's faces, heard their voices, crying, "Dad!
Da-*dee!*" His love for her, and them, was like a tumor in his chest, one that
Ran had proved beyond all shadow of a doubt he couldn't live without.
And what do you do then, when the news comes down that you will have
to live without it anyway, no matter if you can or not?

Ransom Hill, right now, is sitting on the floor before the stereo, rocking back and forth, talking to himself, holding in his hand the liner notes
for an album few people listened to and fewer people bought, wishing he
were someone different, someone other than himself.

And then, moved by something, he gets up, puts five twenties in an envelope, licks the flap, and, copying from the tag, addresses it to Alberta Johns,
tying up loose ends.

FIFTY-SIX

*Y*ou look as if you've seen a ghost." The quarter smile on Harlan's lips seems mocking, but there's a new and humorless sobriety in his ginger eyes, from which the haze has burned away. They're clear and deep and there's something smoldering and strangely voided there, not absent, but wiped out.

"Is it really you?" she says. "It is, isn't it?" A thousand currents of crossed feeling run through Addie as she stands before him, still in shock, her finger circling and recircling the orb of polished shell. "They told me you were dead. Two years ago, Harlan, Jules Poinsett stood right there. . . ." She gazes toward the piazza, but doesn't complete the thought. "Oh, Harlan! I thank God for your life." Her blue eyes, which conceal nothing, film at this, and she takes his hand and presses it, and this is genuine on her part. But it's a belated third or fourth response, and its belatedness does not escape her husband, whose hand remains as lifeless in her grip as his memory, these last two years, has been in Addie's heart.

"You seem changed," he offers. Studious, his eyes drop briefly from her face and then come back.

The blood rushes to her cheeks. "So do you! You are so thin, my dear! You are a rail. A very skeleton! Where did you go? Where have you been?"

"I was captured. I've been in prison."

"Prison? But the papers said . . ."

"I've been in prison, Addie," he repeats with a tolerating note, like a teacher reciting a rote lesson to a child.

And can he tell? she wonders. She's four months now. It's so obvious to her when she looks in the glass, but few have noticed yet. And Jarry, oh! He's with the carpenters on the island and will be back any time. How can she get word to him? She can't! And yet she must. What are they going to do? What is this going to mean? "Come, let us sit you down and put some food in you," she says. "Let's find some decent clothes." (*Jarry's things are in the bedroom, though! His nightshirt, draped over the chair! And did she make the bed today? The sheets!*)

"The birds are in the rice," he says, gazing past her toward the river.

"There's nothing but the gleanings left," she answers, absent and preoccupied. "It's in. We have almost forty bushels to the acre."

"Where's my gun?" he asks, as if he hasn't heard.

"It's in the house. But come and eat."

And now she hears the gravelly click as he slings his single item of impedimenta on his back—a burlap sack with "08 25 lb" stenciled on its face, in black. She should know what this means, she thinks, reading it. But she does not. As they pass through the park, he stares at the charred foundations of the summer kitchen, overgrown with briars, encouraged by the fire; he frowns, but, otherwise, it occasions no response.

At the table, two places have been laid, and Addie quickly sweeps up Jarry's plate and glass. She fetches bread and butter, jam—blackberry, from the canes that grow so thickly on the dikes. She spent the morning frying chicken, and before him now she sets the mounded plate. Harlan regards it like Franklin in Paris in his coonskin hat, surveying his first reeking plate of snails. He presses his finger into the warm yellow butter, sniffs and rubs it to nonexistence in the whorls of his own fingerprint, like salve. "You forget there's a world with things like this in it." His tone does not imply that he takes pleasure in remembrance.

"You must eat, though, won't you?" She pours a glass of milk and sets it, foaming, at his place.

"The smell of it revolts me." Pushing it away, he rolls his eyes to white. The lids briefly flutter like a girl's, and this somehow moves her past her fears to an awareness of his state.

"Is there any whiskey?"

"There's wine. Your Jerez. We hid it in hogsheads in the pond. . . ."

"Bring that."

She pours him half a glass, but Harlan puts a finger under the decanter and makes her fill it to the top.

"But, Harlan," she says, sitting next to him and watching as he drains it in a single draft, "where did they take you? Jules said you were drowned in the evacuation. . . ."

"I swam," he says, refilling. "I tried to get to Sumter, but the tide was running *hard against me. I was dazed and wounded. The water deepened and the current tugged and finally swept me off my feet. I grabbed a bit of wreckage and it carried me down Moffit's Channel and, finally, out to sea. Next morning, I was picked up by the coalers on the* Nahant. *They were out to catch a breath of air and saw the circling gulls. I was transferred to Port Royal. They sent us to Fort Delaware. I was there eleven months. I was ill that winter, '63. I don't remember spring. I couldn't tell you if there was a spring that year. . . ."* He looks away, bemused, and she does not know what to say.

"In August, they told us there was to be an exchange. We'd heard it many times before. . . . But this time seemed to be the truth. They sent six hundred of us south to Beaufort. I was expecting to be home any day. They put us on a boat, under a white flag, and told us we were going back to Charleston. The bastards. Instead, we went to Morris Island. There was a pen they'd built—like our cattle pens, but not so good as that. It's on the north end, between Gregg and Wagner." Now, another glass, the third. *"They put us in the line of fire from Sumter. From our own guns. We were shields, you see, to protect their gunners in the batteries, and half the shells our own men fired came down on us. The Yankees, Addie, sat there safe in their revetments, behind the same palmetto logs we'd cut, the sand and earth we'd dug. They drank and laughed, taking bets on which of us would live or die that night, that afternoon."* And, finishing his third glass, he wipes his mouth and pours a fourth. *"We had no shelter, not from weather, not from guns. The first few months, we dug holes in the sand like crabs and tried to hide. It made no difference. Especially from the seacoast howitzers. Did you know that was my gun? Yes . . . Oh, yes. In the Twenty-first."* Another heavy sip. A blink. A wince. *"Then winter. The gales came in. They blew our shirts to rags. We had no coats, no wood for fire, no water, none clean at any rate. Men had to squat and do their business where we walked and slept and ate. So many died they stacked them up like cordwood on the beach. At night, the fiddlers crept out and picked their bones. The guards accused us of eating our own dead. And some . . ."* Harlan looks at Addie now, and then his eyes glaze, seeing something else. *"You could tell those boys, Addie. . . . They kept the rose upon their cheeks. . . ."* And now the quarter smile on Harlan's lips seems almost mocking. *"After a while, when the shelling commenced, we took no notice. We sat in the open, playing cards, betting who would get it, both amongst ourselves and with the Yanks. And those who did, Addie? We considered them the lucky ones."* Three-quarters of the bottle is gone now. He seems dulled and weary suddenly; then he frowns. *"You hear those goddamned birds? Where is my gun?"*

"But I've told you, dear, the rice is in. It's being threshed."

"*Why let them multiply to cause us future harm?*"

He starts to rise, but stops when there are footsteps on the porch. They're light and springing in a way she's come to recognize, a way that means that Jarry's come home happy, bearing news. "They've driven the first puncheons," he announces, and he walks in, smiling, his hat off. Sometimes he throws it toward the upright of the chair, like the ringtoss at the fair, and she can see that he's about to do this now. It's in his hand to go when he sees Harlan sitting there, and he stops cold. His whole posture stiffens and becomes more formal, like a defendant in a court, an enlisted man before an officer. Addie realizes, with a pang, that she hasn't seen him in this attitude for months and has grown accustomed to his ease and naturalness.

"They told me you were here," says Harlan. "I, frankly, doubted it. I didn't believe you'd have the gall to show your face." He looks at Addie now. "You know he fought with them?"

"You must put your differences behind you now," she says. "You both did what you believed was right. The war is over."

"You're naive, my dear, if you think that. . . . I'm curious, though, Jarry. After you betrayed us, after you betrayed your flesh and blood, what made you think we'd take you back?"

"I'm not here because of you."

"Why are you here?"

Jarry doesn't answer this. He can't. Nor can he look at her. All he can do is hold Harlan's stare, his hazel eyes direct, unflinching, like a pair of taps turned to their full flow. All this suffering and death, thinks Addie, all the boys with flushed cheeks running, yelling, up so many hills, hill after hill, four years of it, and it meant nothing. These two brothers hate each other exactly as before.

"What puncheons?" Harlan says.

"My dear," says Addie, "we've come to an arrangement with the Negroes. You must understand. . . . I thought you were dead, and I've had to count on Jarry to advise me."

"I see. And what advice have you received?"

"His plan is succeeding brilliantly," she says. "Everyone else along the river is struggling, and we've had the best crop in ten years. Forty bushels to the——"

"You haven't answered me," he says. "What plan? Who's driving puncheons? Where? For what?"

Her expression drops to one of sober candor now. "I've ceded them the island, Harlan."

"You have what . . . Beard Island, do you mean?"

"Yes."

"Ceded it to whom?"

"The slaves."

"The freedmen," Jarry says.

Harlan blinks at them in turn, incredulous. "Have you, then, lost your minds? On what authority have you done this?"

"The authority you gave me in your will."

"And here I am, alive, so that is null and void, and there's the end of it."

"But, Harlan," Addie says, "I gave my word. They've worked this whole season on that understanding. They've cut timber, started homes. The church is framed. The steeple's on. The puncheons are in for the new wharf. They've done this in my name, upon my promise that the land and half the profits from the rice are theirs."

"And you expect me to accede? These Negroes, half my wealth, have just been confiscated by the same government that allowed my father to acquire them legally, stolen from me at a single stroke of a tyrant's pen, and now you want me to cede, what, a third of what's left to me in land to them in exchange for . . . what? As a reward for their loyalty? As a courtesy? To celebrate the destruction of our state, our country, our hopes, our way of life? You're a goddamned fool, Addie, a greater one than I took you for. You've lived your life in books, where noble heroes make foolhardy gestures such as this, ruining themselves and casting their children into penury. But in real life, no one acts this way or ever will. Starting from this moment, the niggers—the 'freedmen'—can live in the cabins, which I own and formerly provided gratis, and they may pay me rent. They may work the rice for wages and buy the food I once put into their mouths for free. If they don't like it, let them leave. After all, they're free. Their savior, Lincoln, has emancipated them, and you see how his perfidies have been rewarded. . . . Booth, you know . . . They killed him, but thousands more will spring up in his place. You say the war is over, Addie, but you'll soon have cause to know that's not the case."

"Come, man," says Jarry now, "you can't be serious. You've been defeated. At least show the character to admit you've lost."

"What I admit," Harlan rejoins, "is that my country is under occupation by a hostile foreign power."

"But Davis himself signed the armistice," Addie says.

"Jefferson Davis is a traitor and a coward. He betrayed our cause. Many of the notables of our government are in Mexico right now. They've made a treaty with the emperor Maximilian. One day, they'll march north and free us from our occupation."

"With what?" asks Jarry. "A dancing master and an orchestra? Will they waltz the government of the United States into submission?"

"You laugh now, Jarry. Now you're in the catbird seat. But one day soon, one day very soon, men I know—patriots like Booth, who feel as he felt and I feel—will make you acquainted with a branch of sourwood and the end of a short rope. And when they come for you, the night they ride into this yard, we'll see who's laughing then. We'll see what noises come from your black throat. And I'll show you, then, on that day, all the brotherly love you now show me."

Now Harlan gets his gun and goes to shoot.

"He's insane," says Jarry as they watch him stalk off through the park.

"Do you think he knows?"

"If he doesn't, he will soon."

"Oh my God, Clarisse!" Addie exclaims. "She'll tell him, surely. What are we to do?"

"What is there to do, but tell him first?"

"Oh, but Jarry, I'm afraid," she says. "I'm afraid for both of us." She takes his hand and puts it on her stomach now. "Shouldn't we just take the boat and go?"

"And the people?" Jarry asks. "Beard Island? Everything we promised them? All the work they've done? Are we just to leave them to their fates?"

"What else can we do? The will is void."

Now, the first blast of the gun . . . Jarry stares in that direction, and his jaw is tight. "I won't run anymore."

And, oh, at those words, such a lonely pang shoots through her. "Then we shall die of it," she says, and looks away.

"I could slip down there right now," he says. "We could take him up some nameless creek. . . ."

She looks him in the eyes and shakes her head. "No, you couldn't. And even if you did, it would ruin everything. Let me tell him. It should come from me."

And, in the house, as Addie goes to change the sheets, as she bunches them and holds them to her face to catch their scent, she listens to the Purdey's repeated roar from the landing down below. On and on into the afternoon it goes, and the thought of Wordsworth runs through Addie's mind. "We poets in our youth . . . We poets in our youth . . ." But she's too anxious and the rest won't come. All she remembers is the sense: It begins with poetry, and ends in death.

FIFTY-SEVEN

" 'Wash me thoroughly from mine iniquity, and cleanse me from my sin.

" 'Against thee, thee only, have I sinned, and done this evil in thy sight, that thou mightest be justified when thou speakest and be clean when thou judgest . . .' "

Sitting in the chair, her back discreetly to him, Shanté reads as Ransom wrings the sponge over his head, letting the scented water runnel down his face, his chest, his sides, laying tracks down in the hair of his uncovered legs, drumming softly in the iron basin of the tub. The bathroom window is still black, except for twinned candle flames reflected in the eddies in the pane. Burning on the sill and on the pedestal, both are white and both have been reversed, with new tops carved. Each has been dressed from one of Shanté's vials. "Uncrossing Oil," the label says, and at the bottom, among the culch of seeds and roots, there is a broken link of chain.

" 'Purge me with hyssop, and I shall be clean; wash me, and I shall be whiter than snow. . . .' "

Awakened at the partners desk, his head on his crossed arms, Ran followed Shanté to the kitchen, watching, somber-faced with sleep, as she poured herbs in river water she had boiled. There was a yellow flower in the mix, dried and drooping on its stem, head bowed like a discouraged child. Ransom wondered what it was but didn't ask.

" 'Deliver me from bloodguiltiness, O God, thou God of my salvation, and my tongue shall sing aloud of thy righteousness.
    " 'For thou desirest not sacrifice, else I would give it; thou delightest not in burnt offering.' "

As she continues, he kneels and soaks up the spilled water at his feet and wrings it out again, washing, as instructed—"Up to draw," she told him, "down to take away."

" 'The sacrifices of God are a broken spirit; a broken and a contrite heart, O God, thou wilt not despise.' "

Nine times she reads the psalm, nine times he wrings the sponge. Then he collects the water in a basin, waiting, in the cool of morning, as goose-flesh forms, for the air to dry him. Then he dresses in white clothes—a T-shirt and a worn pair of chinos—and sets off down the allée, carrying the basin, barefoot and alone.

A saffron line, no wider than a pencil stroke, has appeared over the Pee Dee, and birds are singing in the yard.

As the sky lightens, Ransom knows what kind of day it is to be. It is that day. In Killdeer there was only one each year, when you walked outside and found that, overnight, the sky had lifted off. The air was clear, the humidity, gone. The smell of bright tobacco wafted from the warehouses on Depot Street downtown, and sounds carried—the ringing of the steeple bell of the First Methodist Church, and, sometimes, from the high school, the warlike whoops of boys and coaches on the football field, like soldiers reenacting some old charge that ended in defeat and yet, each fall, must be remembered and repeated and remembered and repeated still once more. It was the day you knew—or Ransom did—that fall was here and summer gone and not coming back. The feeling in his heart today is the same as it was then—the loneliness of knowing things must end, the grief that stabs, yet Ransom glimpses far, far down—a flash, and nothing more—how the wound, along its edge, is touched with sacredness. And what is this? All these years, Ran has forgotten there was ever such a day as this, yet here, again, it is.

More than anything he's ever wanted, more than anything he's wanted in this life and on this earth, Ransom doesn't want to have to think of what this feeling means.

And he is at the crossroads now. Waiting for a pickup truck to pass—the driver, an old white man in a beaten cap, gives him a suspicious look that Ransom meets, unsmiling—he proceeds to the middle, turns his back, and throws the water, with his essence in it now, over his left shoulder, east, toward the rising sun. And then, not looking back—as instructed by Shanté— he puts Alberta's money in the box and returns the way he came.

In the yard, the excavator's hole is bound by yellow tape. The Odyssey's rear hatch is open. Shanté has taken out her things. Ran can see her, kneeling in the cemetery. With Claire's garden trowel, she pours a scoop of graveyard dirt into the pot, and her lips move, praying as she works. He enters by the creaking gate, and she stands up and wipes her hands. "I guess it's time."

"I guess it is," says Ran.

Uncovering her basket, with quick, effective violence, she takes out the black rooster she picked from her friend's stall. As she hands the bird to him, it erupts with surprising fury, and in the flurry that ensues, Ran's arm is scored and starts to bleed.

"Hold it upside down."

When he complies, the rooster's wings fall loose, its golden eyes grow tranced.

Untying the bundle, she places the palos, one by one, upright inside the pot. Standing behind her, holding the passive bird, Ran experiences a misgiving he hasn't felt till now. When he bought the bird from Shanté's friend, he told himself that it was just a chicken, after all, and how different, really, from going to the grocery and bringing home the pieces in Saran? Now, though, feeling its bony spurs against his fingers and thumb, the soft wing feathers brushing the tops of his bare feet, its body heat against his leg, the whiff of barnyard shittenness—all this drives home the fact that this is not a harmless game he has consented to. Here now, in the cool of morning, to take its life seems no small thing. Suddenly Ran is far from sure a game is not exactly what it is . . . . if not that, an act of reckless, foolish hope.

From a carved box, Shanté has taken out a folded leopard pelt and draped her shoulders. Inside, Ran can see a pile of fine white ash with larger bits in it. There are dried plants, roots and snails, an armlet she slips on. Lifting a staff, she starts to speak.

"Do not be surprised to see us here today," she says, speaking to the air, the old trees in the park, the mossy headstones, leaning silently. In her left hand is the staff; in her right, hanging at her side, the gleam of the thin knife. . . . "We come here to Makulu with offerings, to make Munkukusa, to confess and purify ourselves, so that we may be clean and righteous in your sight. This man, Ransom, and his family have been afflicted with grievances of which we do not know the cause. We come to ask how he has offended you and what it is you wish from him. He is lost, and we are lost, because we have forgotten you. Yet we know that you have not forgotten us. We know only that this pot was made, that you served its maker, and then were turned out in the anthill, consigned to wander restlessly, like them. Today, we call you to return into the nganga, which you see we have prepared for you. It is time for you to journey to Mpemba, to join your mwela there and to live among the bakulu forever. See, then, here is your wine. . . ." And now she pours it on the ground, a splashing cross. "Here, the prenda, here, the menga . . ."

And now she turns, and with a brief, hard look in Ransom's eyes, she grips his wrist and raises it. "Ensuso kabwinda." As she draws the knife across the rooster's throat, the blood spurts, hot, on Ransom's cheek. "Embele kiamene . . . Eki menga nkisi . . ."

She forces him to hold the bird in place, over the pot, and the blood pours, swift at first. . . .

> *Ahora sí menga va corre, como corre,*
> *Ahora sí menga va corre, si señó,*
> *Ahora sí menga va corre . . .*

As she sings, her song is like something Ran remembers . . . some old lullaby someone sang him long ago. But who? There is an ache in Ransom's throat, and an ineffable tenderness and pity well in him toward the bird. His misgiving, where is that? He doesn't know. It simply is no more. And the blood is falling, *menga va corre, como corre,* not horrible, not horrible at all, but somehow connected to the day, this day, to the lifted sky, the lonesome feeling in his heart, the stab of mortal grief, the wound that, at its edge, is touched with sacredness. It is one and the same thing.

It is slowing now, dripping, drop by drop, over the palos, like a soft, warm rain falling in the jungle, running down the branches of the trees, over the stones onto the forest floor, into the black depths of the pot, where it mixes with the earth which itself is living, is human flesh and tissue, bone and blood, the thing that's left, the thing that we become, and reaching the foundation, it touches the old sygill outlined in new white chalk.

"Now the firma is empowered," Shanté says, and, turning, once more to the air, in a commanding voice: "Tell us who you are and what you want."

And Ran, for one moment of unbearable suspense, allows himself to hope. And for that moment, as he waits—for what, he knows not—he closes his eyes and prays in silence, to the air, to the old trees in the park, to whatever power Shanté has called forth, and the prayer he says is, *Give me back my life.*

Now they wait. The moment of unbearable suspense, no longer than a thunderclap, has passed. And another. And the next one after that. And nothing happens. And Ransom, opening his eyes, knows now that nothing will, that nothing can, knows, too, deep down, that he has known this all along. *This is all there is.* His words come back.

Shanté takes a palm nut from her box and breaks it on the corner of a grave. Taking four pieces, she casts them on the ground, observing how they fall, whether with the white meat up or down. Murmuring to herself, she starts off down the rows, casting at the foot of every grave, and Ransom sits and watches. Demoralized and out of gas, he looks down at the legend in the stone:

CAPT. HARLAN P. DELAY
21st SOUTH CAROLINA, C.S.A.
b. Dec. 8, 1820 d. Sept. 1, 1863
Fallen in Defense of Home and Country
Resting Now in Patient Hope
Of Resurrection

Back in the place he was before, having come full circle, Ran knows the answers to his questions now, knows what it was for Harlan, once upon a time, to walk into this park, into the dappled light that fell through the old oaks, as it falls now, and find his name carved on the new stone in the plot; knows what it was like to come home from that Northern prison, after months and years of suffering and privation, to find his wife had grieved and buried him and moved on with her life.

And the sight of Shanté at her work, the woman he once loved, who once loved him, moving grave to grave, observing how the pieces fall, the fact that she would make these efforts of belief on his account, touches Ransom deeply, but in the way that watching Hope or Charlie play some imaginary game might do. As he envies them their childhood, so he envies her her faith, but Ran himself does not believe at all.

It comes home now that all of this—bathing in the herbs and washing down not up, walking to the crossroads, pitching the pot of water over his left shoulder not his right, and east not west, toward the rising sun . . . all this, Palo, hoodoo, Conjure, Congo practice, spirits, magic pots, all are forms of flight that Ransom took from something that he couldn't stand to face, couldn't stand to bear or bear to stand, something in himself. And what was it, the thing itself? It was his pain. It was the pain of human life. Somewhere Ransom had accepted, without ever knowing that he had, that he was too damaged, too afraid and weak, to bear that feeling in its raw and undiluted state, to hold it in his stomach and his chest, to bear it and still breathe, to bear it and still live, to hold it as he held the dying rooster, as he holds Charlie in the rocking chair at night, to hold it as he'd hold a dying child if there was nothing to be done except to gaze into his frightened eyes and be of comfort and stand what he must stand. But it is not a rooster, not a child that Ran is holding now. And when you awaken on that day, *this* day, when you experience the pain of being mortal, when you understand the dying animal, the dying child is you, that we are dying all the time, dying from the moment we are born, when you grasp that this is human life and it is all bound up with death—what then? What would you not do to escape? What price would you not pay to be spared? What drug would you not take?

It is that day now for Ransom Hill, and he has tried them all. He has fled through humor, wisecracks, affairs and feuds and busy-ness and business, through madness, music, alcohol, and art, even art, the place he'd tried hardest to be true. . . . And now the notion of a curse carried down the years inside an old black pot . . . All flight, evasion, fantasy. And why? Where had the break occurred? Where had he experienced the raw and undiluted thing, and opted out? Somewhere far back, far, far back, in childhood . . . an image of his father's flying fists, of curling in a ball against the wall as blows rained down, of wanting not just them, but everything to end. Lying on the kitchen floor of that old shack in Bagtown, in the shadow of the great twin stacks, life, the core sensation, had become identified with pain for Ransom Hill, and he had wished that it might cease. How terrible and sad. And he has been in flight since then—how long has it been?

And the one thing that has never dawned on Ran till now, this moment, watching Shanté move among the graves, is that he might stop and turn around and take it on the chin. That he might hold the feeling in his stomach, in his chest, and yet still breathe, and yet still live, and bear now, as a man, what he could not bear then. Only now, today—which is that day, this day—does it occur to Ran not only that he might, but that he must. But sitting here on Harlan's empty crypt, the thought that he might do so is like the moment when the addict's eyes glaze and his head lolls back, when he tells himself that in the morning he will stop. . . .

Even now, watching Shanté, his old friend, with love and total disbelief, Ransom, somewhere deep inside, is still waiting, hoping against hope for magic to attend, to redeem him and distract him from the burden of himself. . . . *This is all there is.* This is what life is, what it is right now, not what it was or will be, not what it might or should have been, only what it is right now, here in the graveyard, and no magic to attend. There is no escape from self, except death, and perhaps not even then. . . . *Not even then . . .* Only on the second pass does Ransom grasp that a voice is saying this to him, that it's been speaking for some time, speaking all along. It's the voice that he called Nemo, but it isn't Nemo anymore. The voice has changed. And at this moment, above him in the trees, a scarlet flash and a male cardinal alights in the old cypress and starts to sing. Thrusting out his chest, he sings, full-throated, on a limb. . . .

> *I was afraid . . .*
>   *I was afraid that if I freed them . . .*
>   *I was afraid that if I freed them, they might*
> *leave. . . .*

Is this voice in Ransom's mind, or is the cardinal singing human words? Ransom feels so strange, and he can't tell.

And Shanté turns and says, "Come here."

"What is that smell? It's like . . ."

"Cloves," she says.

"Yes, cloves and sour milk."

She nods toward the grave. The nut has fallen, all four pieces, with the white meat up.

Ran scrapes mildew from the name: Percival DeLay. "She put her father in the pot?"

"Por su voluntad," she says. "I'm certain he agreed."

"But why? Why would he?"

"Ask him."

"Me?"

"Ask," she whispers. Shanté's looking at him strangely now. She's gripped his wrists.

Ran stares down at her hands, then up into her eyes, alarmed. "What are you saying?"

"It's here, Ran."

He blinks. "In me?"

"In you. It's been here all along. . . . Now close your eyes and ask it what it wants."

Ransom, for one moment, stares into her eyes, considering the abyss. Then fear strikes him like a viper, and he pulls away and lurches through the gate.

"This is bullshit," he mutters as he heads across the lawn, and Ran feels nothing, absolutely nothing. Yet how long has it been since he felt right? Has it been since that first night?

"*Bullshit . . . ,*" he tells himself, but Ran feels slightly woozy, slightly faint, and the odd thing is, he's been walking for some time, yet he's no closer to the house. It seems to be receding as he goes, and Ransom, as he stares at it, remembers that he's on a journey. Something has been leading him, sowing clues along the way, and though this journey only started in the graveyard moments ago, it's as if he's been traveling the road for years. The journey is a book with many chapters, and each chapter was an adventure and a stage, and some of them were wonderful, some were sad. There are so many now that he's forgotten most of them, but it doesn't matter how many he's forgotten, all that matters is the adventure he's on now, and what will happen next. There's some responsibility involved, and Ransom has the heavy sense he must not fail.

There are people on the porch, observing him. Who are they? It is . . . *Is it Adelaide and Jarry? They're posing for the photograph, which will be taken now. . . . They're going to die, he thinks, and so am I. . . .* But this isn't his thought. Whose thought is it? *Who am I?* For a moment, he must struggle to remember, and Ransom sees that he will never reach them, never reach the house. He experiences a great fatigue. He looks for someplace to sit down. He turns and, just like that, *Addie stands before him.*

"Ransom."

He shades his eyes to look at her. The sun is behind her now. Her silhouette is black against it, and the sun seems common somehow, like a steel disk, like a coin.

"Ran!" she says, and suddenly Adelaide is Claire. "We need to talk. I think it's time."

Oh, how he wishes she were someone else. . . . Or he was. "Can I say something first?"

Her frown concedes.

And Ran must make the effort now, must shake off the torpor that's stolen over him, the urge to sleep. "I don't know if it was yesterday or some other year, but you asked me why I'm here, Claire, and I knew the answer, and I want to say it now. I'm here because I love you. Because I always have, and because there was a time you loved me, too. Even if you don't remember it, there was. And even if you don't now, I'm here because I hope you will again. I want to be the husband you deserve and the father Hope and Charlie need. I'm here to try to be the man I always hoped I might become and never actually was. I hope it's not too late, because I still believe we have a shot at happiness. I'm here for all those reasons, Claire, and because, along with all the rest, I believe if I could write a song like 'Talking in My Sleep' back then, knowing what I knew, then after everything we've been through, there's no reason I can't write an even better one today. And even if I'm wrong, I think it's what I'm here to do. I'm going to keep on trying till I can't try anymore or finally pull it off, Claire, something great, not great for Mitchell Pike, but great for Hope and Charlie Hill, great for you and me."

Claire is silent for a moment, then says, "I hope you do it, Ran. I hope you get it all. I really do. For Hope and Charlie's sake, and most of all, for you. But it won't be for me, Ran. It won't be with me."

"Don't say that. . . . You may feel that now, but you'll feel differently."

"How, Ran?" she asks. "Are you going to make me not love Cell, when I do? Are you going to make me fall in love with you again, when I don't and can't and don't even want to? Ransom, sweetie, listen. . . ."

"Oh," he says, or "Ah," not a spoken word, a groan, a sigh. He bends just slightly at the waist, as though he has been struck, or sledged, or shot. Ran can no longer breathe. His lungs cannot remember how. *The soul is breath. You'll breathe again after your death.* "No," he says, "no, Claire, please, wait, I . . . I can't do this now. I can't."

He looks at her with anguish streaming from his eyes, and Claire takes his face between her hands.

"You have to, Ran. I know it's hard, but you have to hear me. I've waited as long as I can, as long as I'm going to."

"What about the kids? Can't you think of them?"

"I do," she says. "I have. I've thought of nothing else but them. And you. I put you first for twenty years, Ran. I was the colored girl who sang doo da-doo da-doo-doo-doo, and I don't blame you. I made the choice myself, but now I won't be her anymore." She takes his hands.

"To me," she says, "and I'm sorry if this hurts you, Ran, but it's like God or some higher power has put this love in front of me, and I must turn to it, I *must,* like a green plant to the sun. I have no power to do otherwise. When I turn to Cell, my whole life brightens, the lights come on, I feel alive, I feel myself, and I realize how far from it I've drifted in these years with you. I feel seen by him and understood. And when I turn away, the lights go off, I feel tired and old. It's a struggle just to keep up with the kids and make it through the day and find the simple energy to live. It's like this marvelous drug, Ran, only I don't think it's a drug at all, I think this is just what it feels like to be human, fully human and alive and healthy and running on all eight cylinders, and even if it is a drug I don't want to stop taking it. It's how I once felt for you, Ran, but not in a long time. For years now, we've been sleepwalking through this marriage, marking time, and now that I'm awake again, how am I supposed to let it go? If you love me, really love me, you have to let me go. I would you. If you came to me and said this was happening to you, I would."

"Would you?" His voice is soft now. His face is cold. His eyes are hard and bright. "Would you really, Claire? Are you that pure? Are you so sure?"

"Yes, Ran, I would," she answers without hesitation. "I'm sure."

"What if that's what evil is?" he says. "Just a form of intoxicating self-ishness that feels like goodness, feels like it's from God, but really isn't?"

"Then the world is too fucked up for me, Ran. I can't be that complicated and believe that what makes me feel alive is evil and what makes me feel dead is good. That's what I've been doing for too long, and I don't feel any better or holier, I don't feel improved by all my martyred suffering and self-denial, so why not try what actually feels good? Why not try happiness? That's what I mean to do. I don't have anything to lose."

"You stand to lose a lot," he says. "What you stand to lose is everything. Ask me. Ask *me*, Claire. I've felt what you feel. I lived that way for years. It's why our marriage is in trouble. In the end, it's not the answer either."

"Then what is, Ran? *What is?*"

He doesn't answer. Ran has none to give. He looks at her, then up into the branches of the tree. *We are not the peak . . . not the peak. . . .* Beyond, the sky, so blue. It is that day. That day.

"Our marriage is over, Ransom, not in trouble. Over. Don't you see?"

"Can't I change? Haven't I? There must be something I can do, Claire. Something. Hold out some hope for me, some little thread, however thin, however frayed . . . Because if there's *nothing* . . . if I'm so fucked up and irredeemable . . ."

"Then what, Ran? What?"

Never good enough . . . Never fucking good enough, right, lad?

Nemo, now, Ran's last friend, is speaking in his accustomed voice again. Claire's face is wavering like a candle flame in wind, and it is blowing Ransom, too, blowing him away. He's having trouble focusing, trouble answering the question, remembering what the question is. . . . Then what? Then what? What then?

I will tell you a secret, Nemo says, not without compassion, *a quick, violent death solves many things. It isn't painful. Is that what you thought? No. Oh, no. Don't you remember Livingston? The woman, mauled by lions, went into dreamtime, like the Aborigines. She saw higher realms of truth. So will she, Ran. So will he. So, at the end, will you. It will be merciful. And more. It will be mature. Death is simply the end of human striving, dying, no more than going from a hot, sweaty place into an air-conditioned room. And then you're on a road with many others. It's the journey you're on now, in fact, the one you've been on all along. Very soon you'll come to a door. Before it stands a man who holds a book. He'll scan the columns till he finds your name, and you will be admitted. There will be no lapse in consciousness. You'll still be yourself. What is lost—your body and the earth and sex and food and birth and death and change, and her, and Hope and Charlie, everything you've*

*known and been till now, everything you took, mistakenly, to be yourself—all this is,
finally, small. What you'll gain is your True Self, the thing you've sought and cannot
have on earth.*

"Like this, though?" Ransom's voice is pleading. "Not like this."
Like this.

"Who are you talking to?" asks Claire.

He looks at her and blinks.

"Ransom, look at me. Who am I?"

He shakes his head and weeps. "I don't know. I don't know who you are."

"I'm Claire, Ran, Claire. Look at me. LOOK AT ME."

"I can't," he says. "I can't. I can't. I can't."

And Ransom, after all, can't find the strength to take it on the chin, to
bear the raw and undiluted thing, and so, once more, he does what he does
best. He runs.

Here before him is the old slave cabin Claire converted to a gardening
shed. And there, as if at Ransom's thought-command—leaning in the corner where he left it, when he gassed his whacker—is the Purdey, the right
hammer down, the left still cocked upon its unexploded charge. Lifting it,
Ran becomes aware how much he'd like to lie down here and sleep, to fall
into the black and silent night that befriended him so long ago, but something tells him he must not, that he must stay awake, and Ransom takes the
gun outside and sits down, propped against the cabin wall. In the clear light
of morning of the day, this day, he admires the scrolled acanthus on the silver plate, the bluing on the barrels of Damascus steel. Ran holds the shotgun in his lap, feeling comforted and thinking, *What a thing of beauty, what a
mighty thing it is.*

FIFTY-EIGHT

*B*am . . . *bam* . . . *bam* . . . *bam* . . . *bam* . . . *The Purdey's maddening, repeated roar goes on and on through the long afternoon and deep into the dusk. Like a hand through smoke, the shot moves through the flock. And the black river is littered with them now, studded with dead birds, like strange bromeliads, feathered, warm and apple green, and yet they come, again, again, again, as though they're as in love with dying as Harlan is with dealing death to them. And why does Harlan love it so? Because each explosion, each loud, violent jolt shouts down the voices in his head, drowns out the memories, reduces the whole world to white, ringing nothingness and almost makes it possible, for the duration of the blast, for Harlan to believe that he can stand what has been done to him and live.*

For he's heard the rumors long ago. Oh, yes. How could he not? Jules Poinsett told someone what he'd seen. That someone told someone else. The rumor spread. Eventually, it came to him. Harlan disbelieved at first, but at some point that changed. Was it on Morris Island in the pen? Yes, perhaps it was, lying in his shallow hole at night, gazing at the shivering stars as the fiddlers crept over the faces of the dead (he could hear them, when the gusts died, clicking at their work). . . . There, as the star shells arced and burst, as the hot iron rained, as men in nearby holes cursed and groaned and wept and prayed . . . There, as the winter gales blew freezing spindrift over him, reduced to a shivering, half-naked thing, it was easy to remember that his father had loved Jarry

BACK TO WANDO PASSO

best. Paloma had. The Negroes . . . Who, in fact, had not? Race, so big a thing—in the end, what difference had it made? And why should she, his wife, be different from the rest?

Staring at the stars was sometimes too unbearable, and Harlan closed his eyes and remembered standing on this dock, this very dock, his wedding day, with Tom— Tom Wagner, who had his face blown off at Moultrie (Harlan stood not ten feet away)—remembered standing arm in arm and singing, "She Walks in Beauty Like the Night." How long it took to find the music, to get the men together for the thing! But what came back to Harlan in his hole was Addie's blush, the momentary flicker of embarrassment in her blue, mobile eyes, which concealed so little, as he offered her the granadilla, the berry of the passion fruit brought all the way from Cuba, up through the blockade. That became his settled memory of her, and it would come upon him suddenly and he groaned like those around him, each in his own private hell, actually groaned aloud and rolled onto his face, seeking contact with the ground, the cold, cold earth itself, to conduct away from him the hot and stinging shame he felt and feels again right now, as he pulls the trigger, as the tears streak down his face. For a long time, Harlan blamed Poinsett for spreading ugly lies, blamed himself for putting any credence in them. But, imperceptibly, it came to seem to Harlan that Addie's failure to appreciate the pains he took that afternoon was niggardly and mean, one small example on a longer and much heavier list. He came to doubt she'd ever loved or truly understood him, and Harlan ceased to blame himself and, from that point, began to blame his wife. And walking home from Delaware—where the few who made it had been shipped again when Charleston fell in February '65—it seemed to him that Poinsett might not be lying after all. And if he wasn't, what was Harlan going to do? Somehow, he thought, when he got home the answer would be clear, but that was not the case. By the time he got to Powatan, his sole clear impulse was to stop at Pringle's and buy this bag of 08 shot. And here he is this afternoon, knowing only that dark is coming on apace and now, or soon, he's going to have to put the gun away and walk up to the house and look her in the face and ask.

She's waiting for him when he comes. She's at the table with the chicken fried that morning and the lamp is lit. Her hands are folded in her lap. Her face is grave.

"So, Addie," he calls as he sets the Purdey on its stock, "shall we eat?"

"I'm not hungry, Harlan. I've made a plate for you."

He turns. "I'm not hungry either. Shall we retire?"

"I cannot share a bed with you tonight."

He stares. "And why is that?"

"I simply can't."

"I see. You know, Addie, there's been talk. . . ." He pours what's left of the Jerez. "Poinsett told me you'd protected him. . . ."

"I love him, Harlan."

"So it's true," he says.

"It's true."

"You're a whore—you know that, don't you?"

"I am not a whore."

"You've betrayed me."

"Yes," she says, "I have. I betrayed you when I married without love. For that, I ask your forgiveness. But for loving Jarry? For that I will not apologize."

"You bitch . . . you filthy bitch," he says. "It isn't only me. You've betrayed your name, your family, your class, your race."

"But I've been true to something else," she says. "You've suffered grievous harm, and as the woman who was and still is, in name, your wife, I hurt for you. But I believe you suffered in a cause that was unjust. God has judged it so. We posed our question, and He answered the whole South in blood and ruin, and history will have no pity on us, Harlan. No pity for what you suffered on Morris Island, none for me because my dreams that I would be a happy mother and a wife did not come true. We'll die and be forgotten. The grass will grow over our graves. The best we can do now—for ourselves and for each other—is to surrender any claims we had or thought we had and live and let each other live, and do the best we can."

"You made a vow to me in church before Almighty God. You are not released. I do not release you. God does not release you."

"I made a human vow based on human understanding, Harlan. That was our marriage. But with Jarry, God spoke and He corrected me. It was He who told me, love and live. I am under His command, and I will follow it, unto death if need be. But if I die today, if you kill me now, and He asks me to justify my hours, it is to this love that I shall point, and I trust He'll have mercy on me then, even if you, now, cannot."

With this, she leaves and goes upstairs, and Harlan sits there starkly for a while. Then he gets up. He takes the gun. He carries it and goes toward the swamp, the opening in the trees.

Outside the house, he stops and calls. "Clarisse?"

The door opens. Backlit, she holds the little boy.

"You did this, didn't you?" he says. "You did this to bring me back to you. . . . Well, here I am."

"Ya no me importa," she says. *"I no longer care. You cut the heart right out of me. But this—this—is your son. She is carrying Jarry's."*

"I want him dead," he says. *"I want Jarry dead, Clarisse. I want you to give me back my wife. Do this for me, and name your price."*

She frowns into the dark and doesn't answer right away. Then his sister stands aside, and Harlan goes to the last place he has left.

FIFTY-NINE

Sitting by the cabin, Ran stares up into the branches of an oak, and it seems to him the whole of human wisdom is small and negligible beside that tree. *Not the peak . . . no, not the peak . . .* Something from a prior chapter of the book, which he remembers to forget, or has forgotten to remember. It doesn't matter now, does it? Beyond, the sky, so blue. So blue.

Years go by while Ransom is away, before he thinks, *It's time,* before he remembers, *It's that day.* That day. And Ran gets up.

The house, which previously receded, is coming toward him now, coming with relentless motion, relentless speed. He's on the journey once again, he's written several chapters more. But already he's forgetting them. He's on the porch now, the "piazza"—he had to learn to call it that, like pants and trousers, like so many things. A surge of ugly bitterness. Claire was ever free of that. Was this what Ran resented most? Time, now, to be done with all of it.

As promised, here then, at the end, a door. No man. No matter, though. Beyond the door, a room of books, and Ran, returning, knows the book he seeks is there, and maybe it is up to every man to open up the Book of Life and write his own name there, and where else should the story end? There will be no further chapters or adventures after this. How sad that is. It's time, though. It's that day. He puts his hand on the glass knob. Whole worlds, in the facets, are eclipsed. He bows his head against the wood. He feels so tired, so tired.

That's right, open it, says Nemo. *A single step is all it takes. You're out of it for good and never coming back.*

"Is that what I want?"

What's the option? Starting over?

"So true. Too true." The futility requires no comment.

There are voices from within. The knob is turning in his hand. There is a *whoosh,* an undertow, a roaring wind, not blowing out, but *in.* . . .

"*I've been waiting for you.* . . ." *She starts across the room toward him.* Who is she? Ran wonders, feels he ought to know, but doesn't. *She knows him, though, this woman with blond hair, in her dress of white and purple calico.*

She takes his hand. *She says,* "*I can't live this way, do you understand?*" Ran feels the warmth and pressure of *her flesh, her* living *flesh,* against his flesh. "*I can't,*" she tells him, "*this is death, and I've consented to be dead, but now I want to live.* . . ."

The undertow is sucking, sucking Ran—but who is Ransom now?— down into the vortex, down into *the past.* . . .

"*I want to live,*" she says, "*to live.* . . ."

"Do you know who I am?"

"*I didn't,*" *Addie says,* "*but now I do. I looked into the pool and saw only myself; then I looked through, and I saw you—do you understand? Now I do. I do see you. And it was you, Jarry, you alone, who ever made me feel this way.*"

"*Jarry,*" *she calls him,* "*Jarry* . . ." Ransom, thinking there is some mistake, looks down at *Addie's hand, white, on his black arm.*

This is a dream, he tells himself. How can this be?

But Ransom can't wake up, and it's too late for questions now. The door *the door is swinging open. The tall, gaunt, bearded stranger enters with the gun. The first shot comes. Addie blinks her startled eyes. She looks down at her dress. It's torn and ragged. Smoke is rising from the bloody hole.*

Addie tries to speak and something leaves her mouth, hovers near the ceiling like a bird trapped in a room, frantic, seeking the way out. Outside on the river, the boat horn blows. The chittering of ricebirds fills the air.

"*The parakeets,*" she whispers. "*Do you hear them? Jarry, are you there?*"

"I'm here," says Ransom, shaken, shaking, praying, Let me wake up, please, God, if You're there, let me not have killed my wife, let this not be Claire.

Addie sees him now. Jarry's sitting on the floor. Her head is in his lap. He's weeping.

"Dearest . . ."

"Shhh," Ran whispers. "Don't talk. Please."

"I'm dying, aren't I?"

"No," he tells her. "No." His tone is warm and fierce.

And now Addie knows she is.

Against the window, Jarry's silhouette is black against the sun, which resembles a steel disc. Addie can see the edge, not blurred with radiance, but definite, serrated, like a coin. There's black soil in the crenellations, and she can't remember why her aunt said not to look at it, why humans should be afraid of such a common thing. Addie, now, can stare straight into it.

"I must tell you something. . . ."

"Please, don't talk." Ransom, weeping, strokes *her hair.*

She puts her finger to his lips. "No, please, listen, Jarry, please. I loved my life. I loved my family, my friends, I loved this place, my work, I loved it all, more than I ever loved myself, but you were my true happiness. You were the only one who ever looked at me and saw me as I truly was, not even who I was but who I wished to be. The joy you took in me made me take joy in myself. I had forgotten who I was. I needed you to show me. You loved me as I hope God may love me now. I was just that person once, with you. I'm not sad. Jarry, don't you be."

Ransom shakes his head, agreeing. His face *his face is* streaked *with tears.* "No, I won't."

Footsteps approach over the carpet now. The shadow falls over the lovers. Ran looks up at *the silhouette against the light.* He knows *the bearded stranger* now.

"Harlan."

"Yes, it's me." Harlan's voice is soft, but his ginger eyes are red with weeping, and besotted.

I dreamed that I was you and you were me, Ran thinks, but I was wrong as wrong could be, as you were wrong before me, so who was I, and who were we? Through the window, he can see the oaks and the magnolias in the park . . . *Not the peak, no, not the peak* . . . So this is how the story ends, and how else should it be? *Now Harlan puts the Purdey to his brow, and* Ransom gazes down at *his black arm* and understands. I feared and hated what I envied and could never be; I thought I was the killer, but the thing I killed was me. Ransom, seeing through *himself, is going, going, gone, and Jarry bows his head to it, and Harlan fires the gun.*

The second shot rings out. The birds disperse. Their twittering fills the skies, and he is with them now, Jarry's with them. Far below, the boat horn blows, and Jarry hears the clank of metal pots, the musical thunk-tink *of bones. "Hu eh eh! Hu eh eh!" the children cry in an ancestral tongue his mother's mother had already forgotten how to speak. There's a tremendous fluttering of wings, and all around them are the birds, a great invisible flock, hemming them in on every side, guiding him, guiding them, away over the roof, over the trees in the old park, and Jarry, with Addie now, flying with the parakeets into the checkered sun, is free.*

Like spindrift from a breaking wave, the birds hang a moment, a curtain of bright green high in the air, and then they veer and vanish as though never there. A green feather falls. A wind blows through the park, and it is blown, that feather . . . under the old oaks and the magnolias, through the dappled sunlight, onto the piazza, into the pages of a book, and in that book a poem, and in that poem, a man, the old leech-gatherer, staring down into a pool of water he stirs with his staff and he is gone . . . and, at the bottom, finally, when his self is shattered, overcome, there, he sees . . . so long longed for, finally so small . . .

"Ransom! . . . Ransom!"

Still standing on the threshold, he comes to with the Purdey trained on Marcel Jones. . . . All this is a dream, thinks Ran, I dreamed that I was you, and you were me. But who am I? And who is he?

Nothing exists but empty space and you, says Nemo. *Go on and pull the trigger, Ran. Life, death, it doesn't really matter, does it?*

But the woman who was *once upon a time* and is no more *no more his wifewifewife,* says, "You aren't going to do this."

And Ransom, having died already, says, "You're right," and puts the gun beneath his chin.

"No, Ran . . ."

A denial is the final thing he hears before he pulls the trigger and his blood and brains jet up against the chandelier and drop back down in bloody drips, and Hope and Charlie see their father there, they scream and scream and grow to man- and womanhood and have children of their own and pass it down, the bitter, bloody wounds, as Percival passed his, on and on, and round and round, the carousel spits out the same black bag and starts the same sad trip again. . . .

But, no, Ran merely sees this in advance. When he opens his eyes, his finger on the trigger, Shanté is in front of him.

"I understand it now," he says, and he is weeping now, and wild. "I know why he agreed to go into the pot, Shanté."

"Why, Ran?"

"He wanted to atone. And so do I. I want to be a tree," he says, "I want to be clean and do no harm and turn sunlight into life. I'm tired of all the mess, Shanté, tired of all the mess I've caused, and all the mess I am. I'm tired of being me. I'm not afraid to die."

"I know you're not," she answers him. "You have a brave heart, Ran. But not like this. Think of Hope and Charlie. You'll wound them in a place so deep they'll never be the same."

"I already have."

"Then stay and make it up."

"How can I, Shan? I tried, and look at me."

"Close your eyes and ask him."

"I can't."

"Yes, you can."

And Ransom does, he turns into the roaring wind and holds the raw and undiluted thing, and the ghost whispers him the answer Ran already knows, like everyone, and has forgotten to remember, and remembered to forget. . . .

And Ransom drops the gun and sets them free.

EPILOGUE

. . . there was always, deep in the background, the feeling that something other than myself was involved.

—Carl Jung, *Memories, Dreams, Reflections*

I n the turnaround before the house, the Odyssey is packed to go. Ran slams the hatch and turns, brushing off his hands. "I guess that's it."

It's difficult to meet Cell's stare, and yet he does. When the big man offers him a hand, Ran takes it. "Marcel," he says, not Cell, not Cell Phone.

"Good luck, Ran."

Ran nods curtly, once, and Cell, after a brief glance at Claire, turns and walks toward the house.

"Shan's invited Hope and Charlie to Alafia," he says. "I'd like to take them, Claire. I think it would be good for them."

"And you."

"And me."

"I think so, too," she says. "You get your levels straight, and then we'll talk. Here." She hands him something.

Ran opens a folded check: $11,460.32.

"What's this?"

"Your sixty-five percent."

"I don't want this, Claire."

"Yes, you do."

Ran contemplates a crack, but lets it pass and speaks the true thought underneath. "I wanted you to have it all."

"I know, but this is better, Ran. It's more grown-up."

"I didn't want us to have to grow up, Claire, either one of us."

"Neither did I. But we had to anyway."

"You did."

"So did you, Ran. Don't take that from yourself. Or us."

He puts the check into his shirt. "You're sure?"

She reaches out and strokes his cheek, and Ransom takes her hand and presses it.

"I'm sure."

"I guess I've been holding on to something that really wasn't all that great."

"But it was once."

"It was, wasn't it? I'm so sad, Claire."

"So am I. You know what I lay awake thinking of last night?"

He shakes his head.

"Last winter when you took me to the Plaza for my birthday, and we didn't have the rent, and you hired a limo and ordered oysters and champagne. I would never have done that for myself, Ran. And the next morning when we left, the ATM ate our card, remember?"

"I remember."

"And we had barely enough change for two cups of coffee from the deli, and not even enough for the subway and we walked home all the way downtown, and I felt . . . I don't know, like I'd jumped off some big cliff I'd always been afraid of. . . . And you gave that to me, Ran, a thousand times, a thousand different ways, and it made me better than I was, it made me bigger and less afraid. And I'll always love you for it. Always."

Ransom's eyes are like rain-sheeted windowpanes. "When I boil it down to what really mattered, Claire, what made each day worth getting up to struggle through, it was you, and what kills me is that I realized it too late, after you'd already left."

She holds his gaze, neither gloating nor denying the essential truth of what he's said.

"Cell is a good man, though," Ran continues, "probably the best I ever knew. If it can't be me, Claire, he's who I'd choose for you, and I guess if I was honest, I'd have to choose him over me. So, go, baby. Find your happiness."

She kisses her fingertips, presses them to his lips. "Good-bye, Ran."

And she is gone now, too, and Ransom stands, alone, before the closed front door, remembering nineteen years before, how badly he'd wanted it to open and admit him. Under the tumult of his feelings, it's strange to find a thread of clear relief to be outside again. Overhead, the sky so wide and blue.

Going to find the children, he passes the excavation, where water has collected in the hole. As Ran stares down, he sees an image, just a flash, a man down in that hole *digging, digging furiously, covering the bodies. There's a woman standing over him, watching. When he sees her, he looks angry. "You deceived me. . . ."*

"You asked the pot to give you back your wife," she says, and she holds out her hand. . . . And then . . .

And then? The image fades. The ghosts dissolve in sunlight. The curtain falls. Ran loses sight of them. The chapter they wrote has been forgotten. Aye, ages long ago . . .

And now the woman is Shanté. "You ready?"

"Ready as I'm ever going to be," he says.

"How do you feel?"

He shrugs. "Calmer. Otherwise, about like you'd expect."

"Any voices?"

"Not so far. I put the pot into the car. Claire doesn't want it here."

"That's fine, Ran. We can take it. It's just a pot now, though."

"You think he's gone."

She nods. "Can't you feel the difference?"

"I don't know. Some."

"He's been released now, Ran. Percival wanted freedom for his children. You finally gave him what he asked. He's in Mpemba, but he was there for you, just as one day you'll be there for them." She nods toward Hope and Charlie in the yard.

"I hope so, Shan," he says. "I hope I live that long."

"You will. If not, you'll come back from the dead and whisper to them from a song and put the truth into their hearts as he did yours, and this is simply how it is. The living and the dead are bound, and we, for all our knowledge, have forgotten what you paid this price to learn. Feel good about yourself. You turned your life around right here."

As she walks toward the car, Ran thinks of Percival, and suddenly the words are there, the verse he never knew he knew till now:

> *And the whole body of the man did seem*
> *Like one whom I had met with in a dream*
> *Or like a man from some far region sent*
> *To give me human strength . . .*
>   *to give me human strength . . .*
>   *to give me human strength . . .*
>   *by apt admonishment.*

"Daddy?"

When he turns, Hope is standing, tentative, in the checkered light that falls from the old trees.

"Hey, Pete."

"Are you leaving?"

"In a bit."

"Forever?"

Ransom kneels and stares into her solemn, worried eyes. "No, sweetie, just for a few days. I'm still a little sick now, but I'm getting better, and in a week or so, I'm going to take you and Charlie with me to Alafia, where Shanté lives."

"You promise?"

Ransom smiles and draws an X across his heart. "I promise, Hope. And I'll always come back for you and Charlie. Always."

"And Mommy—is she coming, too?"

Ransom holds the little agony of understanding in his daughter's eyes. "I don't think so, Hope," he answers, gently brushing back a lock of fallen dandelion hair. "Mommy and I aren't going to be together anymore. I'm very sad about it. But it's going to be okay."

"How, Daddy?"

"I don't know. I only know we're going to make it be."

She considers. "Do you have time to push us in the swing before you go?"

"Yes, I have time."

———

"Higher, Daddy! High as the morning sky!" Hope cries.

"Not today, Zurg!" Charlie says.

No, not today, thinks Ransom as he pushes them. It was not that day af-ter all. Not the day he thought it was . . . Or maybe it was. And when he cried out of the wilderness, *when I called out from the belly of the whale, did He not answer me?*

Perhaps, perhaps. Or maybe it was just the words of an old song. That chapter, too, already fading. And Ransom Hill, like all of us, will know the answers before long.

And as he pushes them and listens to them laugh, the last verse comes:

> *But I must go now, Nemo's calling for me.*
> *And having had my say, I'm ready to go back.*
> *Because for me at last there is no mortal satisfaction*
> *Beyond the beautiful wild rush of his attack.*

And so the song is done, and maybe it is Nemo talking to Ran now—as the Odyssey pulls down the white sand road and disappears where the lines of trees converge in the allée—maybe it's that other, better man he'd always wanted to become but never actually was, maybe, once again, it's just the little voice that in the morning helps you choose between the blue shirt and the red, or maybe it is simply Ransom talking to himself, wide awake now, saying, *Hold it, boy, don't run, hold the bitter wonder of the world, close your eyes and lift your face toward the sun, love it all you can and listen to the children cry with plaintive appetite,* "Again! Again! Again!"

ACKNOWLEDGMENTS

This note is to thank the many friends and strangers who contributed to this work, both the living, who reached out in person, and the dead, whose spirits touched mine through the ancient spell we sometimes take for granted—words on the page.

First, the people.

I'm grateful, above all, to my wife and children for their love, support, and forbearance through the five-year writing of this book; to my mother and father (the artist formerly known as Quid Nunc); to my brothers, George A. and Bennett; to Bob Richardson, whose library was my phone-less, e-mail-less sanctuary, the place I retreated each day to write and came to think of as my whaling ship; to Joel El Endoqui, who challenged me to deeper seriousness, and without whom I could not have written the Palo sections; to Bob Schofield, owner of Hasty Point plantation, who shared his real garden spot with me and showed me the old map where I found the name for my imaginary one; to Don Dixon, whose soliloquies kept me entertained as they instructed me on the fine points of rock musicology; to Tina Bennett, my brilliant, kind, unflappable agent; to my three editors: Gary Brozek, who encouraged the green shoot; Meaghan Dowling, who lavished such passionate attention on the sapling; and Jennifer Brehl, who oversaw the pruning that made the thing a tree; to the writers who spoke up for it: Lee Smith, Craig Nova, Randall Kenan, Annie Dillard, Pat Conroy; to R and S, who listened to me maunder on about the title and feigned interest, and whose good cheer and bad influence were as reliable as their friendship; to Bob and Terry and the Wednesday warriors, who helped with the instruction manual; and, not least, to the nfumbi of my line.

I would also like to thank Rich Aquan, Seale Ballenger, Pinckney Benedict, Rachel Bressler, Jamie and Marcia W. Constance, Pam Durban,

Bill Emory, Lil Fenn, David Ferriero, Lisa Gallagher, Sarah Gubkin, Angela Haigler, Robin Hanes, Allan Harley, Richard Howorth, Frank Hunter, Svetlana Katz, Barbara Levine, Kim Lewis, Peter ("Pistol Pete") London, Adriana Martinez, Madge McKeithen, Roland Merullo, Kate Nintzel, Nancy Olson, Harris Payne, Dr. Louis A. Perez, Jr., Carol Peters, Ron Rash, Mark Reed, Mary Gay Shipley, Sherry Thomas, Katharine Walton, Dr. M. W. Wester, Jr., Fran Whitman, Joyce Wong, and John H. Zollicoffer, Jr.

The books.

On Palo Mayombe: above all, the great ethnographic works of Lydia Cabrera: *La Regla Kimbisa del Santo Cristo del Buen Viaje, Reglas de Congo* and *El Monte*. (Their unavailability in English is an impoverishment that I hope the current copyright holders will soon address.) Also, the works of Robert Ferris Thompson, and *The Book on Palo* by Raul Canizares.

On Hoodoo/Conjure: above all, *Hoodoo in Theory and Practice*, Catherine Yronwode's work in progress, published on her learned and fascinating website, luckymojo.com. Also, the works of Harry Middleton Hyatt, Zora Neale Hurston, Maya Deren, Ras Michael Brown, and, also on the web, Inquiceweb.com.

On contemporary Kongo belief: above all, *Death and the Invisible Powers* by Simon Bockie.

On Cuba: above all, *Cecilia Valdés* by Cirilo Villaverde, in the Sidney Gest translation, invaluable to me for nineteenth-century Cuban idiom and general period detail. Also, *The Autobiography of a Runaway Slave* by Esteban Montejo; *The Life and Poems of a Cuban Slave* by Juan Francisco Manzano; *Cuba* by Hugh Thomas.

On nineteenth-century South Carolina: above all, *Chronicles of Chicora Wood* by Elizabeth Waities Allston Pringle and *A Woman Rice Planter* by the same author. Also, *Within The Plantation Household* by Elizabeth Fox-Genovese; *The Plantation Mistress* by Catherine Clinton; *Intellectual Life in Ante-Bellum Charleston, Down by the Riverside* by Charles Joyner; *Incidents in the Life of a Slave Girl* by Harriet Jacobs; *A Bondwoman's Narrative, Slave Narratives* by Henry Louis Gates; and *The Black Border* by Ambrose E. Gonzales.

On the Civil War: *The Civil War* by Shelby Foote; *A Rebel War Clerk's Diary* by John B. Jones; *Battery Wagner* by Timothy Eugene Bradshaw, Jr.; *Gate of Hell* by Stephen R. Wise; *Andersonville* by MacKinlay Kantor; *The Killer Angels* by Michael Shaara; and *Robert E. Lee* by Douglas Southall Freeman.